The Snare of the Fowler Series

Free Indeed
Book 3

Carol S. Lacey

The Snare of the Fowler Series
Free Indeed
© 2023 Carol S. Lacey

Distributed by Adriel Publishing

www.CarolLacey.com

What People Are Saying About "Free Indeed"

"In book three of her 'Snare of the Fouler' series, Carol Lacey brings us more twists and turns as we follow Daphne, the former demon-possessed girl of Acts 16, who battles powerful demonic strongholds in her quest to bring the gospel to people who have been deceived by the myth of false gods."

Beth Jones
Author& Co-Founding Pastor
Valley Family Church

"Carol is a gifted storyteller, historian, and messenger of The Gospel. This final novel of the trilogy, chronicles Daphne's life and is rich and alive. It is a story of faith, pure love, hope, and restoration. The characters are well developed, as the reader is taken on a journey that reveals a heart to leave no soul unturned. Carol's personal urgency gives detailed gospel truth that will set people free from bondage. The reader is led in the experience along with her characters. Vivid and accurate descriptions of Roman settings in the 50's AD make this journey realistic and reflects the journey Carol took to write it. Each novel is reminiscent of the combined styles of writers Frank Perreti and Francine Rivers; yet, wholly Carol's. Tension, joy, tragedy, hope, triumph... all are experienced with the characters and the settings. It is a well written and deeply moving story and very difficult to put down!"

Mary Scott, Intercessor, counselor,
short term missionary for years with
Iris Global Ministries

"In Lacey's final installment of the trilogy, she doesn't disappoint. Amidst vivid pictures of the cities, Lacey paints portraits of characters in their daily lives and conveys the longing in each heart to know their Creator. Readers will discover a transformed young woman with a joyful heart and a spirit determined to do the Lord's will. Alongside her growth in faith, the author weaves in the character's heartaches and victories as she trusts the Lord and obeys His calls to spread the gospel to a hostile world."

Lisa Mackinder
Writer for magazines &
Chicken Soup for the Soul books

"Have you ever wondered really wondered what life was like during Biblical times? Carol Lacey not only gives us a glimpse of it, but through her story and characters, she takes us there to experience it! Enjoy her newest book, Free Indeed, the third in a trilogy she has written."

Dianne Martin, author of "A Fishy Story" and other children's books

"Carol Lacey's final book of her trilogy is a masterpiece. The way she takes a minor biblical story and makes it come alive is truly amazing. What a gift she shares with us."

William R. Wieringa
Attorney & Counselor at Law

"FREE INDEED! In this, the 3rd book in Carol Lacey's Snare of the Fouler series, Daphne faces struggles similar to today's believers in Christ. Painful memories, stubborn family members and tough decisions are her lot. This novel is a perfect depiction of the great gifts given to all believers,

prayer and access to God's love and guidance. Enjoy her journey to spread the gospel and bring glory to His kingdom."

Pamela Wellington
Bible Study Leader

"Carol Lacey has done it again. Her third book in the trilogy, The Snare of the Fowler, gives the reader reason to smile. Here, her Biblical character, the demon-possessed slave girl of Acts 16, seeks redemption and hopes for a totally transformed life. Her journey from pagan beginnings to a life lived for Christ is certain to uplift and inspire you!"

Mary Jane Mapes
Founder and President
The Aligned Leader Institute, LLC

"Carol leads the reader on more adventures with Daphne and Nicanor. There's never a dull moment. The reader will breathlessly anticipate the next chapter to see what they will do and where they will go next."

Barbara Johnson
Bible Study Teacher

5

DEDICATION

This book is dedicated to my three children, Kevin, Laura, and Matthew, along with my many grandchildren. You are my source of joy. May you grow in grace and wisdom in the Lord.

ACKNOWLEDGEMENTS

I would like to acknowledge and thank those who have blessed me with their time and love as I wrote this third book in my *Snare of the Fouler series.*

Mary Scott, who spent endless hours pre-editing and improving this book.

Lisa Mackinder, my dear prayer partner, and Dianne Martin, my dear friend and writing buddy, who promotes my books at every chance.

Also, my good friend, Mary Jane Mapes, for her prayers, and whose wisdom helped me stay on track.

And to all those who read a rough draft and wrote kind words, a hearty thanks.

Most of all I thank the Lord, God Almighty who sent His Son to woo me into the kingdom through the power of the Holy Spirit. He is my all and all, my guide, and my counselor in all He calls me to do.

7

PROLOGUE

Jesus' command to the newly delivered demon possessed man of Luke 8:27-39, reads, *"Return to your own house and tell what great things God has done for you. And he went his way and proclaimed throughout the whole city what great things Jesus had done for him."*

At the end of the second book in this series, the apostle Paul's words to Daphne, the demon possessed slave girl of Acts 16, echoed the same directive. *"Take your newly found freedom and use it for Him. That is the true outcome of gratitude."* May these same challenges burn in your heart and mine.

PART ONE:
HEEDING THE CALL

PHILIPPI GREECE 51 A.D.

Chapter One

A man's heart plans his way, but the Lord directs his steps.
– Proverbs 16:9

Chaos covered the courtyard. Orders shrieked, yet bustling slaves waffled as the demands were retracted before there was time to comply. Daphne charged into the turmoil. She dodged a cart headed for *Kupio's* suite and called to a passing slave, "What happened?" He did not hear her.

Nicanor grasped her arm. "Daphne, it is my father. He has taken a turn for the worse. His fever rages and the cold compresses have not helped. I cannot leave, but could you go to Lydia's?" He pulled her close, his face troubled. "Can you do it? I hate having to ask."

"No, I want to help. I will go." Without thinking, she hugged him. Appalled at her impulse, she quickly pulled away, assured him she would be careful, and ran for the stables. Her heart echoed the sound of the horse's hooves on the well-worn path. Where the terrain allowed, she urged the animal to a gallop, and slowed on the mountain's narrow passes.

Desperation on Nicanor's face haunted her. She wanted to be back with him, but was glad to do something...anything. To avoid going through the city, she bypassed Philippi's Northern gate and entered from the East.

She flipped the reins over Lydia's outpost and yelled out her name. What would she do if she was not home? She called again and ran for the door.

The groundskeeper came around the side of the fence. "Lydia is not here, Miss. Can I help you?"

She stared as if she had not heard. "She must be home. I need her to pray. The Kupio's leg has gotten worse and he—"

"I am so sorry. I will tell her when she arrives. What is your name?"

"Daphne. Tell her it is Nicanor's father. She will remember. His leg was injured during the earthquake. How soon do you expect her?"

"It may not be until tomorrow. She went to oversee a shipment of purple dye at the port of Neapolis."

"Please, do not forget to tell her. It could mean his life."

The man watered her horse and promised he would the moment she returned. Daphne thanked him and dragged herself back to her mount. What should she do? She grabbed the reins, "Where can I go for help?"

Call on Me. I am your very present help in time of trouble.

The first time she heard the Lord speak by His Spirit she had panicked, afraid the demon that had harassed her daily for over a year had returned. But now, with joy, she welcomed the gentle voice of Jesus, so different from the evil one's agenda.

She released a grateful sigh. "But Lord, I need someone who knows how to pray. I need someone to pray like the believers at Lydia's pray."

You can pray, Beloved. My ear is attentive to your cry. Call on me and I will answer you.

She fell to her knees as she had seen Lydia do. "All right, Lord. Lydia said you filled me with Your Spirit and that He would help me to pray when I did not know how. Please touch Patharus' leg and heal it." She looked up, surprised at what followed.

11

"And use this crisis to cause him to want You to be his Lord, too."

The ride back to the estate seemed endless. The sun had set, and mountains shadowed the foothills leaving the path hard to see. To her relief, the horse navigated the twists and turns as if it had insight into her need to get home. Had she really followed this path daily into the city? But that had been in daylight. Her mind wandered. What if Patharus did not recover? The thought made her shiver.

Nicanor had agreed to go back to Athens with her after their wedding to find her family and then on to Delphi. But that was when they expected Patharus' healing would not be a deterrent. What if his father died or was unable to run his estate? Medea, Nicanor's stepmother, surely could not do it.

Her grip on the reins tightened. What would she do? God had made it clear she was to return to Delphi and expose the myth of Apollo. She was to witness to what He had done for her. Could she go alone? Should she?

The moment he saw her enter the compound, the stable master was quick to help her dismount.

"How is he? Has anyone said...?"

"Master Nicanor said to tell you to come to his quarters the moment you arrive, Miss Daphne."

He met her before she crossed the courtyard, his face pinched. "I am so glad you are safe. It is almost dark. Are you all right?"

"Yes. Lydia was not home. Only her grounds-keeper was there, but he promised to tell her the minute she arrived. I am sorry...I did not know whether to wait or what."

"No, I am glad you returned. I would not want you out there alone in the dark."

"But how is he?" His hesitation sent a chill down her spine. "Nicanor? What? Is he..."

"He is alive. But Halaten does not believe we can save his leg. He is prepared to remove the infected portion in the morning, before the infection spreads up into his body."

She fell to her knees, weeping. "No, he cannot lose his leg. It is too awful! It is..."

He knelt beside her and held her while she cried. "I love him and I have let him down. I prayed but it did not..."

He rocked her in his arms. "Shhh. Father knows you care about him, and you tried. God is in control. He will not let him die."

"Can I see him? I want to tell him–"

Nicanor hushed her, "No, Halaten has put him into a deep sleep to strengthen him for tomorrow. You get some rest now. Tomorrow will be a long day."

"Medea… has she been told?"

"No, it is best she learns when it is all over. She is not strong, and it would be too much for her."

Daphne walked slowly to her room. Who would tell Medea? The thought of Patharus' sickly wife hearing the bad news brought dread and more tears.

When she arrived early the next morning, Daphne felt the weight of an eerie silence that cloaked the compound. Nicanor was nowhere to be seen.

13

Chapter Two

...and the prayer of faith will save the sick.
– James 5:15

Nicanor had hardly slept. At the first chirp of a ringed plover, he sprang from his bed. The doctor was already at Patharus' side. He retrieved his scalpels, forceps, clamps, and extractors from a pot of water and laid them on a clean white sheet. Beside them lay a jagged-edged saw, its wooden handle carved with upper and lower notches to maintain a sturdy grip. The sight of it sent a chill down his spine. A thick cord and large needles readied with a wiry black thread completed the apparatus.

Halaten observed as Nicanor's eyes swept the equipment, his face pale. "Master Nicanor, you do not have to watch this procedure. Your father arranged a large sacrifice to go to *Asklepios*, the god of healing, yesterday, and I have trained my helpers well. Sometimes it is better if–"

Nicanor took in his father's still form. "No, I have to be here. I told my father I would not leave, and I will not. I have committed my life to the one true God, and it is He I trust to bring forth this healing. I will stay."

He wished he felt as confident as he sounded. Patharus had recognized Halaten's abilities and sent him to Alexandria to attend a school of medicine; and despite the persistent suspicion that doctors were quacks, Nicanor believed Patharus was in good hands. He took a deep breath. "Better yet, Lord, I know you heard our prayers and are with us, ready and able to heal my father."

He thought of Daphne. How could he help her see God still cared and was answering their prayers despite the need to remove part of his father's leg? He pictured how her thick dark hair curled over her face as she knelt, shaken at the news. "Lord, she is so young and has already experienced so much heartache in her life."

Halaten's helpers arrived. "I have already cleansed the tools and washed the leg I plan to amputate. He has ingested the herbs that will help coagulate his blood and help with the pain. The alcohol and opium have had enough time to be effective, so we need to begin." He tied a cord just above Patharus' knee and pulled it tight. "Monitor that closely, Jepo. Until I clamp off his vessels, we must prevent excessive blood loss." The slave nodded and moved closer.

The next several hours were a blur Nicanor hoped soon to forget. Halaten gave distinctive requests for each tool that began with the scalpel. Like a chef with a carving knife, he cut a circle into Patharus' flesh just below the knee. Nicanor hung onto the back of the bench in front of him, unable to look away. A putrid, sweetish smell drifted from the purulent incision. He managed to control his stomach until he saw Halaten reach for the saw. The sound of metal, as it ground bone, was more than he could handle. He put his head between his knees and prayed for strength to not vomit.

The physician's orders were strong. "That is it. Hand me the forceps. There, it is free. Take it away." His helper tugged and the lower section of Patharus' leg was removed. "Perfect. Now loosen the cord, slightly. We want it to bleed some and wash out any remaining rottenness. Good, good. Now tighten it again while I clean up this flesh." He cut away the blackish-red pieces hanging from the knee until only healthy pink flesh remained.

At his nod, a helper handed him one of several heated metal rods. He pushed it firmly against vessels that still trickled blood. The smell of seared flesh made Nicanor's eyes burn. Halaten repeated the procedure until all the bleeding stopped. Patharus' body jerked and Nicanor leapt to his feet. Within seconds, the doctor gestured that all was under control and called for a towel to wipe his forehead.

With practiced skill, the doctor pulled Patharus' loosened skin down around the remaining bone. Deft stitches held it snug before he washed the wound with acetum. He, then, spread willow over the edges and wrapped the stump with strips of clean cloth.

Nicanor's sigh rose from his toes. The doctor wiped the blood from his hands and smiled. "It went well, Master Nicanor. I believe he will heal and one day we will be able to fit a wooden extension to his knee."

"How long will it be before he wakes? I want to be here."

"It could be an hour, maybe two. I needed to make sure he did not come around in the middle of that or too soon after."

"Will he be in a lot of pain?"

"I am afraid so. He has had a major assault to his body, but I have henbane and poppy seeds prepared to keep him as comfortable as possible."

Nicanor glanced at the blood-soaked padding and headed for some air. "I will be back. And thank you, Halaten. I know you did your best."

For the Lord will comfort Zion.
– Isaiah 51:3

Daphne watched the sun clear the wall around the main estate. She considered going to the garden to wait but did not want to miss Nicanor. Hours later, the door to Halaten's chambers slowly opened. She jumped to get a better look and rushed over the minute she saw it was Nicanor. "How is he?"

He stopped, lowered his head, and leaned on his knees. She drew a sharp breath. "Nicanor, are you all right?"

He straightened and put his hand over his mouth. "Daphne, I..."

She took his arm and coaxed him toward the bench she had just left. "Let us sit down."

He sat with his hands over his face and shook his head. "Thank God it is over...it is finally over. I do not think I..." His shoulders shook and his voice trailed to silence.

"It is all right. You do not need to talk." She longed to put her arms around him, but the change in their relationship was so new she hesitated, unsure of what would be acceptable.

The head of the kitchen approached after Nicanor raised himself. "Master, would you care for some breakfast now?"

He waved the man off. "I am not sure I will ever be able to eat again."

His face had drained of color. Daphne set caution aside. He needed her. She reached for his hand and stroked it.

He put his hand over hers and forced a slight smile. "I will be so glad when you are mine and we can hide away and be alone for a while."

She blushed, treasuring the moment and lowered her eyes.

His voice settled. "Halaten thinks the procedure went well. He said it might be hours before my father wakes and he will be in a lot of pain. The opium will take the edge off, but the drastic procedure will take its toll." He shook his head. "It was the worst thing I have ever been through. Not only the gore, but to see him helpless and vulnerable, totally dependent on someone else, so unlike him."

"You are a loyal son. You told him you would stay, and you did. Somehow, he knew you were there. I just wish I had known better how to pray so he would still have his leg."

"No. Paul taught us that we are to ask and believe God answers. But we must also accept that the results are up to Him, and His plans do not always line up with ours."

She nodded but did not look convinced. "I have so much to learn."

Nicanor stood up and stretched. "I had better get back. I want to be there when he comes to."

"You look so stressed. Please let me tell Cook to get you something to eat...maybe some porridge or a bland soup to settle your stomach."

"All right but tell him to send it to Halaten's quarters. There is a cot I can doze on while I wait.

They should have the mess cleaned up by now and, hopefully, that awful smell has faded."

He closed the door and she hurried toward the kitchen.

The cook was eager to help. "Oh yes, Misses, and I will send some fresh bread and fruit too. It could be a long day."

She wandered in the courtyard, sat by the pool, and paced. She wished she could look in on Patharus and see how Nicanor was holding up. His father would remain under Halaten's watchful eye until he was well enough to be carried back to his own quarters.

Daphne sighed. "I may not get to see him for weeks."

She had just decided to spend some time in the garden when Nicanor poked his head out of Halaten's door. "Daphne, my mind keeps going to Medea. I do not want her to fret over rumors. This is not fair as you hardly know her, but she trusts me, so before she hears the servants whispering, could you tell her I asked you to break the news to her?"

Chapter Three

*And when the people heard the bad news they
mourned.*
– Exodus 33:4

Daphne, slowly, made her way to Medea's suite.
All the way, she rehearsed how to explain why they
had to remove part of her husband's leg. She had
spent little time with Patharus's wife. How would
she take the grim news? Would she resent that he
sent her instead of coming himself?

Danatel, Medea's servant, raised her brows. "The
missus has barely awakened from her nap. Did she
summon you?"

"No, Master Nicanor asked me to come. I have
some important news. Please tell her I am here."

She frowned and had reached to shut the door
when Medea called out. "Danatel, what is it? Is
someone here?"

"It is Miss Daphne, Madam. I will tell her to leave."

"No, show her in. I want to see her." The slave
grimaced and stood to one side.

"I am so sorry to disturb you, Medea, but I have
a message from Nicanor."

She hunched away from her pillows. "Oh yes,
My Dear Son." One look at Daphne's face brought a
gasp. "It is Patharus, is it not? I was afraid
something had happened. The servants have been
very quiet. Is his leg worse?"

Daphne prayed for wisdom as she knelt beside
Kupios' bed. "Yes, I am afraid so. Nicanor cannot leave
him, so he asked me to tell you what has happened."

Medea grabbed her hand. "How bad is it? I cannot lose him, too. Halaten seemed so optimistic the last time he was here."

"Yes, Dear One, but yesterday the Kupio's leg no longer responded to the cold packs and the swelling grew worse. Halaten decided the infection was out of control, and in order to save Patharus' life it was necessary to remove part..."

Medea drew back and screamed, "No! No, they cannot! I will not let them. Tell Nicanor to stop them."

Daphne put her arms around her and searched for an easy way to break the news. "Medea, it has already been done. Halaten removed the lower part of his leg this morning." She raised her voice. "It was the only way to keep the infection from taking his life."

Medea wailed. "No! She clung to Daphne and sobbed. "He has always been so powerful. How could this happen? He is the strong one."

She wiped Medea's hair from her face. "Yes, I know. But he will be strong again. Nothing will keep the Master down. Halaten said the surgery went well and...."

Medea's back stiffened. "Danatel, bring me a tunic and some sandals. I must go to my husband."

The servant rushed back into the room. "Missus, you know you cannot...."

"How dare you. Do as I say! Do you want to be punished?"

Panic swept the servant's face. "But Missus, I promised the Kupio...."

Daphne put her hands on Medea's shoulders. "Please, Medea, wait. Nicanor said Patharus will be in a deep sleep for hours."

"But I need to be with him, to tell him I am here and that I love him."

Daphne held Medea again and let her cry. "He knows, he knows."

Danatel focused on Daphne, her eyes pleading for support. "Please Missus, let me give you some of the powders the doctor left to help you,"

Medea glared at her. "I do not want to be put to sleep. I am going to my husband, now!" She pushed Daphne away and slid off the side of the bed. In unison, she and the servant's arms reached to catch her. Medea's voice quivered. "No, let me be! I am going. Danatel. Where is that tunic?"

The servant looked at Daphne and back at her mistress. "I..."

Medea took a step toward her. ""I will have you beaten. I said I..." She collapsed before either could reach her.

Daphne helped Danatel carry Medea, who still insisted she needed to go to her husband, back to her bed. "Perhaps something to relax you would be good for now, Medea."

Daphne moved out of the servant's way. Danatel was quick to hold the mix to Medea's lips and settle her back on her pillows. Daphne sat and stroked her arm, assuring her Patharus would be back to his old self in no time.

Medea's words slurred. "But I need to go..."

She fell asleep, mid-sentence, and Daphne stood to leave. The servant opened the door and shook her head. "Thank you, Miss Daphne. She will soon settle and sleep for several hours. I will send word if she awakens."

"Yes, and I will look in on her later. Please keep a close eye on her, and make sure everyone around her remains positive when they speak of the *Kupio*. And Danatel, you did the right thing."

The servant's face brightened. Daphne smiled as she left. The woman, who shut the door in her face months ago, had become an ally.

Two weeks later, Daphne sat in the courtyard hoping to spend time with Nicanor. By midday, she gave up and decided to go to the garden. She hated eating alone. Maybe I will join the slaves...at least there would be someone to talk to.

Nicanor called out as she rose, "Daphne, wait." His face lit up as he gazed at the lovely peach peplos she wore. Several dresses had shown up in her room after she switched to the main estate. The dress clung to her slender body and enhanced her tawny skin. "You look wonderful."

She blushed. "Thank you. Where are you rushing off to with all those ledgers? I have hardly seen you for days."

He led her to a nearby bench. "I know and I have so wanted to be with you, but Patharus is on a mission to teach me, in a few days, everything he has built over a lifetime. I think he fears he may not make it."

"How is he today?"

Nicanor shrugged. "Definitely better. Halaten thinks we are past the danger of infection coming back. It is a matter of time."

"Is he in a lot of pain? Can I see him yet?"

"Yes, well, soon anyway. Halaten keeps him drugged much of the time, and when he is awake, he wants to make sure I take care of everything he usually handles... and it is a lot. You keep praying for him, all right?" At her nod, he added, "Me too and probably all the believers that meet at Lydia's."

"Oh, do you think we could slip away and join them tonight? I am so hungry to learn more about Jesus. It has been a week since we have been there."

"I miss it too, but I will have to wait till evening and see how father is. Right now, I need to take care of some immediate business he wants done, now. But I will meet you in the dining room this evening." He stood up and whispered in her ear. "I wish I could kiss you but there are too many prying eyes."

She chuckled and waved him off. The late summer sun drenched Daphne with warmth and left her reluctant to go inside. Slaves bustled in and out. Some smiled broadly and others seemed unsure whether to address her. "Femi," she called to a young woman who carried a load of wheat to the grinder. "Femi, wait!"

The girl lowered her eyes. "Miss Daphne."

"Femi, I have missed you…are you all right? Is your little boy over that cough?"

The slave nodded but did not speak. Daphne touched her arm. "Femi, you can talk to me. We are friends." The young woman glanced up but quickly returned her gaze to the ground. "Femi, really, it is all right. You are so dear to me. I cannot count the times you packed me a special lunch or saved food for me when I was late for a meal."

Femi bowed in a makeshift curtsey. "Thank you, Miss Daphne. I had best get this wheat to the grinder."

Rejection hit her chest and loneliness swallowed her hopes as Femi hurried off. She understood why but hated the "us and them" arrangement. Lord, these have been my only friends since I arrived over a year ago. She pictured the slave family she

24

had grown up with in Delphi. I guess I should not be surprised. Other than my nanny, I never talked much with our slaves either.

She decided to visit the garden. Would any of the late summer flowers still bloom for her wedding? The path wound to the pool and bench she and Nicanor had shared. It was midafternoon. What was she to do with her time?

Daphne thought about her desire to search for her family. She remembered how joy would spring on her mother's face and three-year-old Theo would run, like an unleashed puppy, to her arms. Alexander's fate, on the other hand, worried her. How would a young man brought up in affluence submit to an overseer's demeaning, back-breaking commands? Their images inflamed her desire to begin her journey. "I know we cannot leave yet, Lord, but what do I do with myself meanwhile?"

Spend some time with Lydia. She can teach you much you need to know.

Daphne looked at the sky. Would it be proper for her to go into town by herself? "Well, if You tell me to go, God, You will surely make a way."

Chapter Four

And He changes the times and the seasons.
– Daniel 2:21

As shadows deepened, Daphne knew she must leave the garden if she wanted to bathe before dinner. To her, the privilege was a revived blessing. She hurried past the place where Stello, the former overseer, had tried to rape her, determined to bury that memory.

A flowering bush, Kawit had loved, brought her dearest friend to mind. Daphne's eyes filled as she remembered her violent death at the hand of that same overseer. "Oh, Kawit. I still miss you. You were right, I am in love with Nicanor, and I wish you could be here to see us married."

Melita, the young slave assigned to care for Daphne's personal needs, filled her tub. She smiled at the girl. Melita…*"honeybee"*… the name suited her. She slipped out of her peplos. *I could fetch my own water, but it probably would not be proper.* Guilt nudged as she soaked in the scented luxury denied slaves.

She was already seated for dinner when Nicanor rushed in. He looked exhausted. He sat next to her rather than across the table and released a loud sigh. Dark hair, still damp from his bath, curled with unruly gusto around his ears… so like her brother's. She blinked at the sting the memory unearthed.

He smiled and her heart fluttered at the sight of the dimple she had strained for so long not to notice. "Are you hungry? Or did you stop long enough today to eat?"

His knee brushed hers and gave rise to a wink. "Cook kept me well supplied. What did you do with your day? I so longed to be with you."

"I checked on Medea. She misses you. She does seem resigned to the fact that Patharus' procedure was necessary. In fact, her mind brimmed with ideas on how we should conduct our wedding."

His brows raised. "Do I hear a concern? Is she–?"

"No, it is all right. It has given her something to keep her mind off the Kupio. And I spent some time in the garden." She hoped she had diminished some persistent qualms.

His eyes held hers. "Did you sit on our bench?" At her nod, his hand found hers and he whispered, "Did you miss me?"

A servant set a beautiful array of salad on the table. "Shall I serve now, Master?" At his consent, the man filled their dishes with cucumbers, onions, tomatoes, and feta cheese dripping with olive oil and vinegar. Roast lamb and vegetables soon followed, enhanced by an abundance of wine. Daphne had learned to enjoy it without water, but sparingly.

She watched Nicanor enjoy the food, aware of how well he had adapted to the life of Roman aristocrats. Could she leave behind the slave culture she had experienced for over a year as quickly as he had, and return to the ease of her affluent upbringing? She sighed, no longer comfortable with being set apart from the ones who served her.

Nicanor signaled and their table was cleared. Their lovely outdoor dining area, draped with grape vines and flowers, awakened her awareness of change. Back in Delphi, women did not eat with men. The time of her mother's guidance on proper courtship, or lack of it, had been torn away, her paradigm forever altered. Yet, she marveled at how natural it seemed to sit there without awkwardness, enjoying his company after a year of denying her feelings.

Over the fruit and date cakes, she told him she thought the Lord wanted her to spend time with Lydia and asked again about joining the group that night.

He rose and pulled out her chair. "Let me do my quick check and make sure Father is settled for the night and I will meet you at the stable."

The horses were saddled, and they rode side by side where the path allowed. "Nicanor, how long do you think it will be before your father will be well enough to attend our wedding?"

"It is hard to say. Some days he is only awake for an hour or less at a time. Halaten monitors his pain and keeps him sedated much of the time, but he is getting better."

"I am truly glad, but I am anxious to have our wedding so we can leave for Delphi."

Nicanor's jaw twitched. He reined in his horse and reached for her bridle. "You do realize I will not be able to leave until Patharus is able to run the estate on his own, do you not?"

Her face fell. "Yes, of course. You could not leave while he is helpless, but maybe in a month he will be much better."

"That would take us well into fall and the time for sailing will have passed. We will have to wait for spring. The journey would be too dangerous. I am sorry. I know you are eager to go."

The path narrowed and she was glad he could not see her disappointment. "He sounds reluctant, Lord. Is he having second thoughts?"

Joy-filled songs of praise ushered them into Lydia's home. Delight in being there pushed concern to the back of Daphne's mind. Everyone rushed to welcome them, gushing, "So glad you could join us. How is Patharus?"

The music quieted and one of the men whom Paul had established as an elder stood up. "Friends, our beloved mentor, Paul, left us with specific instructions on how we are to conduct ourselves. The magistrates were so mortified by their exposed impropriety that they have given us a wide berth and we should be free to meet and do as we desire. However, our goal is not to irritate or avoid them, but to win them and every other citizen of Philippi over to our Savior, Jesus Christ."

"Yes" and "Amen" rose over cheers and applause.

The elder preached for over an hour on the power of God's love to change lives. "Remember how Paul said, 'and such ones were you,' referring to our unrighteous lives before our hearts were opened to receive Christ for ourselves?"

Murmurs rose and heads nodded.

"Let love be your guide as you share your experience of God's love and acceptance. Our hearts must be ready and expect the Holy Spirit to awaken them to the truth." The room burst into spontaneous worship with hands raised and spiritual songs.

Daphne basked in the man's encouragement. *Let love be your guide, expect the Holy Spirit to awaken....* Surely the Lord had equipped her to explain His love to people. She nodded when Nicanor whispered that they should go. Lydia hugged her and said she would love to have her come and spend some time together.

At a bluff, that overlooked some foothills, he stopped and dismounted. "I wanted you to see this view in the moonlight." He helped her down and guided her to the edge of the rock formation. Beavers had backed up a stream and the water formed a glimmering pond surrounded by lush foliage.

"Oh, it is beautiful. How could I have passed this way so many times and never noticed?"

"It has to be seen at night."

Daphne pointed at the pond. "Look, something is there in the water." She turned and found his face inches from hers.

Nicanor drew her close. "I knew you would love it. But it cannot compare to the beauty of your eyes."

Her heart skipped a beat. His eyes held the same hunger as they had when he discovered her about to ingest hemlock. In a moment of weakness, before fear ran her off, she had briefly yielded to the warmth of his kiss. She opened her mouth to speak but he covered it with his own. This time she had no desire to run from this gentle embrace that soared to a passionate demand she respond.

She could hardly breathe when he pulled back. "This probably is not proper behavior for Roman society, but for days I have longed to be alone with you." Nicanor ran his fingers down her high cheekbones and over her lips. "You are so lovely. I can hardly wait until the day I have you all to myself."

He kissed her again then purposely drew back. "Slaves do not go through all this ritual, they just decide to get married and do it." He kissed her forehead. "Your family probably was very proper too, so I promise not to spoil things by compromising you until we have that ceremony."

Daphne trembled the rest of the ride home, not sure if it was the cold mountain air or their kiss. She had much to learn about this man whom she would soon marry. He had been brought up as a slave not in a wealthy household like hers, and his mindset would surely reflect his background. But, Lord, we both belong to you. What more could we need?

Chapter Five

Walk worthy of the calling with which you were called.
– Ephesians 4:1

Medea's servant knocked on Daphne's door. "Miss Daphne, Madam has asked that you visit her."

Daphne's pulse quickened. Why this seemingly formal summons? She had made it a practice to look briefly in on Patharus' wife every few days. She did a quick check in her mirror, grateful to have the brass looking glass after living so long without any of the luxuries she grew up with.

The black lambs' wool carpet of her new quarters brushed her sandals as she rushed off. Danatel ushered her in.

Medea motioned to a bench near her bed. "Come in, Daphne. Sit here, close to me." The beautifully draped curtains and pillows, in creams and pale colors, complemented Medea's brown eyes and flowing blonde hair. Her own mother had endured much to keep up with that change of hair color. Still, Daphne was amazed that someone who almost never left her room would endure such a process.

Medea pulled herself more uprightly and stretched out her hand. Her smile, meant to put Daphne at ease, gave her cause for wonder. Had Medea forgotten the ugly scene she stirred after she heard they removed her husbands' leg?

Daphne returned the smile. "How do you feel today?" The well styled hair and expertly applied makeup could not disguise Kupios' pasty color or hide the dark that circled her eyes.

"I feel fine. Ignore talk of my limitations and exaggerated need for rest. I can manage much more than they think." She gestured at her servant. "You may be excused, Danatel."

The maid glanced at Daphne. "I will be right outside if you—"

Medea's sharp tone left no room for debate. "I will be fine. Thank you." She faced Daphne. "Now, we can talk in private. I want to hear about you. Nobody tells me anything. It is as if they think I will melt if I hear more than syrupy nonsense!"

Daphne strained to laugh with her. "What would you like to know?"

"Everything. Where you came from, about your family, and this mysterious experience that changed your life. That has been hidden from me, but I do know you were responsible for the rescue of my beloved Patharus when his leg was crushed in the earthquake." Her eyes welled. "For that, I will be forever grateful."

Daphne bowed her head and nodded. "I am so glad Kupio's leg is healing without complications."

"Yes, I do not know what I would do if..."

"Halaten is a good doctor. But I am sure you know that."

"Of course, but before they begin to scold me for my need to rest, tell me about yourself."

Daphne bit her lip. Where should she start? "My family was from Delphi, a small city west of Corinth. My father mismanaged his finances, and after he died, unscrupulous magistrates auctioned off our home and all we owned to pay his debts. The sale included my mother, two brothers, and me."

33

Medea's face clouded. "How awful for you. Where are they now?"

"I have no way to know. We were separated when we reached the slave market in Athens. I have not seen them since."

"I am so sorry." Medea touched Daphne's arm. "But I am glad you ended up here with us, and I am so excited about your betrothal to Nicanor. Such a fine young man."

Daphne relaxed, relieved Patharus' wife appeared to have no reluctance about a former slave marrying into the family. "I love him very much, but we have hardly talked about or planned our wedding. Nicanor loves his father deeply, as do I. Our main concern is his recovery."

Medea's eyes sparkled as she scooted forward. "As is mine, but I cannot keep from envisioning a joy filled wedding." She turned her face to the wall. "It has been so long since..."

Daphne waited but she did not continue. Medea's enthusiasm for a wedding brought a picture of her mother's excitement at the news she had been selected to marry Apollo's high priest. She sighed. That was the only good thing that came from being sold into slavery, to be saved from a forced marriage to the man she watched commit a horrible murder.

She broke the silence, surprised that Medea could be excited about the wedding while Patharus' complete recovery was still uncertain. "You all have been so kind considering my past, but I—"

"Nonsense. Neither you nor Nicanor probably know of my background. Patharus is very private, closed mouth about everything. It is not that he is ashamed. That is just the way he is."

Her ears perked. Had Medea been a slave too? "I would not pry—"

"No, I want you to know. Most Romans, like my husband, would not consider marriage to someone from another country. But Patharus and I met when my father asked me to work with him. My whole family had been trained in horticulture and Patharus wanted a palatial garden linked to his estate, one that would be completely sheltered from onlookers."

Daphne's conscience stung. How many times had she sneaked into that beautiful oasis?

Medea's face glowed. "I loved that type of project and only expected to sketch out possibilities and suggest where to place ponds and specific plants and flowers. Never did I dream it would one day be mine. He loved my ideas and insisted I come daily to supervise its construction." Her face colored. "That led to friendship and then much more."

"Then you are not Roman either?"

"Well, I am now, by marriage, but I was born Greek, same as you and Nicanor." Her smile was contagious.

Daphne could hardly believe what she heard, "Really? You are Greek? Amazing!"

"Yes, we have much in common and if you will let me be a substitute mother, I would love to help you plan your wedding. I have thought of nothing else for days and have lots of ideas on how we could arrange it."

Daphne was quick to hide caution that gripped her chest. Medea had only casually hinted at her interest in the wedding, until now. Is that the way it is supposed to be, Lord? I do remember mother's memories of the elaborate plans my father

35

envisioned, the special carriage, the procession, and intricate details. Maybe I should be grateful she wants to be involved, but I want it to glorify You, Jesus, not some false god.

"I have watched you enjoy my garden all this past year and —"

Her hand flew to her lips. Medea had seen her! "Oh, I must apologize. I know I was not supposed to be in there, but it was so —"

"No, do not fret. I loved seeing you enjoy what I could only experience from my window. I have hoped you might want to have your wedding there."

"In the garden? Oh, that would be wonderful! Thank you, Medea."

"I do so look forward to you and Nicanor living here with us. He is so special...drops in often to check on me. I plan to convince Patharus he needs to add another wing to the estate with lots of rooms for your family." Her eyes drooped. "I do hope they will let me see him soon."

Daphne's heart sank. Patharus' wife had no inkling of their plans to leave. Medea was tired and both were happy to continue their conversation another day. Not having to discount an immediate need for an additional wing or explain what she called *"the mysterious experience,"* was a relief. How do I recount a spiritual miracle to an unspiritual person, Lord?

With love. You tell her about Me, how I died to save her from the kingdom of darkness and to bring her into my kingdom of light. Then she, too, will be able to grasp spiritual things.

Her jaw fell. She had received Jesus as her Savior less than a month before. Would He expect her to explain His plan of salvation to someone when she, herself, still had so much to learn?

You already know what I have done for you. That is what I have called you to tell others. No matter who they are.

She sighed, grateful the Lord knew her thoughts and would guide her.

Yes, Lord. I will tell her. And I cannot wait to get to Delphi and tell everyone I meet about Your amazing love.

Deep in thought, Daphne reentered the courtyard. In light of Medea's previous tantrum, how would she receive the unwelcome news they planned to leave? More to the point, how would Patharus accept the announcement?

Chapter Six

*You will keep him in perfect peace whose mind is
stayed on You.*
– Isaiah 26:3

Nicanor paced. Was it not the time his father
usually awakened? He leaned in to listen to his
breathing and was startled by a sudden snort.
"Nicanor?" Patharus' eyes remained closed, but he
murmured something too slurred to understand.

He laid his hand on Patharus' shoulder. "I am
here, Father. You have been asleep a long time.
How do you feel?"

"Oh, I umm, I am..."

Nicanor pulled a stool closer. "It is all right,
Father. Rest. I will be here when you wake."

"No, I am awake." Patharus tried to shift his
injured leg and moaned. "Clumsy thing! Good for
nothing..."

"It will be easier when it heals. Halaten says it
has come along well, and he can fit you with a peg
that will get you around as fast as ever."

"Ha! That will be the day." He lifted the stump
with both hands and groaned at a stab of pain.
"Listen, I want you to instruct him to quit knocking
me out so much of the time. The pain has lessened,
and I need to be alert. Whatever he uses makes my
head foggy or puts me to sleep more than
necessary."

Nicanor smiled. It was good to hear him give
orders again. "I will tell him, but we cannot let the
pain get out of hand. Halaten says it is better to
keep it under control."

Patharus closed his eyes and lay still so long it seemed he had drifted back to sleep. "Nicanor? Good, you are still here. I think it is time to allow Medea to come see me. Halaten says she is quite anxious, and I do not want her to worry...not good for her condition. Tell him to arrange it as early tomorrow as he can. You or Daphne can tell her maid to have her ready so she can be brought here as soon as I am awake and cleaned up."

"I will send Daphne. She has spent a lot of time with Kupios since the surgery and has asked when she too could see you." He nodded and they talked about the expected harvest until Halaten arrived with his midday parcel of medications. Nicanor corralled him just outside the door and spoke to him of Patharus' wishes.

Halaten's brow twitched. ""I will wean him off some of the stronger pain killers, but you know your father. If he starts to feel like he can get up and get going, he could tear the sutures and we would have a whole new set of problems." They agreed to take it slowly, and Nicanor left to tend some business and find Daphne.

Melita laid Daphne's dinner tunic aside and hurried to answer Nicanor's knock. "I think she might have gone to the garden, Master."

He rounded the path that led to their favorite bench, but she was not there. He continued, softly calling her name. By the time he reached the hemlock swamp with no sight of her, he became concerned. He ran and shouted her name all the way back to the gate but did not find her. He charged through her door. "Melita, has Daphne returned?"

The servant's eyes grew wide. "No, Master. I have not seen her."

"Have not seen whom?"

He spun around. "Daphne! Where were you? I have been so worried."

Her face puzzled. "Worried? Why? Do you not remember I told you that I was going to spend time with Lydia today?"

He closed his eyes and loosed a loud sigh. "Yes, yes. How could I have forgotten? I am sorry, it is just that I...."

She caught Melita's eye. "You can leave. I will call when it is time to get ready for dinner." The servant left and he backed her into the privacy of her room.

She cocked her head. "Nicanor, could the strain of being with your father night after night and throughout most days have affected you? Yesterday, you walked right past me and never even saw me. You have been under such a strain and probably need some undisturbed sleep. Now that Patharus is better, could you not go to your own quarters at least at night? Halaten is well able to watch over him for you."

Nicanor pulled her into his arms and nuzzled her neck. "You are right. I will tell Halaten after dinner." His lips crept up her throat until he found hers. "How did I ever get along without you?"

Behold, You desire truth in the inward parts.
– Psalms 51:6

Strict prohibitions of being around, or ever in, an intimate situation with a man before marriage flashed in Daphne's mind. Gently, she pushed herself from his grip, her eyes on his. "I do not think you should be—"

"I know, I know. I will leave." He ran his hands slowly down her arms before he grinned and reached for the door. "But I am greatly relieved that you are all right. See you at dinner."

She hugged her arms, savoring the tingle of his touch. "Lord, things are not the same here as they were back home. There is not anyone to protect me from myself and I love him so much. I need help to resist him."

The next day, even before she reached Medea's suite, Daphne could hear her giving orders to her servants. She smiled. The *Kupios* sounded happy. Her visit with Patharus must have gone well. Danatel quickly opened the door. "Come in. The mistress has ordered a special luncheon for the two of you. It will be ready shortly."

"Daphne, I am so glad you could join me." Joy bubbled on Medea's every word. "Lunch will be ready soon. Please, sit here by me."

She pulled the bench close. "You look wonderful. I understand you were taken to see Kupio this morning. I am glad it did not overtire you."

"Yes, I finally saw my beloved. He looked better than I expected. His leg was covered, but when I saw the crease in the blanket where his foot should have been, it left me queasy."

Daphne nodded and squeezed Medea's hand.

"But he is strong and there is no way this accident will slow him down. He was already full of plans for that property he acquired before the quake and, of course, for things he wants Nicanor to be master over."

Daphne tried not to wince. "It must have been a wonderful reunion after so many weeks."

Medea chatted on about the visit, her gratitude for Halaten's care, and her hopes Patharus would soon return to his own rooms. "And that leads me to the wedding. I kept the orange veil from my wedding in hopes I would have a daughter, but I would love for you to wear it." She dropped her voice. "But only if you would like to. I have the orange shoes too, but your feet look much smaller, so we will have to order new ones."

Daphne tried to imagine an orange veil. Had anyone back home worn one? Roman weddings must be different. Oh, Mother, I wish you were here.

To her relief, Danatel interrupted. "Lunch is ready, Misses. Shall I serve it now?"

"Yes, and pull over that table so we can talk." The servant placed a wooden tray with sides over Medea's legs and set Daphne's food on the table.

"I spoke to Patharus about adding another wing to the estate and he was all for it. He said he had the same idea."

A quick bite of her date nut muffin became the perfect excuse for Daphne to remain silent. Medea did not notice. She talked throughout the meal, mostly about her ideas for the wedding.

Daphne looked at the lovely fruit salad bathed in a creamy yogurt sauce. Will I be able to keep that down? She held her napkin to her mouth and shook her head. She could not continue this deception. How long before the truth would pour from her lips and cause mass disappointment, especially after Patharus had so generously set her free? She stood. "I am so sorry, Medea. Something has upset my stomach and I think I had better go lie down. Perhaps we can talk again soon."

"You do look pale, *Kalon*. You go ahead and get some rest."

Daphne made a quick exit, moved to tears at the sound of her family's pet name spoken after all this time. Her stomach churned but it was not the food. *I do not want to disappoint anyone Lord, least of all You.*

She needed to talk to Nicanor, and he must see the urgent need to tell his father of their plans.

Chapter Seven

Let none deceive himself.
– 1 Corinthians 3:18

Nicanor cocked his head and squinted at Daphne. "You have been awfully quiet tonight. Is something wrong?"

She pushed her food around on her plate but did not look up. "It is still early. Do you think we could walk in the garden before you look in on your father?"

He eyed the sky. Autumn had swept the trees, and left patches of color amidst the green leaves. "It will not stay light long, but if you are finished, we have time."

He pulled out her chair, and she followed him to the hidden gate. He held her hand as they walked the familiar path. "Are you chilly?"

She shook her head and they headed for their favorite bench. A few crimson leaves already dotted the surface of the pond. She pulled her shawl over her shoulders. How can I help him understand what is happening, Lord? How can I make him see...

He put his arm around her and faced her. "Come on, tell me what is bothering you. It is me. Remember? The one who loves you."

Her face darkened. "It is that I am so concerned about our plans to leave." She felt him stiffen. "I know, I know. It cannot be until spring. I wish it were sooner, but you are right. Patharus is far from able to run things alone and sailing will soon be over, but..."

He drew her closer. "Do you know how beautiful you are?" He leaned in to kiss her, but she backed away.

"Nicanor, please. We need to talk."

"I would rather kiss you."

She jumped to her feet. "If you are not going to —"

"All right, all right. But if we agreed we cannot go until spring, what is the problem?"

She released a heavy sigh. "The problem is your father and Medea both plan on our being here after the wedding. They have no idea we intend to go find my family and then on to Delphi. She has even spoken to him about building a wing on the estate for us...and he has agreed."

His eyes grew wide. "Add a wing to the estate, for us?"

She nodded and returned to his side, quiet while that sank in. "Medea has buried me with ideas for the wedding, and that will work out. But I cannot go on with the pretense that we will settle down immediately, when we plan to leave for a while. It is dishonest.'"

Nicanor leaned his elbows on his knees, with his fists under his chin. "You cannot begin to understand how much my father has come to depend on me. Not just for the many things he cannot do now but into the future. He has given me more and more responsibility over portions of his estate. He even talks about when it will all be mine. I cannot fathom how I can leave."

Her shoulders slumped.

"It all seemed so simple when God told me to go back with you to your home."

"I know. I know, but —"

"Maybe we should go ahead and plan the wedding, and then when things are stable..."

She fought back tears. "You know that would not be right. It is like living a lie. Nicanor, I must be true to what God has called me to do." She raised her chin. "I plan to leave as soon as it is safe to travel. I understand your position," her voice wavered, "but you will have to decide for yourself what is right for you."

A breeze tousled their hair, and he felt her shiver. "Come on, I do not want you to get cold. Halaten says Father will be well enough to move back into his quarters by next week. I need to be sure he is settled and well enough before I give him such unwelcome news. I hate to think how he will take it." He took her hand. "You know how much I want us to be married and together, but I cannot leave until I am sure he can handle things. I will have to wait and see how it goes."

Preoccupied with their thoughts, they left the garden and parted in near silence.

Casting all your cares upon Him for He cares for you.
– 1 Peter 5:7

Daphne tried to hide her relief when Lydia answered the door. "I am so glad you are home. I did not intend to come back this soon but—"

"It is all right, Dear. Come in, and I will brew some tea." She put an arm around her shoulder and instructed her servants to make Daphne's chaperone comfortable and care for their mounts.

Daphne warmed her hands at the fireplace before she cozied into a nearby chair. Fall's chill had arrived. The morning was unusually cold, but

Lydia's warmth radiated like the heat from their teacups.

She pulled up a chair and sat some muffins on a side table. "We have missed you and Nicanor at the meetings. I hope Patharus' leg is not worse."

"No. Nicanor often works well into the evening to accomplish all his father wants him to do, and Patharus' leg is healing well. He may even move back into his own quarters in a few days."

"Wonderful. God has answered our prayers. But you do not look like you are celebrating. What is wrong?"

She focused on the ceiling. "Lydia, what would God think if I did not go back to Delphi, at least for a while?"

"God is on your side, child. He loves you. He is not waiting for you to make a mistake or fail to follow His counsel. He is—"

Daphne's voice rose. "But I know I am supposed to go. Paul confirmed what I already knew when I thanked him for delivering me of that demon. He said, *'Take your newly found freedom and use it for the Lord. That is the true outcome of gratitude.'*"

"Then, what is to stop you? Did you not tell me Nicanor said God told him to go with you? God has no problem with your waiting until it is safe to sail. That is wisdom."

"The problem is not God. It is either Nicanor or it is me. Forgive me, I am so confused. He seems very hesitant to leave his father now that Patharus has put so much responsibility on him. I am not sure he even plans to leave with me in the spring. What will I do? I must go."

Lydia pulled her chair closer and put her hands on Daphne's. "First, My Dear, you need to step back and decide to trust God. He is not the author of confusion. Remember how we were recently taught to expect the devil to interrupt our plans or send distractions to cause doubt, fear, or unbelief? Take that to heart, and decide whom you will believe, God or these circumstances."

She wiped tears from her cheeks. "But what if—"

"No. No what if's. You must decide to trust God to work this out for you. Paul taught us that God works all things for good for those who love Him and are called according to His purposes. He knows of your dilemma. Pour it out to Him in prayer and believe.The Holy Spirit will guide you."

"Do you think He would have me leave Nicanor here and go by myself? How could that be good?"

"I cannot tell you God's will for you. If He has knitted yours and Nicanor's hearts together and wants you to be one, the Lord will work it out. Remember how impossible it seemed when you ran from Him, afraid to return to your master without the ability to tell fortunes?"

Daphne could barely nod.

"And did He not work it out beyond your hopes and dreams? It is always good to remember how He helped you in the past, and to know He is totally committed to guide you now that you are His child."

But how will I know that it is His prompting and not a demon leading me to do the wrong thing?"

"The Lord speaks in a still, small voice inside you, He never demands that you do anything. He is gentle and His counsel is always bathed in peace. That is your determining factor. Examine the words you hear. Do they speak peace to your heart?"

"Oh, Lydia, what would I do without you?"

"It is the Holy Spirit in you who is your helper, Dear One. Call on Him and listen to His counsel. Let Him be your guide." A sly smile spread across her lips. "You have at least five months before you can leave. Surely, you will receive your answer by then."

Chapter Eight

You uphold me in my integrity.
– Psalms 41:12

It took two weeks before Halaten felt it was safe to move Patharus back into the Kopio's suite. Servants would monitor him day and night. Nicanor relished the extra time to examine his priorities and seek God for the right course. Much was at stake: his desire for a life with Daphne or his obligation to his father. Could he manage to have both? In the quiet, her announcement that she was going back to Delphi, with or without him, vibrated like a never-ending gong. What if he lost her? Patharus' plans loomed larger every day. Responsibility, traditionally passed to an heir, came fast and furious. To hear from the Lord and find peace in his decision had not come easily.

Nicanor arrived early for what had become a daily briefing with his father.

After the doctor finished his morning checkup and bandage change, his servant cleared the master's breakfast. "Will there be anything else, *Kupio*?"

Patharus barely looked up. "No, not now." He motioned to Nicanor.

He pulled up a chair. "It is good to see you back in your rooms, Father. Was the move painful? Did it wear you out?"

""No. Well, the transport was not comfortable, but I am glad to be here. Halaten gets on my nerves. He hovers like a hen over her chicks."

Nicanor hid a smile. This was not the time to defend the man's dedication.

Patharus plowed into his plans for the day. "The harvest is our foremost concern these days. The peaches and nectarines are probably about done, but you need to check on the apples and make sure all the figs are picked. The overseer tells me the root vegetables have been stored and the tomatoes and such prepared, as well. Of course, the grapes will need a good frost. Have we had one yet?"

"Nicanor?"

"Oh, sorry, Father. What did you say?"

Patharus' brows flexed. "I asked whether or not we have had a frost, but it seems your thoughts are elsewhere, in fact, they have been for days. What is on your mind, Son?"

The question caught him off guard. Nicanor had rehearsed how he might explain his dilemma to Patharus but felt ill-prepared. There was no way now to avoid it. He uttered a silent prayer for wisdom and to keep his voice steady. "I have something to tell you that may be hard to understand."

"Well, what is it?"

"You remember when you first learned I was attending meetings at Lydia's, the woman who gave Daphne a shawl? You met her." Patharus nodded. "I told you at the time I had found the one true God, Jesus Christ, and that I had made him my God."

Impatience scrunched Patharus' face. Nicanor could almost hear, "So, get on with it.'"

"I tried to explain to you what happened to Daphne the day your leg was crushed by the earthquake, but you were in such pain I doubt you were able to take it in. I know you realized that instead of running to save herself she chose to stay and try to help you, but—"

"I know, I know, and I will always be grateful. You paid off her other two owners, right? Is that what this is about?'"

Nicanor resisted an urge to roll his eyes. His father's disregard for matters he considered trivial was well known and could be maddening. "No, no it is not. But yes, I paid off Sergius and Amplias, and Daphne knows she has her freedom. That same day, she was set free from a demonic power that had enslaved her. She, too, came to accept Jesus Christ the one true God for herself.'"

Patharus shifted on his bed and reached for his water cup. "Well, if gods are important to you, it is probably good that you both have this in common, but—"

"Father, I need you to listen."

Patharus' cup clanked when it hit the table. He folded his arms. "All right, get on with it."

"The thing is, Daphne immediately sensed that our God told her she is to go back to her home city and help others who, like herself, were indoctrinated into Apollo worship. Our leaders taught us that all other deities people worship are false gods, portrayed by demons. She is to expose the myth of Apollo that prevails in her city. He is a false god that binds people and keeps them from the true God who loves them and wants to set them free."

"And you want to go with her." It was not a question.

Nicanor struggled to regain his composure. "Father, before we found that your leg would not heal and needed surgery, I promised I would. I cannot let her go alone.'"

Patharus pulled himself upright and winced. "That is very noble of you. But have you considered your promise to be my son and heir? You were to learn my businesses and to carry them out alongside me, as well as after I am gone. How do you plan to keep that commitment from the other side of the country?"

At the dismay in his father's voice and the disappointment that undergirded his words, Nicanor cringed. He had watched him deal with suppliers and associates and knew he did not tolerate unnecessary upsets of his plans. Nor did he ever settle for less than a fair exchange.

"You probably think I do not appreciate all you have done and given me, but I do. I value that I can work alongside you and learn all it takes to run your estate. I am sorry to have disappointed you, but this is something I must do. We will not leave until spring when it is safe to sail, and you are better able to handle everything again. I plan to return in the fall before it gets too dangerous to sail, maybe sooner, if you will have me back."

Patharus turned his face to the window. His silence cut like pruning shears. "We will talk of this, again. For now, you had best see to the harvest." Before Nicanor reached the door, he added, "And tell Daphne that I wish to see her."

Love does not seek its own.
– 1 Corinthians 13:5

Daphne puzzled at Nicanor's quick wave as he barreled past her in the courtyard for the second time. Was he avoiding her? She walked to the kitchen and asked a worker for some juice. She should visit Medea but dreaded the thought. Now that the Master had returned to his rooms, more pressure to comply with her plans was sure to follow.

She sat on a bench, sipped her drink, and lifted her face to the autumn sunshine. Well, maybe now is the time to talk to her about You, Lord, rather than after she hears of our plans to leave. She tried to imagine the Kupio's response to the news of the Lord's great love but could only wonder.

Not yet.

The Lord's whisper surprised her. I do not understand, Lord, but You must have a reason so I will wait. She rose, deep in thought, startled when Nicanor called her name.

"Daphne, wait. I am glad I caught you. Let us eat lunch, I need to talk to you."

Terra cotta bowls filled with boiled goose eggs and vegetables wrapped in filo pastry were laid before them. Pears, mulberries, and melons added to the colorful spread. She asked for water, but Nicanor welcomed wine to wash down the warm bread placed on the table.

She picked at her food. Had he told his father of their plans or made the decision not to leave with her?

"You are not eating. Are you all right?"

She raised some of the pastry to her lips. "I am fine. How is your father? Did the move go well?"

He cleaned his plate and swirled the last of his wine. "I told him."

"You told him? What did he say? Is he angry with us? With me?" She held her breath.

He relayed the conversation with his father.

"And did you tell him of your intentions?"

"He figured I planned to go with you before I even told him."

Her relief poured in silent thanks. "Did it upset him?"

"Well, he questioned my loyalties, but I assured him we would not leave until spring when he is better and return in the fall."

Neither spoke for a while. She studied his face, trying to decipher his thoughts. The possibility of being separated, of not becoming his wife tore at her heart, but she could not deny his huge responsibility. She fought to keep her voice from breaking. "Nicanor, I want to release you from your request to marry me. I—"

His chair fell as he jerked away from the table. "Wait a minute! What did you say? I do not intend to change my plans to marry you. I love you."

She stammered, unable to quench her tears. "But—"

"No, no 'buts'." A vein that ran on the side of his left eye jutted noticeably as he bundled her up into his arms. "Did you really think I would let anything come between us?"

"No, but I love you and want the best for you. If you leave and it ruins your chance to be all Patharus has planned, I—"

He held her close. "Shhh! My plans are for us to be together, no matter what he or anybody else wants. If that is not to be here, then wherever God leads us. I do not intend to let him down, but I am not tied to this estate or anything in it. Only to God and to you.

"And you told your father that?"

"Well, partly, but he interrupted and waved me off. I thought he might be about to say he was finished with me but all he said was, 'Tell Daphne I wish to see her.'"

Her hand clenched to her throat. "Oh, no. Do you think he will ask me to leave?"

"No, I do not think so. He cares about you, or he would not have given you your freedom. He probably wants to know if you intend to return with me. He asked for you to come first thing tomorrow morning. Do not be afraid. He is a good man."

Chapter Nine

*The Lord our God we will serve and His voice we
will obey.*
– Joshua 24:24

Daphne could not sleep. Every possible thing she
thought the Kupio might say turned to a haze that
lingered like dust over a newly plowed field. Most
held accusations. After several hours, she paced .
What was it Lydia said? "Tell the Lord what is on
your heart and then choose to trust Him with the
outcome." Asking proved easy. To believe and let
go, much harder.

Epaphroditus, the elder Paul appointed before he
left, had preached that God was on her side, for her,
and not against her. She would concentrate on that.
Had the Lord not already answered her prayer
when he convinced Nicanor that being together
was more important than anything?

She fell to her knees. "Father, You know what is
coming and I choose right now to trust You. Thank
You for Your great love for me and Nicanor, and for
Patharus and Medea. Lord. I release the whole
situation into Your hands and determine to leave
the outcome with You."

Sleep finally came, but she awoke, yawning. "Oh,
Melita, thank you. I might have slept till noon if
you had not come. What a long night."

Her servant brought a warm cloth for her face,
brushed out her hair, and bent to lace her sandals.
Daphne's eyes pooled as she remembered how
Belte, her beloved servant back in Delphi,
performed the same tasks. When I get to Delphi,

Lord, could You show me where the slave mongers took her after the auction of my father's property? I so long to tell her I found her Jesus, or I should say You found me?

Dressed, with her hair carefully arranged on top of her head, she left most of her breakfast uneaten and headed for Patharus' suite. How many times, since she arrived over a year ago, had she gone to that door and been ushered in to account for what she had earned telling fortunes?

His beautiful accommodations had over-whelmed her, luxurious furnishings, far beyond those of her family's stately home. And yet, he had always been approachable. He had never taken advantage of her lowly position, nor referred to her as a sorceress.

His servant responded quickly to her knock. "Come in. The *Kupio* awaits your visit." He led her past the area she had been familiar with and into his sitting room. She had spent but a few moments with him since the accident. The first had been at his request. He had thanked her, personally, for getting him away from the damaged building that pinned his leg and threatened to collapse on top of him. The second had been after his leg had begun to heal, simply a brief call to let him know she cared.

His customary furnishings had been replaced with a comfortable bed and seating for guests, much like Medea's. He motioned her over. "Come in, Daphne. Welcome."" He ordered his servant to settle her chair close to him and dismissed him.

Her hands shook, so she gripped the edge of the seat to hide them.

"Well, look at you. You have come a long way from the frightened little waif that arrived over a year ago. You look wonderful."

Daphne blushed and murmured her thanks. Never would she forget being brought before him. She had been a slave to the powerful owner of this gigantic estate, to use in any way he pleased. Filthy and half-starved after weeks in the Athenian slave market, she had trembled, terrified of the rape and beatings she had been warned to expect. Wanting to die was her foremost memory. Mercifully, he had only offered kindness and protection.

She drew a deep breath and reminded herself she had chosen to trust the Lord. "Master, it is so good to see you back in at—"

He went right to the problem. "Nicanor told me about your desire to find your family and revisit your city, and I understand. But you must know it would be a hardship to have him gone for an extended period at a time when he is being newly grounded in the complexity of managing our estate."

She opened her mouth, but he raised his hand. "I want you to know I am very pleased that my son has chosen you to be his bride. Medea and I both look forward to the wedding and to having you here with us. But it would be better, all-around, if you could put off your journey for a year."

Daphne clamped her lips. He sounded like the matter had already been decided. A whole year? How could she follow the Lord's directions and wait a whole year? She swallowed the disappointment that threatened to choke her and sent up a quick prayer.

"*Kupio*, I have no desire to upset your plans for Nicanor, or for us, but I have given my heart to the Lord God. It is He whom I must put first, and He has—"

"I do not ask you to deny your god, just to wait a while."

Tears, she could not stop, coursed down her cheeks. "I know this must be hard for you to understand, Master, but my God has redeemed me from a miserable life controlled by an evil, demonic spirit, and I must do as He has asked. I must go back to Delphi and help the people there, who are under the same bondage, realize they can resist and be set free."

He handed her a cloth. "You are right. I do not understand such loyalty to a god who would require you to leave all you have here to go and do something that sounds impossible. I know the Greek people, and their gods are deeply imbedded in their culture and history." His sigh held disgust. "What pull does this new god have on you? Where did it come from?"

She blew her nose and snuffed back her tears. "In the spring before we lost our home, I came of age and my family hoped I would commit my life to Apollo. He is the god sacred to them. To please them, I went through the rituals and pledged to honor him. At my final review, I was given the devastating news that I had been chosen to marry one of the temple priests at the group marriage ceremonies arranged every fall. That is when I knew I had to find out if Apollo really was a god and if all the lore, taught me by my grandmother, was true."

He leaned into his fist and stared. "Well, was he?"

"To find out, I snuck into the adytum, the bowels of the temple forbidden to all but the priestesses. That is where Apollo's acclaimed divination presumes to originate. While there, I discovered that the priests operate according to what enhances their treasury. And the pythias, the priestesses, the ones who bring forth the divination..." She closed her eyes and shook her head.

"Apollo worshipers believe fumes rise from a crevasse in the floor that holds the decayed body of the dragon Apollo killed centuries ago. These deceived, older women babble as a result of breathing these intoxicating vapors. They have no way to know that demons are their source of what they believe empowers them. At the end of the session, the priests on duty use the gibberish to interpret what they themselves decide is Apollo's will for those seeking divination."

Patharus' lips twisted to one side. "So, this assured you Apollo was a sham, perpetuated by men? Then why did you—"

"I was convinced the rituals were a farce, but while I waited to leave unseen, the high priest broke protocol and dashed into the adytum. A rival priest, who coveted his position, followed and murdered him right before my eyes. The *pythia* witnessed the crime, discovered my presence, and hurled a curse at me. I saw her clutch her chest, collapse, and fall from her perch. Panicked, I tripped, hit my head and was knocked unconscious."

"Terrible. Was there anyone there to help you? Other priests?"

"No one knew I was there. When I awoke, in a daze, both bodies had been removed and I was alone. I had no idea what happened while I was out, but have since learned that the demon, a spirit of divination that had indwelt the dead *pythia*, needed a new home. I was available, unprotected, and eligible by my own pledge to a god other than the only true Lord. That is when I first heard the demon talk inside of me. He had been reassigned to work his divining through me. That became a life of submission to an evil being bent on bringing as many people as possible, with him, into the kingdom of darkness. The demon told me he was a messenger of the god, Apollo. At that time, I did not know there are no other gods than our Lord. Though convinced the temple was a sham, I came to believe Apollo was real. How else could I hear a voice inside that told me things, and at first, helped me?"

She could not discern Patharus' reaction or interest but was unable to stop. "His counsel gave me the ability to earn money by telling fortunes. I clung to it though it clashed with my integrity and filled me with shame." She choked on her tears, "God forgive me, I chose ease and protection at the expense of misinformed, unsuspecting men who sought what they deemed godly counsel. All to keep me from the horrors slavery can inflict."

"And why did your new God not help you?"

"I believe He wanted to, but I had aligned myself with His enemy and He never opposes our will." He waited while she regained her composure. "So, when the apostle Paul arrived in Philippi with the truth about salvation through the Lord, Jesus Christ, I hungered for it and the demon knew it. He began to use me to discredit the man. He took over my body and turned me into a grotesque puppet that disrupted those who gathered to hear God's servant, by mocking both him and the very name of our Savior."

She could hardly finish as the truth of what she had done to save herself reduced her to sobs. "I hated what I did, and at that point I no longer cared or wanted to live. Thankfully, it all ended when Paul commanded the demon to leave me in the name of Jesus Christ our Lord, and it had to obey. That very night Jesus became my Lord and my deliverer. Within days, He showed me I was to testify to His great love by manifesting my gratitude through a return to Delphi to help others see the truth."

Patharus shook his head. His lips parted but he did not speak.

She wiped her eyes. "I am sorry. So sorry to disappoint you. I want to be here with all of you, but I cannot fail to first do what the Lord has laid on my heart."

He reached for her hand and blew a low whistle. "Your honesty and integrity continue to amaze me. I believe that just as you could not find contentment in a life of deceit, or leave me to die under that building, neither would you be able to live with failing to go and do what you were told to do."

He grimaced and she wondered if he was about to suggest she go by herself. He leaned into his fist for several minutes. "There is nearly half a year before you and Nicanor plan to leave, and if you promise to come back next fall, I will do everything I can to teach him what he needs to know before you sail."

She barely resisted an urge to hug him. "Thank you, thank you, Master. Somehow I knew you would understand." She left and raced to find Nicanor, her heart filled with gratitude.

"Lord, You were on my side! You opened his heart and made a way for us to go with his blessings. Thank You, thank You, Lord." Medea's face surfaced. Would she be as gracious?

Chapter Ten

But now having been set free…
– Romans 6:22

Daphne sat by the courtyard pond with her fist under her chin. This was the third time, in two weeks, Medea had refused to see her. Who could she talk to? Nicanor seemed busier than ever since Patharus accepted that they would leave in the spring.

What was she to do about the wedding? Nicanor's patience had worn thin, and her dreams of a beautiful garden wedding faded faster than fall's latest blooms. She had asked him to speak to his father about Medea's recent reluctance to be involved in the plans. What more could she do? To go ahead without her input would start everything off on the wrong foot and leave a strained relationship.

The setting sun quickened her awareness of servants who scurried about with the dinner preparations. Melita would have her bath and clothes ready, a smile on her face, as if she delighted in being a servant. Daphne shrugged. *How does she do it? I hated that someone had control over my every moment.* She left for her room, grateful for Melita's sunny attitude despite her lack of freedom.

She lingered for a moment by the pond. The face of a sullen young servant back home flashed. *They are people…just like me. Nobody should live without freedom to go and be whatever they desire. What about that, Lord?*

Freedom is from within. It is to find contentment in whatever life brings to you.

But to be owned by another...Lord, it is not fair.

True freedom does not depend on your station in life. If Patharus had freed you and the demon still possessed you, would you be free?

No, I only felt truly free when You became my Savior. She left the pond and reveled in the peace that accompanied the Lord's input into her thoughts. His counsel so opposite the turmoil produced by the commands of the demon that had possessed her. Like a gentle caress, His voice rustled in the leaves of a terebinth tree above her.

And so shall they know that same freedom when anyone, slave or free, discovers my forgiveness and love.

His words continued to stir as she submitted to Melita's care and left to meet Nicanor.

Godliness with contentment is great gain,
– 1 Timothy 6:6

Nicanor drew back his chair after they had eaten their sauteed calamari appetizer. "You seem preoccupied this evening." Daphne lifted her eyelids, and he was struck afresh with how beautiful she was. A stark white peplos highlighted her dark hair and tawny skin. He reached over and took her hand, his thoughts on the day he would be free to hold her close and discard conventions that separated them.

"I am sorry, I have been wrestling with thoughts that refuse to settle. How was your day? Did Patharus take you through more of his plans?"

"Yes, his preparations are endless, but I suppose most are necessary. I have become more and more aware of how his strict attention to details has gotten him to where he is today. Now tell me about you. What whirls in that pretty head?"

She leaned into her chin. "Do you ever think back to when you were a slave? I mean when you see the ones who work to make everything pleasant for you, do whatever you tell them to do? Does it ever bother you to think that is what their lives amount to? To do only what someone else has the power to command them to do?"

His brows pinched. "That is the way it has always been. Was it not the same for your family back in Delphi?"

"Yes, but—"

"I mean I do think about my life before Patharus made me his son and heir. I miss the friends I had." He lowered his eyes. "Did I tell you I went back to join them one night after dinner, you know, like we used to gather after the day's work was finished? I longed for the camaraderie we had, but it was not the same. My friends could not get past who I am today and let me be one of them. I guess because I no longer am."

Nicanor's longing brought tears to her eyes. "Hey, I did not mean to upset those beautiful brown eyes." He dabbed at her cheeks with his napkin. "What brought this on, anyway? You were brought up where people served you. It has not changed."

"But should it? Back then, did you not long to be free?"

"Of course, I did. But you know something, there were things about that life that I would prefer over the one I have now. Do not get me wrong, I am thrilled with the opportunities I have as Patharus' son, but I have found there is good and bad in everything. It is a matter of being content with where you are."

Her expression revealed he had struck a nerve, but he decided to drop it. They finished their dinner, and he led her out into the courtyard. "Want to see what, if anything, is still blooming in the garden?"

"No, it would just amplify my regrets."

"Regrets? You mean that it is getting too late to have a garden wedding?"

"Or any wedding at all."

"Wait a minute. What does that mean?" He made an elaborate bow. "Madam, you will become my bride, or I shall sweep you away and—"

"Nicanor, Medea refused to see me again today. I cannot make any plans until she will…"

"Oh, I have been meaning to tell you. I did ask Patharus to speak to her about it. He said she is so disappointed over our plans to leave, that we need to give her some time. He said he thought she would come to accept it before long."

"And you are all right with that?"

"Not much I could do about it." They had reached her door and he pulled her into his arms. "Worst of it is it keeps us from being together the way I dream it will be."

She glanced around. "Careful, someone might see us."

"Let them. I want you for myself, not just dinner and walks in the garden." His lips found hers and she surrendered to her longings, all objections lost in the rustle of the late fall winds in those same terebinth trees above them.

Chapter Eleven

Be angry and do not sin.
– Ephesians 4:26

Daphne awoke early. She had dreamed about Nicanor. She sat on her bed and leaned onto her knees while she rehearsed all that had happened the night before. His words, his kiss... like rays of the morning sun that peeked through her window, the glow of their love and desires warmed her.

She thought of her mother. What would she say about allowing such things before marriage? But her world had changed. No family hovered to protect her, and she was not sure she wanted protection from this man she loved so much.

Melita had yet to arrive. A light tap on her door surprised her. Her servant usually gave a soft knock and walked in. She reached for her robe, "Come in, Melita."

To her chagrin, a girl she did not know let herself in. "Hello, Mistress. I am Zosime. I have been assigned to take care of you. Shall I—"

"No, wait. Where is Melita?"

The girl lowered her eyes. "I do not know, Mistress, but I heard that the Kupios insisted Melita be assigned to her own suite."

Daphne hid her resentment and allowed Zosime to help her prepare for the day. It is not her fault, Lord, but I do not like the sound of this. She refused the offer to fetch breakfast and dismissed her.

At the dining area she hoped to see Nicanor, but a server said he had eaten and left very early. She thanked the man and asked if he were familiar with eggs coddled with *staka*, He assured her they would add the clotted cream and promptly filled her request.

Throughout her meal, her stomach churned like butter at losing Melita. The Kupios would have had the final say. Questions coursed through her mind. Had the girl served Medea before? Had she missed Melita's sunny disposition and wanted her back? Had the Kupios missed her expertise in arranging hair? Had Medea's long-time servant become ill or... Daphne shot from her chair. "No, those are not the reasons!"

Her conclusion spilled loudly enough for two servers to turn and look. She gave them an apologetic nod and stepped out into the courtyard. She did it to get even with me for wanting to leave! I know that is it. Lord, how could she be so small?

Nicanor needed to hear about this. She searched until she found his servant. "I am not sure where he is right now, Misses, but he asked to have provisions readied for a quick trip to the port of Neapolis. Said he would not be gone overnight but wanted food and water for him and his driver. Would you like me to check and see if he has left?"

She sighed. "No, that is a full day. I am sure he is already on his way. Thank you, Batano." She returned to her room, but the walls closed in on her. Her anger grew as she wandered the courtyard. She threw up her hands and left for the garden. Beside the pond, near the bench she and Nicanor shared, the last of the sky-blue asters and harebells drooped. Hope rose in the cream colored gentian and yellow hyssop that still flourished. Maybe they will bloom long enough for our wedding, if we have one. She huffed, at least they would not clash with an *orange* wedding veil.

Lord, my hopes for peace have withered like those flowers. I know anger is not good and I fully intend to forgive Medea, but I am so disgusted that she would stoop that low. I told her when we first met how happy I was with Melita, and she has all the servants she needs. There was no good reason for her to take Melita from me, except revenge.

She continued to pour out her frustrations, aware of the Lord's silence. Her stomach growled reminding her of how long she had been sitting there. She decided to walk but found herself stomping down the well-worn path. Peace eluded her. Finally, she stopped, put her hands on her hips, and cried out. "All right, Lord, I forgive her. Now what do I do about it?"

Forgive her from your heart.

I said I did. What more do you want from me?

Remember how I forgave you? I held nothing back and forgot your offenses?

The rebuke stung. She tried not to whine. "How do I do that, Lord? I cannot be like You. I said the words, but the anger is still there."

You set your will to forgive. Your feelings will catch up. It is a choice, and it includes treating her like she never hurt you.

She wheeled around and hiked back toward the courtyard, her fingers pressed to her lips. Where is that peace I am supposed to feel? *It is a choice,* clanged in her mind. At the gate she stopped and bowed her head. All right, Lord. I surrender my anger and hurt to You. I choose not to hold anything against Medea. Please show me if I should just accept that Melita is no longer mine, or what You would have me do.

Go talk to Medea.

That was the last thing she wanted to hear. She decided to stop for a quick lunch, amazed to find her anger had diminished. Maybe I should go and talk this over with Lydia. Did not the Lord tell me to go spend time with her?

A quickening in her heart brought reproach. God had already told her what to do. She finished her lunch and vowed to obey and trust Him to work it out. Maybe Medea's heart has softened, and I will get a chance to tell her about the love of Jesus.

Daphne waited until she thought Medea's afternoon nap might be over, and with leaden feet approached her suite. Danatel's face fell when she answered her knock. "Oh, Miss Daphne…it is you."

"Yes, I would like to see the *Kupios*. Has she risen from her nap?"

"I, well, ah, wait here and I will see."

She did not know what to expect. Had the Lord not smoothed the way for her to talk to Medea? And why did Danatel seem so flustered? A shriek echoed from the room.

The servant's face was ashen. "I am sorry. The *Kupios* is not up to seeing anyone today."

Daphne stopped her before she shut the door. "Danatel, wait. I have tried several times to see her. Why will she not see me?"

The servant glanced over her shoulder and whispered. "Miss Daphne, I do not know what to do. She is so angry with your and Master Nicanor's plans to leave. It is like she has lost all sense of reason."

72

Medea shrieked her name. "Yes Ma'am, I am coming." She shook her head. "I am sorry. I cannot help you."

Daphne ignored her better sense, pushed past the servant and walked in and over to the Kupios' bed. "Medea, I have been trying to see you for weeks and I would really like a moment to talk with you."

Danatel wrung her hands. "I told her what you said, *Kupios*, I..."

Medea shouted at the trembling servant. "Leave us and send in Melita." Dread spewed from the girl's eyes as she left. "Melita, show this intruder to the door."

Daphne drew closer. "No, wait, please Medea, can we not talk about our differences? I am sorry that I barged in like this, but it is that I..."

She closed her eyes and turned her face to the wall. "Melita. Did you hear me?"

Her hands trembled as the girl put her arm around Daphne's shoulders. "It would be best if you leave now."

Melita's despair dissolved her determination to speak with Medea. She backed towards the door. "I am so sorry to have caused you all such trouble."

Back in her room, she collapsed in a chair and sobbed. What had she done? How could she explain it to Nicanor, and what kind of a report would Patharus get from Medea? She should not have pushed her way into the Kupios' room, but the Lord sent her there, or so she thought. Her whole body shook. "Why, Lord?"

Trust Me.

She refused to let Zosime fetch her dinner. Batano had left word that Nicanor would not see her until tomorrow. Her servant took it upon herself to bring some bread, cheese and fruit and set it upon Daphne's table before she gave in to her insistence she leave for the night.

Daphne cried herself to sleep and awoke while it was dark. She lit her oil lamp and paced. Her sleep had been troubled with dreams plagued with turmoil. She sat at her table and nibbled some of the early grapes Zosime had left, surprised the harvest had already begun.

Put on a garment of praise for a spirit of heaviness, usurped her thoughts.

Epaphroditus had taught them to sing these words from one of the many uplifting psalms an ancient king of Israel wrote in praise to the Lord. Lifted by his counsel that they repeat it when things looked dark, she whispered, "Yes!"

Timid at first, she began, "Lord, I praise You with all of my heart. You have never failed me, You are faithful, and I wish to glorify Your name." Her worship grew in intensity until she found herself praising God in a language she had not learned. The words poured from her lips, but the content was not from her mind.

Tears of pure joy ran down her cheeks, but she did not bother with them. The Lord had visited her, and sleep would come, cradled in His peace.

Chapter Twelve

Confess your trespasses to one another.
– James 5:16

The peace Daphne relished the night before seemed elusive in the morning.

Condemnation swirled. You should not have barged in on Medea. You had no right. Nicanor will be very upset with you. He will see you differently now. Patharus might revoke your freedom, he loves his wife dearly. God loves you, but He is disappointed in you.

Lydia's gentle counsel broke through. "The world, your own thinking, or the devil will try to put lies in your mind. It is up to you to sort out where the input is coming from. God's truth and guidance bring peace, not stress."

Daphne rose and pulled a deep breath, determined to shut out the negative accusations. "Nicanor loves me, and his love will not change. Patharus granted my freedom and that cannot be revoked. And God said He would never leave me or forsake me, no matter how many times I fail to measure up. So, Devil, I refuse your lies and reject my own disparaging conclusions. Flee from me in Jesus' name!"

Zosime arrived and went quietly about helping Daphne dress. "Would you like me to fetch your breakfast, Miss?"

She studied the servant's face. "Is something wrong? You have been awfully quiet."

Her face colored. "No, I uh—"

"Do not be afraid, I want to help. What bothers you?"

The girl released her lower lip. "Miss, it is Melita. She told me what happened in Kupios' suite yesterday. We are both very worried for you. She said she was not sure you would be around following the tirade. The mistress screamed after she commanded you to leave."

Daphne sighed and motioned for the girl to finish her hair. "Zosime, do you have a god?"

She paused mid stroke and withdrew the brush. "I, uh, well, I do give homage to several gods, especially Feronia, Rome's fertility goddess. She is the one our master commanded everyone to worship after he lost his son."

"I have only been here a little over a year. How did the child die and when was that? I remember my friend Kawit telling me they had a boy that died."

"I do not know how he died. I was very young. At least eight years ago I think, but I do remember the great sadness that covered the household, and..." She covered her lips.

"And what?"

"Something we are not supposed to talk about." Daphne's nod buoyed her courage. "I did not grasp such matters then, but later I learned the Kupios sorrowful condition was a result of the difficult birth, and more children would not be possible."

Her mind a whirl, Daphne checked her hair in her looking glass. Poor Medea, no wonder she harbors such anger. "Thank you for telling me this. I will never speak your name in connection with it. But I want you to know I have a God that is greater than this problem or any other. He will show me a way to restore my relationship with Medea and find forgiveness."

Her servant looked relieved. "Thank you, Miss."

She dismissed her and headed for the door. "And please tell Melita that I miss her, and it will all work out."

Both she and Nicanor reached the dining area at the same moment. A smile lit his face. "My beautiful bride, come join me for breakfast." They walked hand in hand to a table set up under vines heavy with ripe grapes.

The smell of dew-covered leaves welcomed her. He moved his chair closer to hers and she smiled. "I missed you yesterday, but Batano told me of your trip to Neapolis. Was it very late when you returned?"

"Yes. I thought to come say goodnight, but your light was already out. Did you have a good day?"

To her relief a servant approached to hear their breakfast choices. He left and she turned the conversation. "Tell me, what was so urgent that you had to rush to the port at the last moment?"

"With all that happened since Patharus' accident he totally forgot about a shipment of oil he ordered from Athens." By the time he shared details of what day the shipment would or had already landed, the servant laid his *andrest-frouteslia* omelet before him. "It was a great relief to find the ship anchored only the day before, and the man who served as port commander for many years had heard of Patharus' accident and took care of it for us."

She glanced at the potatoes and sausage he so enjoyed, and wondered how he could tolerate such heavy food. More importantly, how would he digest what she had to tell him? She finished her yogurt and berries and put her hands in her lap. "Nicanor, I made a terrible mistake yesterday. I am sure you will hear about it from Patharus."

He wiped the sausage drippings from his chin. "What mistake? What are you talking about?"

She reminded him of her frustration with how Medea took Melita from her, but that the Lord told her she must forgive her from her heart and to go see her.

"But that is wonderful, I am sure she—"

"No, it is not. She refused to even give me a moment, so I...well, I pushed past her servant and went into her chambers, with hopes I could change her mind."

"You what? I cannot believe you would do that."

"I know. I cannot believe it either. I was just so tired of this unresolved issue that hangs over our heads. But it was wrong, and I made her very angry. I am so sorry. I am afraid I have made things worse. She has surely told Patharus about it and who knows how he will react." Tears spilled from her eyes. "He may rethink his permission to let you marry me."

Nicanor wiped her cheeks with his thumbs. "No, that will not happen. This has gone on long enough. I am going to see Medea. We have grown closer since the accident and maybe she will listen to me."

"I do not know. She is so angry. But if you can get her to see me, I think the Lord has given me a clue as to what is behind her fury."

"I will try to see her before lunch, and you can tell me about it. I need to go, Patharus will expect me for our morning briefing." He reached over and squeezed her hand. "Do not worry, let me handle this. You pray and we will trust God to give me the right words. No matter what, remember I love you."

Blessed are the peacemakers.
– Matthew 5:9

To Nicanor's surprise Patharus never mentioned Medea or Daphne. His attention lay riveted on the successful delivery of the shipment from Neapolis, elated with what Nicanor explained. He shook his head, compelled to repeat the welcome news. "And my good friend, Gaius, put my goods in storage until I could come for them. Imagine!"

Nicanor assured him again that the oil was being stored, even as they spoke. Patharus' pleasant demeanor made it easier to bring up Daphne's misdeed. "Father, something happened yesterday that you need to know."

Concern swept his face. "What, I thought you said —"

"No, it does not concern the shipment, it is Daphne, and Medea."

"I told you —"

"I know you said to give Medea time, but Daphne became frustrated with the waiting. You know we are both anxious to get our wedding under way." Patharus grimaced but before he could object Nicanor went on to tell him what happened, including Medea's reaction.

"Daphne has overstepped her bounds. But I do know Medea can be difficult."

"Father, Daphne is terribly sorry she did what she did, and wants to ask Medea and you to forgive her, but Medea will not see her. I am surprised she did not report Daphne's uncalled for behavior to you, yesterday."

Patharus released a heavy sigh. "I think it must have drained her. She had planned to be brought to my room earlier, but a message came that she was not up to it. I know she is hurting over this, this..." He slammed his fist on his bed. "I hate not being able to come and go when I want without a production."

Nicanor sympathized with a nod. "Would it be all right with you if I went and talked with Medea? I have not seen her since our decision reached her, and I want to try to explain Daphne's position and assure her we plan to return."

Patharus leaned his head into his hand. He looked up, his eyes heavy with sorrow. "Yes. Go. She thinks a lot of you. Maybe you can help her overcome the disappointment."

Chapter Thirteen

By faith, the walls of Jericho fell.
– Hebrews 11:30

Nicanor headed for the holding barns to make sure the new supplies were being stored properly. Makendon, the estate's overseer, waved him over. "Good morning, Master. Quite a load we brought in last night."

He nodded at the tall man he had come to respect and depend upon. Months before his accident, Patharus had replaced their former overseer with an excellent choice, a savvy leader who was fair but could get things done. Appreciation had filtered from the slave quarters for the new overlord's relaxed approach to disputes, easing past tensions and fears. "Any problems with enough room? I am not sure Patharus realized what was already here."

The wiry overseer smiled, exposing a wide gap between his front teeth. "No. Kupio prefers the olive oil from the Peloponnese, so he ordered enough to last through the year." He gestured at the next building "We will fit it all in or make room over there.""

"Fine, and get some extra sleep if you need to. That was a very late night." The man chuckled and turned to lend a hand to a slave with an oversized crate.

Nicanor slowly walked away, praying, his mind on Medea. *I wonder if she will see me. Cannot hurt to try.*

Danatel's eyes lit up when she saw him. "Oh, Master Nicanor, it is so good of you to come. Kupios will be so happy to..." Her gaze fell to the floor.

"I understand and I hope she will see me. Please tell her I am here and want very much to see her."

He crossed his arms and leaned against the wall opposite her door. What was taking so long? It could not be good.

At last, the servant poked her head through the frame, her face drawn. "Master, she says she is not up to a visit. Perhaps another time."

He stepped to the door and lowered his voice. "Listen. You tell her I will return after her afternoon nap, and I will not leave until she sees me."

The maid's face clouded but she nodded. He left, almost hoping not to run into Daphne. A check on the apple crop took longer than he planned so he skipped lunch and arrived back at Medea's suite about the time he thought she would awaken. He pictured her confined day after day to her room. Must be hard to have so little strength one cannot perform normal tasks or get through a day without a nap.

Her servant was quick to answer his knock. She did not look hopeful. "The madam asks that you make it brief. She is not having a good day."

He nodded and walked into her receiving room. She lay, propped in a semi-upright position, supported by mounds of pillows. He smiled. "Medea, it is good of you to see me. I hear you are not doing well." He took her hand, surprised at how cold it felt.

She returned a slight smile and lowered her eyes. "I am all right. I have missed you."

"I know and I am sorry. Patharus has kept me so busy with all there is to learn to run his estate and —"

Her voice exploded. "It is your estate, too, and you need to learn all those things and you need to be..." Her voice caught and she withdrew her hand. "You need to stay here and help him."

"Medea, I—"

Sobs choked her words. "No, I do not want to hear it. You have chosen to leave right when we need you most."

He stood and pulled her shoulder to his chest, his voice gentle. "Medea, it is going to be all right. I would not leave if Patharus were not healing well, and I promise we will return by fall."

She sniffed. "No, Daphne wants to go back to her own family, and we will never see you again."

"Of course, she hopes to find her loved ones, but this is her home now and she wants to live here with me, with us."

She pushed herself upright, her eyes piercing his. "Then why must she go? And why now when your father is still unable to handle so many things?"

He drew his chair closer, his face near hers. "Listen to me. Makendon, our new overseer, is very competent and loyal. He will handle anything Patharus cannot yet do while I am gone. And you know how much I care for him and how much I care for you, do you not?" She wiped her cheeks and nodded. "Then I want you to hear me with an open heart. Did Daphne tell you what she went through after she was brought to Philippi as a slave?"

She huffed. "She told me she lost her father and was brought to the slave market at Athens where she was separated from her mother and brothers."

"Would not being alone be awful enough for a young girl? But there is so much more."

She looked puzzled. "More?" Her expression softened.

"Yes, I think it is time you knew about the nightmare she lived through, possessed by an evil demon with no way of escape. How she was forced to lead unsuspecting people into a relationship with a false god, knowing his plan was to destroy them. How as a fortune teller she helped people lie and cheat and take advantage of others, all in order to escape the abuse and horrors of slavery should she refuse."

"That sweet little girl you chose to marry did that?"

"Yes. She told me of a young woman, pregnant with her first child. She was terrified that the baby might be a girl and be discarded by her husband. To her delight the demon told her she carried a boy, but it was born imperfect, and her fears were justified. Daphne said the poor girl lost her mind and carried about an empty blanket that she believed held her child."

Her hand flew to her lips. "A baby? How could he?"

"She became so distraught upon hearing a man took his own life after she took part in causing him to lose his land and his family, that I found her at the end of the garden about to ingest Hemlock. The loss of her integrity overwhelmed her. And worse yet was being forced into an almost inhuman creature, publicly screaming insults at the one True God. Finally, she was delivered of the demon when God sent a man here to teach us about the power and forgiveness in His Son, Jesus Christ. But then she faced a life of slavery without the special ability that kept her safe. Still, she chose to stay and help Patharus at the cost of a very dismal future."

Medea hung on every word, her face aghast.

"You need to understand, the God who set Daphne free asked her to go back to her city and expose the horrors that worshiping a false god can bring. She has chosen to follow Him because she, personally, experienced what that bondage can do to a person. She feels compelled by the Holy Spirit of our God to spread that truth to as many as she can. She could not live with herself if she did not do what she knows she has been appointed to do. But her intentions are to return with me and make our home here."

Medea pressed her hands to her cheeks. "So that is the mysterious happening that no one would tell me about. The poor dear. How awful. I had no idea what choosing to put Patharus' life before her own happiness might have meant for her."

She looked him in the eye. "I cannot say that I understand this need to do what a god tells you to do. I gave up putting my hopes in gods when...well, a long time ago." She put her hand on his arm. "But Nicanor, you cannot possibly know what you mean to us. We cannot lose you."

He took her hands in his. "Before Patharus' leg went bad, I promised Daphne that I would accompany her on this journey. Now that Halaten is confident father's healing will continue, I must do this for her, and our hope is that you can accept Daphne's need to follow her heart and believe we plan to return and make our home here."

Her shoulders sagged. "Promise me Nicanor. Promise you will come back to us.""

"I promise. Now promise me you will see Daphne and help us get this wedding under way." She nodded and he kissed her cheek. "You will make a beautiful mother of the groom."

On the way out, he winked at Danatel and whistled down the hallway. Now he wanted to find Daphne, and soon.

Chapter Fourteen

Your love to me was wonderful.
- 2 Samuel 1:26

Daphne's chaperone stuck his head through the door. "Perhaps it would be best if we left, Miss. I believe a storm is approaching."

She gathered her things and hugged Lydia. "Thank you, Dear One. You are such an encouragement."

"Listen, My Friend. You have grown so quickly in the Lord, that soon you will have to teach me."

She hugged her again and allowed the servant to help her mount her horse. "Goodbye. Give my love to the believers. I hope Nicanor will soon be free early enough for us to come join you."

Black clouds hovered and the wind already whipped their outer robes, but her mind was on Lydia's counsel. *Not by might nor by power but by my Spirit says the Lord.* The words spun through her thoughts and repeated themselves almost at will. "Lord," she whispered into the wind. "I release Medea's anger to you. I have no power nor might to make her forgive me so right now I yield to the precious Holy Spirit who alone can change things."

Part way home, a loud clap of thunder spooked her horse. He reared and she flew from his back. She struck her head and blackness closed in. She blinked at the darkness and whispered, "Nicanor, are you here?"

Several hours later, she tried to open her eyes, but they refused to cooperate. She turned her face and pain seared the back of her head. "Umm."

Someone ordered Melita to wring a cloth in the fresh well water. She was quick to comply.

"Here, *Kalon*, do not try to move. Rest and let this cold compress ease the pain."

Daphne's brows furrowed. Was that Belte? Mother? Panic grabbed her. Had she heard the demon again? She forced open her eyes and tried to focus. A figure loomed over her, and a deep voice drifted in and out.

"Be at ease, Daphne."

She tried to rise, to cry out, but no sound left her lips.

The figure pushed her back on the bed. His touch was gentle. "It is Halaten, Daphne. You have had a nasty fall, and you must remain still."

Halaten. Relief flooded her. She was safe. With a raspy voice, she whispered, "Water." Someone put a cup to her lips, and she sipped the cool liquid.

The soothing voice whispered, "It is all right, Halaten. I will stay with her."

"Yes. Good. But call me if she tries to get up or begins to thrash about. We must keep her calm."

"I will keep watch," echoed through Daphne's mind, but she could not decipher where she had heard that voice before. She tried to open her eyes, but the room swirled. Darkness beckoned and she drifted with it, her head against an icy cloth.

But let him ask in faith, with no doubting.
– James 1:6

Nicanor stepped back into the room, shook his head, and spoke quietly. "You must get some rest. You have been up for hours. I have briefed Patharus on her condition and I will stay with her now."

The woman sighed. "All right. Halaten's instructions are that she stays calm and does not try to rise. Also, give her a sip of water if she asks but do not try to wake her."

He signaled her nearby help. "See that she gets back to her room and gets some rest." The servant looked relieved, took the woman's arm, and they left.

Halaten checked again after a few hours had passed. "Has she been awake at all?"

Nicanor shook his head. "Is that a bad sign? She does moan now and again."

"No. Rest is the best remedy for now. Here are some blankets, I knew you would not leave her."

"Should I have Melita change her damp clothing...find her a night dress?"

Halaten checked her arms. "She does not feel cold so do not disturb her. And send word if...well, if there are any changes."

Nicanor dismissed Melita and made a pad on the floor beside Daphne's bed. He stroked her hair. "Sleep well my beautiful bride. And come back to me. I could not bear to lose you."

He stared into the dark, his eyes wide with worry and fear.

Call on me.

"Oh, Lord, I feel so inadequate, so new at praying."

Just talk to Me.

"Right. Paul told us that we should ask." He took a quick breath. "Lord, we have been taught that the blood You shed on the cross paid for our healing as well as our sins. Daphne has hurt her head, Lord, and she needs Your healing. Please touch her, and do not let this injury have any permanent effects. I love her so much. Thank You, Lord. Amen."

He kissed her cheek, swiped at the smears under his eyes and lay down. Every time she moaned, he rose and watched for signs she had awakened. Near dawn, he heard her ask for water. He jumped from his pad and rushed the cup to her lips.

She opened her eyes. "Is that you, Nicanor? Where am I?"

"Daphne! You are here, with me! Oh, My Love, I have been so concerned. How do you feel? How is your head? Wait, I have to go get Halaten."

She reached for his arm. "No. Please do not leave me. Why must you call for Halaten?"

"You fell and hit your head. Do not move. I will be right back. I must fetch him."

The doctor hastened to the room. "Ah ha. And how is our patient this morning?" He bent close and examined the lump on her head.

"Oh, that is sore. When did I fall? I have no memory of it."

Nicanor drew close to the bed. "You were nearly home from visiting Lydia yesterday when a storm hit, and you were thrown from your horse."

She frowned, "All I remember is mounting the horse and waving goodbye."

Halaten looked into her eyes. "Does your head hurt?" She nodded and he asked her to follow his finger as he waved it back and forth in front of her.

She kept pace, blinking. "It is fuzzy. How did I get home?"

Nicanor took her hand. "The servant who traveled with you carried you the rest of the way. You were both soaked to the skin, and he was terrified, sure you had died."

"Oh, the poor man, I must thank him."

Halaten put some salve on the cut and picked up his bag. "I think you will be good as new in a couple of days. Your vision will clear and your head will heal, but do not wash your hair until the wound stops oozing."

Her mind raced to the time she fell in the adytum. Had she not heard those same instructions? The doctor turned to Nicanor. "See that someone stays with her all of today. I do not want her prancing around, yet."

He left and Nicanor lifted her hand to his lips. "I am so grateful you are better."

"I know. I heard your prayer, but I could not wake enough to thank you."

"Would you like something to eat?"

"No, I feel a bit queasy, but you go ahead and have breakfast."

"All right. I am going to fetch Melita and have her help you clean up. You must have landed in a muddy stretch by the looks of your peplos."

"Melita? Do you not mean Zosime?"

Nicanor grinned. "No, I mean Melita." He was gone before she could question him further.

Chapter Fifteen

As for God, His way is perfect.
– 2 Samuel 22:31

Daphne had nearly drifted off, pleased that somehow Melita would be the one to help her.

The soothing voice she had heard before asked, "How is she this morning?"

Melita returned the whisper. "Halaten says she will be fine in a few days. I planned to help her clean up, but he said if she is asleep, I should not disturb her."

"You should fetch her some fruit and juice, and maybe some yogurt. She may want to eat when she wakes. l will stay right here with her."

Melita hesitated but left for the kitchen.

Daphne opened her eyes and found herself face to face with Medea.

She blinked several times. "Kupios...what? Why are you...?"

Medea stroked her forehead with a cool cloth. "Hush. Do not try to get up, *Kalon*. You must lie still and rest."

"But you, you should not be here. You —"

"Do not worry, I want to be here. We have much time to make up."

Confusion surged and she shut her eyes. It was Medea's voice I heard last night. But why? She should not be out of bed. Daphne forced open her lids, sure it was a dream. Had not the Kupios refused to see her for weeks?

Melita returned with food and drink. Daphne smiled at her former servant. "It is good to see you again, Melita."

The girl glanced awkwardly at Medea and blushed. She stepped close to Daphne. ""Would you care to eat something…maybe drink some juice?"

Her eyes closed and Melita spoke softly. "Maybe you would rather sleep. We can get you cleaned up and changed later."

Daphne's mind whirled. Medea was there, but why and what did she mean by much time to make up? She turned her face to the wall. "I am sorry, I am not able to stay awake. Please do not fuss over me. I need to sleep."

Melita pulled up her blankets. "I will be right here if you need me, and I am sure Master Nicanor will be back soon to look in on you."

Daphne turned at a touch on her shoulder. Medea looked pale. "Please rest and get well, *Kalon*. I, also, will check back on you." She patted her cheek and Melita alerted Danatel that the Kupios was ready to leave. They had reached the door when Melita gasped. Daphne twisted around in time to see Medea's servant catch her. Melita ran to help and the two of them steadied her onto a nearby bench.

Danatel held her while Melita went for Halaten. He took her pulse, listened to her heart, and looked into her eyes. "Kupios, you cannot be away from your suite like this for hours. You are too weak, and likely to faint and get hurt. I have sent for help, and we will get you back to bed and rest."

Medea did not spurn the gentle scolding and by the time a strong young servant arrived, Nicanor appeared. He insisted he carry her back to her suite himself. Danatel followed, clucking like a hen. "Keep her head up. Careful. Do not trip on her peplos."

Nicanor retraced his steps, pulled a bench close to Daphne, and took her hand. "So much commotion. How are you? Does your head ache?"

"It is not too bad, if I remember not to roll my head on that side. I am worried about Medea. How was she? Will you check on her and let me know?"

"She is worn out so I left, but I will look in on her later."

"She should not have been here. Did you know she spent hours here the night I fell?"

"Uh huh. She insisted she stay, and you know Medea, once she sets her mind on something, she—"

"I do not understand. She would not even talk to me the day before."

He grinned. "Did not Epaphroditus tell us God works in mysterious ways?"

"Nicanor! What happened? What is it you have not told me?"

He bent over and kissed her forehead. "Do you remember my saying I was going to see her?"

Her brow flinched. "Yes, it was while we ate breakfast yesterday...or, what day is this?"

He chuckled. "You are right. I insisted and Medea finally agreed to see me. I wanted her to understand what you had gone through the past year with that demon. No one had explained to her the horror or the trauma of being delivered of that evil. And I told her of your gratitude and your determination to follow what God has called you to do. She was awed. I assumed you had told her yourself."

"I planned to, but it never seemed to be the right time."

"That is because it was not. God knew what was to come and that this would be the right time."

She blew a deep sigh. "And what you told her changed her mind?"

"That and when she realized what you sacrificed by refusing to leave Patharus."

"Do you think she will talk to me now?"

"I am sure of it. She was so worried about you she would not leave, even when her strength failed like this morning."

Daphne's eyes filled. "I cannot wait to thank her."

"You need to get better first. I am going to call Melita and have her get you out of those dirty clothes."

"Melita! She must have given her back to me.?"

He stood and smiled. "That should tell you how her heart has changed." He bent over, and she circled his neck with her arms. "Get well fast, I think our wedding is just round the corner." She kissed his nose. He laughed and left.

My heart is severely pained within me.
– Psalms 55:4

A few days later, Nicanor arrived for his morning briefing with Patharus. "How is Daphne? Does Halaten feel her head has healed properly?"

"Yes, she is doing fine, concerned about Medea. Do you think she is still all right with our plans to leave?"

Patharus hunched his shoulders. Nicanor regretted the question Was the subject still raw? What could he say that would help? A moment passed before his father spoke, his voice muffled. Nicanor stooped, not wanting to miss what he was not sure he wanted to hear.

"You were probably too young to remember when Medea and I finally had a child, a son. He came down with a fever when he was only four. The doctors tried everything to save him, but he died in my arms. We were devastated, especially Medea."

"How awful for both of you. I do remember my mother cried when she told me about it, I must have been about six. We children were not allowed in his play area, but I saw him over there a few times."

Patharus nodded. "I had no idea it still haunted Medea with such intensity. She blamed herself. She loves you like her own and I guess the thought of losing you brought it all up again."

An uneasy silence followed. Nicanor squirmed, hating the problems their need to leave created. "It must have been hard for you, too."

"My pain included the loss of my only chance for an heir, until..." His voice cracked. "Until you became so important to me."

Nicanor blinked at the water that welled in his eyes. "He laid his hand on Patharus' shoulder. And you are the father I always longed for. I hope you can believe and trust that you can count on my promise to return and take my full place as your son when we return next fall."

He cleared his throat. "Yes, well, enough of that. Now, tell me about the grapes. Makendon says the leaves have turned and should be ready for harvest."

Nicanor agreed and left to instruct the overseer and fulfill his father's other requests. Later, Daphne felt strong enough to meet him for lunch. He spoke at length on the busyness of getting the grapes picked and ready to be crushed.

She listened and asked. "How is Patharus? I have not seen him for weeks."

"The same. His leg gets stronger every week. Halaten has him doing exercises to rejuvenate the muscles so he can walk on the peg he has carved to fit his leg."

"Is he concerned about Medea?"

"He knew how she remained with you and that she collapsed, but for the first time, he talked to me about the death of their son. He was only four when he died from a fever."

"Really? Would you believe Zosime mentioned the child's death to me recently? But Patharus seems so private...I am surprised he talked about it."

"Me too, but I think it did him good. You should have seen the pain in his eyes, when he shared how it had nearly destroyed Medea. And then he choked up and said his relationship with me eased his pain." He shook his head. "I do not deserve all he has—"

"I think you do. You have been a loyal son. He truly loves you and Medea does too." She squeezed his hand. "Matter of fact, so do I."

He beamed at her devotion. "So did Medea come back to see you?"

"No, not even after you said she had regained her strength. But I was relieved she did not try too soon."

"Then you plan to see her today?"

"Yes. And I am a little nervous."

He pulled her up into his arms. "Just dazzle her with that smile I love." He nuzzled her neck and kissed her. "See if the two of you can get our wedding going. I can hardly wait."

She playfully pushed him away. "Nicanor, someone will see us."

"I do not care. I never get enough of you."

Chapter Sixteen

First be reconciled to your brother...
– Matthew 5:24

Daphne waited until Medea would have awakened from her afternoon nap before she knocked on her door. Over and over, she had rehearsed what she would say, how she might ease the strain that had built like a thundercloud between them. She gave Danatel a weak smile. "Has the Kupios awakened?"

The servant ushered her in, her smile broad. "I think she expected you might call. I am so glad that—"

"Who is it, Danatel?"

She swallowed her dread. "It is I, Daphne. Are you up to a visit?"

"Oh my, yes. Please come in. Sit here by me. I am so relieved that you recovered from your fall. Danatel, fetch some refreshments."

She drew a bench close to Medea's bed. Each spoke at the same time. "I am so sorry..." Both stopped and they laughed. Medea reached for her hand and tears mingled as Daphne hugged her.

Medea assured her that she now believed that both she and Nicanor planned to return in the fall. "And I do respect your integrity to fulfill a promise."

"It is beyond integrity, Kupios. I do not know how much Nicanor explained about our God, but it is a relationship that—"

"Well, call it what you want, *Kalon*, but I do understand your need for a strong creed to attach your hopes to, especially after what you went through."

97

Daphne sent up a quick prayer for guidance. "Yes, but it is so much more than a simple belief. It is to know a God that loves you and is continually there for you."

"But you must be careful, Daphne. Those gods can turn on you for no reason and..." She cleared her throat. "But tell me about your plans to find your family."

"I am sure Nicanor explained we will not leave until it is safe to sail. We will go to Athens first and see if we can find where each was taken and by whom. Then we will buy back their freedom with the generous gift Kupio gave me."

"I am so happy for you. You deserve to be rewarded for what you did to help him."

"God had a hand in that, too. He has seen Patharus' good heart and wants you both to be a part of His family."

The servant arrived with tea and sweets and Medea made much of the timely interruption. "Thank you, Danatel." Both sipped spiced tea and expounded on their love for each other and hopes for a future family together.

Their cups were removed, and Daphne repositioned her bench. "I want you to know I do understand your concern over our plans with Patharus in a somewhat weakened condition, and how hard it would be for you both to lose Nicanor." Her eyes filled and she touched her shoulder. "Honestly, I want to assure you that—"

Medea drew her arms across her middle. "I know you mean it, but you do not truly understand. No one can."

"Beloved, are you referring to the loss of your son?"

She nodded and Daphne went on. "You are right. Only someone who has shared your same heartache can really understand. Loss is loss, only mine came to me differently."

"But there is a chance you will be reunited with your loved ones. That door is closed to me."

She wanted to tell her she would see her son again in eternity but sensed in her spirit the time was not right. Empathy drove her to continue. "I have heard of the great sadness that covered you and Patharus and your whole estate when the fever overtook your son. So tragic, to lose a child you have waited for and loved. You must miss him, still."

Tears streaked the heavy makeup that covered Medea's pale cheeks. "There is not a day that goes by that I do not picture him as he followed his father around or chased butterflies in the garden. He used to love to snuggle here beside me, ask for a story, or wrangle a treat from the servants."

Her recollections brought an image of Theo and the imaginative games and similar ploys he too used. She swallowed the lump in her throat. They were about the same age when she last saw her little brother.

"I cannot help but wonder what he would look like now. What he would want to do with his life..."

"I imagine he would be much like Patharus. A young man of strong character."

Medea snuffed but did not respond.

Daphne stroked Kupios' arm. "You know, I wonder if Nicanor may have become a vicarious stand-in for your son. Perhaps, he became a place to pour out your love, to fill a vacuum that vaporized when your son did not live."

Medea closed her eyes, her voice low. "He is that son to us. I felt so bad about Patharus' loss of an heir, especially, after it became clear there would be no more children."

"How you have both suffered! But the true Son of the living God came into the world and He—"

Medea sprang up from her pillows, her words laced with bitterness. "I prayed and sacrificed to every god I had ever heard of, but nothing changed. After our son died, Patharus was so hurt and so angry. I could only listen and be there for him. I tried. I really tried. I even suggested he take a concubine and bear a son through her, but he would not hear of it. I love him so much and I have failed him so."

At her loud sobbing, Danatel rushed into the room. Daphne waved her off, rubbed Medea's back, and let her cry. *Her heart is so closed, Lord. How can I reach her?*

Love her and listen. My timing is perfect.

After she quieted, Daphne whispered. "But you have suffered too. Your only child, I cannot imagine the pain."

The Kupios held her head with her hands and Daphne put her arms around her. "Patharus had you to lean on, but who was there to help you grieve your loss? Maybe that is what made it so hard to think of losing Nicanor, your hope of a family and grandchildren."

She sniffed and Daphne rocked her in her arms. After her chest stopped heaving, Medea looked up, her voice a mere whisper. "You may be right. Once the bond between Patharus and Nicanor grew beyond master and favored slave, grief lost its hold on him. He decided to make Nicanor his legal son and I came to love him dearly. He is so much like Patharus and his smile and dimple remind me of Elias. That was our son's name, Elias."

Speaking his name brought more tears. She drew a deep breath and let it slowly drift. "Maybe I have hung onto the painful void I have carried, but how does one let go? How do I stop the pain and accept I will never see him again?"

"I know. I still struggle with that possibility. It is understandable. And you have a mother's heart, and he was your baby. In fact, it was not until God brought Nicanor into my life that I began to see I could let go of what was and dare to care again." She smiled, surprised at the truth she had not yet deciphered for herself. "Maybe he has become a substitute for both of us, a way to go on."

"You are wise beyond your years, *Kalon*. Nicanor is lucky to have found you."

Daphne gave Madea's shoulders a squeeze. "No, I am the one who is blessed. I lost my family and God has given me another to love. And if there is wisdom, it is from my God. He loves you and wants you to become His own so He can carry all your burdens and pains."

She grew quiet and Daphne sensed she should leave and let Medea rest. Her eyes focused on Daphne, groping for hope. "Promise me you will come by tomorrow and we can talk about the wedding."

"I will, but please do not overdo it. I need your input with the plans."

She let herself out, surprised that she really did look forward to Medea's help.

Chapter Seventeen

...to give you a future and a hope.
– Jeremiah 29:11

Six weeks later, grapes became juice ready to age into wine, olives were harvested and pressed for oil, and the air held a definite chill. The wedding date had been carefully chosen to be sure it did not coincide with a bad omen. Daphne had let Medea decide. No past evil could override the Lord's blessing, no matter what day was picked. In two hours, she would become Nicanor's wife. The thought both thrilled and left her, somewhat, on edge.

Melita helped her into the bridal undergarments. "The day is warm for early winter, but your hands are like ice. Misses. Are you all right?"

"Just nerves. I wish my mother were here. Things were so different in Delphi where I grew up. A bride would never have spoken to her groom until the marriage ceremony. It was not even unusual for her to never have laid eyes on him until then. Fathers committed their daughters based on economic gains, an agreement was signed and gifts exchanged. I do not even have a dowry."

"Marriages here are similarly arranged, Misses. Yours has been different because you and Master Nicanor live in the same household. And I suspect he could care less about a dowry, or the Kupio either."

Daphne's voice turned dreamy. "I know, but back home the groom comes in a chariot and sweeps the bride away to his parents' home where families and friends gather to celebrate. It is so daring and romantic. My mother would be appalled to know that Nicanor and I have spent time together, even kissed." She blushed and turned her face.

Melita pretended not to notice. "Misses, from stories about your lovely mother and how she leaned on you when your lives were upended, I suspect she would be happy for you and so proud."

"Thank you, I am sure you are right. You have become more than a servant, Melita. You are a good friend."

She grinned. "Would you like me to bring you something to eat? It will be quite a while before the feast, and I would not want you to faint from hunger."

"Maybe some fruit and yogurt, although, I am not sure I will be able to keep it down."

She left and Daphne stared at her wedding dress. The white, wool peplos would reach the top of her sandals. Belted with the Knot of Hercules, she had agreed to wear it to satisfy Patharus. He firmly believed that the celebrated victor was the guardian of wedded bliss. She tried to picture Nicanor as he followed the tradition of the groom's duty, in the privacy of their chamber, to untie it. Did those born into his former culture practice the rituals of their master? Did it matter?

The veil Medea had given her lay on the bed. The Kupios' enthusiastic joy, when she had presented the gift, was too great to ignore. Why orange, still mystified her but the color did complement her olive skin and dark hair.

Daphne had woven a few hearty blossoms of the sowbreads that still flowered, along with their ivy-like leaves, into the customary wreath. Later, she would attach her creation to the top of her veil and send the replica she fashioned on to Nicanor.

For the third time, she picked up her looking glass and checked to see if her hair still held in place. Melita had outdone herself with curls that topped Daphne's head and cascaded over her ears.

From her endless storehouse, Medea had given her lotions, foundations, and makeup. Daphne had tried them, but returned most, preferring a more natural look. She took great care to not overdo with what she kept, and added a touch of vermilion to her cheeks for color. *Malachiti* shadowed her eyelids, and with a mixture of charcoal and olive oil, she drew a line below and above her lashes.

A knock on the door surprised her. She reached for her robe and opened the door a crack. Medea smiled. "It is just me, I could not wait another moment. Are you nearly ready?"

She invited her in. "Yes and no. Melita has gone for a bit of light food. She is worried I might faint if I do not eat."

Medea laughed. "She adores you and worries about how the day will go."

"I know. She is dear. But how are you? Should you not rest right up to the last minute? We all want you to make it through the whole celebration."

"I feel fine, and I rested until Danatel did my hair and helped me dress."

"Well, you look beautiful. That pale green peplos matches your eyes. But please, sit down. You will need all your strength to survive the ceremony and the feast."

"You do not mind if I stay a while? I never had a daughter to—"

"Of course. You are my substitute mother, remember?"

Medea's face glowed. She reached for Daphne's hand. "*Kalon*, are you concerned about...well, I mean do you have any questions I can help you with about, about...I mean after the feasting is over?"

How should she respond to the Kupios' obvious discomfort? ""Thank you for your concern. It was kind of you to ask, but my friend Lydia has helped me to understand what to expect."

Medea looked relieved. "Good. You will make a beautiful bride."

"Thank you. And I must thank Patharus. I so appreciate that he wished he could walk beside me." Her eyes watered. "My mother told me how much my own father looked forward to this day. But I want you to know I am grateful both of you are willing to take their place."

Melita brushed through the door and laid out Daphne's lunch. "Kupios, can I get you something to eat or drink?"

Medea shook her head. "I will leave you to finish now." She rose and walked in an unsteady gait toward Daphne. "I wish you the best of everything, from this moment on."

She hurried to her side. "Melita will walk you back to your suite. Please rest until the last moment. We could not go on without you."

Upon her return, Melita assured Daphne that Danatel would oversee the Mistress' care. She sighed. "It is hard for her to accept her limited strength. I do so hope she is able to be with us throughout the whole night.""

"Danatel said they have arranged everything so she can remain seated and still be a part of it all."

"Good. I hate when I see her wobble about like that."

And let your saints rejoice in goodness.
– 2 Chronicles 6:41

Nicanor paced. How could a day go so slowly?

He tried to picture the crowd. Surely, Patharus had invited half of Philippi, well over the required ten witnesses.

Batano covered a smirk. "All right. One last time, do you have the ring?"

He patted the pocket of his tunic and shoved his fists onto his hips. "Are you mocking me?"

His servant failed to hide a broad smile. "Of course not."

Despite Batano's good-natured joy in his discomfort, Nicanor defended himself. "It is not every day a man gets married, you know. Is it time? Should I put on the wreath Daphne sent?"

His servant went to the window and peered at the sundial in their courtyard. He forced a straight face. "Oh, about ten minutes since the last time you asked."

Nicanor picked up the wreath and turned it over. *My beloved made this with her own hands.* He tried to imagine her expression when at last she would be presented to him. A smile scrunched his face as he pictured them together, husband and wife, having a family. He held the wreath to his chest, sure he could smell her fragrance in the blooms.

Patharus' admonition returned, "You know, Nicanor, the main reason to unite in marriage is to produce children, heirs. I hope you will instruct your leader to include a sacrifice to Feronia, the goddess of fertility. A marriage is not fully consummated until the first child is born."

He had winced. How could he please his father but avoid sacrificing to a god he did not believe in. *Let those who are not mine sacrifice what they wish*, had been his heavenly Father's way of escape.

Batano stood, "Let us make sure your tunic is straight. It is nearly time." He brushed Nicanor's finely woven toga and centered the gold chain with the pendulum Patharus had given him for the occasion. Nicanor handed over the wreath. His servant placed it squarely on his head and secured it into his thick hair with a well-hidden clip. He stood back. "You look good enough to get married,"then ducked in time to dodge his master's hand.

Nicanor entered the garden where tables were set for the feast and chairs had been arranged in a semi-circle that opened down the middle. He walked immediately over to the Kupio and Kipios who were seated at the front. "How are you both? Are you warm enough, Medea?" Patharus' leg was propped up on a stool and both assured him they were comfortable.

Her eyes shone. "You look so handsome."

He reminded her that he had predicted she would be a beautiful mother of the groom. As their guests filed in, greeted them, and took their seats, Patharus groused that he was unable to stand and receive them properly.

The lilt of flutes signaled the bride's entrance. Nicanor's eyes misted, and his knees felt strangely weak.

Chapter Eighteen

...and they shall become one flesh.
– Genesis 2:24

Daphne told herself to put one foot in front of the other. Those who were not yet seated made way so she could pass. She kept her eyes lowered, grateful that the dense veil hid her face. Feminine oohs and ahhs filled the air along with whispers of how beautiful she looked. Halfway to the front, she chanced a peek at Nicanor. He beamed like an athlete just presented a crown. His expression sent a lump to her throat. Lord, I am so blessed. I am about to marry the man I love, not one of Apollo's priests or some stranger my father chose. Thank you, thank you, thank you, Lord.

He stood to the left of Epaphroditus with his hands behind his back. She hardly recognized the beloved leader in his official wedding tunic. He looked pleased. She inhaled the essence of the exquisite bouquet Nicanor had sent to her room. Where had he acquired white roses and lilies? The fragrance calmed her senses and enhanced her peace.

She smiled at the pleasure that graced the faces of Patharus and Medea. Despite her past, they had accepted their son's choice over dozens of hopefuls. Servants had been instructed to seat Lydia next to them. Daphne's heart skipped as her dear mentor's face momentarily evolved into a likeness of Hebee, her mother.

She gasped and missed a step. Seconds passed before she gulped and steeled herself against what could not be. A few quick blinks and a deep breath revived her senses. Today is a day of joy. No sadness will plunge me beneath waves of sorrow. One foot in front of the other.

Patharus was pushed on a moveable chair to the front where he could make a sacrifice to Feronia, the goddess of fertility. She looked at Nicanor and both lowered their eyes as the Kupio poured out his libation and asked the deity to bless the couple with a large family. He was returned to Medea's side and Nicanor stepped forward.

His voice was calm and confident "Oh Lord God, we give you the sacrifice of praise and thanks for this day. You who made heaven and earth and each of us and everything that ever was made, we bring You glory and honor and praise. Thank you for the abundance of blessings You have bestowed on this house and each of us, and for making new life possible for all who worship Your Holy Name." He lifted his hands. "Accept our homage, All Mighty One, and bless this our union of marriage today and always."

Those who met at Lydia's house responded with praises and thanksgiving. Others listened with furrowed brows. Most of those expected the usual bestowal of wine or delicacies to follow his sacrifice. When the ceremony skipped to the presentation of Daphne to Nicanor, heads shook and shoulders shrugged.

Patharus was brought forward. He took her right hand. "My son, as Daphne's protector, I give to you one who has become like a daughter to me. Guard and protect her with your very life." He placed her hand in Nicanor's, enacting Rome's traditional silent commitment and was returned to his place.

The music faded to a soft hum and a hush fell over the crowd. Epaphroditus stepped to the front. "Well, Nicanor, Daphne, we have looked forward to this day for weeks. This is the first Christ-centered marriage I have been called to perform, and I believe the Lord our God is pleased." He glanced at the crowd. "And did He not give us a lovely warm day for the wedding?"

Cheers rose from the small band of believers, while the eyes of Patharus' guests darted to catch his reaction. At his obvious consent, nods and smiles followed. Daphne relaxed. They had worked hard to have a ceremony that would offend no one and honor the true God. Nicanor had handled Patharus' request without courting any offense, and Medea's suggestions concerned mostly the setting, flowers, and menu choices. Surely You are with us, Lord. Oh how I thank You.

Epaphroditus began again. "Some of you are not familiar with Nicanor and Daphne's God, the Lord, Jesus Christ." He followed that with a condensed explanation of God's creation, how sin entered the world, men's rebellion and God's grace-filled gift of His Son, Jesus.

"It is not good for man to dwell alone, so our Creator gave Adam a wife, and thus He has given our lovely Daphne to you, Nicanor, to leave your family and to cleave to her alone for as long as you live. This kind of love is a replica of how Jesus loves those who are His people. And He charges you, Daphne, to obey and cherish your husband, as you each follow the Lord and put one another's needs first."

She returned Nicanor's frequent squeeze of her hand as their spiritual leader continued, pleased that the man they loved and respected managed to entwine the good news into the ceremony. When his message was finished and they had repeated vows of endless commitment, he asked for the ring. Nicanor raised her hand, pressed it to his lips and slid the ring on her third finger in honor of the Roman custom, believed to connect a vein directly to her heart.

Epaphroditus smiled. "I now declare that you are husband and wife."

Nicanor turned and lifted her veil. She expected the wedding kiss, but he fell to one knee. "Daphne, to remove this veil signifies you have been permanently transferred to my family. I want to proclaim to you my endless devotion and my appreciation of who you are in Christ. Your character and integrity under fire, and your faith and determination to serve our Lord inspires me. I love you, my bride, my wife."

He took her hands. Tears, she determined to control, flowed down her cheeks and dripped on her flowers. He rose and kissed her, tenderly, on her forehead. Her heart nearly burst with the joy of what her heavenly Father had brought into her life.

Medea made her way to the front and presented them with the traditional cheesecake. "This has been offered in your honor to Jupiter."

Beautifully decorated, it had been layered with an almond and apricot filling, fluted with whipped cream, and sprinkled with almond shavings. A servant cut the cake and Nicanor and Daphne fed it to each other before they were led to the area where tables were set for the feast.

Patharus had spared no expense, ordering Peloponnesian ham, roasted pig, squid, and every side dish imaginable to complement the meat. Wine filled huge craters, with a special, herbed concoction poured at the start for Patharus to make the first toast.

When everyone was seated, he raised his glass and the chatter quieted. "Friends, please join me in a toast to my son, Nicanor, and Daphne, his lovely bride."His voice trembled. "You are all well aware of the struggles I have faced after my accident, but I am here, today, to say I owe much to this loyal son of mine and to his selfless bride. With deep appreciation, I give you my children, Nicanor and Daphne."

Cheers and "hear, hear" came from every person. At his signal, the feast began. "Please enjoy yourselves, eat and drink to your heart's content."

Throughout the meal, toasts interrupted the chatter, enjoyed by all. Jatel, Nicanor's birth father attended the krater. He had avoided all contact with her once she moved to her new rooms, and she had yet to see him make any effort to congratulate his son. She sighed. "I wonder what he thinks."

After they had eaten, she walked over to the tables where Lydia and those with her had been seated. The women embraced her and complimented her gown. The men smiled, broadly.

Nicanor caught up with Daphne and they approached a group of Patharus' contemporaries, Amplias and Sergius among them. Sergius's eyes swept her form. "Well, I see you..." Nicanor put a protective arm around her, and the man's voice shrank to nothing. They received good wishes from those seated with him and quickly moved on.

The dancing and celebrating became louder and less inhibited with each additional cask of wine. Daphne made her way for the third time to check on Medea. She assured her she was fine, but strain leaked from her eyes. Suddenly, she stood, looked around and gave an impish grin. In a loud voice she called to Daphne. "*Kalon*, come quickly, hold tight to me."

Nicanor stepped up, his tone stern. "No. Come, My Bride, come away with me!"

Daphne gripped Medea's arm with both hands. "No, no. I cannot leave my mother."

He circled her waist and pulled her to himself. "But you are mine now." He swept her into his arms and headed for his suite.

Daphne feigned her remorse. "Mother, Mother, save me!"

Most of the guests gathered to watch the traditional farce. They threw dates, figs, nuts, and small coins as Nicanor ferried her off to the call of blessings from the believers. Patharus' guests followed with raucous laughter, bawdy songs, and obscene jokes.

Nicanor carried her over the threshold, snagged the door with his foot, and shut out the rest of the world.

PART TWO:

THE JOURNEY BEGINS

Chapter Nineteen

The righteous are bold as a lion.
– Proverbs 28:1

Daphne awoke to find Nicanor watching her sleep. "Good morning, Beautiful, did you sleep well? Was last night...all right?"

"Yes, I am deliriously happily married to the man I love." He reached over and brushed a curl from her forehead. She clasped his hand and held it to her cheek. "Promise me we will always be together like this."

"Of course, we will. Nothing could ever keep me from you. We —"

She shot up and clapped her fingers over her lips. "Oh, no! Nicanor, I forgot, I was not supposed to stay here all night." She reached for her robe and swung her feet over the edge of the bed. "My mother always left for her own rooms after, after..."

He pulled her back to himself. "No, that is not how it is going to be with us. I know Medea has her own suite, but I talked to Patharus and told him I want us together, not in separate quarters and he had no problem with it." He laughed. "So, you are stuck with me."

She melted into his arms. "Really? I guess I can get used to that."

Hours later they rang for their first breakfast as husband and wife. They ate in Nicanor's sitting room. She pretended not to notice the servant in the bedroom changing their sheets. She had seen the red stain and knew he had too.

He met her glance and smiled. "My Love, you are such a gift, I would do anything for you."

She cocked her head and laughed. "Anything? We will see."

When their wedding week was over, he continued his daily meetings with Patharus. As often as he was free, they met with the believers at Lydia's. On the way to dinner one night, she caught up with him, breathless. "I am so glad you finished earlier. We must go to Lydia's tonight. She told me Epaphroditus received a copy of a letter Paul wrote to the Thessalonians and he is going to share it with us. Is that not exciting? I cannot wait to hear from the Apostle himself."

Every believer had gathered for the reading. When the leader reached the part about "turning to God, from idols to serve the living God," her heart leapt. She had flung the idol she once depended upon into a herd of swine the very night she believed. Thank you, Lord for accepting me as Your own even before I fully grasped the demon's wicked agenda.

Everyone wanted to reexamine Paul's letter and discuss each line, so it was late when they returned. Medea's lights still burned. Nicanor grimaced. "Patharus is concerned about her weakened condition.'"

Daphne lay awake after they prayed for Medea. What the letter said about Jesus' return to earth, billowed in her mind. I believe your promise, God, to bring back those in Christ who die beforehand, but the wedding celebration sapped Medea's strength, and she is not doing well, Lord. She needs to receive you before it is too late.

By mid-morning the next day she knocked on Medea's door. Danatel beckoned, "Do come in. I will see if the Misses is up to a visit. She has been very tired."

She waited, relieved, when the servant motioned her to follow. "Medea, how are you? I have missed you." Behind a hug, she hid the shock of the *Kupios* drawn face and ashen skin.

"I am glad to see you too. Forgive me for postponing a visit, I have just been so... tired."

"Please, no need to explain. I am sorry the wedding added strain to your health. You were so brave to see it to the end. What can I do for you? Halaten has probably said rest is crucial, so I will not stay long."

Medea reached for her hand, "No, please do not go. To lie here alone for hours tires me more than company. Tell me, how have you adjusted to marriage? Is Nicanor as considerate as I suspect he would be?"

"Yes, he is so wonderful, and I love him more every day. Yesterday he had to meet very early with Patharus so he left a love note beside my pillow and ordered breakfast of all the things I like best."

She nodded. "So like his father, I remember when..." Her voice faded and tears trickled down her cheeks.

Daphne squeezed her hand. "If Nicanor is as devoted to me as Patharus has been to you, I will consider myself more than blessed."

Medea swiped at her tears. "Yes, he is awesome. Most people see a strong and confident leader, but I know the sensitive man he hides from the world. His love has never faltered, even when I..." Her head drooped. "When I could no longer be a wife in every way."

"Unconditional love is rare. I am just learning the reality of it in my God, the Lord, Jesus Christ. It is a love that will never fade." You are blessed to have had a husband who demonstrated the Savior's love for you.

The Kupios briefly closed her eyes. She blinked and pushed herself up on her elbows. "Tell me, how you came to be so sure of the one you call your God, to develop such trust in Him?" Her voice rose. "The gods I called upon never seemed to hear or accept my offerings, or else they simply did not care."

Daphne drew her chair close, silently seeking the Lord's wisdom. "It surely did not happen overnight. When the apostle Paul came to Philippi I began to learn about the great love of the Almighty God, our Father."

Medea's brows pinched. "So, upon hearing about the love of this God, convinced you to put your trust in Him? Did you not want some proof, some evidence it was true?"

She pondered her answer. "No, I guess it was because His words rang with more credence each time I heard them. Even the demon that possessed me recoiled at the powerful name of Jesus. He did everything he could to keep me from the knowledge of the freedom and peace that comes to all who believe what God did for us through His Son, Jesus."

Medea's lips mouthed, "Peace."

"It is His gift to us, *Kalon*, and He wants to give it to you. From the very start I realized the Father's love was real. But it was not until after God's servant delivered me of the demonic, evil creature that controlled my life, that I realized there was a greater power, and I wanted to know more about it. My dear friend, Lydia, explained the truth about our Savior's power, His forgiveness and acceptance to me that same night."

Medea fell back into her pillows. "You were fortunate to have someone to run to or talk with. Sometimes I feel so isolated."

"Oh, Dear One, I know. I felt the same way when I was brought here as a slave. But Jesus changed everything. When He comes into your life, He is always with you, to listen and encourage you. It took a while to dare to believe that His love could include me, but when I understood my heart leapt and I asked Jesus to be my God. Dearest Medea, I found such joy and freedom and He wants you to have it too."

She sighed. "Every god I have ever heard of demands things like homage and sacrifices. I cannot imagine that there is one that really cares." She drew herself up until they were face to face. Her eyes challenged like a hawk over its prey. "Tell me, would your God have kept my son from dying?"

Daphne's breath caught. "Oh, Medea, I cannot say for sure, but I do know that He loved Elias and did not want him to die at such a young age. God's plan is always a long, full life, but I have experienced evil, demonic powers that work in this world, ready to kill, steal and destroy. The good news is they can be overcome through prayer and spiritual warfare. The blood Jesus shed on the cross paid for our protection as well as our healing and salvation."

Medea's head collapsed into her hands and her voice lost its edge. "I miss him so...I miss him so much."

Daphne put her arms around her. "Dearest *Kupios*, the God I serve promises that we will once again see our loved ones who have died, when we get to heaven. Your son will be waiting there for you the moment you leave this earth."

"Are you sure? Are you really sure I will see him again?"

"Yes, I am sure. God said it and He never fails to do what He promised. He knows of your broken heart, and He cares. Jesus wants you to come to Him so He can mend every hurt and disappointment you have ever carried."

She raised a tear-stained face. "It sounds so good, but I do not know if I can trust in a god again. It is too painful. I am happy for you, glad you have found such peace, but I do not know...I just do not know."

Daphne's heart went out to her. To believe something so wonderful was a gift, hers for the asking, had been her struggle too. "It is all right, Medea. God understands and He is willing to wait for you as long as it takes. But could I pray for you?"

She nodded and Daphne took her hand. "Dear Lord, thank you for Medea and Your great love for her. Please reveal Yourself to her and give her peace. Amen."

Chapter Twenty

Through deceit they refuse to know Me, says the Lord.
– Jeremiah 9:6

By midafternoon, Nicanor left the oversight of trimming the grape vines to Makendon. Winter's colder temperatures had settled in, and the job was nearly over. He hoped to visit Medea before he cleaned up for dinner.

Danatel gushed, "Oh, Master Nicanor, she will be so happy to see you." Like many of the servants, she adored Patharus' adopted son. He had been one of them and treated them with respect.

Medea brightened at the sight of him. "Nicanor, it is so good of you to come."

He smiled. "You appear much more rested than when I last saw you. How do you feel?"

"I am doing all right. How is Daphne? I have not seen her for a while."

"We do not want to wear you out, but I will tell her if you are ready for another visit."

She nodded and called for refreshments. They chatted about the change of seasons and how Patharus, at last, looked forward to getting around on a peg leg.

Her fingers worried her multi-chain gold necklace. "I know he is doing well but cannot help but wish you and Daphne were not leaving so soon. Three months will pass so quickly."

He raised his brows. "Medea, we have been over this and—"

"I know, I know. I just could not bear to lose another son."

His voice was firm. "You are not going to lose me, and you can see your little son again in heaven if you put your faith in Jesus."

Uncertainty burned from her eyes, and she stiffened. "That is what Daphne said. Babies and children who die go immediately to be with your God."

"She is right. Our God loves and cares about all of us and wants everyone to come to Him like a trusting child." He cocked his head and winked. "Even you."

She looked away and he reached for her hand. "Medea, God would not have sacrificed the life of His only Son for any who would believe if He did not long for you to be His own. You lost a son. Surely, you can relate to the enormity of such a gift."

Her face contorted. "But I had no choice in the matter. My son is gone, and the gods did not care!"

He reminded himself to stay patient. "There are no other gods. Like you and I, most Greeks never had a chance to hear of the only true God till recently, probably few Romans either."

"Well then, why all the celebrations and festivals?"

He ignored her sarcasm. "God put the desire to worship within all of us but people are prone to worship whatever has become a god to them. Or in ignorance, they worship myths that demonic powers create. Most of the world did not receive the evidence of the only true God's unconditional love until about fifty years ago. That is when God the Father sent His Son, Jesus, to earth to show us how much He cares."

"So, He is alive? I thought you said He became a sacrifice. Have you seen Him for yourself?"

"No, people who were jealous of His power and growing followers killed Him."

"They killed him? He is dead? Then why do you—"

"Jesus did die, but the Father brought Him back to life." He raised his palms. "I know, I know. That is against everything we Greeks believed, but it is true. Ours is a supernatural, powerful God. Jesus rose from the dead, and over five hundred people saw him during the forty days before the Father called Him back to heaven."

She frowned. "He actually came back to life? That is hard to believe."

He released a heavy sigh. "Amazing is what it is. But believing is a choice. Everyone must decide for themselves if God is real and that He rewards those who seek Him. It is a gift, and it transforms lives. You did not know Daphne before she became a believer. She was a fear-driven, timid, mass of confusion. She did not trust anyone except her friend, Kawit, who was tragically taken from her. She would not allow herself to love or care for anyone after that. She lived behind a wall she erected to survive."

Her jaw dropped. "She is not at all like that now."

"No, that all changed after she became a new person in Christ Jesus. That is where she found the courage to stop and help Patharus, despite the terror she knew she would face as a slave without power to perform as a sorceress."

"And I will always be grateful to her. It is just that—"

"Look, God's ability to change lives and set people free is what is driving Daphne. She feels called to go back to her city and help people renounce the same myths we once believed."

Medea grew quiet and he knew it was time to leave. He stood and put his hand on her shoulder. "I had better go. It is not my intention to badger you into accepting what has become a great blessing in my life. It is just that...that we love you and want to know that you are safe in the arms of the true God."

"Nicanor, I..."

He jumped on her pause. "No, you owe no explanation. Just know we love you and I will stop in again soon."

She did not object when he picked up his outer cloak and left.

Weeks later as he and Daphne waited patiently for their evening meal, she touched his arm. "So, what are you working on now that the vines are trimmed and even the root vegetables are stored?"

"Oh, there is plenty to do. Patharus always does an annual inventory of everything we have stored from animal fodder to household provisions. He wants an accurate tally of the herds and of the condition of the sheep." He shook his head. "And would you believe he keeps a detailed list of his slaves, their abilities, who died, and how many gave birth each year? The man is more than organized!"

She laughed. "Well, he must be doing something right, his estate has certainly prospered."

He shrugged, "I wish his soul would prosper. He waves me off if I mention our Lord."

"I know. Medea too. I spent the afternoon with her yesterday and her bitterness is hard to deal with. She mentioned feeling isolated and lonely and I considered asking Lydia to pay her a visit. They seemed to enjoy each other at the wedding feast. Maybe the Kupios would benefit from the wisdom of someone nearer her age, I feel like I have failed her."

"That is a lie from the enemy, but it is early, let us get to tonight's meeting and ask her. If Patharus would come to Christ, Medea would surely follow, but she needs Jesus now."

Chapter Twenty-One

The troubles of my heart have enlarged.
– Psalms 25:17

Daphne laid the last of her peploses and outer robes out of their bed. "Melita, I do not know which of these things I should pack. It is less than four weeks before we leave, and I cannot make up my mind."

"Misses, they are all lovely. You have a large trunk so why not take most of them?"

"Nicanor's clothing needs to fit in, too. I wish I knew what was proper. I try to picture what my mother wore in the Spring. I had barely been allowed to wear adult clothing before we were sold into slavery and lost everything."

Melita picked up part of the clothing. "Here, let us do a practice packing and see what fits. Or maybe you should ask the Kupios. Surely, she would know."

Daphne rolled her eyes. "No. I cannot bring up anything about our trip without enduring her displeasure. She seemed to understand my need to go and was supportive throughout the wedding, but something has changed, and it is like there is a wall between us."

"She is worried, Misses. Danatel tells me she has become difficult to please, obsessed with the fear you will not return."

"Fear is an awful taskmaster. I will always be grateful the Lord's perfect love removed its hold on me."

"Perhaps you could tell her about that."

"Believe me I have tried, but she shuts the door on any such conversation."

"Maybe she will listen to your friend. Danatel told me she paid the Kupios a visit."

Daphne pressed down the contents in the trunk and shook her head. "Lydia said she was pleasant, seemed pleased she had come, but would not allow the discussion to delve into anything that mattered."

"That is a shame, maybe..."

Both startled as Nicanor charged through the door. "Daphne, it is Patharus. Something is wrong! Quick. Halaten is with him. Hurry!"

He was halfway to the *Kupio's* suite before she caught up with him. "What happened? Why is Halaten with him? Is he sick? Did he fall?"

He shrugged, breathing hard. "I do not know. I had been in the south barn with Makendon when Patharus' servant ran in. Did not make a lot of sense...said the *Kupio* is not right. I asked him what he meant, and he said my father tried to get up and seemed to almost fold onto the floor. He ran and told Halaten and then found me."

She followed him into the master's suite. "I do not understand. What did he mean 'he is not right'?"

"Halaten is examining him. He will know." He put his finger to his lips, and they entered the bedroom where the doctor hovered over Patharus. "How is he? Do you know what happened?"

"He has come to, but he is not able to make sense."

Nicanor pushed past Halaten. "Father, I am here. What happened? Did you fall?"

Confusion etched deep lines into Patharus' face. "Asha bah, ayana."

Nicanor gasped, horrified at the terror in his father's eyes. "What is wrong with him? Can you not give him something?"

Again, Patharus called out "Ayana," and tried to sit up. Halaten pressed a vessel to his lips and coaxed him to lie back down.

"I have given him something to make him sleep, that should help. I do not think he injured himself when he fell. Sounds like he passed out and slid to the floor."

Sleep soon quelled Patharus' agitation. Daphne nudged Nicanor. "There is something wrong with his face. The left side of his mouth is hanging as if he cannot close it."

He grimaced and moved toward Halaten. The doctor nodded and ushered them into the next room. "I know it is a shock to see your father like this. I am sorry to have to tell you he is in serious condition."

Nicanor nearly shouted. "But what? What is wrong with him?"

"I believe it is *apoplexy*, a condition that hits a person as if he were struck violently from within."

"But why? Did the removal of his leg cause it? Was there more that should have been done?"

Halaten gently urged them toward a settee. "Please, sit down. *Apoplexy* is something that has been recognized for over 2000 years. No one knows why it happens and there is little we can do but let it run its course and hope the effects are mild" His voice dropped. "It can be overcome but that is not always the case."

Nicanor pressed. "What 'effects'? What do you mean?"

"It is most likely why he fell. A sudden weakness made him lose his balance." He looked at Daphne. "And you noticed how his mouth drooped? That is a common sign."

She scooted to the edge of her seat. "What else?"

"He may have significant loss of strength on that same side of his body and could lose sight in that eye. You can also expect him to be confused and unable to speak clearly, as we just heard."

Nicanor stood. "This cannot happen. He is a strong man. Why him?"

Halaten shook his head, his words tender. "Nobody knows, Son. I have seen cases where the patient does not live long after the onslaught and cases where, in time, the person regains nearly all of his strength and speech."

Daphne grabbed Nicanor's arm. "You mean he could die?"

"It is a possibility, but not likely. Let us not get ahead of ourselves. Right now, he is resting, and I will keep vigil."

Nicanor put his arm around Daphne's shoulder, and they clung to each other. "I cannot leave him."

She lifted her face to his. "Remember we have a great and powerful God, and He has promised to never abandon us."

"I know. But how much can one's body take? First his leg and now this. I must stay here in case he..." His voice broke. "Will you arrange an escort and go to Lydia's? We need serious prayer."

She glanced out a window. "The sun has not peaked, I can get there and back before dark."

He nodded and by the time she had changed for the ride, her escort had the horses ready. He checked on her every few minutes, until she smiled and assured him she was fine.

The day was cold, but the sun took the edge off. Patharus' distorted face came to mind as she passed bushes that sprouted the promise of new leaves.

She prayed, "Oh, Lord, please be with Patharus and touch his body with Your healing power. I believe You are with us and that You are our very present help in this time of trouble. But please, direct Halaten to do exactly what is needed to bring about Kupio's recovery. You, Oh God, are the great Physician and my trust is in You."

To her relief, Lydia was home. She fixed them some tea and listened while Daphne explained what had happened. She hugged her distraught friend. "I am so sorry to hear this."

The gesture released the tears she had yet to shed. "I am sorry to be such a baby. It is Patharus who needs help. He is not yet a believer and the doctor said he could even die. Fear spilled from his eyes and Nicanor is beside himself."

Lydia took Daphne's hands and prayed a powerful prayer for healing, hope, and victory over the attack from the enemy. "You know we will pray tonight, at the meeting, and keep Patharus in our prayers."

Daphne mounted her horse. Halfway home, it struck her that they had finally arranged passage to sail from Neapolis to Athens, then to Corinth and on to Delphi. She jerked her mount to a stop, her hand over her lips. Oh, Lord, what will happen to our plans? We will not be able to leave. Father, I so want to be obedient to what you told me, but now Patharus will need Nicanor more than ever. What do I do?

Her escort looked back and spun his horse around. "Are you all right, Misses? Is something wrong?"

His urgent tone jarred her musing. "No, no, I am fine. I am sorry. Let us get home."

Nicanor helped her dismount. "I am glad for the longer days, Are you all right? Was Lydia home?"

She filled him in on their visit and of Lydia's prayer and promise to tell the others. "But how is your father? Is he any better? Has he spoken to you?"

He shook his head. "No, when he awoke, he just kept repeating that same word, 'ayana.' I have instructed them to set up a bed for me and bring my meals. I need to be right there."

"I will arrange to have dinner there with you tonight."

He pulled her close. "How did I manage without you?" He gave her a quick squeeze and hurried for Patharus' quarters.

He was already out of earshot when she thought about their trip. She sighed. It is just as well, he does not need to think about anything now but seeing his father regain his health.

Back in her room, Daphne paced. Melita had put away the clothes and she was glad to be alone. Patharus' pathetic attempt to talk haunted her. "Oh, Lord, how can I help?"

From seemingly out of nowhere the answer came and she could not wait to tell Nicanor.

Chapter Twenty-Two

...that God would grant me the thing that I long for.
– Job 6:8

Daphne tiptoed into Patharus' bedroom where Nicanor stared at his father. He jumped, startled, when she laid her hand on his shoulder.

"I am sorry. How is he? Has Halatan's potion kept him asleep?"

Nicanor nodded and led her back into the sitting room. "Let us sit here where we will not disturb him." He sighed and put his arm around her. She snuggled close. "He has slept, mostly, but at times opened his eyes long enough to mutter those same words before he falls back asleep."

Her eyes sparkled. "Nicanor. I asked God how I could help, and I believe he has shown me that when Patharus says 'Ayana,' he is trying to say 'Medea.' Think about it, Ayana could be his slurred effort to call for his beloved."

"Ayana." The meaningless word rolled from his tongue. "Ayana, I believe you may be right. Makes sense when I think about the fear I saw in his eyes. Probably thought he was dying and desperate to see Medea before it is too late."

"What shall we do about it? I cannot imagine telling her about this. She has barely accepted that he lost his leg, and...and what about her condition? This could be way too much for her."

His chin fell to his chest. "I do not know, but she will have to be told. How do I tell her? You know how quick she is to become aware when something has happened and she has not been informed." He leaned into his fist and shook his head.

A servant arrived with dinner, set it on a nearby bench, and poured their wine. She thanked the man and took Nicanor's hand. "Let us pray and ask God to show us how to handle Medea. He loves her and knows her limitations."

They had finished eating when Halaten came to check on the Kupio. Each head shot up when they heard Patharus call out. Nicanor pushed the bench aside and hurried to his father's side. "Ayana, Ayana," Patharus muttered.

He took his hand. "I am going to get her, Father. Just relax and let the doctor take care of you till I get back." The promise appeared to calm him.

Halaten followed them out of the room, his brows pinched. "You are going to tell the Kupios?"

"Yes. We must. We have no choice. If there is a chance he will not make it, she has to be able to see him and he needs her. Make sure you are ready in case she needs help, too."

The doctor nodded and returned to Patharus. Nicanor grabbed Daphne's hand. "Come on. I know she has probably retired for the night, but we need to go right now and tell her."

"Are you sure I should go? She has been very put off with me for weeks."

He stopped and pulled her to his face. "You are my wife and as much a part of things as I am. Medea needs to get used to that."

"It is that I am concerned..."

He put up a hand, his mind set.

Surprise flashed from Danatel's face when she answered the door. "Master Nicanor, I was about to get the Kupios bedded for the night. Did she expect you?"

"Something has come up and we must see her at once. Tell her we are here."

The maid backed and they entered. She returned in minutes and gestured toward Medea's bed chamber.

Daphne followed, well behind Nicanor. As Medea rose on her pillows. both bid her good evening.

"Good evening to you, but what is this about? Is tomorrow the day you plan to leave?"

He drew close and took her hand. "Medea, we have not come to say goodbye. Something has happened that you need to know about."

Her eyes grew dark. "I knew it! You are here to tell me that you have decided not to return."

Daphne could feel Nicanor's tension, but he remained calm. "No, but it is not good news, Kupios." He proceeded to explain what had happened to Patharus and what Halaten believed caused the awkward conditions of her husband's body. He left out that Patharus could die.

Like a baby bird, her mouth hung and remained ajar. When he finished, she became hysterical. "I do not understand. Tell me again what happened." Over and over, she cried, "I do not understand."

Daphne stepped to her side. "Medea, I am so sorry. Halaten is with him and Patharus asks for you. Do you think you could come with us? I believe your presence will assure him he will be all right."

She stared as if she had been asked to climb a mountain. The words finally took root and she repeated, "Go to him. Of course! I must go. Danatel, fetch that woolen robe and some sandals."

They bundled her up and with their support, she walked to Patharus' suite. At the sitting room, Nicanor stopped her. "Kupios, Father will not look like himself. One side of his mouth is not able to close, and he cannot speak clearly. Try not to show your shock and do not let him see that you are afraid or worried. He just needs assurance you are there. Understand?"

She nodded and took a deep breath.

Daphne's eyes welled at the sight of Patharus' relief at seeing Medea. He tried to reach for her hand but could not move his arm. "Ayana," he whispered, tears running down his cheeks. "Ayana, Ayana," he repeated.

She buried her face in his chest. "I am here, Beloved. You just rest and get well. I will not leave you." He laid his other arm across her back and murmured words that made sense to only him.

Silence descended on the room. Halaten began to pace. "I think I should give him something to sleep through the night. I cannot imagine how she is going to hold up. She has no idea there is no quick cure for this."

Nicanor stood. "I will get her." He went in and found them just as before, eyes closed and arms entwined. He touched her shoulder. "Medea, Halaten thinks it best if we let Father sleep now. Come, let me help you back to your rooms."

She slowly rose and patted Patharus' chest. "I will come back in the morning, Love. Get some sleep and do not worry. Nicanor is here and he will take care of everything."

They bundled Medea up and returned her to Danatel's care. He walked Daphne back to their quarters. "I hate to sleep without you by my side, but I need to make sure he is all right."

She put her arms around him. "Of course, you must, but I will miss you too."

Chapter Twenty-Three

If I still pleased men, I would not be a bondservant of Christ.
– Galatians 1:10

Nicanor kissed Daphne's cheek and walked slowly toward Patharus' door. Medea's words rang in his ears. *Nicanor's here and he will take care of everything... take care of everything...*

Momentarily, he sat on the bench by the sundial and tried to quell the echoes in his head. Lord, what am I going to do? I promised Daphne I would take her home, but I cannot leave with Father in this condition. I do not even know if he will make it through the night. And this is way too much responsibility to leave on Makendon. What if I left and Patharus died?

The evening chill brought a shiver that spurred a need to get back to his father. He whispered a prayer into the night, "Help me, Lord."

The wind rustled the trees but carried no answer.

Two weeks passed before the fear he had seen in Patharus' face turned to anger and frustration. He was usually propped into a sitting position and though it was awkward, he could feed himself with his good arm. His speech had not improved, but he tried harder each day to make himself understood.

Medea had concluded her morning visit and left to rest, so Nicanor entered his father's bedroom. "Makendon reports the land is ready to plant vegetables. Dry weather allowed for early tilling of the soil, so we will be able to get the cabbage, onions, beans and the rest in with plenty of time to harvest the barley and the wheat next month."

Patharus nodded and motioned with a jerk of his head. Nicanor drew close. Wonder what's on his mind. Olives, wine, and the orchards were harvested in the fall just after the grains were planted so that could not be it.

"Oo saa?" It sounded like a question.

"What was that, Father?" He hated that he had not a clue what Patharus said.

"Oo saa?" he repeated, louder but no better.

Nican ran the sounds through his mind. What could he possibly mean or want me to know? Surely not the crops. He knows Makendon is more than competent.

Daphne's discovery that "Ayana" was his father's version of Medea led him to ask the Lord to tell him what he needed to know. "Oo saa...Oo." That could be you, meaning me. "Saa." What would that be? "You saa." Instantly, he knew what it was.

"Are you asking if I am going to stay, Father?"

Eyes conflicted with dread and expectancy, Patharus nodded.

Nicanor's thoughts ran to the conversations he and Daphne had struggled with, what to do about their plans to sail in only a week's time. Neither could imagine him leaving Patharus in such a helpless condition. Yet, he ached for her even in the midst of disappointment over the tragic turn of events.

He put his hand on his father's shoulder. "I would never leave you while you are unable to take care of things here. I will be here as long as you need me."

Patharus covered his son's hand with his own and loosed a deep sigh. The working side of his lips strained to smile. Nicanor returned the effort. "You get some rest now and I will be back after I check on Makendon's progress."

He alerted Halaten of his leaving. Out in the courtyard, he paused. *Well, I guess that makes it final.* He had known all along that he would not leave, but hated having to tell Daphne they must postpone their trip. He decided to wait until after dinner and went to find their overseer.

A man's heart plans his way…
– Proverbs 16:9

Despite her servant's objections, Daphne straightened their living quarters for the third time. Fearful she had not completed her tasks to her mistress' liking, Melita said, "I will do that for you, Misses."

"No, it is fine. You are dismissed for now." She waved her off and thought about a visit to Patharus. He mostly slept, and she did not want to disturb him. His sad state brought her brows together. *How will he ever accept his condition? He is used to being in charge. To not be in control of things must eat him alive.*

Time hung like a heavy carpet strung for cleaning, oblivious to the gentle nudge of a breeze. She rang her bell and Melita quickly appeared. "I am going to spend time in the garden if Master Nicanor should happen to look for me." She nodded and started to leave. "Wait, Melita. Would you care to go with me?"

Her eyes grew wide. "You want me to go with you? I have never been in the garden. It is off limits to—"

"I know, but why not? Your work is done, and it is a beautiful day. You will love it."

Her servant smiled and followed out through the courtyard to the nearly hidden gate. At first, she stayed several steps behind, but as her mistress pointed out flower after flower they chatted and enjoyed each other's company.

They had walked for an hour when Daphne gestured for her to join her on the bench by the pond. "This is a very special place. It is where Nicanor and I used to meet before we were married. Makes me wonder, is there a special man in your life?"

Melita blushed. "No Misses. No one has spoken for me yet."

"Does that bother you? Do you want to be married?"

"'I guess I do, but I am in no hurry. My mama had three children when she was my age and then had five more. Sometimes she looks so tired."

Daphne thought about her own quest as a child, to find the freedom she longed for. "What do you want from life, Melita? What would you do if you were suddenly set free?"

She paled. "Oh, Misses, I did not mean to complain. You are so kind to me and—"

"You have not. I asked what you would do?"

She looked down at her sandals and twisted her hands, "I would like to learn to read and write, Misses. And I would like to go to faraway places and see some of the things slaves talk about when they speak of their former homes."

Daphne cocked her head and stared for a moment. Merchants had once seen her as property, someone's to command as they pleased. Melita is not a fixture, Lord, she is a person. "I think that is admirable, and when Nicanor and I get back from our trip I am going to teach you to read and write. That is a promise."

They returned from the garden and Melita fetched her bath and helped her dress for dinner. Nicanor had sent word that he had arranged for them to eat under the grape arbor.

They met part way and he reached for her hand. "The leaves are just sprouting, and it may be a little chilly, but I cannot resist being out here after such a beautiful day. Are you warm enough?"

She assured him she was fine. "But what about your father? Is Halaten with him?"

He confirmed that the doctor was there and would stand by while Medea made her evening visit, so he and Daphne could relax and enjoy some time to themselves.

The meal ended with their chef's specialty, a puffed pastry filled with almond paste and drizzled with honey. She shared her joy in taking Melita with her into the garden, and he caught her up on the spring plantings. Silence fell as he pushed his desert about on his plate. Something was on his mind. He never left sweets uneaten. "Nicanor, what is wrong…is your father not coming along?"

He looked troubled. "No, nothing much has changed. Let us take a walk." They went into the garden, but he stopped by the pond, and they sat on their bench. He told her about Patharus' effort to question him and that he had finally understood that he was trying to say, "you staying?"

It took a minute for her to realize what he meant. Her voice dropped. "'You staying'? He was asking if you intended to cancel our trip or to stay."

He nodded. "He has been stewing about my leaving."

"Of course, he would wonder." She tried to keep her lips from quivering. "What did you tell him?"

"The only thing I could say. That I would never leave him while he needed me here to watch over things."

Her head fell. He reached over and lifted her chin. "I know how disappointed you are about our plans, but there is nothing else I can do." He wiped the tears from her cheeks. "You know I would do anything for you, and I promise we will go as soon as I am sure Makendon can handle things."

"I know. I have known for days that it must be, but my heart hoped something would change. Your father needs you. I truly believe that, but something inside just cannot find peace with putting off my going." He pulled her into his arms. She looked up into his face and forced a half-smile. "Well, at least Medea will be happy to have things her way."

"It is not her way. It is God's way. His plan is different from ours. But you watch, somehow His timing will work out for the best."

She sighed and snuggled against his chest. Lord, I know you asked me to go, and I want to be obedient. Please help me sort this out.

Chapter Twenty-Four

For Your name's sake, lead me and guide me.
– Psalms 31:3

Lydia answered Daphne's early morning knock. "Come in. This is a surprise."

She followed her into the house. "I hope I am not intruding."

Lydia listened while she poured out her concern. "What am I going to do? I cannot quiet this urgency in my heart that I must get back to Delphi."

"Have you prayed about it? Is Patharus any better? Any chance Nicanor would feel free to go?"

"No. Patharus' whole left side has been affected. The doctor does assure us that it is not likely to take his life."

Lydia poured some tea. "I knew a man back in Tyre, before I moved here, that faced this tragedy. He recovered some mobility, but he was never the same."

Daphne stilled a shudder. "The Kupio would have such a hard time with less than a full return to his former self. What did Epaphroditus say when you told him about it? I know he is praying."

""He was shocked as we all were and asked the believers to keep Patharus in their prayers. You know how our beloved leader cherishes God's word. He has some of the few scrolls in our city. Recently, he shared a portion of it with me. It was a psalm written eons ago by an ancient, Jewish king named David. In one he mentions those symptoms, a useless hand and a tongue that cleaves to the roof of the mouth. So, it is certainly nothing new."

"Did that ancient king say how long it takes to recover his speech or mobility? Halaten seems pretty sure Patharus will improve eventually."

"No, I do not think so, but I do know God will guide you and give you peace as your search for His will. Paul said we are not to be anxious about anything, but to pray with a thankful heart about everything. When you do, the Lord's peace will rule in your heart."

Daphne sighed. "You are right, I am afraid my prayers have focused on a way to make my desire prevail. I had better be off. Thank you for listening, Dear Friend. I do not know what I would do without you."

Her mount descended toward the estate, with Lydia's reminder of Paul's counsel affirmed with each clop of its hoof. *Pray about everything...refuse to be anxious...be thankful and the Lord's peace will rule in your heart.*

Back at the estate, she finished lunch and left for the garden, fully intent on seeking God's counsel. Despite her efforts, her thoughts floundered. Why can I not hear You, Lord? I am listening.

Frustrated, she began to walk. The beauty of flowering trees lifted her spirit and she found herself singing one of her grandmother's favorite songs.

Heavens open up to me, leak your secrets, gloriously
Let me know the joy of spring.
Hidden treasures ever bring.
Who awakens life asleep? Dares to nature's chamber
    creep.
Give my eyes new light to see.
Beyond my wonder set me free.
Beyond my wonder set me free.

She reexamined the message of the familiar tune. Secrets of heaven, hidden treasures, eyes that see the light, be set free? Surely God had revealed Himself and the treasure of knowing His Son, Jesus, to her. And had He not opened her heart and set her free? "God, You heard the unspoken cry of my heart when I had no idea You existed. And still You called me to be Your own."

She nearly danced down the path, her dilemma all but forgotten. Songs of praise sprang from her heart and evolved to a melody that rose from her deepest being. Words flowed that she had never learned. Joyfully spent, she knelt by a patch of violets. "Thank You Lord, thank You. I came to find answers to my questions, instead, You filled me with Yourself. I know You care, and I believe You will show me what to do."

She plucked a few blossoms and carried them back toward the gate, but hesitated when thoughts not her own, whispered to her spirit.

Have I not called you to follow My lead and to speak of Me and the freedom I gave you, back in the place from which you came?

"But, Lord, we cannot go now. Nicanor cannot possibly leave his father."

I called You to follow My lead. Nicanor must hear for himself what he is to do.

She gulped. "You mean I should go on alone? Go without him?"

Have I not promised I will be with you, that I will never leave you or forsake you?

"Yes but...but, Lord, he would never agree to that. And could I do it? Travel all by myself back to Delphi?"

Trust Me. I will clear the way.

144

They had finished dinner when Nicanor reached for her hand. "You are awfully quiet. Are you still mourning our postponed trip?"

Daphne's insides cringed. Should she tell him? She had to. Lord, You told me I am to go on alone, but I can only imagine his reaction. How do I make him understand? I could never leave without his blessings, but You promised to clear the way. What do I say?

She swallowed her dread and focused on his eyes. "I spent a lot of time with the Lord in the garden this afternoon and I know there is no way you can leave your father right now. But..." she hesitated and refolded her napkin.

"But what? Did He assure you He understands why we must wait and go later?"

She took a deep breath. "No, what I heard the Lord tell me is I am to go now, by myself...alone."

He shot from his chair. "Alone? You mean He told you to go alone, without me?"

She shrank in her seat. "That is exactly what I heard Him say. I had a wonderful time praising Him and it seemed to open the door to hear what I could not grasp beforehand."

The disbelief on his face made her mouth go dry but she pulled herself upright and went on. "He said that I was to follow what He has asked me to do, to speak of the freedom I have found and that He would be with me."

"And you heard that to mean you were to go alone?"

"Yes, He said I was to go as planned and that you were to do what you must do."

His eyes darkened. "No. I could never let you go alone on a journey where there is so much

145

unknown. Your message is likely to meet with violent opposition and who knows where that would lead."

"But God said He would go with me and He—"

"No. You are my wife and there is no way that is going to happen."

His expression left no room for discussion. It frightened her. Was this the way of a godly marriage? And why would he not want her to obey and trust in the Lord's protection? "Nicanor, please, could you at least pray about it?"

"I will not subject you to dangers you cannot yet imagine. Let us not speak of this again." Without his usual parting touch, he pushed in his chair. "I need to check on Father."

Stunned, she watched him go, leaned her face into her hands and wept over the gulf that had sprung, like a flood, between them. "Lord, peace ruled in my heart when You showed me what I am to do, but now what? And did You not say You would clear the way?"

Chapter Twenty-Five

Be angry and sin not.
– Ephesians 4:26

That night, Nicanor did not return to the suite he and Daphne shared, but moved his cot back near his father's bed. Halaten's brows raised but he said nothing when a week passed and Nicanor had not returned to his own quarters. When he came to do his nightly check, the doctor found him there with his head in his hands.

Nicanor turned from the doctor's curious stare. "I just feel a need to be here at night."

His father slept quietly most nights, but awakened at first light. Nicanor heard him stir and rolled off the cot he had slept on all week. He started for the door. "I will get Halaten."

Patharus groaned. "Where's Daphne?"

Either his father's mumbled attempts at conversing had improved, or Nicanor found it easier to decipher what he wanted. Daphne? Why would he be asking about her? "She is probably still asleep, Father. Hold on and I will get Halaten to attend to your needs,"

He slurred his request. "I want to see her."

Nicanor walked back to his father's bed. "You want to see Daphne?"

At his nod, Nicanor touched his shoulder. "I am going for the doctor, but I will be back after I give Daphne your message." He made sure Halaten knew he was leaving and entered the bustling courtyard. Slaves greeted him warmly but did not linger. A wave of loneliness for his former friends washed over him. "Who do I have to talk to?"

Talk to Me. Call on Me and I will answer you.

He was quick to recognize the still, small voice and wished he could disappear. Surely, the Lord had seen his harshness with Daphne and knew he had separated himself from her. What had Epaphroditus emphasized a few weeks ago? *Do not let the sun go down on your anger and give the devil an opening.* There was no place to hide.

He found an out-of-the-way bench and sat in the quiet trying to sort it out. "All right, Lord, I am sorry. I know I have not reacted properly, but surely You would not have told Daphne to go off on a dangerous trip without me. How can I make her understand it is because I love her so much and I could not bear to let something happen to her?"

Do you trust me, Nicanor?

"Yes, but Lord, I—"

My ways are not your ways, Beloved. Commit your worries to Me, believe I am in control, and My peace will rule in your heart.

He dragged himself toward their suite, reluctant to accept what the Lord seemed to indicate. How could he let her go? It was not a matter of trust. It was insane. Women did not travel alone, and Daphne was naive to the ways of the world. Was she not?

A man of understanding has wisdom.
– Proverbs 10:23

Daphne had risen early after a week wrought with tears. Why would Nicanor stay away like that? Was he done with her? Her heart ached. Could a disagreement cause him to leave her for good? She sank to her knees, frustrated that her attempts to give her cares over to the Lord returned with questions but no answers. She jerked around when the door suddenly banged, and he charged into the room.

"Daphne, we need to talk. I am sorry about everything. The thought that you would leave without me was more than I could bear. I hope you have thought it through."

She rose from the floor and stared into a countenance foreign to her. The sincerity of his apology greatly diminished by his self-justification. Think it over? It was not her idea to go alone. The Lord asked it of her. How could she make him understand? "Nicanor, I..."

Oblivious to her pain, he stepped close and put his hands on her shoulders. "Tell me you will not go. I love you and could not stand to think of you unprotected and alone."

She shook her head, unaware anger flashed from his eyes "I..."

He dropped his hands and stepped back, his tone rigid. "Father has asked that you come see him." The door closed before she could fathom how to reply.

She thought her heart would break. "Lord, this cannot be of You." Sobs choked her plea. "You would not ask me to choose between obeying you or my husband. I do not understand, I just do not understand."

Trust me, Daughter, and believe that I will work all things for your good.

She dressed for the day and allowed Melita to bring her some fruit and yogurt. A reminder of Patharus' request drew a quick gasp. Oh, the Kupio

149

wants to see me. Lord, I am not up to a confrontation with him, what do I do?

By late morning she knew she should go. Patharus would have had time with Medea and it would not interfere with his nap. Halaten met her at the door. "The master is doing very well, considering. Be patient with his speech and do not stay long. He tires easily."

He led her into the bed chamber. Patharus held out his good hand. "Daphne."

She hurried to his side and returned his effort to smile. "Oh Master, you look better every day. Are you in pain?"

He shook his head and bounced his finger on his chest. "Father, I Father."

"Yes, Father." She swallowed tears, touched that he considered her a daughter.

With much frustration he asked about her plans to leave, but she was able to grasp the gist of what he wanted to know. What should she tell him? Did he know how Nicanor felt about her going and that they had not been together for a week? Could he possibly understand her dilemma? She bent close to his ear. "Master...I mean Father, Nicanor will never leave you while you cannot attend to things. He cares deeply for you and Medea as do I."

"But you...remember your strong need to go, soon. Do...what your God asked."

She listened patiently while he struggled to get out what he wanted to say. He repeated several words and she finally understood. Her throat caught and she could not stop her tears. "I..."

He squeezed her hand. "Take all...money needed. And servants...do not go...alone." His eyes held hers. "You waited...all winter. Go, and return to us."

She snuffed her tears and hugged him. "Thank you. Your blessing means the world to me. If Nicanor gives me his blessing, I will leave as planned in a week and I will surely return. This is my home now."

Why are you troubled? And why do doubts arise in your hearts?
– Luke 24:38

Nicanor worked alongside the overseer most of the day. Makendon spoke to him three times before he realized he addressed him.

"Oh, sorry. What was it you wanted?"

He stated his question but added, "Look, we are nearly through with the planting. Why not let me see to the rest of it, and you go deal with what is on your mind?"

He grimaced at the smile that curved his overseer's lips. "All right. Guess I have not been much help. See you in the morning." He walked over and washed his hands at the well and went to report to his father. *I hope he does not ask about Daphne again. I wonder if she went to see him and what that was about?*

The walk back ended too soon, His heart wanted to go to Daphne, to hold her in his arms and reunite in the wonder of the love they shared. He pictured her in the mornings–tousled hair, cheeks warm with sleep. "Lord, what am I going to do? She is determined to go and I am so afraid to let that happen. I cannot lose her."

Fear is not from Me. My perfect love casts out fear.

"But, Lord, You know the dangers that could await her. Am I not supposed to be her protector?"

151

Could you ever protect her from everything? I am her shield. Nothing can touch her unless I allow it and My plans are for good.

"Then change my heart, Lord. Somehow, show me Your will."

He had skipped lunch, so he ordered a servant to bring his dinner along with his father's. To his surprise, he found him propped in an almost upright position. "Need not...stay, Daphne waiting..."

Nicanor squirmed. He could not tell his father they were hardly speaking. He kept it light. "No, I want to dine with you. Good to see you up a bit. How do you feel?"

His father brought it back around. "She... sweet girl, came...we made good...plan."

He stared. A good plan? What did he mean? He was about to ask when a servant brought their dinner and arranged Patharus' tray so he could feed himself.

It would have to wait, but Nicanor would leave and get to the bottom of it as soon as they finished.

Chapter Twenty-Six

The valley of Anchor as a door of hope.
– Hosea 2:15

Nicanor was unable to get Patharus to speak further about Daphne's plans. Right after dinner he indicated he expected Medea soon and felt a need to rest. Nicanor waited outside the bedroom until she arrived. *I wonder if she is in on this "plan."* He met her at the entry door. "Good evening. You look wonderful, are you satisfied with Kupio's progress?"

She shrugged. "According to Halaten, thus far it may be as much as we can hope for. His speech is much improved but the weakness in his left side and his discomfort with that peg leg makes me wonder if he will ever be able to get around. And you know how hard that would be for him."

He touched her arm. "Try not to be discouraged, time will work wonders and it is important to be positive for his sake."

She smiled and patted his hand. "I know. But the best thing is that you and Daphne will be here to help with what he is unable to handle for now."

He did not miss her not-so-subtle implication: *I am the parent, and this is what I expect of you.* He assured her he intended to keep his promise, signaled to Halaten, said goodnight to his father and left. *Lord, I am grateful she obviously is not in on some unspoken plan, probably knows nothing of Daphne's desire to leave without me.*

His feet faltered in the courtyard, wanting to see Daphne but unsure of what to expect. Had she and Patharus made some sort of agreement? Could

153

father have assured her that he would be fully behind our plans to leave as soon as possible, and she is at peace with the delay?

The likelihood lifted his mood and he scurried for their suite.

My heart is in turmoil and cannot rest.
– Job 30:27

Melita returned Daphne's half-eaten dinner to the kitchen and tidied the room. "Would you like me to help you with your nightdress, Misses?"

"No, you are excused. I can manage." She wandered around the rooms she and Nicanor shared. At her dressing table she admired a beautiful broach he had given her. "Lord. I miss him so. What is to become of us?"

Ugly scenarios of being deserted and doubts of his love bombarded her, thoughts she knew were not her own. "No, I am not going there. In Jesus' name be gone from me Satan and take your lies and flee my presence."

She jumped when their outer door opened and Nicanor entered their bedchamber. "Who are you talking to?"

She rose, mouth ajar. "I...no one. It was nothing."

At her vulnerable demeanor, his expression softened. He walked over and took her hands. "I have missed you, Daphne. Do you still love me?"

She snuffed tears that threatened to spill. "I will never stop loving you, I..."

He swept her into his arms and hushed her lips with his. "Beloved, I do not ever want to be away from you again, not for a moment. You are everything to me."

Her arms circled his neck, tears smearing his cheeks, fingers stroking his hair. "Oh, my love, I have missed you so much."

Solving their dilemma faded like the light from their bedside lamp, briefly flickered in both hearts, fizzled, and disappeared beneath the heat of rekindled desire for oneness.

In the morning, she left him sound asleep and went into their receiving room. At Melita's knock she instructed her to order a huge breakfast and bring it back to their suite. The servant's brows rose. Face aglow, Daphne could not suppress a smile. "He is back."

Melita resisted an urge to hug her and left for the kitchen.

Nicanor sat up and rubbed his eyes. "What is that wonderful aroma?"

She grinned at the memory of Theo, her little brother, how he woke up with the same look and demanded honey cakes. It felt good at last to smile and not despair at the reminder of him. "The roosters crowed a good while ago and your favorite omelet awaits you."

He pulled her down beside him. "How about my favorite wife?" In time she sent Melita back to re-warm their food and they enjoyed a leisurely breakfast. Before he left to meet Patharus, he took her hand. "I am so glad Father helped you accept our plan to go the Delphi when he is better. I—"

She backed as if he had struck her, "Your father? Nicanor, I do not know what you mean. Patharus and I made no such agreement."

His brows twitched. "Then what did he mean? He said the two of you had a plan."

"He asked me about my desire to leave now and said he thought I should go. That he would give me

155

all the money I need and send servants along to help and protect me. When you came back last night I thought he had told you and you were all right with it."

The cloud she hated returned to his face. "Well, I am not alright with it. I cannot agree to let you travel that distance without me at your side." His voice grew louder. "It is not going to happen no matter what my father promised."

The door slammed and she slumped into a chair. "Lord, what can I do, he will not listen."

Epaphroditus' teaching loomed. *Cast your care upon Me and I will carry it. Do not set aside your confidence, trust has great reward.*

She spent some time in prayer and ended up praising the Lord. "You have it all worked out for the best, Lord. I cannot change Nicanor's mind. Help me to leave it in Your hands."

But where can wisdom be found? And where is the place of understanding?
– Job 28:12

Nicanor was too angry to meet with his father so he sent word with a servant that he would be working with Makendon in the storage barns. Patharus' detailed fall inventory left little need to sort out which work assignments were a priority, but he made busy work of going over the lists, anything to keep his mind off his troubles. What is the matter with her, Lord? Does she not remember she vowed to obey when we married? Why is it she will not listen to me?

A nagging thought refused to be hushed. *Go talk to Epaphroditus.*

He threw down the carton of seed he forgot he held. "Makendon, I have to attend to something. Go ahead and finish here and assign what you think is needed most." Without telling anyone of his plans, he saddled his horse.

Epaphroditus' wife welcomed him. "Some of the believers have come to help harvest wheat in the west field. I am sure you will find them if you ride out there. And could you take along this water? The dust makes them awfully thirsty."

He thanked her and left feeling guilty. I have never offered to help our leader with his crops. He has a family to care for too, and study and prayer must eat into his time. Nicanor made a mental note to see what he could do to help in the future.

Those assisting with the harvest called out. "Welcome, brother. We have missed you and Daphne at the meetings...everything all right?"

He returned their greetings, excusing their absences with Patharus' stroke and added responsibilities. They thanked him for the water and told him he would find Epaphroditus back at his barn where he sharpened the curved blades of the sickles.

At the sight of him, their leader smiled broadly. "Nicanor. Good to see you. We have missed you and your lovely bride. What brings you here in the middle of the day?"

Nicanor asked about the spring wheat harvest, made small talk, and hemmed around until Epaphroditus put his hand on his shoulder. "Alright, now what really brought you out? Sorrow or trouble is written all over your face."

He grimaced. "It is Daphne. You remember how we planned to return to Delphi to fulfill her call to expose the myth of Apollo and turn people to Jesus?"

He nodded. "Yes. She certainly took to heart Paul's admonishment that action was the true outcome of gratitude."

"And you know about Patharus' stroke?" He nodded again and Nicanor explained how because of it he could not leave now. "And Daphne is determined to go on without me. She is sure the Lord told her to go on next week as planned, alone. Does that not seem contrary to the Lord's ways? To tell her to do something so dangerous for a woman?"

Epaphroditus did not hesitate. "God never calls us to do something He does not first equip us to handle. I cannot tell you He is not telling Daphne to go, but she has had a zeal to help people who are as blind as she was to the devil's plans." He paused and looked him in the eye. "And I do not believe she would want this if God had not put it in her heart. Could you not send people you trust along with her?"

Disappointment flared and his eyes widened. That was not what he wanted to hear. He shrugged and mumbled a disclaimer. "I have a loyal servant I know I could trust and maybe one other. But they are slaves and who knows if being far from home and less likely to get caught, they might flee. I do not know what to do. I cannot let her go without my protection."

Epaphroditus stroked his beard. "You know, I may have just the solution you need."

Chapter Twenty-Seven

Shall we not much more readily be in subjection to
the Father?
– Hebrews 12:9

Nicanor stared at their beloved leader. What could Epaphroditus possibly have in mind? Surely something to assure Daphne it was alright with God for her to wait and go later.

He laid down the sickle he had been working on. "Son, you remember how all this last month we collected an offering for Paul?" At his nod he went on. "Well, in about ten days my grain will be harvested, and the planting finished, so I have arranged to take that money to Corinth myself and spend some time with Paul. I want to glean more of his wisdom and understanding of all Christ accomplished for us on the cross. Daphne could travel along with me if her passage could be changed."

Nicanor's jaw dropped. Lord, is this your answer? To give me someone I can trust to travel with Daphne.

"I am sailing from Neapolis, was that your arrangement?"

He swallowed his disappointment. "Yes...it was, but—"

"Well, what do you think, could you trust Daphne to my care?"

A half-hearted response rose from the battle his heart still waged, to hang onto the outcome he wanted. "I... I guess I could."

Epaphroditus graciously waited. Finally, Nicanor surrendered his will to what God assured him was

His solution. "I would have to send a servant to rebook her passage and cancel mine." His jaw flexed as he reworked the details aloud. "And I would want to send Batano, my personal servant to protect her in case you come home sooner. And she would need Melita to attend to her needs..."

Epaphroditus smiled. "Sounds like you have it all worked out. Stop back at the house to get the ship's name and departure date and let me know how it goes."

Despite a lingering uncertainty about wisdom in relenting, as he rode home he rehashed his gratitude for the solution afforded him. He snorted at his own reluctance. "I knew it was You who nudged me to go see him, Lord, so I guess I need to rejoice in the guidance I asked for."

By the time he reached the estate the Lord had given him total peace in Daphne's going on alone. Praise poured from deep in his heart. "Your love is amazing, Lord. Even when I would not consider any plan but my own, You still made a way. Thank You for Your mercy, for making a way when no compromise seemed possible.

He signaled at a stable hand to take his horse. Daphne is going to be so relieved.

I will turn their morning to joy, will comfort them and make them rejoice.
– Jeremiah 31:13

Daphne was beside herself. "I just cannot do it. Not while Nicanor refuses to let me go on ahead of him."

Melita prepared to put away the clothing her mistress retrieved from her trunk. "Misses, you were not a slave very long, but those of us who have

160

never known anything else have a different mindset. We treasure the things we do have because we know that at someone's command, they could be torn from us at any time...especially people. Could it be that Nicanor has not yet truly grasped that things are different for him now? That he need not fear you will be taken from him?"

Daphne leaned on her fist and studied her servant's face. Melita put her hand to her lips. "Oh Misses, I am sorry. I had no right—"

"No. No, Melita, I am grateful for your insight. Sometimes I forget Nicanor was brought up with a background different than mine. I grew up with the same luxury I have here. Anything I wanted or needed was provided and servants were at my beck and call. You have helped me understand his hesitancy to let go and trust that God would be with me."

She looked pensive. "Can I ask you something, Misses?"

"Of course. You are more than a servant to me, you are my friend. I have told you things I know I can trust you will keep to yourself."

"It is about your God. I hear you talking to Him as if He were a person right here in the room with you. How can you tell He hears you?

Daphne lurched with joy at her interest. "Well, from words written by men who walked alongside Him or wrote truths by the leading of the Holy Spirit. Everything I know about God has come through learning He sent His Son, Jesus, to show us His love and forgive our sins if we ask Him to be our Lord.

"The Holy Spirit? What is that?"

Daphne smiled. "Come, sit beside me and I will try to explain what I have come to understand."

It was nearly time for dinner when Melita asked one last question. "Does your God care about slaves like me or just free people?"

She chuckled. "Oh, my friend, I asked that same question when I was a slave. Let me assure you—"

Nicanor barged through the door. "Daphne, I am home. Have you had dinner? Come, go with me to the dining room. I have something to tell you."

Melita jumped up. "I am so sorry, Misses. I did not help you prepare for dinner, I—"

"It is not a problem, Melita. I can go as I am, and we will continue our talk tomorrow if you like." The servant nodded, stepped past Nicanor, and left.

"Is she upset? She looked it."

"No, she is fine. But you, are you all right?"

"Come let us go. I have some wonderful news." He took her hand and she followed, astounded by the change in his demeanor.

A few days before she was to leave, Nicanor brought his personal servant into their suite. "I want you to get to know Batano. He has agreed to go with you on your journey and I know I can trust him to keep you safe."

Since their marriage, little interaction with his personal attendant had come about. The young man appeared in Nicanor's dressing room at a moment's notice. He never spoke but occasionally she saw him enter or leave. He always ducked his head to avoid bumping the door frame that his muscular body all but filled.

He nodded and she smiled, neither sure what to say. She cleared her throat. "That is very kind of you, Batano. I hope it will not be too hard on your wife to have you gone several months."

162

He looked at Nicanor and back at her. "I do not have a wife, Misses."

Daphne flushed. "Oh, I am sorry...I mean, well, I hope you do not mind being away from home."

He appeared anxious to get the encounter over. "I am happy to do whatever my master asks."

Nicanor chuckled. "That is fine, Batano. See to whatever clothing and whatever else you will need and be ready to go in just a couple of days. The servant bowed his head and made a quick exit.

Daphne chewed her lower lip. "Do you think he is all right with going? He seemed very uncomfortable with the idea."

"He will be alright. That is the way he is, rarely says much but is as loyal as they come. He will be there for you and do whatever you ask." He drew her close. "Besides, he is the perfect bodyguard against anyone that comes near my wife." He nuzzled her neck. "I am going to miss you."

She lifted her face to his, her eyes filling. "I cannot tell you what it means to me to have your blessings." A smile curled his lips. His thoughts on her squeal at the news and how she floated like a swan on a serene pond through the week that followed. She brushed the tears from her cheeks. "It took me a while to grasp how hard it was for you to let me go,".

"God helped me over that hurdle. But always remember how much I love you." He kissed her wet eyes. "Have you told Melita she is to accompany you? How did she react?"

"She is so excited. We have grown so close it is like having a good friend going along with me. I have been teaching her to read and you know what? She is asking questions about our God. I think she may soon be one of us."

He smiled his approval. "Listen, be sure you find time to visit Medea before you go. You have only a few days now and Patharus said she is concerned for your safety."

"I will. I will tell her Batano is going along so no one will dare bother me."

Nicanor left to meet with Patharus and she made her way to Medea's. "Lord, I have dreaded this visit. Please grant me grace to deal with her bitterness and to ignore any guilt she lays on me. I am determined to love her through the power of Your Holy Spirit."

Daphne raised her hand to knock on Medea's door, when a woman she had never seen before barged out of Medea's suite. She swept a long black robe over something she carried, gave Daphne a patronizing nod, and left.

She let herself in. "Danatel, who was that? I have never seen her here before."

She shrugged. "I do not know who she is, Misses. She has been coming to see the Kupios for a while now and my mistress makes sure their talks are private."

Chapter Twenty-Eight

*And this is the spirit of the Antichrist which you
have heard was coming and is now already in
the world.*
– 1 John 4:3

Daphne went directly to Kupios' bedside. "How are
you, Medea? I see you were up to having a visitor."

"Oh, Daphne, come in. It is...ah, good to see
you." She averted her eyes and became engrossed
in the need to rearrange her blankets.

"I do not want to tire you with too much
company. You look tired. Are you alright?"

"I am fine. Now, tell me about your plans...when
is it you leave? Tomorrow?"

Her defensive tone and quick change of subject
bothered Daphne, but she did not pursue it. "No, it
is three days from today. I am excited but I will miss
all of you very much."

Medea's face softened. "We certainly will miss
you too...I know Nicanor will be counting the days
till you return."

"Melita and Batano are going with me, along
with Epaproditus, our spiritual leader, so he is
assured I will be safe."

She did not respond, merely reshuffled her
pillows, and reached for a small two-handled cup
on her bedside table. Nothing was said about her
concern for Daphne's safety nor did she ask about
her plans to find her family.

Danatel stepped inside the doorway. She looked
apprehensive. "Shall I prepare lunch for you and
your guest, Kupios?"

She huffed. "Did I not tell you water will do for today?" Her servant backed from the room and Medea quickly filled the silence with talk of hope for good sailing weather.

Twenty awkward minutes later, Daphne rose to leave. She took her hand, "I will say goodbye for now. Do take care of yourself and Patharus."

Relief flashed in Medea's eyes. She squeezed Daphne's hand and uttered a rushed goodbye. Her servant showed Daphne to the door. "Danatel, what was that about her wanting only water? She looks so thin. Is she not eating?"

She kept her voice to a whisper. "Oh misses. I am so worried about her. Ever since that woman has visited, there are several days a week when she will not eat, saying self-discipline is giving her secret knowledge of her spiritual essence." Daphne assured her she would speak to Nicanor about it.

Later, at lunch, she poured out her concern. "Nicanor, it was mystifying. First, seeing a strange woman leave Medea's suite, someone she obviously did not want to talk about. Then, to have her so preoccupied with whatever that was about, she could hardly wait for me to leave. She was not herself. I could not believe she did not condemn my leaving without you, or even point out the possible consequences. It was as if something had become so vital to her she had no interest in anything else."

He frowned. "A woman? Who was she? Medea seldom has company."

"I do not know and neither did Danatel. She said her mistress insists she not interrupt them for any reason. She looks so thin… have you spent any time with her recently?"

He shook his head.

"Medea's is not eating and the bizarre explanation she gave Danatel concerns me. Her trying to find knowledge of her *spiritual essence,* has become dangerous to her health. When I went daily into the city, I heard of a lot of peculiar things people believed about attaining a spiritual perfection and none of it lines up with what we have been taught."

"I will ask Patharus. He will probably know what it is about. Such a beautiful day, let us forget it for now and take a last walk in the garden."

She linked her arm in his, her heart overflowing with the joy of their oneness. They walked the whole path and sat on their bench. She took his hand. "Promise me you will pray for me every day and every night. I cannot wait to go and do what the Lord has asked of me, but honestly I do not have a clue as to how to go about it."

He pulled her close. "My little warrior. I would not know either, but I know you will know when you get there. When I talked to Epaphroditus he reminded me that God always equips his children to do what he calls them to...that His callings are His enabling."

The day before she was to leave, she visited Patharus. "I have come to say goodbye. Nicanor tells me you have been up trying out your new leg."

"Darn thing, how can I hold on to this crutch with a gimpy arm and walk on a peg that will not stay in place?" He laid it aside. "But I am glad you came."

She smiled. It had taken her a while to know his persistent gruff manner was not who he really was. "I know you will master it. You have never let anything defeat you. How are the exercises coming?"

He snorted. "Halaten comes every day and puts me through a dozen paces he says will strengthen these weak muscles, but I do not see much progress."

"You will, it takes time."

He fixed his gaze on the poplar tree that swayed outside his window. "Time, I have, but who knows how much?"

Mas...I mean Father, nobody but God knows and each of us are in His hands. He watches over and keeps us safe until it is time to come home to Him."

"You really believe that?"

"With all my heart. That is why I can go to Delphi confident He will bring me safely back to all of you."

He cocked his head and squinted at her. "This God of yours, how does he choose who he will accept and who he will not?"

She sent up a quick plea for wisdom. Patharus had never shown any interest in spiritual things. "Our God has an enormous capacity to love anyone who comes to Him. He desires that none be left out or separated from Him. All He asks is that you believe in your heart and say with your mouth that His Son, Jesus, came as a man, died for our sins and was raised again to life."

"That is a lot to swallow."

"It can be, considering what has been taught for centuries. But it is true. God loves you just the way you are and wants desperately for you to become His child."

"What convinced you he wanted you?"

She thought a moment. "Well, when His servant Paul, followed the Lord's instructions to deliver me from that horrible demon, I knew it was an act of pure love...why else would He care about the misery I lived with?"

He looked her in the eye. "You are quite a girl, Daphne, and I am going to miss you. By the way, I want you to know I have signed Melita over to you. She is your property now to do with as you please."

She ignored what might be improper and hugged him, her eyes brimming. "That was not necessary but thank you. I will miss you too. Think about what I said, promise?"

He could not hide his pleasure, but the conversation ended. She left, forgetting she had intended to ask him about Medea.

The next two days were a blur of preparation, but at last they were on their way to

Neapolis. The ride brought a swirl of memories, poppies bobbing in the breeze, strange pink birds with long black legs, and the swamp with its colorful birds and flowers. She marveled at the changes in her life in less than two years. From free to slave and from slave to a free, made new in Christ and married to the man she loved. She reached for his hand.

He smiled, put the reins in one hand, and whispered, "How will I manage without you? You are the best thing in my life."

In the back of the wagon, their passengers chatted among themselves. Epaphroditus voice rose above the others. "Well, it is because His presence within us gives us the confidence to say and do the right things." His explanation hardly faded before Melita peppered him with another question.

Nicanor nudged Daphne. "I think your servant is about to become a Christian and I hope Batano gets an earful. I find it hard to get him to sit still long enough to listen to anything."

Daphne giggled and snuggled closer. "Melita may not be the only one." He drew back in wonder as she told him about her conversation with Patharus.

"Really? He has never asked me anything or encouraged any talk about God. I think you have a special gift."

"Maybe, but I have never gotten anywhere with Medea. I hope you can spend some time with her. I am concerned about that strange visitor." He nodded and she sighed. "I will think of you every morning and dream of you every night."

"You had better, or I will haunt you. Look, there is the harbor and that is probably your ship moored just out from shore."

Chapter Twenty-Nine

For by grace you have been saved – it is the gift of God.
– Ephesians 2:8

Daphne did not stop waving until Nicanor was but a speck in the crowd around the port. Melita and Batano stood behind, wide eyed at the enormity of the great body of water neither had ever imagined.

Despite the captain's objections, Nicanor had ridden out in the dinghy with them to make sure their passage was secure, and that Daphne's special quarters were safe. Epaphroditus kept close. He would bunk along with Batano and a few male passengers in the lower part of the ship. The captain pointed out the common area for women, but Daphne insisted Melita stay with her.

The evening meal finished, they stood by the rail and watched the sunset. Melita Had eaten little. "Is this like your trip to Philippi?"

It took a moment for the question to register. "Oh my no. I had spent weeks in the dreadful Athenian slave market before I was sold to strangers who took me to a ship. The captain took me to a room for women slaves. It was on the ship's lowest level, crowded, dank and smelly. We were given little food and water. At the halfway point, the ship stalled for lack of wind and things grew worse, less food. little water and unbearable heat."

"How awful...were you scared?"

"Terrified, but mostly of what was to come. I contemplated jumping overboard but was too cowardly to follow through."

Melita's hand shot to her lips, and she reached for a chair back. "Misses, thank you for keeping me with you. Your room is small, and you would have been more comfortable without—"

I could never have let you sleep in a hovel like that. You are my friend. Are you alright?

"I...I think my stomach does not like this ship's motions. But that is what I love about you, you care and are so unselfish."

"Not always. But my Lord, Jesus has taught me many things and helped me see what is important. Here, sit down. You will soon adapt to the ship's roll."

"Do you think your Jesus could change me?"

She took her servant's hand. "I do not know what changes you want, but I know Jesus loves you and wants to fill your life with goodness."

"Will you help me to ask Him?"

Her heart nearly burst with joy as she led her in a prayer to receive Jesus. Melita repeated every word with such sincerity, Daphne choked on the "amen." She looked into her eyes. "That makes us sisters in the Lord...I am so happy for you."

She wiped the smears from her cheeks. "Am I now really the same as you even though I am a slave?"

She hugged her. "You surely are. God says we are all one in Him, slave and free, male, and female. It does not matter. I was still a slave when I asked Him to be my Lord, and He gladly received me as His own. Now He is your Lord too and He will hear your prayers as quickly as anyone else's."

Melita's face lit up. "Epaphroditus will be so surprised? I cannot wait to tell him."

Daphne laughed. "Somehow, I do not think so. But while we are aboard ship you can learn a great deal from him...he loves to teach new believers."

The days passed quickly. Batano hovered like a wary warrior while Melita spent all her spare time quizzing Epaphroditus. Without a spring storm or lack of wind to disrupt their voyage, they soon sailed from the Aegean Sea into the *Saronic Gulf*

As the *Cenchrean Port* opened before them, excitement built, and everyone clung to the rails. Rome had constructed piers on either side to make the entrance wide and deep enough for large ships to carry in goods that would enhance commerce, Epaphroditus guided them into the line of those who waited to depart. "Stay close to me when we exit the dinghy."

Melita eyed the swells and clutched the little boat's sides. "Is this Corinth?"

The sailor who manned the oars rolled his eyes. "No, this is *Cenchrea*, a city on the outskirts. Corinth is six miles up the Isthmus."

Memories of the day Daphne arrived from Delphi struck like an icy blast. Her brows pinched as she looked for the great high walls that enclosed the marble road her family had been forced to traverse, chained to one another. "I remember high walls leading into the city the last time I sailed into Corinth. What happened to them?"

The sailor cocked his head. "Did you arrive from the Gulf of Corinth, Madam?" She nodded. "Then you would have sailed into the *Lechaem Port*. That is on the western shore, four miles across from here. That is where you saw the double walls of the *Lechion*

Way. They are an impenetrable fortress built to protect the city from invading armies in times of siege."

Had the horror of that day had confused her memory? Upon reaching the shore her eyes filled. How close she was to Delphi and home. Oh mother, I want to find you and... She swallowed the lump that swelled her throat. There was no home to go back to.

Melita's head whipped from one shop to the other, until Daphne grabbed her arm to keep her from falling behind. They made their way through the crowds until Epaphroditus found the place to rent a carriage to ferry them into the city.

The line was long. They sat on their trunks and watched the crew unload its cargo. Goods meant for the east were placed onto carts that would cross the Isthmus, the narrow strip of land that joined the Peloponnese to the mainland.

Batano's gaze did not waver from a large group of slaves. The owners of the freight paid the hefty fee and the port overseer picked up his whip. Batano winced as the slaves strained to haul the wheeled carts down the *Diolkos*, a flagstone tract embedded with deep groves laid with fat smeared, wooden rails.

Epaphroditus joined him. "Those barrels and crates will be loaded onto ships harbored in the Gulf of Corinth's port and thus avoid the dangerous journey around the Peloponnese." Daphne shook her head in wonder. How did a Jewish convert to Christ, from a small Grecian city, know so much about so many things?

Seats in the carriage were small, and while the three of them made do, Batano pushed his huge frame as close to the back railing as possible. She noticed again how uncomfortable Batano was with such close contact. The driver urged his horse through the *Cenchrean* gate and up

the road that led to the city.

Even Epaphroditus was awed at the overt display of wealth they passed. Houses were constructed of marble or rock hewn from nearby mountains. Every turn held pillars and monuments to city leaders or elaborate fountains and statues. In their midst stood temples and various places of worship to the many gods.

The driver took them to an inn on the city's outer edge and helped them with their trunks. Epaphroditus paid him and waved him off. "This inn was recommended by a recent pilgrim to Philippi. He was sure it would be clean and safe."

She nodded her thanks and Melita followed her to a second-story room with a balcony that looked over the city. The only private room was small, but she was grateful, and there was ample room for Melita's pad. She was told Batano could bunk with the help, but soon discovered he would not sleep anywhere but on a mat outside her door. She ordered a tub of hot water, sank below the surface, and enjoyed the luxury not available at sea. The warm water revived the memory of her first bath after months as a slave, and her friend Kawit's holding her nose in response.

They all gathered at the communal breakfast the next morning and chatted with the inn's other guests. Epaphroditus beckoned to her. "I have found where I am likely to find Paul working, and am going to see him. If he plans to teach this afternoon or evening, perhaps you would like to join me."

Her eyes lit up. "Oh yes...I would cherish an opportunity to hear him. The only time I heard him before he left Philippi was his goodbye speech at Lydia's."

She invited her slaves to explore the city with her. They passed the gymnasium, theater, city baths and the arena where chariot races highlighted the Pan-Hellenic games that honored Poseidon. She did not want to miss Epaphroditus, so they left the rest for later and hurried back for lunch. He had not yet arrived, so she sought out the innkeeper. "Sir, could you tell me how far it is to Athens and where I might find transportation to get there?"

The man looked at her strangely. "Why would you want to leave us so soon, Misses? Corinth has much to offer our visitors."

She was taken aback by his answer. "I...well, I need to go there to...to find someone."

"It is bigger than Corinth, you know. I hope you have people there...you will need help to find your way around. But I will inquire and let you know what I find."

She left to find Melita. Her mind ran to the five or six days her family had been forced to walk over the mountains from Corinth to Athens. Food and water had been sparsely doled out and cold nights sleeping on rocky ground had been miserable.

"There you are Misses. They announced lunch and it smells wonderful."

She laughed, Melita's appetite had returned. "Has Epaphroditus returned?"

"No. Maybe Paul was speaking, and he could not bear to leave."

"I hope we get to hear him. I plan to leave for Athens in the morning."

Chapter Thirty

Idle babblings and contradictions of what is falsely called knowledge.
– 1 Timothy 6: 20

Nicanor did not find time to visit Medea for days after Daphne left. Patharus had shrugged off his inquiry about his wife's strange visitor and changed the subject.

Danatel greeted him warmly. "Yes, Kupios will see you, but requests you do not stay long, she tires easily."

"Medea. How are you? I am so sorry I have not been by. Patharus keeps me busy." He reached for a chair and hid his shock at how notably thinner and pale she had grown.

" I am fine...so glad you stopped by. How are you getting along without your precious wife?"

"I miss her terribly. It is lonely, especially in the evening after a long busy day."

She sighed. "Yes. I am so grateful Patharus is now well enough to have dinner with me most nights...even if it must be in his suite. You should join us."

"I will do that, but you are looking so thin, is something wrong? Are you having trouble eating?"

She turned her face from his. "No, nothing is wrong, I just have days when I choose to deny this evil body and purge myself of all fleshly indulgences."

"Medea, our bodies are not evil. The Lord says they are a temple, a dwelling place for His Holy Spirit."

Hostility flared on her face as she turned back to him. "Not everyone believes that. Some have

177

discovered that our bodies are a prison we can escape through instruction and knowledge that prepares us to be reunited with God at death."

He shook his head. "No, no, Dear one, it is only through believing on Jesus that one can be united with God after we die. Who is feeding you this rubbish?"

She stiffened and drew up from her pillows. "You know, son, it may be you who has received faulty teaching. The Supreme God is way beyond our reach, unknowable to mere mortals." Your Jesus did not come in the flesh, he attained divinity through knowledge. He had a phantom body that only appeared human to his followers." He opened his mouth to speak, but she ignored it. "We may have a spark of divinity or seeds of light in us, but an enlightened believer who achieves spiritual fullness matures only through special intuitive knowledge."

He could hardly believe what he heard. The voice had been hers, but it was as if she had been tutored to recite the mantra word for word. He searched for a way to reach her. Lord, what has influenced this woman who formerly was so turned off by spiritual talk, that she was quick to abort every effort to help her see You?

His gaze fell on an empty pedestal that had held a vase she especially favored. "Medea, what happened to that unique vase Patharus gave you? I hope it was not broken...I know how you loved and cherished it."

She looked as uncomfortable as one asked to propose a toast to a despised colleague. "It is, I mean...it was part of my quest for enlightenment.

To give to the point of personal poverty opens the door to deeper understanding."

His jaw dropped. "You gave it away? You gave away that beautiful, expensive gift from your husband? To whom, Medea? To whom?"

"It was mine to do with as I please. To fast and give is part of our rigorous, self-discipline."

Nicanor fought to suppress his anger. "Our? Who is our? Who is teaching you all this nonsense?"

She put her fingers on her temples and let her head droop. "Perhaps we can talk again sometime. I am afraid you will have to excuse me, I am very tired."

He wanted to shake her, to find who was behind this. "I will leave for now, but someone is feeding you a dangerous heresy and it has to stop."

And they were all filled with the Holy Spirit and began to speak with other tongues.
– Acts 2:4

The next morning Daphne paid the carriage driver the fare for herself and Batano. Melita was to wait for her at the inn. They had attended Paul's meeting last night and been encouraged by his teaching and explanation of their need to be baptized in the Holy Spirit. Upon learning that this opened the power to be the Lord's witness, along with Melita, she had gone forward for this special prayer.

A great peace had come upon her and on the way back to the inn. She yielded to the unction Paul spoke of and quietly released an unknown language of prayer. Times she had experienced this blessing without understanding its source, affirmed God's will for her to return to Delphi. The joy and assurance it brought left her torn between her quest to go find her family, and a desire to learn more.

Epaphroditus and Melita rose for the early morning sendoff. He spent some time with the driver before he rejoined Daphne and the others. "This driver does not go directly over the mountains, which is shorter, because there is no place to lodge. He says nearly twenty leagues is much too far to go in one day so he stops halfway at a small inn, but you will be in Athens the next night."

The reality of not having Epaphroditus along to see to such things fluttered a wave of apprehension. She steeled herself. Oh, Lord, thank You that I will never be alone, even after he leaves for home. You will always be with me. "Did he recommend a place to stay in Athens? And will he bring me back when I am finished?"

"I have given him the address of an inn recommended at the meeting last night. It is run by believers, and the driver understands you do not know how long you will be. He said he would put you in touch with other drivers if he cannot wait."

Batano helped her into the carriage and rode up front with the driver. Melita put her hands on the side of the carriage. "I do not know, Misses. I feel like I should be going with you, what if you—"

"I will be fine. tI will save two fares and if I find my family, I will need the drachmas to buy them back from their owners. Enjoy the time and feel free to accompany Epaphroditus to hear our esteemed apostle whenever possible.

The driver flicked his whip, and the horses took off at a swift pace. The sun had fully risen before they passed out into the foothills. Daphne leaned back in her seat and enjoyed the abundance of wildflowers and especially the poppies. The driver stopped by a swift flowing creek at midday to allow the horses to drink. She pulled out the package of food the inn had prepared for her and Batano.

Her attempts to draw him into conversation fell flat. He refilled their jugs in the stream, and they were on their way again. Later, that afternoon   In the late afternoon, a sudden jostling shook her awake. She righted herself and rubbed her eyes. The lurch brought memories of the near disaster she and her mother had experienced when their carriage slid halfway off a cliff in Mount Parnassus.

Her mother. The memory triggered possibilities of how she might find her. Did the slave market keep records of who bought each slave? She would start there. Did slaves keep track of one another when one was sold off? And would they open what they knew to her? Would estate owners tell her if her mother was there?

Twilight was waning when they reached the inn. Batano helped her down and reached for her trunk. A plump woman with a scarf tied at the nape of her neck came out to greet them. She called to the driver. "Hello, Stafune. It has been a while since we have seen you. How many passengers?"

"A lady and her servant. Can your boy attend my horses? I'm spent."

They were ushered into the main room and told dinner would be shortly. Batano, she was informed, would sleep and eat in the outbuilding with their servants. The woman showed her to the women's quarters and left. Daphne's brows raised. The room held only one bed. A chair covered with clothing and an open trunk sat on the other side of it. She peered at the belongings. Did they belong to the owner? She went to the wash stand to wash her face and hands but found only soiled towels. Was this normal? Did she dare ask for replacements?

She sat on the edge of the unmade bed. The door opened and a short, stocky woman entered. She gave a nod and pointed to herself, "I Baronda."

Her accent was so heavy Daphne wondered where she was from. She touched her chest and said, "Daphne." To her relief, Baronda said no more, simply turned and began to clear the chair.

Was she expected to share the bed with this stranger? Dread widened her eyes and her skin crawled. At the sound of a bell, Baronda patted her stomach, and motioned for Daphne to follow her down to dinner.

The table was heaped with plenty of food, a rich lamb stew, biscuits, vegetables, and a fruit compote. The owners joined them and soon the clatter of utensils and porcelain covered the conversations. The day had been long, and she ached to retire. She approached the owner. "May I please have fresh towels to wash off the day's dust?"

The request appeared to surprise the woman, but she opened a drawer and handed her a towel. Daphne thanked her and asked the driver what time they would leave in the morning.

"Before sunup. We have about the same distance to cover."

She went upstairs. The cool water felt good on her face. She opened her trunk and pulled out a nightdress, laid her clothes neatly on the floor and with much apprehension climbed into the furthest edge of the bed. Her sleep was fitful; until something woke her. A figure bent close to her side of the bed, rummaging through her trunk.

Chapter Thirty-One

Speak each man the truth to his neighbor.
– Zechariah 8:16

Nicanor left Medea's and headed straight for Patharus. Outside his door, he hesitated. How do I explain the urgency of this situation to a man who probably will not understand? According to Epaphroditus, the things of God are spiritually discerned. Would Patharus be able to grasp the danger Medea is courting?

He shrugged. He had to try.

"Nicanor, glad you stopped by. Makendon sent a report that some of the slaves have grumbled about there being less food at the evening meal. It is spring and we have gone all winter on what we stored, but there should be plenty. I want an inventory of what is left, and you need to find if there is any validity to their complaints. I think—"

"I will see to it first thing tomorrow, Father. But I need to talk to you about Medea."

"Medea? What?" He sounded irritated. "She is alright is she not? She was with me last—"

"Yes, she told me about dining with you, but have you noticed how pale she is...and how thin?"

Patharus responded as if he had come in on the middle of a conversation. "Medea? I do not know, what do you mean...pale, and thin?"

"Exactly what I said. I just came from a visit with her. Father. She does not eat regularly and I am worried. She has always been slight, but her face is gaunt and the circles under her eyes are darker than usual. She does not look healthy."

Doubt pinched Patharus' his face. "You sure? Why would she not eat? If there really is a food shortage it would not affect her." He patted his middle. "My portions certainly have not been slashed."

Nicanor pulled up a stool. "It is not a food shortage, Father."

"Well, you know, she wears those long shawls over her tunics so it would be hard to see a difference, but I —"

"Listen, you may find this hard to understand, but both Daphne and I have talked to her about our faith, and she has always rejected the help God has for her. She has asked questions that dwelt on the loss of your son, but it is obvious his death still troubles her...in some ways it has kept her from going on with life, but —"

"Well, that is understandable. She is a woman and women hold onto such things. They have a harder time getting over loss than most men."

"Yes, that is probably true, but she has changed, Father. That strange woman who visits her is teaching her things that are contrary to the laws of God and the affect is not good."

Patharus twisted in his chair. "I know you and Daphne feel strongly about your faith and that is fine. But if Medea sees things differently, you must leave her to decide what's right for her. You know —"

"Alright, but do you know this woman has Medea fasting several days a week? I am telling you she is not healthy enough for that. You are going to lose her if this does not change."

Patharus blanched at the possibility. "Alright, alright. I will ask her about it over dinner."

184

Nicanor stood to leave. "You also need to know that besides not eating that woman has convinced her that taking a vow of poverty is the way to salvation. Medea has accepted that releasing her hold on material things will help her break free of this world and satisfy a need to purify herself. So, while you are at it, ask her to whom she gave away that beautiful vase you bought her last year."

Patharus shot a startled look.

"Someone is taking advantage of Medea, Father, and it needs to stop."

The right hand of fellowship.
– Galatians 2:9

Daphne sat up with a start and tried to clear her head. "What?"

Baronda turned from the candlelight. "Oh, mistake. Thought it my trunk." She moved to the other side of the room and busied herself with her nightdress.

She stared, her heart racing. The woman looked disgruntled as she bent and blew out the candle. She climbed into bed showing no signs of remorse, and as if nothing had happened, her snores soon wracked the room.

Daphne replayed the incident, unsure of what to do *There is no way that woman mistook my trunk for hers. What did she hope to find?* Her hand clasped the money bag hung on her chest. Nicanor's instructions popped like water on a hot skillet. *You are never to take this off, Daphne...night or day, except to bathe.*

She shuddered. That had to be what the woman was after *She is a thief! The innkeepers seem well* acquainted with her...are they in on it? Should I tell them" Would they believe her story and deny what I saw?

A fresh awareness she was on her own, kept her awake. I need to guard my possessions and not take their safety for granted. She rose before dawn, dressed, packed her belongings, and locked her trunk. Batano arrived and she instructed him to load it into the carriage. They ate a hasty breakfast of cheese and barley bread and were outside before the driver arrived.

All morning, she stewed over the incident. The woman had not yet risen and there had been no opportunity to tell the owners. By noon, she decided to tell the driver when they stopped for lunch. Surely, he would want to know what future passengers might face.

He frowned. "You sure she did not forget she did not have the room to herself, and assumed it was her trunk? She lives there and helps the owners with meals and does other chores."

"I find it highly unlikely. A candle still burned, and she could hardly miss my form in the bed.

He shrugged, opened her door, but did not look at her. "We need to be on our way." Batano had drawn close. The remainder of the way, he rode inside.

They pulled up to the inn recommended to Epaphroditus. The driver said he would not be available for her return trip and bid her a hasty goodbye. She had Batano carry her trunk into the inn, grateful to be out from under the driver's auspices.

An older man with a crooked smile welcomed her. "Come in, come in. My name is Asher, and this is my wife, Leah."

Daphne relaxed, knowing the owners were believers. To her relief, she was given a room by herself. Dinner had been earlier, but the woman said she would be glad to warm up something for her and her servant. While they ate, they shared backgrounds. Leah peppered her with questions about Paul's ministry in Philippi. Daphne gave a brief update and asked the same about his time in Athens.

Leah's eyes closed briefly, and she shook her head. "He preached daily in the marketplace, but word was that when he shared the good news on Mars Hill, except for a few men who were with Dionysius the Areopagite and a woman named Damaris, none received the revelation of Jesus as truth. They just could not accept that the Son of God Paul preached, was raised from the dead."

"How did you hear of Jesus...did you hear Paul speak?"

"We are part of a Jewish community and of the synagogue who were blessed to have Paul speak. Asher and I received the good news before he left. It is such a shame... the unknown God whose altar stood among all those false gods, was finally explained but not believed."

Daphne sighed. The unknown God. Back in her beloved mountains, she had wondered if He were the God who created all its the beauty. Awe of the Lord rose. Even then He had tried to reach her.

She blinked away her reverie and convinced Batano he need not sleep outside her door this night. On her knees she thanked the Lord for His generous provision and flopped into the bed. In the morning she discovered the inn's owners held a wealth of information and suggestions on how she might find her family.

Asher advised her not to go to the place where they had been held. "No one there would have any authority. You need to go to the office of the man who owns the slave market. I do not know where it is but when you get to the agora someone will be able to direct you. Do not let the owner intimidate you or take advantage of you...but do be prepared to pay a bribe if it will help."

Leah added, "It is not far into the city, but if you decide to hail a carriage ask ahead of time about the charge or they will double the fare. Keep an eye on your possessions, there are a lot of unsavory people and beggars out there. Here is lunch enough for both of you. Sometimes good food is hard to find."

Daphne thanked them, relieved she could leave her trunk without worry. She set off for the city with Batano close behind. The Port of Piracus could be seen along with the walled path that led to the harbor. Memories surfaced of Patharus taking her aboard a ship whose destination she was not told.

A smile passed her lips. I thought my life was over, but though the voyage led to a year of great pain, God used it to bring me freedom and marriage to the love of my life.

A pang of loneliness hit with a gnawing awareness of how much she missed him.

Chapter Thirty-Two

Our hope is lost and we ourselves are cut off.
– Ezekiel 37:11

Two days of sitting left Daphne glad for the opportunity to walk. Blue skies and a warm temperature inspired thanks for spring's loveliest gifts. The rising sun shadowed half of the walled walkway, but she and Batano soon reached the city's edge. To her delight, sunbeams highlighted one side of stone buildings and lit up the *agora*.

Shop owners bustled to prepare for the day. The scene replicated her trips into Philippi to ply the only option open to her...earn money for her owner by telling fortunes. The ploy had given her protection and kept her from an overseer's abuse, but sadly had opened the door to the horror of becoming fully demon possessed. She shook off the memory. Thank you, Lord, for setting me free from Satanic bondage as well as slavery.

She wandered down the same corridor into the city she and her family had been led, bound to a passel of people owned by the same slave trader. A vendor approached selling sweets passed. Her little brother's innocent plea rang in her head. *I wants a honey cake. Daphne, tell that man to give me one.* Then as now it brought tears to her eyes.

Food sellers gave way to booths she had seen then, Beautiful jewelry, fabrics, and home goods. Her friend, Cassandra's face flashed. The rejection still stung. The girl's mother unable to believe it could be me, and my friend not brave enough to

189

stand up and respond to my plea for help. I wonder if she ever thinks about it, but I forgive her, Lord.

From the end of the market, she could see the dilapidated buildings where she and her family were kept. She did an about face, vowing to never go near that place.

She found the city's *bema*. A man up on the stage-like platform expounded outrage over some newly established Roman tax. She questioned his wisdom, but few appeared to listen. An older gentleman stood to one side, paying no attention. She ramped up her courage and approached him. "Sir, forgive me. I am new to your city. Could you direct me to the office of the man who owns the slave market?"

His chin drew to his neck, and he frowned. "The slave market? It is at the end of the *agora*."

"No, sir. I need to know where to find the office of the man who owns or runs it."

"The office, huh? Well, Marcus' office is about five or six doors down from here. He pointed to his right. "Same side as the *bema*."

She thanked him and followed his directions. A sign on the door read, Marcus Olestess, Personal Property Management. She read it again. Personal property? That could mean lots of things...but Marcus was the name the man used, so she took a deep breath and knocked.

A young girl opened the door. She was dressed in slave garb, probably a few years younger than herself. "Can I be of help?" Her smile did not reach her eyes.

Her manner of speaking triggered doubt she had always been a slave. Daphne returned the smile and spoke kindly to the girl. "I need to see the owner."

She ushered her and Batano into an outer room. "Please wait here," She returned moments later and led them into the owner's office. Beautiful couches with polished tables circled the room. Silk draperies that reminded her of Patharus' office covered windows that opened to the courtyard.

A slender man with a thin face and a long nose rose to meet them. Batano remained standing while Daphne sat on the seat closest to the door. He spoke sharply to the girl and waved her out of the room before his attention turned to Daphne. Abruptly, his tone changed. "Please, sit down. What can I do for you, Madam?"

"Two summers ago, my family was brought here as slaves." The man raised his brows, glanced at Batano and back at her. She ignored his skeptical expression. "I was separated from my mother and two brothers and taken to Philippi where my owner set me free." To clear any question about her current status, she added, "I am married to his son."

The man squinted, assessed her wardrobe, and eyed her slave. She refused to squirm and drew a quiet breath. "I am on a quest to find my loved ones and to buy their freedom from whomever bought them at your market. Is it possible that you would have a record of who purchased them?"

"Two summers ago?" The man barely covered a smirk. "We keep no such records. If it had been a few weeks, I might have been able to offer some help, but at this point there is no way to trace their whereabouts. We process hundreds of slaves each month so what you are hoping to find is highly unlikely."

He stood, making no secret he meant for them to leave. "You are a fortunate young woman. Enjoy your new life and forget the past."

She gestured to Batano, and they left. The man's callous suggestion made her bristle. Forget the past? Maybe he could forget a loved one torn from his side and sold into a life of misery, but what decent person would? They had walked well into the *agora* when a young voice stopped her.

"Misses. Misses, wait up." She turned, surprised to see the owner's young slave. Her lungs wheezed. "I overheard your desire to find your family. I only have a moment before I must return with my master's lunch, but I understand your pain. My family too...well, anyway, I have a suggestion. If you can remember the name of the man who brought you to the auction, he might remember your family and have an idea who bought them."

Daphne's heart went out to her. She touched the girl's arm. "You are so kind to try to help me. Thank you for risking..." The girl pulled back and nodded, ready to run. Daphne longed to reach out to her. ""Is there anything I can do to help you?"

Hopeless eyes met hers. "Listen, I know things look futile, but I have a God, His name is Jesus, and I will pray that you will be released from slavery...from that man. My God answers prayers and He will find a way to set you free."

The girl's eyes filled, and she backed away. "No, I have been shamed. There is no hope for me but thank you." She ran off before Daphne could say more.

Batano followed her into the courtyard where they replenished their jugs and opened the parcel of food. She picked at her lunch. Her heart ached for this one who had not escaped the same fear that plagued her while a slave. Why is she so heavy on my heart, Lord? I know many suffered her fate.

I am calling you into a ministry of caring for those who suffered what you suffered. To comfort with My truth just as you have been comforted, that slaves may become My freed men and women.

The huge white clouds that drifted above reflected His glory. Yes, Lord. Lead me and help me to find the path You have laid out for me.

In time, the young slave's suggestion settled like fresh dew. Daphne searched her memory but could not find the name of the man who had purchased her family from the ship's captain. Had she even heard it? She knew his assistant's name was Hurle. He had overseen their trek over the mountains and checked on her in the camp. But how would she find him?

It dawned on her that if she went near to the buildings that had housed her and her family, she might spot him herding his latest group of slaves through the streets to sell at the auction. She shuddered at the thought, but led Batano to a spot near the end of the agora where she could see him approach or detect new arrivals at the slave quarters.

When the bench grew hard, she paced. Shops began to close for the day, and they needed to return to the inn.

Batano never pushed his opinion, but her discouraged posture brought a quiet suggestion. "Misses, you look tired. Would you like me to hail a carriage for you?"

"No. The walk will do me good. We may be in for another long wait again tomorrow."

193

Chapter Thirty-Three

When I spoke you did not hear.
– Isaiah 65:12

Nicanor's mind had been elsewhere all day. Frustrated, Makedon finally asked, "Anything I can do to help?"

He sighed. "No. We need to finish these supply records for Patharus' sake. Did you assure cook he did not need to cut back on food for our help?"

"Yes. Seems some newly assigned assistant did not understand how we store things and convinced him we were short on staples. Cook should have known better."

"Well, you know *Kupio*. He has to be sure so this report should put it to rest." They finished the summary and Nicanor gathered what they had documented and left for the day. When asked days ago, Patharus had not confronted Medea about the influence of the strange woman but did admit she frequently begged off joining him for dinner.

In case she came tonight, Nicanor decided to wait and take the report to their morning briefing. Dining alone under the grape arbor, he wished Daphne were there with him. She has been gone two weeks...how will I bear being without her all summer, Lord? Patharus is doing much better...maybe Makendon could handle things and I could...

Hope drifted to doubt, and he knew it. There was much more to see to than the overseer's responsibilities. Patharus' strength had not fully returned, and though his speech had improved, slurred words hampered communication and his intermittent confusion made decisions difficult. From sunup to sundown, Nicanor met with associates, managed his father's leased properties and business investments, and answered inquiries about frequent consultations which Patharus normally attended. No. There was no way he could leave.

He lay awake, too wound up to sleep, his mind on Daphne. I hope Epaphroditus returns soon and has news of her progress. "Lord, watch over her, and help her find her family. And please open the right doors for her in Delphi." His mind wandered and the next thing he knew Batano's substitute called for him to wake.

Patharus fidgeted and hardly glanced at the records he brought the next morning. "Medea dined with me last night. I asked her about the woman who visits her and about the not eating. She convinced me she is fine...thinner but she ate a good dinner. So, I—"

"But did you notice the dark circles under her eyes and the—"

"Son, you have not known her long enough to realize she has a... well, a woman's condition that has kept her nearly bedridden for years."

"That is true but the physical and emotional changes I see now, compared to a year ago, disturb me. They have escalated even from the time of my wedding. In her condition she may not be able to discern the damage that woman has caused, and I think you would do well to step in and forbid those visits...for the sake of Medea's health."

Patharus grimaced. "I do not discount what you are saying, but for now I am going to give it some time...wait and see." He cleared his throat. "She has asked that you not bring it up to her again and I

195

think that is best for now. "He reached for the inventory. "I will look this over later, but for now please check on the crew assigned to that land we use to the east of us. I have not had a report in days."

Nicanor left, too frustrated to remind his father that a report on that venture had been given just the day before.

Weeping may endure for a night, but joy comes in the morning.
– Psalms 30:5

At the end of the third day of monitoring the slave market, Daphne rose from the bench. "We may as well go back, Batano...does not look like this is the way I will find my family." He nodded and they returned to the inn.

Leah met them at the door. "No sign of them?"She shook her head. "Why don't you take a break and go visit the Parthenon and the Acropolis tomorrow. It will do you good to take your mind off it for a spell."

A pleasant dinner and a good night's sleep left Daphne in a better mood the next morning. As a slave, she had regretted no opportunity to see it up close and decided to follow Leah's advice.

Batano seemed as excited as she was to see the sights of Athens... days of their unsuccessful vigil had weighed on them both. They wandered over the city amazed at the number of shrines. The enormity of Zeus' temple with its cone shaped entrance and gigantic columns that reached several stories, made her jaw drop. She hurried past the Apollo temple, appalled at the number of people lined up before it. They have no idea Apollo is but a myth, Lord. Who will tell them about You?

Truth will come in great power to this city. My timing is perfect.

They watched a change of the guards before the Roman council's ornate building, their red hats, black bibs, and white robes shone in the sun. Walls of stone houses and buildings boasted of beautiful frescos, adorned with well-tended gardens. She bought fruit-filled sweets at the market to add to their lunch. To avoid the dreadful sheep and goat shed where she had been kept was not an option, to climb to the Acropolis it had to be passed.

She hurried past and focused on the Parthenon's sun-drenched, endless columns. Few people walked along with them. Cassandra's explanation returned. *It is now no more than an ancient landmark that serves no official function.*

Nearby, the beautiful temple of Athena with its statues of the virgin goddesses took her breath away. She sighed. So much honor given to demonic powers posing as gods or goddesses that do not exist.

At the top of the Acropolis, they looked down on endless olive groves and the theater with seats carved from the mountain side. She gazed at Mars Hill, where Asher said Paul had spoken. She wished it were not so far away. It stretched out beyond the valley, its monuments hidden behind a green canopy. They had nearly returned to the path when a woman's voice cut into the quiet. "Master Adonis, you get right back here by me and your sister."

She gasped, spun around, and screamed, "Belte? Belte, is that you? Belte it is me, Daphne."

The woman dropped the girl's hand and clutched her chest. Her lips mouthed, my baby. "Daphne, is that really you?"

Before she could move Daphne was at her side. Belte clutched her to her chest and hugged her like a long-lost child.

"Belte, oh, Belte, how I have missed you." Through a wash of mutual tears she held her at arm's length, studied her face and hugged her some more.

The little girl drew close to her nanny. "Belte, I want to go home."

Daphne grabbed Belte's arm. "No, you cannot leave." She pulled out the sweets she still carried and offered them as a distraction to the children. It worked.

Each spoke at once, hardly able to contain their joy. Daphne could not contain herself. "Where do you live? Are you a nanny to these children like you were to Alexander and me? Does your new master treat you right? Is your family with you...that little granddaughter you loved, your husband?"

Belte related that her husband, granddaughter, and the child's parents had been bought by her same owner. The rest of her family had been sold to a different man and she never saw them again. At the familiar tale, Daphne's eyes watered with hers. "But your mother, and your brothers, are they here in Athens with you?"

"No...oh, Belte, I have so much to tell you." The children grew impatient again. They pulled on their nanny's tunic and begged to move on. "I know you must go, Belte, but I need to see you again. I need your help. Would your new owners be willing for me to come visit or let you meet me in town tomorrow?"

"They are less likely to free up my time than your family was, but I believe the misses would be alright with a visit. Their estate is on the other side of the city. Have a driver take the main road North and tell him it is the estate of Bacchus. He owns the largest olive groves around. Everyone knows where it is."

Daphne waved goodbye. Tears of joy and hope mixed with a sorrowful warning. Belte will be devastated when she learns the fate of my mother and brothers. She and all my father's slaves had been sold and taken away before it was announced that his family would also need to be sold to pay his debts.

She hated to have to tell her. But maybe she can help me know where to find them.

Chapter Thirty-Four

And God will prepare the way before me.
– Malachi 3:1

Daphne's excitement at finding her beloved Nanny far outweighed her desire to see more of Athens. She chattered to Batano as they hurried back to the inn. She told him about being separated from slaves she considered family. Belte, Jasper their overseer, Sarvya their driver and all their children. She had grown up with them, all torn from her life along with her mother and brothers.

He listened with uncharacteristic attentiveness. Her background, from free to slave to free again was not news, but her relationship with those she considered family or friends, invoked his interest. To her surprise he even asked her to expand on those relationships. She told him about how Belte corrected and mothered her, about watching Sarvya tend their horses and how Jasper watched over her like a favorite uncle. Batano did not comment but she sensed that his view of her had changed.

The innkeepers were happy to hear her news. Asher said he had once met Baccus at a city meeting. "He is not part of our Jewish community, but he has a good reputation."

"My former nanny thought they would not object to a visit, but Asher, would you consider going with me...to kind of smooth the way, introduce me to her owner?"

For a moment he was silent. "I am not sure Bacchus will remember me, or if I could be of any help, but yes, I would be happy to go with you."

The next morning, she wanted to hire a carriage and leave right after breakfast, but Leah convinced her to wait. "Households are busier in the morning and by noon most chores are finished." Daphne agreed and informed Batano he need not come, but he insisted Nicanor's instructions were for him to always accompany her, so she relented.

The driver drove them to Bacchus' estate and said he would await their return. Batano agreed to stay with the carriage while Asher accompanied her to the front door. The sprawling stone house had two stories with large porches on both ends. A middle-aged slave with a pitcher in hand answered the door. She invited them into a large foyer. "Wait here and I will see if master Bacchus is in."

A portly man in a Roman tunic entered the room. He gazed at her and at Asher without any sign of recognition. He stepped forward. "Good afternoon master Bacchus. You may not remember me but I am Asher, the owner of an inn on the other side of the city. We met last fall at a meeting of the city council."

Bacchus squinted and cocked his head. "Yes, of course, ah, Asher. What can I do for you?"

He introduced him to Daphne, explaining that the nanny to Bacchus' children had once belonged to her family and that a chance meeting had happened the previous day near the acropolis. "This young woman is visiting from Philippi and if you have no objections would like very much for your permission to have a short visit with her former slave."

Bacchus frowned. "Highly unusual. I am not sure it would be proper for a —"

A slender woman with a wide smile entered the room. "What is it Bacchus? Do we have company?" Before he could answer she looked at the visitors. "Oh, my. Is that you Asher? I have not seen you at the market in weeks...how is Leah and who is your friend?"

Asher greeted Bacchus' wife, explaining that a friend had shopped for them because his wife had not been well. "But she is better now. Thank you for asking."

"And is this one of your guests?"

Asher repeated Daphne's request with one eye on Bacchus. The man appeared unsettled with the interchange. "Well of course she must see Belte, alright, Bacchus?" He gave a concessionary nod and she continued. "Come with me, Daphne. The children are at their afternoon rest so this is a good time." She held out her hand and led her from the room.

Asher said he would wait in the carriage. Bacchus gestured to his servant, but made no attempt to be hospitable.

Bacchus' wife looked at Daphne. "How amazing that the two of you ran into each other, My name is Anna. You may sit here on the porch in the sunshine, and I will send Belte right down."

Daphne thanked her, awed at her kindness. Belte soon arrived with refreshments Anna had insisted she bring. A wave of resentment at her nanny's belonging to a another's family rose in her chest, but she rebuked the senseless thought. "What a kind lady you have as a mistress, Belte, I am so glad for you."

"Yes, she has been good to us." Her voice dropped. "The master sees things differently than your father did...but look at you! All grown up." Now tell me about your mother and your brothers."

She smiled. "Is Theo still insisting on honey cakes for breakfast?"

The moment she dreaded had arrived. "Belte, you and all of father's slaves had been taken away when the magistrates decided my family also had to be sold to finish paying my father's debts." At Belte's audible gasp she stopped and took her hand. "I am sorry, you could not have known but we were sold to a terrible slave monger, taken to Corinth and resold to a man who brought us to the slave market here in Athens." Her voice caught. "We were all separated, and I have not seen any of them since."

"No, not your precious mama...not little Theo and Alexander. I cannot believe it. How you all must have suffered. I am used to being someone's property, but you...and your lovely mother...no."

"It is true Belte, it was awful. I was taken by ship to northern Greece where I... oh I do not think I have time to tell you the whole sordid story, but after a year the owner's son fell in love with me and I with him. His father set me free, and his son and I were married last fall. I am here in Athens to try to find what happened to my family and hopefully purchase their freedom."

"Oh, my poor baby. I cannot believe what you have told me...your mama a slave..."

"Is there any way you could find out what happened to her or my brothers, Belte? Do slaves know where other slaves go...who buys them?"

She shook her head. "In nearly two years they could be anywhere. Sometimes slaves know about other's whereabouts...they run into each other on outings for their masters or word gets around. There are a lot of slaves in this household, and I promise I will ask every one of them if they know of a woman named Hebee with a five-year-old boy, or a young man named Alexander. They might have stood out because of their different background."

Anna appeared at the porch door. "Belte, I am sorry, but the children have awakened."

She rose. "Yes, I will be right there."

Daphne stood and put her hands on her shoulders. "Thank you, friend. But I have one quick thing I must tell you. After an agonizing year as a slave, I became a believer in Christ."

Belte clutched her chest. "You have? You made Jesus your Lord?"

Daphne hugged her. "Yes, do you remember you told me about Him when I struggled so to find a way to save my father's estate? Even then my heart knew you were right, but I was too afraid to deny my family's god."

Tears rolled down Belte's cheeks. "I knew it would happen one day!" She looked up. "Thank you, Jesus, You answered my prayers. Thank You, thank You, Jesus."

Daphne could not stop grinning. "I could not wait to tell you...now we worship the same God. You go along now, I do not want to get you in trouble with your mistress, but I will be back if they let me."

"Yes. Goodbye, my baby. And I will see what I can find out about your family." With a spring in her step, she hurried from the porch.

Anna saw Daphne out the front door. "Thank you so much for allowing this visit. Would it be too much if I returned one more time?"

"You just come when you want. And do not mind the master...he can be difficult, but any friend of Asher and Leah is a friend of mine."

Chapter Thirty-Five

A door was opened to me.
– 2 Corinthians 2:12

On the ride back Daphne nearly bounced in her seat as she savored Belte's joy at the revelation one she loved and helped raise had become a believer. And her promise to ask around about Daphne's family inspired new hope.

Asher reveled in her joy. "Leah will be so glad to hear you met Anna."

"She seemed happy to see you, have you known her long?"

He grinned, but would only say, "Wait until you tell Leah."

She met them at the gate. "Tell me all about it, Daphne. Was Bacchus alright with a visit? Did they let you see your former nanny...Belte was it? Did you—"

Asher held up his hand, "Hold on, you are not going to believe who Bacchus' wife is."

The crease between Leah's dark brows deepened. Daphne waited, twisting to study one then the other.

"What are you talking about, Asher? Who Bacchus' wife is? Honestly, sometimes you—"

"Alright, alright, listen. Anna, the woman we often talk with at the market is Bacchus' wife."

Leah drew a short breath. "Really? Anna is married to Bacchus?"

"Sure is. And if it had not been for her, I do not think Daphne's visit would have come about."

Daphne chimed in. "He is right, she could not have been nicer, took me right in to see Belte, and even said I could come back anytime."

Leah pursed her lips. "Well, that explains why she does not join us at the synagogue."

"You mean that Anna is Jewish? Married to a Roman?"

Leah motioned to the door. "Let us go in. It is a long story, but I will try to clarify it." They settled over some tea and *rugelach.* After Leah passed the sweets, she began. "Anna told me that her family was forced to sell her to prevent them all from starvation. Her owner bought her to assist his wife and the eldest son fell in love with her. Eventually he convinced his father to let them marry." She shook her head. "I cannot believe that Bacchus was that son."

Daphne's chin quivered. The familiar tale brought the hopeless face of the girl they encountered at the market owner's office. Lord, how many girls have been torn from their families and sold into a life of misery?

Leah refilled their cups. "Anna was so closed off from her family that she put aside all reminders of her heritage, but in time she longed to connect with God's people again. She is a strong believer in Yahweh, but married to Bacchus, I..."

"It is heart wrenching to be severed from your family, does she ever see them?"

"I believe they left the area to find land more suitable for their crops."

"So sad. How wonderful that you and Asher have been able to bring her the fellowship of those who worship the Lord, God."

Leah smiled. "Yes, and she was so excited when we told her about the apostle Paul's visit. Each day before her father made the tormenting decision to sell her, he faithfully read the Scriptures to his family so she knew the ancient prophesies that promised the coming Messiah."

"I would so like to learn more of the background of our Lord's people. Epaphroditus, our leader, has shared many of Scriptures that pointed to Jesus, but what a rich heritage those of you who were born into it have to draw upon."

"We do, but even more I value the grace to believe the freedom given through the death of our Savior...so many have not heard or received it."

Everyone was quiet for a time.

Daphne broke the quiet. "Do you remember I told you my nanny, was a believer?" Leah nodded. "Well, she was thrilled to learn I am one too. Do you think either Anna or Belte know the other is a child of God?"

"I cannot say. I do not recall Anna ever even mentioning their nanny nor does she bring her to market. Anna likes to do the shopping herself...I think it is her opportunity to get away and be out with people."

Daphne excused herself and went to her room to rest. Her thoughts jumped from the possibility that Belte would find information about her family, to gratitude for Anna's willingness for her to come again. Lord, how soon do I dare make another visit? I want to give Belte plenty of time but what do I do if no one remembers my family?

For the next two days she went into the city with Batano and watched again for her former owner. The *agora* was jammed with people the second day.

She inquired and soon learned the slave auction would take place that very day. "Batano, stick close to me. We are going down there and see if I can find my former owner or his overseer."

The crude bantering of the crowd and the aurora of despair that hung over the place sickened her, but she found a place where she could see buyers and sellers move about. By mid-afternoon she was ready to give up when she spotted Hurle's huge bald head. She jumped up and shouted. "There he is! Hurry, Batano. I must not lose him."

Batano muscled his way through the crowd with her close behind, until they reached the man who had supervised her for her former owner. Batano tapped him on the shoulder."Excuse me sir, my mistress needs to talk to you."

Hurle turned and looked at her. "You want to see me?"

"Yes, please give me a moment." He nodded and she explained who she was and of her hopes he might remember her family. "It was less than two years ago, and we traveled with you over the mountains from Corinth." To jog his memory, she added, "You let my little brother ride in the supply wagon. And I was sold to some Romans. You took me to the port where they waited to take me aboard.

He glanced at Batano and back at her. "You do not look like a slave."

She explained that she had been set free and had the money to buy her family's freedom. "I hoped that you or your owner might remember to whom my mother and little brother were sold, and my other brother, a boy of about thirteen years."

Hurley stroked his chin. "I do remember a woman with a little boy in the women and children's stable. We do not get many that young. But once the auction starts my job is usually over. Perhaps my master could help, but he does not pay much attention to the people he brings to the market."

"Oh, please, could you take me to him? Even if it is unlikely I would like a chance to see if he remembers anything."

He shrugged. "You can try. I think he is eating over at the tavern." He led them through the crowd to the building. "Wait here."

Neither man came out for longer than seemed necessary, but she determined to wait. At last, the owner approached. His eyes burned with curiosity. "My man, Hurle, has filled me in on your dilemma. I am sorry, I do not keep records on who buys my goods, but I do remember a family who did not look like they had been born into slavery, and the woman did have a small child." He cocked his head and frowned like something had come to mind. "Did I buy your family from a ship's captain in Corinth?"

Daphne's heart raced. "Yes! Yes, that was us. We walked over the mountains with you from there. I was sold to three men from Philippi, but do you have any idea who bought my mother or my brothers?"

The man shook his head. "I am sorry, I have nothing to do with the actual auction and have no idea who buys any individual. I am only there to pick up my profits. I can tell you that around that time the owners of olive groves and those who had produce farms around here were short on workers, so there is a good chance your family remained in the area, but there is no way to know."

His last statement resounded with a painful finality. She thanked him and gestured to Batano. Another dead end. Lord, my only hope is that one of Belte's fellow slaves will remember something. It began to rain. Large drops mingled with sorrowful tears that insisted she give up. "No, tomorrow, I will go back to Bacchus'."

The rain almost drowned out the man's call. "Young woman, wait a moment. You should check with the city council. They would know the larger growers here." He pulled his himation over his head. "Maybe you could contact each landowner and ask about your family." He shrugged. "Be worth a try."

She called back over her shoulder. "That is very kind of you, sir. I will look into it."

Chapter Thirty-Six

Diligence is man's precious possession.
– Proverbs 12:27

Upon hearing the man's suggestion, Asher spoke up. "Daphne, if you like I will make that inquiry for you. I can get the information you need without raising anyone's curiosity."

"Oh, thank you, Asher. I have not had much success on my own. I planned to go back to Bacchus' tomorrow, but I will wait and see if this venture goes anywhere."

He returned by midmorning the next day with a list of four large farms besides Bacchus'. "Again, I do not mean to intrude but if you want I will go with you."

"Oh, I would welcome and appreciate your help. You and Leah have been such a blessing to me, this would have been much harder without your help."

He smiled and left to arrange for a carriage. Upon his return, he handed her a crude drawing. "Here, I mapped out a route, so we do not cover the same ground twice." He pointed to a name. "We will start with this one. It is a large produce farm that owns hundreds of slaves."

Daphne stepped into the carriage along with Batano. She tried to dismiss a picture of her mother picking vegetables from dawn to twilight. They reached the first farm before noon. Asher accompanied her to the door, and they were welcomed in to await the owner. He listened to her tale, his head bent to catch every word.

"My mother's name is Hebee. She is in her early thirties and has a little boy of five and an older son,

Alexander, about fourteen years. We were from Delphi, a small city on the north shore of the Gulf of Corinth. I would be so grateful if—"

"Wait, let me see if I can find my overseer. He would be more likely to know if any of them are here. I do not know if we can be of much help, things turn over and a lot changes in two years, but please be seated and I will see what I can find out."

The man instructed his maid to bring them refreshments and left. Daphne looked at Asher. "I am amazed at how concerned he is, as if he really hopes to help me."

"God is for you, Daphne. Do not ever let that fade from what you believe."

The owner returned shortly with another man. "I have given my man all you told me. He doesn't believe your mother is here but wants to inquire about your older brother."

The possibility of finding Alexander brought a gasp. "Yes, what do you need to know?"

"I have a young man of that age we bought around that time...very educated. He is just outside, perhaps you could look and see if he is one you are looking for."

She leapt from her chair. "Oh, yes, please."

The man led them through an outer door where a young man waited. Her hopes crashed like the boulders she and Alexander pushed over the cliffs on Mt Parnassus. She put her hands over her face and wept. Asher put his arm around her shoulders. "Try not to be discouraged, we have several more farms to check out."

She gave the owner her appreciation and by the time they reached the second farm she assured Asher she was prepared for whatever came. The second owner listened to why they were there but eyed them with suspicion. "My slaves are not for sale."

She took a deep breath, determined not to cry. "Sir, I understand, but would you at least consider inquiring as to whether or not one of my family might be here. We were not born into slavery but were from a family such as yours. My father died and we were falsely stripped of our home and sold to pay debts for which the settlement had already been arranged."

His expression softened. "Wait here, I will send for my overseer and see what he might know."

Daphne released the breath she had held. Within moments a tall man with a gruff voice addressed them. "Something I can do for you people?"

While she explained the whole story again, she watched his face for any sign he recognized her family "No, nobody here fits your descriptions. Most of our people are not from Greece but were brought in from other places, sorry."

They had not yet left when the owner stopped them. "Have you been to the Andreas vineyards yet?"

Asher checked his list. "No, we are headed there next, why?"

"Well, Andreas can be touchy. Tell him you were here and that I had my overseer cooperate. It might help."

They stopped midway and ate the lunch Leah prepared, sharing the plenty with their driver. As they approached the vineyards, Asher touched her arm. "Let me do the talking when we first get there, alright?" She nodded. The gate keeper looked them over carefully but finally decided to let them proceed. At the door Daphne stepped back and let Asher speak.

The man did not invite them in but listened. His demeanor changed when Asher told him how his fellow owner tried to help them. He too called forth his overseer with the same disappointing results. "We have a woman with two young children but no one that sounds like your older brother."

They rode to the last farm in silence and received the same report: no one here of that description. Daphne went straight to her room when they returned, too disheartened to cry. Belte's my last hope, Lord. How can I leave this area knowing my family is likely close by and I have no way to find them? She fell into an exhausted sleep until Leah called her to dinner.

The next morning, she announced plans to go back to Bacchus' that afternoon. "Would you like to go along and visit with Anna while I am there, Leah?"

She brightened at the idea. "Well, I could. Anna never invited us to come visit but now that we have made this connection, I think she would welcome the company."

They arrived at the same hour as before and Anna invited them in, delighted to see her friend. She brought Belte out, excused herself and rejoined Leah.

Daphne hugged her. "Oh, Belte, you cannot imagine my joy at seeing your face. I treasure every memory of growing up with you, always there to care for whatever I needed...even correction."

Belte chuckled. "You could be a handful but were always one of my own...special. I remember the day you left for the festival to join your parents' temple, remember? You were so excited, especially after having to wait a whole year longer than most of your friends."

She sighed. "Yes, it was supposed to be the best day of my life and instead it was the beginning of a year of horror. But tell me, were you able to find anyone who thought they might know of my family? I went to several farms yesterday, but no one knew of them."

Belte lowered her eyes and shook her head. "I contacted every slave who lives here, and nobody was aware of anyone of your mother's description, or Alexander either. I am so sorry, Little One."

Daphne tried to hide her tears, but Belte's sad face undermined her intentions. She let the waiting arms of her dear one enfold her. "I know you tried,"

She quieted and Belte asked, "What did you mean after the festival your life was a year of horror? Did your owner abuse you?"

"No, at the temple I was invaded by an evil demon, and you remember father was killed on the return trip."

She nodded, "Such a good man. But what do you mean by an evil demon?"

"I do not know how much opportunity you have had to learn about God's enemies. But they are servants of Satan, a force of evil whose agenda is to destroy people, especially before they come to know our God."

Belte's face was blank so she explained how she had come to be possessed by a demonic being who at first paraded himself as angels of light sent to help her. Belte listened as she filled her in on her whole year of despair and of her deliverance.

"Oh, my poor baby...and no family around to comfort you."

"People cannot begin to understand how devious they are. Most do not experience what I went

215

through, but these demonic imposters harass even believers. Their plan is to distract us from living a life that makes our witness effective and draws others to our Savior. They specialize in putting thoughts of fear, doubt or unbelief in our minds."

"Daphne, I wish — "

Anna's voice interrupted. "Belte, I am sorry, the children are awake, but we will get together with Daphne and Leah again soon."

Her eyes locked on Belte's. Neither was sure of Anna's intentions. They hugged goodbye, each hurt over the loss of one another.

Daphne stared without seeing anything on the ride home. Lord, what am I going to do? I have followed every avenue to find my family and gotten nowhere. I cannot just leave.

Trust Me

Leah sympathized in silence until Daphne volunteered Belte's sorrow at not finding anyone who knew of her family's whereabouts. She patted her knee. "I am so sorry and I know this will not make up for your disappointment, but you will find it hard to believe the door our connection with Anna has opened."

Chapter Thirty-Seven

Beware of false prophets who come to you in sheep's clothing,
– Matthew 7:15

Nicanor stewed. It had been over a week since Patharus made it clear he did not intend to prevent visits from the woman Medea had welcomed into her life. How could anyone believe such nonsense, Lord? You are the way, the truth, and the life...salvation your unearned, undeserved gift. Why is it Medea cannot understand that it is available for her...for everyone? Surely, she has seen that nobody has ever attained enough knowledge, done enough good or disciplined themselves to the point of resisting wrong...except Jesus.

Patharus' mandate returned. *Medea has asked that you not bring it up to her again...*

Unable to concentrate, he laid aside the records his father asked him to study. He tried to recall Epaphroditus' sermon that warned of dangers of a fast growing, false teaching that had infiltrated the body of believers. What he did remember sounded exactly like the regimen Medea spoke of.

Frustrated with his lack of recall, he decided to go see Lydia. She answered his knock. "Nicanor, what a nice surprise. Come in and let me get you some cool water, it seems summer has arrived early."

They shared their desires for Daphne and Epaphroditus' journeys to go well and for timely returns. "What brings you out, you seem a bit troubled? I am sure Daphne will be fine."

"It is not her, but I sure miss her."

"What then? Your family?"

"Of sorts." He filled her in on his concern for Medea. "I tried to remember what our leader taught us about this threat of what is falsely called knowledge. It seems all that stayed with me is that you cannot attain spiritual oneness with God through special enlightenment and self-discipline. Do you remember what he said they believe about Jesus? I need to understand so I can help her see the truth."

"Well, for one, that Jesus was not fully God or man, but one of the semi-divine beings that bridge the gap between God and the world. That is the bases of their error. We know and believe Jesus is God, the Son."

"Right. Now I remember. And did he not say they do not believe Jesus came in the flesh as a human but attained his position through knowledge?

She refilled his glass. "Yes, and some even insist He had a phantom body that only appeared human, that He was never resurrected and has no authority or ability to meet our needs."

He squinted at the glass he held, deep in thought. "Denying His deity and the pursuit of knowledge to attain eternity seems to be the mainstay of their beliefs."

"And that the body is nothing so no matter what you do, good or evil, it is alright."

"What do you think about Medea giving the woman her treasures? Do you think she is taking advantage of her and keeps them for herself or is this vow of poverty a legitimate part of their beliefs?"

"I honestly cannot say. Epaphroditus did say that vow was part of their beliefs. But whether this woman is truly committed to the concept or is taking advantage of Medea, who knows?"

"Even if I confront her, I have no way to know if she will tell the truth."

"No, not by your own wisdom, but remember the Holy Spirit's discernment works within you, so if it comes to that, you will know. One more thing, Epaphroditus also told us about Alons, remember? Lower gods formed by the demiurge, an evil creator god, and gods of the upper world who attain their status through soul perfection. It is all part of the deception about semi-divine beings."

He shook his head. "Lower gods and upper gods, they make it so complicated. I am so grateful God revealed His truth to me." He rose and thanked her for her help.

"Wait, let me pray with you." She put her hands on his shoulders and asked the Lord for wisdom for him and for Medea's eyes to open to truth.

He did not hurry his mount on the way back but mulled over all he had learned. How could he make Patharus see this false teaching was harmful and could leave Medea in serious trouble? *Lord, I must help her see the truth before it's too late.*

Pray. You have the Spirit within, and you will know what you need to do.

He rubbed his forehead, grateful the Lord confirmed Lydia's counsel. "Yes, Lord. I trust You to lead me. Please go with me, I am going to see her as soon as I get home."

Danatel welcomed him. "It is good to see you Master Nicanor. I will see if Kupios will..." She frowned. "I will see whether she is up to another visitor."

"Wait, you look worried. How is she...does that strange woman still come around?"

Medea's servant was indignant. "Yes, and she has left with many of my mistress' treasures." Her tone softened. "Master Nicanor, I have been maid to the mistress for more years than I remember...way before her son died. I do not want to be disloyal, but I do not know what to do...who to alert. Kupios grows weaker every day. She can hardly stand alone or even walk to relieve herself. Night after night she has me send word to Kupio that she will not join him for dinner." She shrugged. "Maybe he is not able to find what is happening to her, but somebody needs to." Tears rolled down her cheeks. "I am afraid we are losing her."

"You are doing all you can, Danatel. I am going in there and do not worry, I will make sure she knows I did not wait for you to ask permission."

Medea's eyes were closed when he entered her bedchamber. The slight hump her body raised brought a grimace. Beneath dark, sunken eyes, pasty skin strained to cover protruding cheekbones. He whispered to her servant who had followed him in, "Danatel, bring some nourishing broth. She needs to eat."

She returned with broth she kept ready. He pulled a chair close to the bed and gently shook her arm. "Good afternoon, Medea, I heard you missed lunch and I wanted to share this time with you."

Her lids fluttered, then opened wide. "Nicanor...how nice to see you."

"And you...it has been weeks. How do you feel? Can I help you raise up on your pillows?"

She looked about. "Where is Danatel? I—"

"I told her I wanted to surprise you. Here, she brought you some broth."

Medea glanced at the bowl and back at him. "I am not really hungry, I—"

"Danatel said you have not eaten...do you not think you should?" Medea turned her head. She searched the walls like she hoped to find a forgotten exit. When nothing materialized, she sighed, took the bowl, and sipped a little broth.

"Have you heard from Daphne? No, of course not, ships take a long time to get back to Neapolis. But I am sure you will hear before long."

"Our leader will bring word. He is scheduled to arrive in about ten days."

She gazed at the ceiling "You mean the head of the group you and Daphne look to for spiritual fulfillment? Such a shame, it is likely he has misinterpreted Christ' message."

He was tempted to pounce, after all, she brought the subject up. He ignored the remark and squelched an urge to defend Epaphroditus. That she eat more important than an argument. "Tell me, have you been having dinner with Father? He has not mentioned it lately."

It has not worked out recently, I—"

"And why is that?"

"Sometimes after a full day I am just too tired."

He was not about to let her off that easily. "And what is it that fills your days? Visitors?""

"Some, how about you? Has Patharus caught you up on all his endeavors? I know very little about what they are, but he used to talk about them over..."

Nicanor hid a smirk. Her effort to change the subject had cracked a door she did not intended to open. "It is going to be a lovely evening. Perhaps Halaten could assist Father and the two of you could join me for dinner under the grape arbor."

Medea sat the broth down and lay back on her pillows. "This is not a good day...perhaps we could —"

He refused to relent. "Why not, Medea? What really keeps you from eating?"

Stripped of excuses, her patience evaporated. "I have days I choose not to eat. Did not Patharus pass along that I did not want to discuss this with you?"

"He loves you too much to deny you anything, Medea. But I care too, enough to be concerned about whatever causes you to starve yourself. Do you not understand this could end your life? And without Jesus you would face eternal separation from God?"

"The secret of my spiritual essence mirrors a restoration of divine nature. Knowledge superior and much greater than the doctrine you profess. My guide says I have nearly attained that status, and she —"

"Medea, Medea. You are being exploited by false teachers. The destructive heresies that deny the Lord Jesus has enslaved them and will bring you into bondage straight from the pit of hell. Do you want that? There is no secret knowledge or elite people. We are all the same in God's sight. He shows no partiality, all are welcome, but no one comes to the Father except through Jesus Christ."

Medea's body grew rigid. "You have much to unlearn about your Jesus, but I must ask you to leave now. Please excuse me, I am very tired and need my servant's help. "Danatel, please show Master Nicanor out."

At the door, he sighed. "I am sorry to have upset her, but do not despair, I will see to it that—"

Medea's shrieked and both startled. "Danatel, help." A crash interrupted her frantic cry. Both rushed to her bedchamber. Her crumpled body lay next to the table that had held her broth.

Danatel screamed and knelt beside her. "Mistress, Mistress, I am here, I..."

Nicanor pulled her away and checked Medea's pulse. "She is still with us. Help me get her back into bed." He picked her up, aware of how little she weighed. "Send for Halaten, she probably fainted when she tried to get up, but he needs to look her over."

He waited in the outer room until the doctor had examined her. He came out wiping his brow. "Well, she did not break anything when she fell but she must have hit her head on that table, she has a good-sized lump on her head."

"Has she regained consciousness?"

"Somewhat. She will be sore from the fall but should come fully awake soon. Master Nicanor, I am shocked at how thin she has become."

He closed his eyes and rubbed the back of his neck. Maybe Halaten should be told what was going on. Maybe he could get Patharus to see Medea needed help. "When you finish here, Halaten, I would like you to stop and see me before you report this to Patharus. There are things you both need to know."

Chapter Thirty-Eight

Be ready to give a defense to everyone who asks you a reason for the hope that is in you.
– 1 Peter 3:15

Until she mentioned Belte, Daphne was so discouraged she hardly listened to what Leah said about her visit. "Anna was so excited when she heard her children's nanny was a believer. She is anxious to see if Belte has spread the good news to any of the other servants."

"That is wonderful, but what did you mean by an opened door?"

Leah's smile lit up her eyes. "I told Anna about your being possessed by a demon and how you came to be a slave. I hope you do not mind, she just seemed so hungry to hear more of how the Holy Spirit brought you to Christ."

"No, that is alright, but—"

"Here is the best part. Anna wants to hear your whole story and she wants their slaves to hear it too."

Daphne faced her. "Really? Her slaves? Would Bacchus allow that?"

"Evidently she thinks so. I get the impression he does not deny her much."

"But I know how Romans feel about anyone who teaches customs which are not lawful for their citizens to receive or observe...especially if it denies their Emperor's deity. That is what got the apostle Paul in trouble in Philippi."

"I asked her about that, and she said since it would be on their private estate, and if her husband approved, it would not matter." She drew close, hardly able to bear her excitement. How do you feel about it? Would you be willing to tell what Christ has done for you?"

"Oh…I do not know. I have never spoken in front of a large group of people. I am not sure I could do that."

They arrived at the inn and Anna patted her arm. "Well, you pray about it and trust the Lord to lead you. If you decide to do it, Anna suggested we send word as to when and she would arrange for the slaves to come listen if they chose to. She said after dinner would be best. That would not interfere with work."

Daphne could not sleep. Disappointment over her failure to find her family pushed Anna's invitation to the back of her mind. She moaned a prayer. "Lord, what am I going to do? I came all this way to find my family and now I do not know where to turn."

Place your cares in My hands and remember what I called you to do.

With tears, she recommitted her family to His care and began to mull over promises she knew and loved. *I will never leave you or forsake you...when my heart is overwhelmed lead me to the Rock that is higher than I... He is our very present help in time of trouble.* Peace descended and she was close to sleep when the last part of the Lord's counsel invaded her thoughts.

Remember what I called you to do.

The prompt was so strong she sat up, almost expecting His presence to light the dark room. Her mind cleared and she whispered, "Lord, I remember Paul's admonishment, that my gratitude should lead me to use my newly found freedom for

You. But I thought You meant for me to go back to Delphi and expose the myth of Apollo worship to families like mine."

How many oppressed people have touched your heart?

It seemed a strange question but as she thought about it. Patharus' slaves and those owned by others that she knew came to mind. Her father's, torn from their families, those like deaf and dumb Nectari, sold to a brothel at the slave auction. The slave who suffered an undeserved whipping by their overseer. Kawit and those like her who struggled with the heartbreak of separation from loved ones. The distraught girl at the market owner's office. Some she had only heard about through Melita, but all still on her heart.

You are not limited to Delphi. Many need to hear from you of the love of God.

"But Lord, I cannot teach people, I do not know enough, I —"

I have called and equipped you by my Spirit to be my witness. To tell of your past life, and how I rescued you out of the kingdom of darkness and brought you into the kingdom of My dear Son.

She swallowed the lump that rose in her throat. "Yes, Lord, I will do whatever you ask. I know You will go with me, and Your strength will be my guide."

Sleep forsaken, she was wide awake. Her thoughts grappled with what she would say to those who might accept Anna's invitation. Leah's call to breakfast found her sound asleep but she hurried and joined the others.

Asher teased. "You look sleepy. I hear Anna wants you to come tell your story...are you going to do it?"

She sighed. "Yes. I am a little nervous, but God has assured me He will be with me. I can hardly believe how this all came about. My stay with you two, being at the Parthenon at the same time as Belte, your friendship with Anna that allowed me to meet with her, and now a chance to tell others about the love and mercy of the Lord. Surely He had this all planned before I ever arrived."

Leah laughed. "Actually, before the world was formed. Shall I send word to Anna that you will come?"

Daphne raised her brows and held out both palms. "It seems to be what the Lord brought me all the way from Philippi to do." Silently, she commanded the apprehension that threatened to unnerve her, to leave in the name of Jesus. ""Yes, tell her I will come as soon as she would like...and I hope you two will go with me."

Word was sent and received that this very night would be good. Daphne gulped at the quick response and told Batano to be free to enjoy the day to himself. Most of her day was spent in prayer and seeking the Spirit's guidance. "And Lord, please prepare the hearts of those who will be there, to open to Your amazing love and grace."

Leah prepared an early dinner so the four of them could arrive right after Bacchus' slaves were fed and finished their duties.

Their master did not object as Anna led the four of them out into a large courtyard. Daphne clutched her arms to her sides and took a deep breath. The place was jammed with men and women sitting on serving tables or benches. Mothers casually nursed their infants while they corralled toddlers and called older children to come sit.

Quiet descended in unison when Anna stood before them. "This is Daphne, Belte's friend and former owner." Many turned to Belte and smiled their approval. "She has come to share with you her journey into a freedom greater than any earthly bondage bestowed upon you at birth."

Daphne willed her voice not to waver. "Thank you for coming tonight. You have heard that my father once owned Belte and all of her family, and to this day I thank God for her love and influence on my life." Her former nanny beamed. "I am sure you all wonder how I would need such a freedom, born a wealthy landowner's daughter."

Their vigilant attention spurred her on. She scanned the crowd, made eye contact with many, and swallowed hard. Lord, I yield to your strength.

She told of her decision to override her doubts and join the temple of Apollo for her family's sake. She explained her panic when it resulted in being assigned to marry a temple priest, and how she snuck down into the bowels of the temple to find if its claims were true.

"It was there I found its world-renown divination to be a sham. But while I waited for a chance to leave unseen, the high priest charged into the room chased by an underling who murdered him before my eyes. The priestess on duty discovered me, cursed me, fell from her stool, and died. I tried to flee, tripped and was knocked unconscious."

As one, an audible gasp rose. Her confidence grew and she continued. "I was totally unaware of the spiritual world that surrounds us. There is the one true God in heaven who desires to help us and do us good, but there is another force. He is called the god of this world, but he is not a god, he is Satan, the ruler of the underworld. He wants nothing more than to lead us into his kingdom of darkness and destroy us. He is a liar and the father of liars, and he sends out evil, demonic beings to harass and even possess unprotected people.

"Because of my commitment to a false god, the door of my soul was open to evil. While I lay unconscious, a wicked demon of divination left the dead body of the priestess and invaded my vulnerable being."

Skepticism rose among the men and fear in the women. Wide eyed, mothers clutched their children. She sent up a desperate prayer. Help, Lord, I do not want to fail you. She took a deep breath and continued. "Even then, God our heavenly Father was with me. He had already devised a plan to bring me to Himself and free me of a life of horror." To her relief, the people relaxed, their postures signaled she go on.

"On the way home from the temple my father was killed in a storm. Soon after, my family discovered he was deeply in debt. A friend arranged for the deficit to be handled, but the magistrates decided our estate had to be sold immediately. Everything went up for auction including our slaves. When the proceeds were not enough, they callously decided my family also must be sold to satisfy the city's claim."

Heads turned and murmurs rippled at the announcement. "My mother, two brothers and I ended up at the slave auction here in Athens. There, we were separated from each other." She cleared her throat. "I have not seen any of them since." She wiped tears from her cheeks as many of the women nodded compassion born of a similar experience.

Chapter Thirty-Nine

By this my Father is glorified that you bear much fruit.
– John15:8

Daphne filled her lungs and regained her composure. Nods from Leah and Asher, along with Anna, encouraged her. Batano stood off to one side with Belte, their attention on those who focused on Daphne.

"Three men from Philippi found I possessed a *teraphim* and bought me with the intention of using me to tell fortunes. I had no idea how to do that or how they would profit from it. Soon, I discovered it assured me of an easier life and protection from the lustful intentions of their overseer. At first the demon acted like a friend. He wooed me to believe he wanted to help people. Each day, I went into the city and followed his instructions on how to tell fortunes.

"The endeavor was successful for my owners but devastating for me. To keep safe and secure, I took part in a ritual that led unscrupulous men to triumph over innocent people or one another. Each session ended with the demon coercing my solicitor to commit his life to a false god, and his money to Apollo's temple. Once the demon convinced them of his ability to grant their desires, he had no problem securing that commitment. Those who did not follow through, he led to destruction. My integrity was compromised to a point where I once tried to kill myself. I had opened my soul to evil and helped men make the same mistake. The demon claimed to be a spokesman for the god, Apollo, but as with all false gods he was an evil spirit from the pit of hell. His task was to keep men from the knowledge and truth of the one True God and His Son, Jesus Christ."

A muscular man with a shaved head slowly made his way to the front of the group. He glared at her. She ignored him and concentrated on her story.

"For over a year I lived out this horror, torn between my conscience and my need for protection. Near the end of that period, thankfully, a true man of God and his helpers arrived in Philippi. They began to teach people about our Heavenly Father and His Son, Jesus Christ. My heart yearned to learn of this God, of the love, grace, and forgiveness they spoke of, but the demon made it nearly impossible. Because he recognized the power in the name of Jesus to save any who came to believe in Him, he would threaten and punish me if I even dared to listen. He forced me to follow these men, to curse and mock their mission. Through my lungs, he screamed warnings of the consequences to any should they forsake Apollo. I had been cursed by him with the evil eye and many who heard my ranting ran off in fear. This went on for several weeks." Her voice caught. "By this time, I ceased to care if I lived or died. All I wanted was to be free of this voice within me, but as of yet I did not know what he was, nor of the power to make him leave."

The baldheaded man had worked his way to a bench in the front row. His arms were folded across his chest and his body rocked from side to side as if ready to pounce. The hood of darkness that covered his face made her shiver.

"The final time the demon forced me to follow and revile these godly men, he pushed me right up front so I could scream taunts into their faces. Their leader's patience evaporated and at last he balked at the lying accusations. He stood up, pointed directly at me, and commanded in the name of Jesus for the demon to leave me. Because of that powerful name, the evil spirit had no choice but to obey. I was thrown to the ground, torn and bruised, but finally free. The oppressive load I had carried was gone!"

To her surprise, except for the disgruntled man, the slaves shouted and clapped their hands. She knew from a year of living as one of them, how stories were loved and passed on. She smiled and whispered, "Lord, help me make them see this is not just another tale."

They quieted and she continued. "A woman named Lydia, a convert of the true God, took me into her home and explained why the name of Jesus had power to deliver me. That He is the Son of the Most High God who loved us so much that He came to earth and willingly spilt His sinless blood on a cruel Roman cross to set us free. From the beginning God ordained that without the spilling of blood there is no forgiveness of sin. His Son, our Lord Jesus became the sacrifice for all mankind, and if we believe in Him our sins are canceled, our spirit comes alive in Him, and we are born again by the Spirit of God. She told me that Jesus died on that cross, but God, the Father, raised his body from death and took Him to heaven. And that same promise is ours when our time on earth is over. He loves and desires each of us to receive that same eternal life. You will never deserve it and cannot do anything to earn it. It is a gift, free to any who believes." She paused long enough to let her emotions quiet. "Lydia helped me pray and ask Jesus to come into my heart and be my God."

The bald man jumped to his feet. "You people have not swallowed this have you? There is no freedom for people like us. We were born into slavery and that will be the end of us. No God cares about you and me. This is our lot, and it will not change. A man who died on a cross cannot do anything for us. He cannot change our lives." His lips curled in a vicious sneer. "There is no 'one true god,' Jesus is a myth. Do not listen to her, there are many gods...stay with the one you know."

Murmurs ran through the crowd, his years of dominant influence unsettling. He jerked his head back toward her as if he was about to go on. She swallowed her panic. Lord, how do I answer this? I am afraid I will lose them to these lies.

Remember who is the father of liars, the same one who sent the demon to destroy you.

She glanced at the crowd. Confusion etched many faces. Lord, what shall I do?

Take the authority I have given you and do what my followers did when you were forced to persecute them.

A picture of her harassing the believers flashed. A man she later learned was Silas, one of Paul's team, pointed directly at her and commanded she be still. She recalled the pain in her hip as the force of his words threw her to the ground. Her heart raced but she drew upon God's promise to be with her. The man turned and faced her. She raised her hand, pointed at him and commanded, "Be still in the name of Jesus Christ."

The man backed a step, fell over the bench, and lay still. A gasp ran through the slaves and whispers of "What kind of power is this?"

Anna quickly moved through those who gathered around him. Most believed he was dead. "He is alright, people. Please take your seats." She gestured to their overseer who took the man to his quarters. Undaunted, she addressed her slaves. "You all know that Daragus has lived a life you may not want to adhere to. The one true God Daphne is telling you about, is my God too and I encourage you to hear her out." Her revelation sent nudges of acceptance through the crowd. A handful of slaves left the compound but most stayed, awed at Daphne's courage.

Assurance enveloped her. "I am sorry that was necessary, but the Lord wants you to hear this message and give you the opportunity to become His children. The ruler of darkness intended to lead this son of disobedience to blaspheme His holy name, but God has not allowed it."

The slaves settled and she went on. "After I prayed and asked Jesus to be my Lord, joy and deep peace came upon me. But Satan shattered that peace when Lydia told me   God says unless a slave's freedom is granted, they should remain in the state in which their new life began. You see God sees His children as one in Christ, whether male or female, Jew or Greek, slave or free. To return to my master without the demon's input meant I could no longer tell fortunes." Her voice shook. "I was terrified of losing my protection and reassigned to the horrors some of you may have experienced in the past.

"Lydia, advised me to obey God and trust Him to work it out, but fear engulfed me, and I left in the night. As I ran, an earthquake hit our city and I found my master trapped under a large section of a broken building. I fought an urge to leave him for someone else to find but I could not do it. He had always been fair and kind to me.

"I tried to free him but was not strong enough. Aftershocks shook what was left of the building above him and he commanded me to leave. I kept trying anyway and about that time his son came along and the two of us finally freed him. My owner was so grateful he granted me my freedom."

Sounds of "awe," ran through the crowd. "To this day I praise God that obedience was the path God laid out for me to receive the deepest desire of my heart."

Her smile was broad. "So, I went from a pampered daughter to slavery and back again, but the freedom I have experienced in the Lord, Jesus Christ is the greatest thing that ever happened to me. I have discovered how much He loves me and that I can trust Him with my life, even when things look hopeless."

Compassion urged her on as she gazed at the slaves. "I am not telling you that if you chose to make Jesus your Lord you will be set free, but that no matter what you face in this life, He will be with you and take care of you. Plus, you will spend eternity with God. I am still learning about Jesus' great love and power, but if you have any questions, I would be glad to try to answer them."

A young woman stood up. "If your God is up in heaven, how is it you say He will help us?"

Daphne smiled. "That is a good question. Father God knows that because Jesus returned to heaven, you would need someone here to help to live out your new life in Him. So, He sent the third person of His Godhead, His Holy Spirit, to come and reside in each believer. As soon as you become His child, you will be indwelt with this precious gift and He will be with you and in you forever to comfort, guide, protect, and give you wisdom and so much more."

More jumped up and asked questions. She raised her palm, "Wait, one at a time." She took a deep breath and whispered, "Holy Spirit, please give me the right answers." It grew late and she did not want to impose on Anna's household. "Dear ones, we need to leave now and tomorrow I am going back to Corinth, but it is my hope that my friends over there," she pointed to Leah and Asher, "will come frequently and strengthen you in your new journey with God.

"Now, if any of you would like to receive Jesus as your Lord tonight, come down here by me and we will pray." To her delight many nodded and hurried to her side. "Alright, here is what we will do. If you now believe in your heart that Jesus is God's Son whom He raised from the dead, you must speak it with your mouth. I am going to lead you in a prayer and after me, you must repeat the words aloud. Please bow your heads before Him." She swallowed the fountain of joy and excitement that billowed and led the slaves in a prayer for salvation. At her, "Amen," many voices followed.

She motioned to Batano, who was deep in conversation with Belte, that it was time to leave.

Chapter Forty

The heart knows its own bitterness.
– Proverbs 14:10

Daphne wiped the last of her tears as her carriage left Athens. Most flowed at the finality of not being reunited with her family. Some at leaving Asher and Leah, but the pure joy of how God moved the night before, refilled her eyes much of the trip.

Once again Batano rode up top with the driver. Asher had made sure the driver was not the one she had arrived with, nor did he plan to stop at that same inn. The ride would be long, but she relished the solitude, so much to think about, to plan. Lord, You were so faithful last night. I could have never answered all those questions on my own. Thank you for the prompting of Asher and Leah when I faltered. I learned so much from them and I believe their input will make it easier for the slaves to accept them as mentors and teachers.

Her thoughts ran back to Corinth. It will be good to see Melita and Epaphroditus. Maybe I can stay a few days before I leave for Delphi. I would love to hear Paul again. She grinned. Melita will probably be about to burst with what she has learned.

Daphne's mind hopped from one thing to another. The maze lulled her to doze until the driver stopped for lunch at the same creek of the first trip. Batano joined her for the feast Leah had packed. A lamb mixture wrapped in grape leaves, fruit and Leah's special bread. As usual, he was quiet. She chatted about the majestic mountains and the wildflowers for a while, then asked him about his talks with Belte.

"Oh, just about her time with your family. She thinks a lot of you."

"She was very dear to me, always looking out for me and taking my side."

"It's not like that for us."

"You mean at Patharus' estate?"

"Yes."

"But you and Nicanor seem to have a good rapport."

"Oh, he is good to me, not hard to please."

"What then?"

"I did not really know him before he became Patharus' heir, we were not friends."

"And now?"

"No complaints. It just is not like what you had with her and your overseer...Jasper, was that his name? It sounds like they were almost part of the family, friends. Most slaves do not have that. Did you before Patharus set you free?"

She shook her head. "No. Patharus was kind to me, and I sensed I could trust him, but he never talked to me about anything other than what he had given me to do. And I never met his wife."

"Well, your former nanny said it is good where she is but not the same as at your father's either. Maybe 'good' is the best slaves can hope for. She seems content, but she still is a slave and who knows where she will be tomorrow." He paused and Daphne waited, silent.

He watched a hawk circle before he looked back at her, disgust scrunching his brow. "Some have it hard, like when Stello was our overseer. Each day we wondered what reason he would find to beat someone. We are better off than most, but our lives still are not our own. Patharus could hire another 'Stello' any day. "

At the driver's signal, Batano jumped out to refill their jugs before they left. She sipped the cold water and welcomed his choice to avoid the hot sun and ride inside. Both were quiet, him feigning a preoccupation with the scenery, her sifting his point of view. The same longing, for freedom she had felt, rekindled by memories of Stello's abuse.

"Batano, I am not that far removed from your desire to be free, and Nicanor is not either. I wish freedom were mine to grant but of course it is not. But I do know what the difference in my family was, at least between Belte and me. It was love. Even before she came to Christ, she loved me because it was her nature to love, especially children. But as I grew, her knowledge of the love of Jesus increased, and that is why she can be content though her circumstances have not changed. My response was to love her back. That is the way it is with Jesus, He loves us first and we respond to that love. That is how it is with people in the Lord too, they give love and draw it from others."

He leaned back, cocked his head, and studied her. When he did not respond she yielded to a check in her spirit that confirmed for now she should drop the subject. Still, she cherished that he had shared his heart with her. Is that why you allowed me to become a slave, Lord? Were you preparing me to be one people like Batano could relate to? Please heal his resentment and reveal Yourself to him. It is so hard to grasp freedom that liberates peace in your soul when you are a slave.

By the time they reached the halfway point and the driver pulled into the inn, both were ready to get out and stretch, have a quick dinner and get some sleep. To her relief, their accommodation was fine and they were back on the road at dawn.

It was nearly dark when they pulled in front of the inn where Melita and Epaphroditus waited. She rushed out, gushing with joy at Daphne's return. "I knew I should not go tonight. Could that have been the Spirit telling me you would arrive, and I needed to be here?" Her head bobbed with expectation. "Are you all right? Did you find your mother? Tell me everything. Have you eaten? No of course not, I will run ask the owner to fix you both something."

She was gone before Daphne could catch her breath. Batano joined her and they munched on pita bread filled with leftovers and listened to Melita's version of Paul's teachings. "And the worship is so wonderful. Hundreds of voices would sing in the Spirit and blend into beautiful praises to our Lord. Oh, I am so glad you are back, Misses. I hope you get to hear him many times before we leave."

"Me too." Daphne shared parts of her unsuccessful effort to find her family before she suggested they leave the rest for morning. "Has your stay here worked out all right? Do we have the same room?" Melita nodded and they waved Batano off to sleep with the workers. He hesitated but she assured him she would be safe and led the way up the stairs. "I would love to stay up and see Epaphroditus, but I am so tired."

Melita's breath caught. "Be sure to be up to see him in the morning, Misses. He leaves for home before noon. He has so hoped you would return in time to give him a report for master, Nicanor."

She grimaced. Lord. You showed me in Athens I can do anything with You at my side, but this means I am truly on my own, apart from You if course.

I will be with you, and I will perfect that which concerns you.

The promise whispered to her spirit, restored her peace. Thank You, Lord. I believe You.

At breakfast Epaphroditus lingered over their food, each filling the other in on all that happened the nearly two weeks she had been gone. "I have learned so much more of the depth of the Son of God's finished work on the cross and I cannot wait to get home and share it with our people. Paul is steeped in the history of those of us who are Jewish, and he ties it all to the Messiah. Back home, we have hardly stuck our toes in the water of the power of the Holy Spirit, or of God's grace and favor that make all things possible. I need to explain more fully of the blessing of being filled with the fullness of God and the power to witness that comes after being baptized in the Holy Spirit. I could go on and on."

Daphne sighed. "I never tire of hearing it. I wish you were not leaving so soon."

"Me too, but my family awaits my return and our church needs to hear more of the revelation that came with God's Son. I will pass on all you have told me to Nicanor. I am so sorry you did not find your family but do not give up, God still has a plan."

Melita and Batano joined her to wave Epaphroditus off. "Do not hesitate to send Nicanor word of your plans by the ship we arrived on. The captain said he would be glad to carry your messages to Neapolis."

Melita spent the morning washing Daphne's clothes while she caught up some sleep. She bathed and Melita washed her hair. "Thank you, friend. It is such a relief to have you doing my hair again. It is so thick I am afraid it looked unruly while I did it myself in Athens."

"I am sure you did fine. Did I tell you Paul often speaks in the afternoon at one of the believer's homes? Her name is Chloe, and she holds church in her courtyard on the Lord's day. Would you like to go, or do you need more rest?"

"No, I mean I would love to go. Between what you and Epaphroditus told me, I missed a lot of good teaching."

They had lunch and Batano and the two of them set off for the city. Melita led the way past the temples and shrines to the outskirts of the city where small homes filled the streets. She pointed at a somewhat larger house with spacious surroundings. "There it is. See all the people, that means Paul is going to speak."

They entered through the gate and were greeted by smiles. A wiry woman with grey hair hurried over. "Good to see you, Melita. Who are your friends?"

She introduced Daphne and Batano. "Welcome to our meeting. I am Chloe and I am so glad you could come. Please find a seat. Paul will be here shortly."

The area soon filled with people. Daphne whispered to Melita, "Is this where he speaks at night, too?"

"Not usually. Those crowds are even bigger, so he uses that large building in the city where we first heard him."

The chatter quieted when someone started praising the Lord in song. Soon, most joined in. A spirit of worship descended, and Daphne found herself carried into a deeper awareness of His presence than she had ever known. The music ebbed just as Paul stood before them.

Chapter Forty-One

Poisoned by bitterness.
– Acts 8:23

Nicanor gave Halaten a quick overview of what was happening with Medea. He explained the destructive beliefs taught by her visitor, though the doctor probably would not grasp their importance. "The woman professes a vow of poverty is a necessary part of rigorous self-discipline, while she carries off Medea's treasures." Halaten listened politely, but his brows rose at Nicanor's emphasis of how those vows included denying oneself through fasting.

"These people teach the body is evil, a prison to escape in order to be united with God at death. I have tried to talk sense to her but have gotten nowhere. Somehow Medea has latched onto the idea that excessive fasting will bring her that assurance and the peace she so badly needs."

"And who is this woman? Does Patharus know of all this?"

Nicanor sighed. "To a point, yes. I have tried to make him see how dangerous this is granted Medea's poor health, but she has convinced him she is fine. Either he refuses to see the changes so obvious to you and me, or he does not want to confront or upset her. Halaten, I am worried. Could this extreme fasting take her life, or am I overreacting?"

"No. I too am concerned. Her pulse was quite weak, and her skin has the touch of one who is dangerously dehydrated. Not good in her ongoing condition." He stroked his beard. "Trouble is, you cannot make someone eat or drink if they decide not to. But if she does not reverse this pattern, we could very well lose her. Thanks for informing me. I fully intend to make Patharus understand the danger she is in. I will let you know what course he decides to take."

He followed the doctor to the door, making a mental note to pray for an opportunity to explain to this caring man the difference between religious activity and a relationship with the one true God. "Thanks, Halaten. I hope he listens to you."

The next morning, Patharus did not mention Medea's fall or Halaten's visit, so Nicanor chose not to bring it up. After a full day of assigning priorities with their overseer, meeting with a man Patharus had contracted to do some work on a storage building, and several other matters, he decided to check on Medea. He arrived at her suite just as a woman in black garb was leaving. In her arms she carried one of Medea's tapestries, a favorite of a mother deer and her fawns drinking from a brook at sunset.

The woman put her head down and attempted to hurry past. "Just a moment, madam." She looked up and he drew a sharp breath. "Tanis...is that you?"

She tried to get around him, but he blocked her way. She drew herself into a defensive stand and glared at him. "Please excuse me."

Momentarily, he reasoned within himself, this could not be the same woman who used to attend Epaphroditus' meetings, could it? But it was, she had sat next to the jailer's wife for months after Paul's visit. "Tanis, what are you doing here? I cannot believe you are the person who has carried off Medea's treasures. What are you thinking? I have not seen you at our fellowship for a while and now it seems you are spreading untruths about Jesus not being the way to God the Father. Why have you departed from the faith?"

Her face wound into a snarl. "I do not have to answer to you. "You and your precious bride think you are better than anyone else because somehow you conned the mighty Patharus to make you his heir." Her lips curled like a vicious dog. "My husband invited you to visit our adjoining property so you could meet *our* beautiful daughter and you did not give him the courtesy of an answer."

Bitterness spewed as she vented "I was at Lydia's when you used to sneak out and come to her meetings. People treated you like someone special, but I knew you were nothing but a slave who came into all you own because of Patharus. Now I have found people who understand blessings do not fall on someone who professes Jesus as the only way to God, but on those who diligently seek superior knowledge and earn it through sacrifice."

Nicanor's jaw hung. How could she turn what she took to be rejection into such jealousy and anger? He could hardly believe what gushed like a crack from a broken cistern.

Tread with mercy, the Holy Spirit whispered. Vengeance has opened the door of her heart and Satan has lodged like a squatter in the void.

Instantly, Nicanor's need to defend himself vanished and left only sorrow he had offended her family, and sadness at such spiritual deception. "Tanis, I am so sorry to have offended you, but—"

"Do not be sorry, I have discovered a better way to connect with God." She lifted her chin. "I have reached a spiritual essence that those of you who think you will find it in Jesus will never know. He was not God, He was just one of..."

He held up both hands. "No. that is enough. You have been badly misled. That self-willed opinion you have adopted is independent of the truth. Medea is a hurting, confused woman and you will not feed her this garbage any longer." He reached out and jerked the tapestry from her arms. "I do not know what you have done with all her things, but I suspect this covetous practice and your bent on revenge is a phony vow of poverty. It appears you have used your zeal for these doctrines of demons to add to your own treasury.

Her face blushed a bright red. "Well, I, I..."

"I do not want to hear anymore. You are to leave, and I forbid you from coming here ever again. But I promise to pray for you, that you will seek God's forgiveness and find your way back to His unlimited grace."

With a loud huff she left, leaving him shaking his head. Oh, Lord, how could that happen? I did not purposely ignore her family's invitation. In Your mercy, please open her eyes to the truth.

After she cleared the gate, he sent word to Rybic, their gate keeper, that the woman was never to enter again. A soft knock on Medea's door quickly brought Danatel. "Oh, master Nicanor, I gave her some sleeping powders after that woman left and she is sound asleep. I do not think I should wake her."

"No, do not. How is she doing? Has her head healed?"

"Yes, the bump is about gone but she suffers headaches. Halaten gave her some powders, but I suspect it is partly because she hardly eats."

"Have you received any instructions from Patharus about her refusing food?"

"No, the Kupio has not sent messages of any kind. I have tried to get her to go dine with him, but truth is she's too weak to get there."

"Danatel listen. I met up with that woman as she was leaving, and I told her she was not to ever come here again. Here is the tapestry she was about to make off with." The servant's eyes grew wide. He held up his hand. "Do not be afraid, put it aside for now. I do not want the Kupios to know what I have done just yet. Let us wait and see if she will let it go and get back to eating. If the woman shows up or anything goes wrong with Medea send word right away, all right?"

Two days later a young servant knocked on his door. "Master Nicanor, the Kupios' servant asked me to tell you her mistress is not doing well and please to come as soon as you can."

He laid aside plans he had been studying and hurried to Medea's suite. Her servant opened the door on his first knock, her eyes red and her face puffy. "Danatel, what is it? Has she fallen again?"

"No, she will probably have me beaten again but I —"

"Beaten? What do you mean? Medea had you beaten?"

"Yes." She showed him the welts on her arms and legs. "She is sure it is my fault that the woman has not come around. Says I must have told her not to come or done something to stop her." She burst into tears. "She is asleep now, but I do not know what to do."

"Danatel, I am so sorry. I did not mean for you to take the brunt of Medea's frustrations. How long do you think she will sleep?"

"Usually a couple of hours."

"Listen. I will be working at my place this afternoon and I want you to send word the minute she wakes, understand? We need to get to the bottom of this."

She nodded and he left. A confrontation was necessary. The question was, should Patharus be in on it?

Chapter Forty-Two

I received from the Lord that which I also delivered to you.
– 1 Corinthians 11:23

Paul's gaze swept those gathered to hear him "Beloved, grace and peace to you from our Father and our Lord, Jesus Christ,". Daphne sat on the edge of her chair, eager to hear every word. He introduced a young man named Timothy and asked him to begin the meeting with prayer.

She whispered to Melita. "He was with Paul in Philippi."

Melita smiled and gestured toward a man standing off to the side. "They call that one, Luke, was he there too?"

"Yes. How excited Nicanor would be to see him. He tried to help find me before the earthquake shook the jail where Paul and Silas were held. Is Silas here too?" Melita looked around and pointed out a man leaning on a staff.

"I did not get to meet them at the last meeting before Paul left, Have you ever met them or talked to them?"

Melita nodded and both grew quiet as Paul began. "There is power in the name of Jesus to overcome any attack of the enemy. We all need a firm understanding of the exceeding greatness of the working of His mighty power toward believers." Daphne could not stop mulling over his admonishment. How she would need that power when she arrived in Delphi.

The thought sent a shiver of wonder down her arms, and thanks that it would be his power, not hers. Paul continued. "Beloved, the same power that raised Christ from the dead and seated Him at the Father's right hand is in you. Every other name that can be named is under His feet."

Her heart leapt with gratitude. God had revealed that Divination was the name of the demon that had possessed her, its evil agenda conquered by the powerful name of Jesus. Paul preached for several hours but no one left or wandered about. After he and his helpers prayed for those who were sick or had needs the meeting closed with an invitation to join him that night in the city.

She wanted to tell him again how much his ministry had done for her, but people clamored for his attention, and they needed to get back for dinner if they wanted to attend tonight's meeting. Chloe caught up with her and Melita before they left. "Daphne, Melita told me some of what you went through back in Philippi. Paul is not available to speak tomorrow afternoon, would you be willing to share your testimony with our people?"

She stared, so taken back by her request she could hardly process what the woman proposed. Why would people who hear Paul want to listen to her? Before she could respond Chloe touched her arm. "It sounds like you have quite a story and it would encourage us to hear it."

Daphne swallowed the lump in her throat. How could she refuse? Was this not what God asked her to do? "I... I would be honored to if you really think it would bless someone."

"Wonderful. Could you be here right after lunch?"

She agreed and Chloe promised to be in prayer for her. People smiled at her as Chloe circulated and passed the word.

The three of them arrived at Paul's evening meeting in time to squeeze into the nearly full room. She grinned at what Batano thought of all he heard, being he was somewhat of a captive audience. Lord, open his ears, I know you want him for your child.

That night Paul taught the need to be aware of the enemy's tactics and the discipline of daily covering oneself with God's armor, likening it to the protective covering a Roman soldier wore and listing each item.

On the way back to the inn, everyone was caught up in their own thoughts. Daphne mused. Lord, I know You are preparing me for battle. I am going to need salvation's helmet to protect my mind from drifting or forgetting my position in Christ. One by one she prayed over each piece of spiritual armor, especially the shield of faith to ward off the devil's attacks. I know how he works and ask for grace to send him sprawling when I speak Your word.

Again, Paul had put great emphasis on depending on God's power and not one's own. He ended the meeting with prayers for the sick. She was awed at the instant healings that followed the teaching of God's word. A man's crippled limb was restored. A child's blind eyes lost their scales, and a woman deaf from birth shouted God's praises as her ears opened to their first sounds.

After breakfast the next morning Daphne spent time alone in her room, praying and seeking God's direction. Speaking to Anna's slaves seemed less daunting than what Chloe had asked of her. How could she share the little she knew with these more knowledgeable people? "Lord, help me."

Be at peace, daughter. Remember all I have asked of you is that you bear witness to what happened to you and how it changed your life.

"But those people, Lord, they have heard Paul teach the oracles of God."

You are the only one who can tell your story. Trust me with the results.

Melita knocked and informed Daphne that the early lunch she requested was ready. She rose from her knees with peace that God would be with her. They arrived at Chloe's before the crowd trickled in. The meeting began with songs of praise and grew to be a courtyard full of people. She walked to the front with an assurance God would lead her.

Chloe introduced her and she began, slightly unnerved, when someone near the back shouted for her to speak up. As at Anna's, she gave a brief background of her life in Delphi. How her pampered life dampened her reluctance to join Apollo's temple and led her to pledge to the false god to please her family. She told of her inner turmoil that resulted in sneaking into the temple's adytum to find if Apollo was truly a god and finding it a sham.

Many of her listeners knew of the fallacy of Delphi's temple and nodded. Some, having been there, murmured as she told of seeing the high priest murdered, a fact the new leader had successfully blamed on a disgruntled patron. They listened intently as she discredited the divination and gasped as she told of the *pythia's* curse and the demon who invaded her body.

Everyone hung on to every word, sympathizing with her father's death and the slavery it brought upon her family. Quiet intensified as she told them of the demon's agenda to use her to tell fortunes and lead men into the kingdom of darkness and from the knowledge of God.

Unlike the slaves at Anna's, the people didn't cheer when she told how she was finally delivered by Paul from the horror of being possessed by an evil power of Satan. Instead, murmurs of "Praise You Jesus, thank You Lord," sounded throughout the courtyard. She ended with a short account of helping to free her master after the earthquake and his gratitude that led to her freedom.

She concluded by giving all the glory to the Lord. "I have nothing but praise for our glorious Savior who rescued me and brought me into His kingdom of light. Thank you for coming and patiently listening to my story."

Before she could leave the makeshift platform, several people rushed to see her. "Please," a woman said. "I believe I too have been harassed by a demon. It continually tells me I am not worthy of God's love. Will you pray for me?"

She saw herself nod, feeling inadequate. Lord, please give me how to pray. "Thank You, Lord, for my sister in Christ who is asking for your power of deliverance to set her free of this ugly demon." Daphne opened her eyes and laid her hand on the woman's head. "You demon of rejection who has been lying to this woman about the love of her Savior, Jesus Christ, I command you right now in the name of Jesus Christ to lose her and be gone forever. You are trespassing where you have no right and in the name of Jesus I take His authority given me and tell you lying spirit to flee in the precious name of Jesus."

Just as when Paul had prayed, the woman floated backwards into the hands of a man who had positioned himself behind and gently laid her on the ground. Many of the people began praising God and before she could grasp what it meant another woman took her hand. "Please, I too have battled a demonic spirit of infirmity. It threatens my life and keeps me from caring for my family. Will you pray for me too?"

She nodded and before most people left, she prayed for six or seven people who had been harassed by demonic spirits. Chloe came up and hugged her. "Thank you for being so open and unpretentious. People appreciated your humble spirit and your honesty."

Daphne released a deep sigh. "Thank you for asking me, I am awed at the response. I saw people fall to the ground after Paul prayed for them, but I had never experienced it myself. Everyone seemed to praise God when it happened. What does it mean? "

"Oh, my dear, what you saw were people being slain in the Spirit. Sometimes when people receive a blessing from God they are so overwhelmed by His presence they simple cannot remain standing. It is a good thing. A true sign God heard your prayers and desired to deliver them from the jaws of the evil one."

Her awe brought tears. She motioned to Melita and Batano and they left. As she walked, she whispered, Lord, I have a feeling You brought this all about for a reason. Is this what I will face in Delphi?"

Chapter Forty-Three

A friend loves at all times.
– Proverbs 17:17

Daphne remained in Corinth for a week, reveling in the opportunity to learn from Paul. She met Pricilla and Aquila, friends who worked alongside him making tents and hosting meetings. At a dinner in their home, she learned of his close involvement in their lives, and gleaned wisdom as they shared their journey.

Pricilla touched her hand. "Enough about us. Tell me about the effects of Paul's ministry in Philippi."

Daphne told of the trial Paul and Silas endured, and the growth of the church he established. They asked about her personal testimony, and she shared her story, along with Paul's challenge that determined her need to go to Delphi.

Pricilla smiled. "And you have been baptized into the fullness of the Holy Spirit and received power to be His witness?"

Aquila had been quiet but at Daphne's nod he spoke. "Then God will be with you and bless your obedience. Always bear in mind, young woman, that your sufficiency is from Him. You will not be alone." She left comforted by their vow to pray daily for her mission.

Batano accompanied her to the Lechaem Port the next day where she arranged for the three of them to leave for Delphi in the morning. That settled, they caught a different carriage to the Cenchrean Port to see if there was word from Nicanor. The ship they had arrived on was not in port, but a

255

dockworker pointed them to a small building where he said messages were kept.

An older woman appraised her with a suspicious frown. "And your name?" Her lisp was so pronounced Daphne hoped that was all she required. The lady disappeared into an inner room and returned with two messages. Daphne clutched the letters to her breast. Her heart soared as she tore open the first and found Patharus grew stronger each day. Nicanor ended with his love and hope to join her soon. The second, dated two weeks later, left her concerned and disappointed. Medea was not doing well, and he was afraid she might not survive. It too ended with his longing to be with her and a promise to send along any changes.

She kept her answer brief, Epaphroditus would have told him of her progress and of not finding her family. *I plan to leave for Delphi tomorrow and do so wish you were with me. Please pray I follow God's plan and people accept the good news I bring. I love you and miss you terribly."*

With sleepy indifference the old woman scribbled which ship was to carry the letter, but her attention quickened at the *denarius* handed her. "I know the captain of that ship and I assure you I will hand deliver it to him," Daphne wondered if she would follow through.

On the third day they arrived in Delhi. The accommodation had been cramped but compared to her first trip from the inlet off the Gulf, it was a delight. The small, familiar port revived memories of her family tied in a wagon, waiting to be shipped to a life of slavery. She blinked back tears and chastised herself. You cannot fall apart at each memory, or you will get nowhere.

They boarded a one-horse carriage that would take them, where? The driver awaited her request. "Oh, ah, to that inn in the city." She hoped it still stood. Melita was full of questions about Daphne's former life, but the misery on her mistress's face soon silenced her.

They neared the road to her former home. She lifted her chin and looked in the opposite direction. The inn was not busy, so she booked their largest room for herself and Melita. Again, Batano would bunk with their slaves. He followed her around the city the next morning while Melita freshened their clothing. Daphne passed familiar homes and market stalls, but turned her face from any who might recognize her. That afternoon she decided to try to find the only friend who had not deserted them when her family lost their freedom.

She left Batano by the gate and walked to the door of Cyrene's former home, expecting to hear she had married and lived elsewhere. A slave left to fetch Cyrene's mother. An immaculately dressed woman with a pleasant face welcomed her. "Good afternoon. My servant said you are looking for..." She cocked her head. "Daphne? Daphne, is that you?"

Her throat caught, touched to be remembered by someone from her former life. The past seemed long ago, as if it belonged to someone else. "Yes, it is me. I hoped to find Cyrene. Is she married? Does she live in Delphi?"

"Do come and sit down. How we have wondered about you and your family. Are they with you?"

The kind inquiry burst her resolve to stay her emotions. The woman offered her a small linen cloth and Daphne snuffed back her tears. "No, we were separated, and I was set free about a year ago. I do not know where they are or even if they are alive."

She led her inside to a chair. "Oh, my dear, rest here a few moments. Cyrene was married and lives very close. It will do her good to see you and hear of your family. I will send my servant and I know she will come the minute she hears you are here." She instructed her maid to bring water and left the room.

Daphne looked around the lovely alcove and tried not to envision the home her family had lost. She pictured Cyrene with her auburn hair and hazel eyes, her comical way of twisting her lips. I wonder what her mother meant by "It will do her good to see you?" A familiar voice called from the hallway, "Daphne? Daphne, are you really here?"

She stood and they rushed into one another's arms. They cried and laughed, hugged, and parted, and hugged again. "Daphne, look at you! You are beautiful! All grown up. I am so glad to see you. What? Has it been two years? Come sit with me, I want to hear everything."

Like the barely-teenagers they had been at their last meeting, both talked at once, each anxious to hear every detail of the other's life. Cyrene's mother joined the conversation and as Daphne fleshed out the details of her mother's fate and wiped her eyes.

"So that is how it happened. I never saw my family again after I was taken to from Athens to Philippi."

Cyrene's mother shook her head. "How awful. "Your poor mother. She was so delicate, such a perfect lady."

Cyrene turned to Daphne, "But you? There is something different, and it is obvious that you are not a slave now. What happened to you in Philippi?"

"It is a long story, but I ended up marrying the son of the man who bought me."

Cyrene squealed. "You are married? To his son? Tell me about him, he is not old then?"

Daphne laughed and told her all about Nicanor. "He is wonderful, and I love him with all of my heart."

"I cannot believe he let you come all this way alone."

"Things are not as rigid in Philippi as they are here and there are reasons I will get to later. He really cared about my desire to find my family."

Cyrene's voice fell. "That has to be love. I am so happy for you." She cleared her throat. "And you have just come from searching for them in Athens?" The smile was back in her voice.

"Yes. I spent weeks there but did not find them. Had no real assurance they remained in the area. But tell me about you. Your mom said you were married and live close by."

"Was married. Do you remember the family with the large estate near the east end of Delphi?" Daphne nodded.

"Yes. Well, the owner's wife died, and my father arranged the marriage. He was not real old, maybe my father's age, but after a year he was gored by a bull and died. The animal escaped and he tried to corral it by himself and... well, it was a long, agonizing death. Because he had no heir, his brothers stepped in and took the estate. They did give me enough money to buy a home here in the city close to my family."

Daphne reached for her hand, "Cyrene, I am so sorry."

She held up her hands, her lips curling like Daphne remembered. "Do not be. He was a good man, but it was an arrangement. I know he hoped I would produce a son." She sighed. "That did not happen. Now, tell me. Where are you staying?"

At Daphne's answer Cyrene insisted she come stay with her. "We have so much catching up to do. I want to hear more and wait till I tell you what became of Helene."

Chapter Forty-Four

So that they may know the truth.
– 2 Timothy 2:25

Nicanor paced. He had not felt this unsure of himself since becoming Patharus' son. *Lord, what do I do? Medea is out of control...may be dying. Patharus has not acted upon Halaten's report and does not comprehend the danger she is in. How I wish Daphne were here. She had a way of discerning what was really going on and how best to deal with it.*

Call on Me. I am your very present help in time of trouble.

He fell to his knees and leaned his head on a couch. "Lord, forgive me for trying to solve this instead of bringing it to You. Please open my eyes to what is behind Medea's struggle and show me how to get Patharus to see she needs help." He stayed and poured out his heart until peace descended and quieted his mind.

He rose, confident he had heard from God. Shortly, he found the doctor. "Halaten, I need you to come with me and either get Patharus to Medea's suite or her to his."

"Well, she is too weak to leave her quarters, but maybe his servants could help get him to her. What is going on, is she worse?"

"Yes and no. I will explain when we get to father."

Patharus' brows knitted when he saw Halaten enter behind Nicanor. He looked from one to the other. "So, what is this about? My healing off schedule...something wrong?"

Nicanor drew close and gestured for the doctor to join them. "No, Halaten says you are doing fine, Father. I believe he told you about Medea's passing out and falling a few days ago and of his concern for how thin she has become. Well, I—"

"Nicanor, we have been over this." His voice collapsed to a mumble. "I told you we have to let her decide for herself what she wants to believe. I send servants each day to make sure she is all right and she sends back that she—"

"And exactly when did you last see her, Father?"

Patharus opened his mouth but only exhaled.

"Think about it. We know she has been way too weak to join you for dinner for a long time and you still are not able to leave your quarters on your own."

"Well, yes. It has been a while and I miss being with her, but—"

"Father, you need to let us take you and see her for yourself. Halaten is as concerned as I am. He has arranged for your servants to carry you. We will be right behind and make sure you arrive safely."

"All right. All right, maybe in a few days I—"

"Father. I insist we do this now. Medea is out of control. Not just starving herself but this morning I found she had her long-time servant, Danatel, beaten for something Medea only imagined. We need to get to the bottom of this and help her while we still can."

Patharus sighed. "All right." He looked at Halaten. "Find a way to get me there."

"Danatel said she was asleep when I stopped earlier, that the powders put her out for about two hours so she should be awake by now."

Patharus nodded and Halaten left to figure out how they would transport him. He returned with two strong slaves who carried a sturdy, wooden plank. "I know you have walked some on your new leg since the apoplexy, but I am going to have you sit on this and they will carry you. Do not want to take a chance on a fall."

Nicanor whispered a quick prayer. Thank You,Lord. You made him see he should go, now please, prepare her heart to hear us.

Danatel's eyes grew wide when she opened the door and saw the Kupio. She glanced at Nicanor. "Master, I —"

"It is all right, Danatel. Is she awake?"

The servant nodded and stepped out of the way. The young men carried Patharus through the doorway. "Take him into her chambers," Nicanor said.

Medea called out, her voice weak. "Danatel, what is it?"

"It is me, Patharus said. I have come to see you." The others stayed in the receiving room while his servants helped him into a cushioned chair at her bedside.

Medea blinked as if she could not believe her eyes. "Patharus, you are here."

He covered his shock at her appearance, reached over and took her hand. "Yes, beloved, I have missed you. I know you fell and hit your head. Are you all right? You look so pale...and thin."

Nicanor left them to themselves for a while and then ordered Danatel to take some lunch into the room. She announced her coming and carried in a tray of soup, bread, and fruit, along with water and wine.

Patharus waited while Danatel propped Medea up. "Looks wonderful."

The table that broke when Medea fell had been discarded. Danatel carefully arranged her mistress's food on her tray and made sure everything was in reach for Patharus. He picked up his spoon and some bread and began to eat. Danatel returned to the outer room where Nicanor and Halaten waited. She looked at Nicanor and shrugged.

He nodded. "Wait until he sees she will not eat."

Soon, they soon heard, ""Medea, why are you not eating?" Her reply was muffled but they clearly heard Patharus begin to coax her. His plea turned to begging her to hear him. "Medea, you cannot go on like this. Halaten says you are in danger of losing your life." Nicanor sensed his father's growing frustration and signaled for Halaten to accompany him into the room.

"Father, I wanted you to see this for yourself." He nodded at the doctor who went to Medea's bedside. She glared at each of them while Halaten rubbed his hand over her arm and felt her forehead.

The doctor frowned. "I want you all to know how serious this is, The *Kupios* is dangerously dehydrated. To deprive yourself of enough water for a long period, some of which comes through the food we eat, can lead to death."

Patharus' voice cracked. "Why, Medea? I do not want to lose you. Why are you doing this?"

She shook as she pushed herself up on her elbows. "You do not understand. None of you understands." She glanced from him to Nicanor. "I am becoming an enlightened believer through

264

special knowledge, and I hope soon to break free of this world and reach a oneness with God."

Nicanor sighed and stepped close to her bedside, his voice tender. "Medea, you cannot earn your way into God's kingdom by denying your body. Salvation is a gift, free to anyone who asks. No one comes to the Father except through Jesus. He is the only way, the truth and the life."

Patharus clutched his wife's hand in both of his, "Please, Medea. Give up this, this religion or whatever it is. I do not want to lose you like we lost Elias"

She looked at him and whispered. "I am doing all I can to see him again. I have to know Elias is safe."

Patharus leaned onto the edge of her bed. "Beloved. Elias is gone. We have his ashes in the urn you keep here in your suite. You cannot—"

She screamed. "No. You are wrong! I will be with him again if I continue to escape the demands of my body. Do you not see I must remain disciplined and deny myself food and luxuries so I will qualify to be with Elias? I must, I must..." She gasped and her upper body folded toward the bed. Hysterics silenced her rant.

Patharus' jaw fell. He reached for her, but she pulled back, forced herself upright and clutched her hands to her chest. "You all need to leave. Danatel, come help me. Danatel, come this minute or I..." She paused, arrested by the shock on their faces.

Chapter Forty-Five

For you will be His witness.
– Acts 22:15

The next day Daphne moved from the inn into Cyrene's home. Her husband's brothers had been generous, and the house had rooms enough for Melita and Batano, but he decided to bunk with Cyrene's servants.

Cyrene suggested a walk around the village. She pointed to a well-worn road at the edge of town. "And that is the road to Janaze's home. We did not see her for a year after you left but when she finally produced an heir her husband softened and allowed visitors."

"Was he not pretty old when they married? I remember—"

"Yes. And stuck in the old ways, that a woman should not have a life outside her home. What a miserable time of it she has had." They continued and she recounted the changes in the lives of people Daphne once knew.

They drew close to her former home. "That Roman who bought my father's estate, does he still live there?"

Cyrene sighed and shook her head. "No, but he still owns it. I heard that right after your family left, he received a highly regarded appointment from Rome. He found an overseer willing to run it for him and left soon after. Who knows if he will ever return."

"I am not surprised. It meant nothing to him. He cheated my father out of it and would not find it hard to leave. Poor man, money and position were all that mattered to him."

Cyrene gave her a quick sideways glance and put her arm around Daphne's shoulders. "He will get what is coming to him one day, you will see."

Just before they turned from the main road through the city, a vehicle approached. Both stared at the unusually luxuriant carriage. Cyrene huffed. "That belongs to the temple. Wonder what it has come to the city for."

A face Daphne hoped to never see again stared at them from the rear seat. The man turned and leaned forward, straining for a better view. His jaw fell, disbelief replaced by an expression that struck fear in her heart. She covered her lips with both hands.

"Daphne! What is the matter? You look like you've seen a ghost."

The carriage wound out of sight before she could speak. "I think maybe I did. A part of my past I hoped never to revisit." Her voice shook. "Come on, let us go home and I will explain."

They arrived back with time to bathe before dinner. Daphne sank into the tub Cyrene's servants provided and had Melita help her wash her hair and get dressed. Cyrene's mother had insisted that they join her tonight and the three of them were soon seated. Daphne smiled at Cyrene's mother. "What a blessing to have a warm bath. You cannot imagine how I missed that when I was—"

Cyrene passed one of the many trays laden with food. "When you were what?"

"Oh, let us leave it until after dinner. Tell me what happened to Helene and about your family. I have not seen your father or your brother yet."

Cyrene's head cocked. "No. Father never stops until twilight. I wish for mother's sake he would slow down and enjoy life. Something drives him for more land, more crops, and more slaves. It is all that matters. He never lets up on himself or my brother, and I know the slaves resent having so little time with their families."

"That is sad, but on the other hand we might never have lost our home if my father were not so busy trying to make his father and the world see what a success he was. He spent money he did not have and was not a good steward over all he inherited. Now, what happened to Helene? You said I would not believe it."

"Well, you remember how thrilled she was to marry Minos' son. Turns out he is of the mindset that the more children the better. She had twin boys and then a girl and she is expecting again. By the looks of her, it could be more than one for the second time."

Daphne chuckled. They returned to Cyrene's home about an hour after dinner, where she settled them into a cozy nook that overlooked her garden. "All right. You have not old me a thing about your life as a slave in Philippi. What happened?"

Daphne's eyes closed and held for a few seconds. "Cyrene, it all started here in Delphi. You may find what I am going to tell you hard to believe and I need to have your word that you will keep it to yourself until I can fully explain it to others. Most people would never believe me or understand, but I trust you."

Cyrene's face darkened. "Something happened here before you left that I did not know about? But of course, you can tell me anything and it will go no further, we are friends."

Daphne squeezed her hand. "Thank you. Do you remember the time when the four of us, you and me and Helene and Semiele met at Helene's house shortly after the festival where I became part of Apollo's temple?"

Cyrene chuckled. "Yes. That was the time Helene brought out her family's idol and we tried to find out to whom our fathers had betrothed us." She grinned. "And you came right out and said Mino's was going to ask for her hand to marry his son, and you were right. How did you..." Daphne's troubled expression stifled her question. "I am sorry. Please go on."

"No, forgive me, I am trying not to let the memories get to me. It is hard to explain, but actually it was at that very festival that I knew I did not believe Apollo was real. Neither did I want to be a part of his temple, though I made the pledge."

Cyrene's brows shot up. "But I remember how angry you were when the rest of us became eligible the year before. Like that was the deepest desire of your heart."

"I thought it was, but I struggled with doubts even before that. My grandmother was an expert on Apollo's lore and the more she drilled me the more skeptical I became. Being accepted into the temple was the biggest thing that happened to girls like us, you know that. But as I look back, the glamour of the ceremony is what drew me and in spite of my doubts I could not let my parents down."

"You went through the ceremony. I remember watching—"

"Yes. I did. That is where my nightmare began." For the next few hours Daphne told her friend everything about being assigned to marry a priest and how she panicked and snuck into the adytum to try to find if Apollo could truly be a god. She told

269

of how the pythia babbled on her stool, followed by the priests who made up divination that best increased the temple's treasury. When she described how the current high priest slayed the former leader, Cyrene's hands flew to her face.

"So, was that who you saw in the carriage today? The high priest?"

"Yes. He does not know I saw him commit murder, but you remember he chose me to replace his deceased wife at the marriage of the priests that fall? Well, he was very angry when I was taken away, even came to the slave market in Athens with plans to purchase me. When the men who bought me refused to sell me to him, he insisted I tell them who he was, to confess that I rightly belonged to him. I decided to take my chances with my new owners rather than be married to a man like him. I told them I had never seen him before in my life. He was livid."

"Seeing him today in that carriage threw me for a moment. But I am covered by the protecting blood of Jesus, though he could make things hard for me."

"But back to the adytum. Right after the murder, the pythia saw me. She pointed at me and uttered an evil curse, clutched her chest and fell from her stool. I tried to run but fell and was knocked unconscious. Waking in a haze, I began to hear a voice although no one was around. Eventually, the priests came to see what kept their leader. I was terrified of being discovered, but the voice that spoke within me showed me how to remain hidden and got me out of there unseen."

Cyrene grimaced. "A voice that talked inside of you? Must have been a result of your fall."

"I wanted to think so, but remember that on the way home in a storm, my father was thrown from the carriage and killed. Meanwhile, my mother and I clung to our seats as it slid halfway out over a cliff and dangled like a child's toy. We expected to die but that voice directed me, and we escaped unharmed. Without his guidance I do not think we would have survived.

"We buried my father, and the voice spoke to me often, but it was not until that day at Helene's that it used me to tell someone's future. I did not know it at the time, but that voice was not a messenger from Apollo as I was coerced to believe, but a demonic spirit sent from Satan. A demon skilled in the deceptive practice of divination. The pythia he operated through for years was dead, so he exited her body and entered mine. I became his new assignment, to mold into a fortune teller who would deceive people to believe Apollo was real and to keep them from the truth."

Cyrene frowned. "I do not understand. Is a demon like one of our gods? And hell? Is that the awful place the gods take people through after they die?"

Daphne sighed. Lord if I cannot make my friend understand how will I help people know the difference between You and demons that pose as gods?

Stick to what happened to you.

"Friend, the reality of an afterlife spent in *Hades* is much worse than what we were told. It does not evolve into a happy place of music and joy. There is a God who is real, and He has made a way to be with us now and in the life to come. But, let me get back to what happened. I will always treasure the picture of you and your mother standing there

271

while our estate was auctioned off and we were forced into slavery. No one else cared about anything but were there to possess all we owned at the sale."

"I remember how painfully helpless we were to do anything."

"I know, there was nothing you could do. We were sold three times, and I was separated from my family. Three men who thought I was a sorceress bought me and took me to Philippi. I am ashamed to say I cooperated and learned to tell fortunes for my owners because it gave me a higher status. It kept me from a hard, degrading life that would have rendered me vulnerable to men's lusts."

Cyrene reached over and rubbed Daphne's arm. "How awful for you, but at least—"

"I know. It does not sound so bad, but you cannot imagine how it weighed on my integrity. To help men lie and cheat and even steal from unsuspecting neighbors or friends was hard to ignore. After I heard about Jesus, the true God, the worst thing was to have to demand each solicitor vow his allegiance to a god who was nothing but a cover for the evil one."

Cyrene shook her head and pulled Daphne up beside her. "I do not really understand all you have told me. Demons, the evil one, a God named Jesus. But the light in your eyes that tells me you believe what you have shared, and I want to understand. Let us get some sleep and you can tell me the rest tomorrow."

Daphne hugged her. "Thank you for taking me in and for listening. The God I have found is wonderful and I do so want you to know Him too."

Chapter Forty-Six

I will have compassion on whomever I will have compassion.
– Romans 9:15

Danatel stepped part way into the room but backed up at Nicanor's gesture. He put his hands on Medea's shoulders and eased her back into her pillows. After she quieted, he took her hand and spoke kindly to her. "Medea, I have talked with the woman who told you that you must fast and give up things to get to spend eternity with the heavenly Father.

"She is an angry, jealous woman who wants to get back at Patharus' household through you because I did not choose her daughter for my wife. She has become a slave to a corruption that promises freedom but brings bondage to any who receive it. I will grant that she may believe what she teaches, but her heart is not right, and her twisted truths will bring swift destruction that may destroy her...and you."

Patharus looked from Nicanor to her and back again. His brows flexed. "Why have I not been informed of this, Nicanor? Who is this woman?"

"She is the wife of your neighbor to the west. He insisted I visit his estate at a gathering after you introduced me as your heir. It was not hard to figure the invitation hinged on meeting his daughter. I am sorry to say I neglected to go, and the girl's mother has pounced on Medea's pain to extract revenge."

Medea's face fell. "But she, she told me..." She turned her face to the wall and whimpered like a puppy separated from its mother. "Please, please leave me. I..."

Halaten stepped over and took her pulse. "I think it would be best if we let the Kupios rest now."

Patharus opened his mouth to object, but Halaten's expression silenced him. He reached over and patted Medea's trembling body. "Get some rest, my love. I will be back to see you tomorrow." Halaten accompanied Patharus and his servants and soon only Nicanor remained.

He spoke quietly to Danatel. "Send word immediately if she, well, if she gets out of hand again. And do not be afraid. I hope we finally got through to her."

For the next week Medea continued to refuse food but did not mention the woman. Patharus came daily but she slept through most of the visits. Nicanor looked in on her, aware as the others that Medea was dying.

Danatel refused to give up. Daily, she coaxed her to no avail to eat or even drink. She retrieved the tapestry Nicanor had wrestled from the woman out of a closet where she had stuffed it, to hang it where her mistress could enjoy the peaceful scene. Behind it, with a few things that had belonged to Elias, sat the little boy's carved wooden boat. She took it to her mistress's bedside in hopes the memory might cheer her.

Medea stirred at her footsteps, blinked, and lifted her head. "His boat. It is Elias' boat!" She reached out and Danatel quickly to put it into her arms. "Yes, this is it." She cradled the toy to her chest as

274

tears ran down her cheeks. Several minutes passed before she called her servant back. "Danatel, send for Nicanor and be quick about it."

He arrived moments later and bent close to hear what Medea said. "Look, Nicanor, it's Elias' boat. It was his favorite. See how the cabin door opens and closes and the sails go up and down? He played with it for hours in the pond in the courtyard."

Nicanor stared at the toy, encouraged by the brightness in her eyes.

She rose on one elbow and pushed it toward him. "Do you see? It is the sign."

He started to protest but had no heart to discourage this latent spark of life. "What do you mean, Medea, what sign?"

"I asked the Supreme God of heaven for a sign that Jesus is His Son, and see, He has given it to me." She stroked the boat's smooth bow. "When Elias left to go find his father the day he became sick, he said to me, 'Mama, I want you to take care of this for me and bring it with you when we, when we...' Her voice cracked. "Do you not see? It is my sign. That was the last thing he said to me. I want to go to be with your Jesus where Elias waits. Will you help me. I know I do not deserve to be there but—"

"No, that is not how it is, Medea. No one could ever be good enough to deserve this amazing gift. The shedding of our Lord's sinless blood has paid for the sins that separated you from the Father. If you ask Him to come into your heart and be your God, He will instantly cleanse you of all sins and past failures, even your doubts. And He will never even remember them. They will be gone forever."

"But He must know I am asking because I want to see my son again."

"He wants you to surrender your life to Him, Medea, exactly as you are, trusting He loves you." She nodded and he could hardly get the words past the lump in his throat as he led her in a prayer to receive Jesus as Lord. With a sigh, she smiled and plummeted into her pillows with a force that sent them billowing around her head. He held her hand and listened to her labored breaths. Two days later she was gone.

Everything that pertained to the estate's needs was put on hold. Makendon handled the demands of what needed to be done daily and assigned the most capable slaves. Everyone did their jobs without a word, reluctant to break the silence that draped the estate like a rainy mist.

Upon Halaten's pronouncement that Medea was gone, Patharus insisted his slaves carry him to her suite where he placed the traditional last kiss on her mouth and closed her eyes. Danatel was granted permission to wash and prepare the body to be laid in state in his receiving room. There, to maintain the tradition, he laid a coin over her lips before friends and colleagues paid their respects.

The day before the procession to the burial grounds Patharus sent for Nicanor. He choked on his request. "Son, I am afraid I am going to have to ask you to represent me tomorrow. I do not want to have to be carried to the cemetery."

"Of course, Father, but you need to tell me what to expect. When slaves like my mother died, we held a simple gathering to say goodbye. Surely this will be different."

Patharus explained the order of the procession, the reading of the eulogy and the protocol of who and when libations were to be poured out in

Medea's honor. "And like most of my peers, years ago I arranged for a marble tomb to be built and decorated with appropriate symbols. Her remains are to be buried there, not burned." His head drooped as tears ran. "And place our son's boat in her arms."

The nine days of mourning passed, and Patharus hosted the traditional feast. Libations were poured again before the tomb. Neither he nor Nicanor took part in the ritual. Patharus had little use for gods of any sort but allowed for those who did. Nicanor, who had managed to avoid it at the gravesite, refused to honor anyone but the Lord, God Almighty.

A week later Patharus sent word to Nicanor that he needed to see him. Nothing special had come up at their morning briefing but he hurried over. He had arranged to have dinner with his father most nights, concerned that he refused to speak of Medea. Lord, I do not know how to help him. I know he hurts but he has closed me out and will not talk about it.

Patharus motioned at a chair. "Nicanor, there are things that need to be settled here and now. I am aware of how well Makendon handled things while..." He cleared his throat, "while we were busy with Medea's arrangements. And Halaten says except for some weaknesses I am continuing to improve and heal from the apoplexy."

"Father, I—"

Patharus held up his hand. "Nicanor. You have been a true son to me. I could not have asked more if you had been born of my flesh. I am sure I have not mentioned it, but I am more than aware of how you have spent morning to night to accomplish things I could not do when my leg went bad and after this last setback."

"Father, you are —"

His glance begged silence. "Losing Medea has brought to mind how temporary life is and who knows how much time anyone has. It would please me immensely if you would make your plans and be quick to join Daphne. I want the two of you back here as soon as possible. Between Makendon and myself I believe we can handle it all without a problem."

A jolt of relief shot through Nicanor. Before Medea's condition had grown serious, he had tried to calculate how soon Patharus might be stable enough for him to leave. Her condition, followed by her death had buried all speculation. "Father, have you thought through the weight of all the decisions here at the estate and of each of the other —"

"Son, I was doing it before you were born, and I know I am ready. I have lots of good people I can lean on if necessary, but I will be relieved to have you back as soon as possible."

"Medea would be pleased to know you have done so well, Father."

"Yes, I sensed a surprising peace in her the day before she..." He stared out at the courtyard.

Nicanor had not shared his last conversation with Medea. Somehow, the time did not seem right. "If you are sure, I will see to arrangements for my trip as soon as possible. Hopefully, Daphne will have finished her quest and be ready to come home." Quietly, he shut the door, sure of his plans.

Chapter Forty-Seven

They are utterly consumed with terrors.
– Psalms 73:19

It was well after midnight when Daphne agreed they should leave the rest of her story until morning. She stared into the darkness. Cyrene seems receptive to what I am telling her Lord, but there is sadness behind her eyes. Please show her your love and desire for her to believe.

When she slept a nearly forgotten reoccurring dream returned. Once again, the high priest chased her, and she woke in a start. But this time she demanded that in the name of Jesus that the dream be gone. "Thank You for Your assurance, Lord. I know You will be with me no matter what comes."

The next morning Cyrene wasted no time. "Come on, Daphne. I could not stop thinking about the things you said last night. I want to hear more about that voice that talks to you and how you regained your freedom."

They settled across from one another. Each mentioned their delight in the morning sun as it streamed through windows that faced the gulf. Daphne sighed. "It is so beautiful here. There were times I thought I never would see Delphi or the gulf again. Your home is lovely, Cyrene."

"Thank you, I love it but living alone can get lonely."

Daphne nodded. "I quickly learned for myself that living in the midst of strangers without loved ones around, can be lonely." She ran her hand over the soft covering of the settee and sighed. So, I told you that three men bought me. One seemed to be in charge. He announced that I would live at his estate."

"What was he like? Were you afraid of him?"

"I was terrified of being owned by someone who could do whatever he wanted with me. Slaves I met in Athens convinced me I should expect to be beaten and raped by my owner, so I panicked when he called me into his inner office shortly after we arrived."

Cyrene scooted to the edge of her seat. "What happened?"

"He asked me a few questions then moved toward me."

"Oh Daphne..."

"I fell to my knees, sobbed, and begged, 'please do not.' He just stood there, looking at me like I had lost my mind. Finally, he pulled me to my feet, asked me how I came to be a slave, where my home was and about life in Delphi."

"Really! Then what?"

"He explained what he expected of me and assigned me safe living quarters. As I look back, I am sure he knew what I thought was going to happen. To stay at his estate proved to be a blessing. One of the other owners was a greed-driven businessman who continually looked for opportunities to rape me, almost succeeded once."

Cyrene shuddered. "Oh, what you have been through. So, you started right out telling fortunes? How did you know how to do it, to get people to trust you?"

"It was scary. My owners expected a profit, and I did not have a clue how it was done. But in the city I saw an old woman tell fortunes, so I followed her and learned how to get customers. The voice told me what to say to each one, but it did not take long to realize his counsel was grounded in evil. He cared nothing about people. He took advantage of their lack of knowledge and in return demanded they pledge to honor Apollo as their god. Once that happened, he was able to blind them to the truth and fulfill his agenda: take as many people down with him as possible."

"Then why did they want his advice?"

"Greed. Sometimes revenge. Mostly because he revealed things that brought the results they sought. I grieved for those who did not follow his demands. Like one man who took his own life after he lost everything. His family, like mine, sold to pay creditors."

"That is terrible. It should never be allowed."

"And I am still haunted by the face of a young woman terrified her baby would be destroyed if it were not a boy. The voice confirmed she carried a male child and that soothed her fears." She huffed. "What he neglected to add was the baby would have club feet and the father would not accept it." Her eyelids drooped. "Heartbreaking, Cyrene. Grief destroyed her mind and her husband had her 'disposed of.' When I confronted the voice, he just laughed it off."

"Despicable, to kill innocent babies, I mean." Her tone escalated. "If I had a child, I would run off with it before someone tried to kill it." She waved off an alarmed servant. "I would, I..." She shook her head and changed the subject. "But I do not get it, Daphne. How did that voice, or whatever it is, how did it know things people could not know? How did it know that girl's baby was a boy?"

"I did not know it then, but later I understood that the demonic spirits Satan sends have a limited amount of insight and power and that they use for evil purposes. I know this is all a lot to understand but I learned that after the first man God created sinned, his fall allowed Satan to become the ruler of our world."

"And who is this Satan who has so much power? Is he a god?"

"No. Satan was a mighty, beautiful angel God created before the earth was formed, but pride entered his heart. He wanted to be equal with God, so he rebelled, and God thrust him out of heaven. Sadly, a third of God's angels fell with him. He rules the kingdom of darkness where at his bidding these fallen angels became demons that harass people."

Cyrene leaned on her fist. "But we have been taught that Zeus is the all-powerful god. That he controls the world and gave his son, Apollo, to be our preeminent god. Everyone I know reveres him, so how can you deny his blessings or his wrath on those who do not honor him? You have seen it."

"Only because of what I have lived through and learned. The demon that possessed me used his power with amazing expertise. He convinced people Apollo was a powerful god. Behind everything good or bad that we attribute to Apollo or any deity, is a demonic spirit who poses as a god and uses the deception to draw people from the truth."

Servants brought them lunch and they talked through it. Daphne hardly noticed what she ate until she tasted her dessert. "Cyrene, this is wonderful, what is it?"

"Oh, it is my favorite. A combination of dates and nuts in a cheesecake mixture. But go on. When did you realize that to bind people to Apollo was such a horrible thing?"

"I am not sure. Most of the year I did not realize what their commitments meant in light of eternity. Maybe it was when I began to shut my heart to quiet my conscience. Being protected from the worst of slavery became more important than anything, even peoples' lives or their destiny." She stared out at the gulf. "But I could never fully convinced myself I was not as guilty as the voice. The faces of men I lied to stayed with me, especially the ones who died or caused great hardship on innocent people."

Cyrene curled her feet beneath her and leaned back, her voice choked with compassion. "I do not know how you kept your sanity, stripped of your family and all alone."

"I was not entirely alone. For over half of the year, I had a wonderful friend, her name was Kawit. You would have loved her. She was the most loyal, giving person I have ever known. Like a light in a dark place to me."

"What happened. Did they sell her off?"

Daphne's eyes welled. "It is hard to even speak of it." She snuffed the tears that constricted her voice. "The overseer of our owner's estate was a cruel, devious man. Because she refused his lustful advances, he found ways to make things hard for her. One day he trapped her alone in the laundry, beat and raped her." She cleared her throat. "She died in my arms."

"Oh, how awful for you."

"It was harder than losing my father. She was all I had, and I loved her with all of my heart."

"What about the man you married? Was he there for you?"

"Not then. He had no idea of the person I had become or of the demon's hold on me. At that time, I was so afraid of being abused I kept him at a distance. I knew he cared for me, and I loved him from the moment we met, but he became the owner's adopted son. So that meant he too owned me and could do with me as he pleased."

"Did he try?"

"No but he found ways to be alone with me. Eventually he challenged my feelings for him and told me he loved me and intended to marry me."

"Did you believe him?"

"I wanted to. I longed to be with him but could not believe his father would let him marry a slave."

Cyrene moaned. "Such turmoil. Where on earth did you find strength to go on?"

"There was a time I did not think I could. I am ashamed to say I once tried to take my life but failed. I believe even then God intervened to save me from myself."

"Oh, Daphne, I am so glad you survived, not sure I would have made it."

"Well things grew worse when God sent the apostle, Paul, to our city to spread the truth about Jesus. Each encounter was a nightmare."

"Encounters? Did the demon beat you?"

"No, worse." She put her hand to her throat. "He would take control of my body and force me to follow the small band of believers."

"Were you unable to refuse, to run or do something?"

Daphne sighed. "No. By that point he had such control over my mind that I had nearly lost my will to object or refuse his evil intentions."

Cyrene rubbed her upper arms. "How awful. I cannot imagine having something control my body or my mind."

"It was so disgusting." She shuddered and reached for the water the servants had left. "I could feel the demon transform me into something you would not have recognized, almost snake-like with a putrid stench and an evil eye to mock the leader's message or any who opposed me."

"How humiliating! Were the people afraid? Did they flee?"

"No, the first couple of times it happened one of Paul's team stepped forward and commanded in the name of Jesus that I stop the harassment. The force of his words sent me flying. I landed on my back in the dirt. The demon feared the name of Jesus and left at the sound of it each time, leaving me at the mercy of Paul's followers."

"What happened? Did they hurt you?"

Chapter Forty-Eight

We speak what we know and testify what we have seen.
– John 3:11

Daphne shuddered at the memory. "Beating anyone's slave who offended you, was an accepted practice. I had seen it done, so I ran. They did not come after me, but watched to make sure I did not come back. I wanted badly to stay and learn about the freedom the man taught, but I did not dare. If I made any attempt to hear it, the demon would punish me or taunt me with reminders that without his input I would lose my protection. That terrified me."

"Punish you...how?"

"Well, one time he found I had gone to the river where Paul usually taught. On my return he provoked a cluster of crows. The whole flock dove at me. I can still see their beady eyes as their wings brushed my face, and their claws tore my tunic. They would not leave but screeched like the wails of paid mourners. He did not call them off until I begged his forgiveness."

Cyrene shuddered. "Crows. They just look evil. I remember that picture of Apollo with his crow, always gave me the creeps."

"Me too. The attacks against Paul went on for days. You cannot imagine how I dreaded going through that mutation time after time."

"You must have felt helpless, trapped."

"I did, but thankfully things climaxed when the demon forced me to harass Paul in front of a huge crowd in the city and..."

Both noticed movement in a curtain that separated the nook they occupied. A young man with a stocky build said, "It is just me, Cyrene. I let myself in." He walked over and kissed her cheek. "Did not mean to intrude, Sis. Last night when Mother sent me over to invite Daphne to dinner, I heard you talking and was so fascinated by what she was telling you I almost forgot what I came for." He gave her his sad puppy face. "Forgive me? I should not have eavesdropped."

Cyrene flicked at the stubborn cowlick that continually covered his usually laughing eyes. "And you came back this afternoon?"

"No, I snuck away from Father a short time ago, but I would like to hear more."

Cyrene shook her head. "Well, say hello to Daphne. Remember when her family lived near here?"

He reached for her hand, looking sheepish. "I am Demas. It is good to see you again. I hope you will forgive me and come to dinner again tonight. It would save me from Mother's ire."

Daphne laughed. "Of course, and after this just come and ask me whatever you would like to know." He left and she sighed. "He reminds me Alexander, my brother. I wish I knew..."

Cyrene nodded. "Life can be cruel. Come on, let us get ready for dinner. Mother puts her heart and soul into all her meals and will not like it if we are late."

Her father welcomed Daphne but said little, though her mother and brother were full of questions about life in Philippi. Finally, her father spoke up. "So, tell me about your husband's estate. What kind of crops does he grow? How many

287

slaves? Are seasons long enough to get a good harvest that far north?"

Daphne answered the best she could, careful to minimized how much greater Patharus' estate was than most in Delphi. The man looked uncomfortable when questions about her life as a slave were asked. Right after the last course he excused himself and signaled to Demas it was time to do nightly rounds.

Demas grimaced. "I will get to it shortly, Father." After his mother left to instruct the servants, he looked at his sister. "Would you mind if I joined you and Daphne later? I would really like to hear more, ask some questions she might be able answer."

Cyrene raised her brows. "I know how irate father gets if you do not follow his orders, how can you—"

"I will make fast work of the rounds and come right after, if that is agreeable with you both."

Cyrene looked at Daphne and both nodded. "All right, be as quick as you can. Anyway, we will spend a little time with mother before we leave."

In less than an hour the three of them were settled in Cyrene's nook. Daphne gave Demas a brief overview of what had happened to her and ended it with being forced to harass Paul.

Cyrene broke in. "You were about to tell me what happened the last time he forced you to badger the leader."

"At that point, the throng that gathered were mostly people who had not heard Paul's message. They were intrigued with his teaching, but the demon was sure they would scatter when I arrived, that it would end Paul's mission in Philippi for good.

288

"By then I no longer cared what happened, I just wanted to be free of his evil presence. The crowd began to close in on me. Angry voices, convinced I was the embodiment of an ancient, evil spirit, called for my death." She shivered. "I expected to die. But the demon was not deterred. He thrust me, mocking, and screaming right up to the teacher. I trembled at the man of God's demand I be brought close, yet relieved that at his order the people backed off.

He ignored my taunts and my evil eye, looked me boldly in the face, and spoke right to the demon. "In the name of Jesus Christ and in the authority, He has given me, I command you, you unclean spirit to leave this body."

Cyrene and her brother both gasped. "What happened?"

"Oh, it was horrible. At the name of Jesus, the demon threw me to the ground where I writhed like a snake, helpless and foaming at the mouth. I felt a shrill scream rise in my throat and something disgusting spewed from deep in my chest. It was the demon, forcibly leaving my body. Paul took my hand and gently raised me to my feet. He smiled and assured me the demon was gone forever."

Cyrene covered her lips with both hands. "Oh, Daphne, I—"

"I know, it was terrible. Imagine sprawled on the ground, vomiting like one who drank too much wine. But I am so grateful it happened. I had no doubt it was true, the demon was gone, and I was free. I stood there shaken and disoriented, with no way to comprehend what had happened. A believer by the name of Lydia took pity on me and took me to her home. That is where, for the first time, I understood that the voice within me was a demon and not a messenger of Apollo. She explained that it was power in the name of the Lord, Jesus, that released me."

Cyrene looked troubled. "But we both pledged ourselves to Apollo along with probably everyone who lives in Delphi. If he is but a demonic spirit, are we all destined to be condemned?"

Daphne shook her head and reached for her friend's hand. "No, no. What either of you did in innocence will instantly be washed away if you ask Jesus to become your Lord. He loves each of us with an unconditional love and will completely forgive your past and accept you as His own child. That is what I have come back to explain to people. It is God's heart that everyone hears this message and comes to believe."

Demas' brows touched and he leaned forward. "How does one sacrifice to such a God? What do you—"

"Oh, dear ones, there is no sacrifice grand enough to give Jesus. All he wants from you is your belief that He is God's Son, that He shed His sinless blood and died on that cross to pay for your sins. To believe that the Father raised him from death to give you new life, simply because He loves you."

"New life," Cyrene repeated the words so softly Daphne was not sure of what she said. She squeezed her hand. Lord, please touch her and heal that wound she carries.

Cyrene closed her eyes and turned from them. "So, you were free of the demon but still a slave. When did that change?"

Daphne sighed. She won't let me in, Lord. How can I help her?

Love her and pray. Give her time to process all she has heard.

"Lydia insisted I stay with her until morning. We talked well into the night and despite all the evil I had been a part of, she said the Lord loved me and wanted me for His own. I was given grace to believe it and she guided me into receiving Jesus as my Savior too. But before we said goodnight my heart fell at her mention that the Lord expected me to go back to my owner in the morning. I told her I could not go back without the ability to tell fortunes, but she said I just needed to trust the Lord."

They startled at a soft knock, then grinned. How was it that they all felt guilty? "Forgive me, Misses, I did not know —"

"It is all right Melita. I realize it is late, I will take care of my needs. You are excused for the night."

Demas' eyes followed the petite girl who blushed at having blundered into their meeting. He watched her leave and turned to Daphne. "Who was that?"

"That's my servant, Melita. She is a wonderful girl, gave her heart to the Lord on our trip from Neapolis. I would be lost without her."

Cyrene yawned. "I want to hear about what you did about returning to your master but I am tired. Can we talk more in the morning?"

They hugged goodnight but before Demas left, he spoke up. "Daphne, I know it is late, but could you stay a little longer? I will not be able to get away from Father tomorrow and I have so many questions."

Chapter Forty-Nine

Therefore if the Son makes you free you shall be free indeed.
– John 8:36

For two hours Daphne filled Demas in on her story. She answered question after question. When she explained the difference between myths and the one true God, he quizzed her further about the Lord's beginnings.

She tried to keep it simple. How God the Father, the creator of all things, had set up a covenant with his people. They would make a yearly sacrifice of the blood of animals to pay for their sins and He would forgive them. How it was a rule of laws, and no one could ever keep all of them. "So, He sent Jesus, His Son, God in the flesh to earth to teach us about the Father's love and desire we become His children. Jesus paid the debt our sins created once and for all time with His own sinless blood on the cross."

When she added that the Holy Spirit, the power sent to live in and help believers was also God, he would not let up until he grasped the mystery.

He smiled as if the sun had broken through a dark forest and highlighted his path. "So, all three are separate parts of the Godhead and yet they are one." It was not a question.

She was grateful Epaphroditus' teachings had riveted many answers to her memory as his questions dug deep into the character of God.

Concern shrouded his face. "You know you are facing a daunting task, to try to convince our

292

people that Apollo does not exist and the god they worship and sacrifice to is actually a demon."

"I know. In my own strength or ability, I could not even try. But when I expressed my gratitude to the Apostle Paul, he said I should take my newly found freedom and use it for Him, that it is the true outcome of gratitude. I knew instantly what the Lord wanted me to do, so here I am."

"I admire your commitment, Daphne. You are quite a woman but that is going to work against you. Most men do not believe women should even be seen in public."

She stood and declared a treasured promise, "With God nothing is impossible," and bid him goodnight. When she finally hit the pillow, she grinned into the darkness. "I believe I have found the first person here who is going to become a believer, Lord."

The next morning Cyrene met her on the stairs. "You look a little sleepy. Did Demas keep you up half the night? He can be as determined as ants around a honey jar when something is on his mind."

Daphne snickered. "He was determined but I enjoyed our time together. He is very bright, catches on or figures things out for himself."

"It is going to be a beautiful day. Would you enjoy spending some time on the gulf? I could have a basket made up and we could spend a leisurely afternoon watching the waves."

"Oh, yes! I would love to. Sometimes when I was so far from home, I pictured myself there on the sand, mesmerized by the surf. Would you mind if Melita joined us? She has been a bit cooped up and I think you would enjoy her company?"

Cyrene's lips pinched. "Well, yes, of course. I had kind of forgotten her until last night."

They arrived at the gulf and walked to an unoccupied cove. Daphne squealed. "Oh look! There is my log. One day before we were taken away, I spent time here, and decided to swim. I stayed in the water a long time and afterword, fell asleep with my head on this very log. I cannot believe it is still here."

Cyrene eyed her like a mother. "That could have been dangerous, there are a lot of sailors in port who might have wandered down here."

They wadded and splashed around in the waves for a while then rested while Melita laid out their lunch. After they finished, she repacked the basket and addressed Daphne. "Would you like me to move down the beach aways and give you some privacy?"

Cyrene touched her arm. "No, please stay, I want to hear about your life with Daphne." Melita blushed and looked at Daphne.

"It is fine Melita, join us."

"Daphne told me you have also come to believe in her God. Do you like serving her? I remember she was very fussy about what she wore, and her sandals, she must have owned a dozen pairs."

Daphne laughed. "And if it were not for our maid, Belte, I could never find the ones I wanted."

Melita looked uncomfortable. At Daphne's nod she spoke. "Yes, I am so blessed to be with my Misses. She treats me better than she should and never looks down on me because I am a slave."

"And what made you decide to make her God yours?"

"I've never known anyone to be so kind and loving as she is. I see her everyday with people and she is always the same. I wanted to be like her and the more she told me about Jesus the more I realized it was because of His presence in her heart. She assured me God loves me as much as he loves her and so I asked Him to be my God and now I understand His power to change people."

Cyrene stared. "But do you resent not being free?"

"Oh, Misses. I am free. The freedom I received in Christ has given me a contentment that surpasses earthly desires."

Daphne snickered. "You can probably tell Melita was able to hear Paul teach the three

weeks I was in Athens. She probably learned things I do not yet know."

Cyrene leaned against the log. "Amazing. A God that sees all people as equals." They watched the waves in silence until she spoke again. "Daphne, you never finished telling me about having to go back to your owner after you were delivered of the demon. What happened? You must have been anxious to tell the man you married about your new freedom."

"I did not know it at the time, but he too had become a believer. Lydia said the Lord expected me to count my master as worthy of honor, to go back and do whatever he required of me. I just could not do it. I had seen what the majority of slaves are subject to, and I panicked. My owner's overseer was the man who raped and killed my only friend, and I could tell by the way he looked at me I would be next."

"What did you do?"

"I decided to run away."

"You ran? Where did you go?"

"Well, my plan was to find my way to Neapolis, that is the port where I first arrived. I would find work to earn passage to Athens and try to find my family."

"Did you get there?"

"No. As I left Lydia's, a strong earthquake struck. I had woven my way through most of the city's damaged streets when I heard a man cry out for help. I did not want to stop but I could not just ignore him, so I stepped closer. There, trapped under a large part of a fallen building lay my owner."

"Your owner! Did he see you? Did you run?"

"I wanted to, but I could not. The man had always been kind and I just could not leave him there. The rest of the building swayed dangerously and threatened to fall and crush him."

"What did you do?"

"I tried every which way to free him, but I was not strong enough. I was beside myself when his son, who had been out on a search for me, heard his father insist I leave before the building collapsed. He joined us and the two of us finally freed his father and pulled him out of danger."

"What a relief. Did he survive?"

"Yes. His leg was badly injured but we managed to get him home to his doctor." She made no effort to hide her tears. "Cyrene, my owner was so grateful that I stayed and tried to help him that he granted my freedom!"

"Your freedom? Oh, Daphne, that is awesome."

"Yes, God arranged complete freedom in less than a day. Freed from slavery, and even greater, freed from the bondage of demonic powers. I shall never stop thanking Him."

Cyrene grinned. "And free to marry your owner's son. I am so happy for you."

"Thank you, my friend. And like I told Demas last night, God has called me to use my gratitude to help others find the freedom in Christ that I found."

"How will you do that? Do you think people will listen to you?""

"I hope so. I know that in my own strength I cannot do anything, but if the Lord opens a door no man can close it. I will tell my story to any who will listen, but my heart longs to help people who are enslaved, either to an earthly master or Satan himself."

Cyrene looked at the sun. "Looks like we had best head back if we want to bathe before dinner. And, Melita, you join us, no sense in your eating alone in your room."

They had almost reached Cyrene's house when they heard footsteps pound from behind. She frowned. "Demas, what are you running from?"

"I am, I...." He gasped to catch his breath. "I have looked all over for you two, three I mean. He smiled at Melita."

"We spent the day on the gulf. What—"

"Mother told me." He looked at Daphne. "I had a chance to share what you have been through with a friend of mine, and he wants to meet you and hear your story for himself. Even has a couple of other friends he thinks might want to hear it too. Would you be willing to meet with them?"

Chapter Fifty

Only be strong and very courageous...
– Joshua 1:7

The long day at the beach left Daphne ready to retire early. Melita brushed her hair. "I think the sun kissed your nose."

"Oh, I loved it. Did you enjoy the gulf? I noticed you did not get into the water."

She hung her head. "I, I am ashamed to admit I was afraid, Misses."

"Afraid? Of the water?"

"I had never seen huge bodies of water before we came from Philippi. And when we had to get into that dingy...I almost ran back to our quarters. As a child, I heard stories of terrible monsters and gods that live under the water and I—"

Daphne shook her head. "Oh, My Friend, there are no sea monsters in the Gulf of Corinth. And you know there are no other gods besides Jesus, right?"

"I know. I am grateful you taught me to read and write. I am learning. Our great Paul taught that there is no fear in the perfect love of God, so I asked Him to forgive my doubts."

They were about to blow out her lamp when Daphne patted for her servant to sit beside her on the bed. "Melita, Paul also taught us that Jesus said if two people agree in prayer about anything it would be done for them. Remember?" She nodded.

"You and I are the only believers here in Delphi that I know of. So, I want you to believe with me that Demas and his friends will be drawn by the

Holy Spirit to hear and receive the good news I have been asked to share."

Melita's eyes filled. "I am honored that you would ask me, Misses." To Daphne's surprise, she began to beseech the Lord to be with Daphne, to help her to discern the exact words that would open their hearts, and for the Holy Spirit to convict them of their need of a Savior.

Daphne hugged her and said good night. In the dark she wiped her eyes at the wonder of Melita's rapid grasp of God's faithfulness and power. "Lord, apart from You I can do nothing. Help me to keep my eyes on You and my ears open to what You would have me say. It is Your mercy and You alone who enables hearts to believe and receive the gift none can achieve on their own. Please do not let me get in the way."

The meeting was set for after dinner the next night. Demas invited Cyrene to join them, but she excused herself as the hour would be late. Daphne spent much of the day in her room, praying and seeking God's wisdom. She confided in Melita. "I wish it did not have to be so late in the day. I have battled the 'what ifs,' all day."

Melita gently reminded her what they had agreed on in prayer.

Daphne smiled. "You are so right. I wish Cyrene would join us."

"Her heart is troubled. God has instructed me to pray diligently for her."

Cyrene welcomed them to her dining area with a smile that stopped short of her eyes. "I asked my cook to create this special dish. I hope you like it." Platters of poached sea bass drenched in a buttery cream sauce with seasoned vegetables arrived, accompanied by bread fresh from the hearth.

Daphne licked her lips. "Oh, Cyrene, this is wonderful, I love *lavnak*. What a gifted cook you have."

She laughed. "I know. Mother has threatened to steal him more than once."

"You have been so generous, and I do not want to overstay our welcome. Perhaps, I should —"

"No, do not even think of staying elsewhere. I love that you are here. You are welcome for as long as you like."

Demas arrived well after they finished. "Sorry to be late. It is hard for Father to let a workday end. Are you still willing to go?"

"Yes, and I am not concerned about the time. But, will your friends wait?"

He assured her they would and ushered her, Melita, and Batono to a small carriage. "I had to borrow Cyrene's to keep my plans from Father." Irritation couched his words.

The ride to his friend's home was short. Batano chose to stand beside the door, but she and Melita were seated in a comfortable receiving room and offered refreshments. Demas followed. "Abiron, this is Daphne and her servant, Melita."

Their host appeared to be several years older than Demas. He was a tall, slim man with an engaging smile that put Daphne at ease as he passed out wine and water. Demas surveyed the room. "So, will the others come?"

"Baltos and Kerpos said they would be here. Like you, Kerpos and his wife live with his family and his father is not well. He may not live out the year. Baltos, always, has to make sure every detail is in order before he leaves his estate. Both would have sent word if..." A knock sent a servant to the door. "That is probably them."

To everyone's surprise four men entered. Abiron welcomed them.

Baltos handed the servant his wrap. His 'in command' kind of manner reminded Daphne of Patharus. His broad shoulders and impeccable dress were so like her father-in-law's. "Hope you do not mind. Word got around and Orestes and Cronos were anxious to hear what is happening in Corinth too."

Abiron nodded. "Great. Come on in and I will introduce you." The men all knew one another, and introductions to Daphne and Melita finished with some raised brows as they learned Melita was her slave.

"You all probably remember Tribia, Daphne's father. It has been about two years since he was killed in an accident on the way home from the temple. We were all aware when the magistrates, underhandedly, called in his loan and decided to auction off his property."

Orestes shook his head, his face pinched with anger. "I remember. That Roman who wanted the estate for himself was the force behind it. Everyone knew it but nothing could be done. I have met with several other owners who are concerned about the crooked ways Rome works, and we have vowed to be there for each other if another shyster tries a similar takeover." He glanced at Baltos who nodded in agreement.

Several chimed in on the unfairness of the situation but Abiron soon brought them back to why they were here. "Good, then you all know the family was also sold off when proceeds from the estate and the slaves were not enough to satisfy the debt, or so they said.

He held up his hand when Orestes started to add his indignation at the fallacy. "Before it gets too late, let us hear from Daphne, Tribia's daughter. Her former owner is a highly respected Roman with a large estate in Philippi. He granted her freedom and she is married to his son."

"Thank you for your understanding. It was a very difficult time for my family. I am not sure how much Demas has told you, but I have returned to Delphi to tell all who will listen that there is a God in heaven who cares about you and wants to give you new life. He is the only true God and all the gods we learned about, especially Apollo, are nothing but a myth. Philippi is one of the cities where this good news first arrived in Greece. That is where I was blessed to witness the Lord's power to change lives for the better." She knew her words had gushed nonstop but when she finished, a calm akin to watching the sun escape the grasp of a dark cloud swept over her.

Orestes leaned forward. He sounded eager. "What do you mean by 'one true god'?"

Cronos spoke up, so quietly, she was not sure she heard him correctly. "And how did you get your freedom back?" He twisted his hands and shrank at her attention. Younger than the others, his slight build hardly filled his tunic.

Daphne hesitated. "Maybe it would help if I started at the beginning." They all nodded, and she began with her dubious decision to please her family and commit herself to Apollo. "His most celebrated temple is here in our city, so I want you to know what I experienced that day."

She told how she hated to be chosen to marry a priest and that she snuck into the adytum and what she saw. Heads nodded as she revealed the phoniness of the pythia's being enlightened by fumes from the decaying dragon, and how the divination process was a farce.

Baltos broke in. "I have long suspected that. The whole temple facade is nothing but a way for those priests to extract money to live their lives of ease."

Daphne was relieved that all but Cronos added their agreement. He looked worried, or was it fearful? Once again Abiron had to corral the discussion.

"While I hid and watched all this, Talsta, the current high priest rushed down the stairs and chased Molonda, the former priest, into the adytum and killed him."

Cronos gasped and Orestes jumped to his feet. "I remember that, but nobody knew who did it." His eyes grew wide. "And you saw him do it?"

Baltos snickered. "Molonda was a pompous ninny. Every time he paraded himself into the theater I wanted to leave."

Comments erupted throughout the room.

"He deserved it."

"I wonder what Talsta would say if he knew someone saw him?"

"Are you kidding?"

"He rules the priesthood with an iron hand...but that was cruel."

Similar remarks bounced from one to the next. Abiron looked at Daphne and shrugged. They gave up and let the discussion flow.

Chapter Fifty-One

Nor is there salvation in any other...
– Acts 4:12

The men quieted, asking for details about the murder. Daphne affirmed that Molonda was slain by Talsta's sword. "It was brutal, hard to watch. The pythia was in a drugged stupor so she did not react until she saw the mutilated body. She threw back her head, saw me, and screamed. In my panic, I had neglected to remain hidden. She clutched her chest, hurled a vicious curse at me, and fell from her stool, dead. I was so frightened I backed and tried to run, but tripped and was knocked unconscious."

She told them she awoke to a voice inside her head. "At first, it seemed to want to help me. Much later, I learned I had been invaded by the dead pythia's demonic spirit of divination who posed as a messenger of Apollo. At the slave market in Athens, buyers discovered I had a *teraphim*, so I was sold as a sorcerer. That concurred with the demon's agenda: tell people how to get what they wanted so they would think Apollo was a god and commit their lives to him."

Orestes broke in. "But we have been taught that the dead are carried away by Hermes and taken on a journey that eventually leads them to a joy-filled place. If a demonic spirit had taken control of the pythia, what happened to her after she died?"

Daphne had not anticipated that question. She hid a gulp and asked the Lord's help. "Only God can know what is in a heart. His desire is that everyone come to Him and become His child. But if people refuse to believe after they learn the truth, they are still in their sin and will face judgment. Nothing sinful can stand in our holy God's presence."

"But if a person did not know of this God and the love and forgiveness you spoke of, then what?"

"God has made Himself known to man from the beginning of time. Surely each of you can remember a time you saw something...a newborn baby, a sunset, a mountain, and knew in your deepest being that someone greater existed and created this world."

Heads nodded, so she went on. "Everything changed when the truth that God had sent His Son, Jesus Christ to redeem the world reached Philippi. I was almost totally under the demon's control by then, but the little I did hear of this God made me want to know more."

She described the horror of being forced to harass those who followed Paul, and of being transformed into a creature people ran from. "Finally, the man of God took the authority given him in Christ Jesus and commanded the demon to leave my body. The presence convulsed me and left me shaken and confused but free of its control."

She answered question after question that followed. What happened to Paul afterwards...what was the reaction of her owners...was the crowd skeptical or did they believe it was the power of this God? When she told of the humiliation of the magistrates who had beaten and jailed Paul and Silas, not bothering to discover they were Roman citizens, they wanted to hear it all.

Kerpos laughed. "Whoa, that must have been a scene. Can you imagine our magistrates in that situation?" Sniggers and a few shrieks erupted throughout the room.

Abiron paused in front of her, a tray of drinks balanced on one hand. "So did this Paul take you aside and explain things to you?"

"No, he motioned to a believer named Lydia and she took me to her home. He used the incident to teach how the love of God could deliver an unclean spirit even from a pitiful creature like me."

As if he needed permission to speak, Cronos raised his hand "She did not care that you were a slave?"

Daphne glanced at Melita. "No, you see there are no free or slave, no man or woman, in God's kingdom. We are all the same in His eyes." She gestured at her servant. "Ask Melita, whom you met. She is my slave, but she has come to believe in Jesus, so while her situation has not changed, her life has. She knows the Lord sees her the same as He sees me."

He cocked his head and spoke directly to Melita. "Is that how you see it?"

Used to standing when someone addressed her, Melita rose, her voice soft but steady. "Yes, My Lord. Since I have come to believe in Jesus, my life has a whole new meaning. I was just a servant before, I did what I was told and expected nothing out of life. But now..." Her face took on a glow that captivated everyone in the room. "Now I serve my mistress with great joy. I know in my deepest being that God loves me and cares about me. No matter what life brings, He will be there for me because He has my best interest at heart."

No one spoke until Daphne blinked back her tears and nodded to Melita.

Abiron's eyes followed her. "Whew! I would like my servants to gain that outlook."

Daphne's voice shook. "It is Jesus in her. Perhaps, we could arrange for them to hear about our Savior. We have seen the lives of many slaves as well as free people changed when they learn of His love and acceptance.

Orestes lips twisted with impatience. "So back to this woman, Lydia. What did she tell you about this Jesus? Is Zeus His father too? Where did He come from?"

Daphne reminded herself to be patient. "No. Zeus is as much a myth as Apollo. He is another demon, whose assignment is to pose as Greek's foremost god. But our God, the Father, has no beginning or end. He created this perfect world and everything in it. He began with a group of people whom He taught how to live, but it did not take long for them to rebel. Sin separates us from God and leaves a debt we are helpless to pay. That is why He sent Jesus.

"Jesus was born a little over fifty years ago, but the priests and rulers of His people did not like the message of forgiveness and mercy He brought thirty years later. It threatened their dynasty of control and power, with a religion of laws and rules even they could not live up to. In some ways, it was the same as Apollo's priests when they make demands and flaunt their authority over us. These priests hated Jesus and contrived a plan that ended with Him being beaten and crucified on a Roman cross."

Orestes held up his hands. "Wait a minute. Why would people who believed in His Father hate

Him? When Zeus gave us Apollo there was rejoicing."

"These priests and their elders' hearts were so hardened they refused to believe Jesus was God's Son. But the miracles, the healings He did in His Father's name, and His message of love and caring for others convinced the ordinary people He was their long-promised Messiah."

"Could He not have forced them to let Him go...His being a god?"

"Yes. He could have called and His Father would have sent angels to rescue Him, but He chose to sacrifice His life. He died so we could be forgiven and become God's children."

Cronos stood to his feet. "But... but why did it have to be so horrific...so bloody?"

"Because from the beginning God's plan of redemption requires a blood sacrifice. Before Jesus came, each year animals were killed, and their blood became the sacrifice for each man's sin. When Jesus shed His sinless blood on the cross, it was for everyone who believes and receives it as the payment for their sins, now and forever."

Boltos had yet to speak. Quietly he asked, "So He died? I thought gods lived forever."

"Yes, He did die. The soldiers made sure of that. He was buried but three days later, just as He promised, His Father resurrected Him. Over five hundred people saw Him, and after forty days of teaching his disciples, many watched as He ascended back to heaven. But He has promised to return one day and take all who believe, with Him, into eternity."

The room grew quiet. "Look, I know this is all new to you...maybe even sounds strange.   But the fact is God has opened the doors of heaven for us through Jesus. I hope I have made it clear that if you can believe and accept this as truth, you will become His child and one day be in heaven with Him.

"This good news is spreading. Jesus returned to heaven and Paul and his fellow disciples were sent to bring it to all people, not just his countrymen. Paul reached Greece and taught it in Philippi where I first heard of Jesus' love. Then he traveled to Thessalonica and a few other cities before he came to Athens and on to Corinth where it turned their world upside down.

"When I fully understood that Jesus loved me just the way I was at the time, my heart just leapt. Hope came alive, deep in my spirit. At last, I knew He was what my soul had longed for, way before I committed my life to Apollo. Lydia explained that if I confessed aloud that I believed Jesus was God, died for my sins and was resurrected by the Father, I would be forgiven and become His child. I will be forever grateful that He opened His kingdom to me."

Tears of joy she did not try to hide slid down her cheeks. "To believe is a choice. Then and there, I decided to believe. My prayer is that one day you too will make that choice."

She expected people to leave but questions continued until Demas stood and held up his palms. "It is really quite late. Maybe, we could get together again if you would like to hear more."

Abiron agreed. "I will get the word out in a couple of days. We can meet here again if you like. Feel free to bring anyone you think might be interested."

Positive comments and unanswered questions ushered the visitors out the door. Daphne thanked Abiron for having them as Demas helped her with her wrap,

He reached for Melita's and carefully placed it around her shoulders. She blushed as his face drew but inches from hers. He smiled as he guided her to the door. "Thank you for sharing your faith with us."

Daphne followed, but Abiron stopped her. "I am thinking about having you and Melita speak to my slaves. Would you be willing?"

She smiled. "Oh, Abiron, I would be glad too. Ever since I experienced firsthand how they feel, my heart aches for those enslaved by anything."

The ride back to Cyrene's was not long enough to thank the Lord for the doors He was opening.

Demas lingered after the others went inside. "Daphne, it struck me when you talked about the times in our lives when we saw or felt something we knew had to be from somebody bigger than anything we had known. Once it was a tree decked out in golden leaves with the sun blazing through its branches. It took my breath away and left me with a desire to worship but I did not know what. And there have been other things. What I am trying to say is I have come to believe it was your God calling me to Himself. Will you pray with me to make Him my God, too?"

"Oh, Demas, I knew in my heart that God was about to bring you into His kingdom. I am delighted to pray with you."

Chapter Fifty-Two

...I will joy in the God of my salvation.
– Habakkuk 3:18

For the next several weeks, Abiron arranged for
Daphne to continue to share her story in his home.
Everyone returned except for Cronos. A constant
question was, "So how did you escape slavery?"

She repeated the oft told story of her fear of
slavery without the ability to earn money by telling
fortunes. She told of the lust-filled owner who had
tried to rape her, one she was certain would take
advantage of her loss of status. "So, I decided to run
away. But as I ran, an earthquake hit and I came
upon my master pinned beneath a damaged
building. I struggled for hours to free him but was
unable to move the debris that trapped him. His
son arrived and together we released the heavy
weight and pulled him to safety. My master was so
grateful, he freed me that very night." Their
approval encouraged her.

Those who attended the original meeting
brought others. Some brought wives or sisters.
Abiron, soon, ran out of space and moved the
group into his larger receiving room. Each
afternoon, Daphne sought God's wisdom in prayer
for the nightly meetings. She sighed. "Lord, how I
wish Epaphroditus were here to help me with some
of these questions, but thank You for what I did
learn from him and from Paul."

Melita gave a soft knock and entered. "Cyrene
sent word dinner is ready."

"Thank you. I will be right with you."

"Lord, please show me how to reach Cyrene. I know she needs you." Once again, she refused Daphne's plea that she join them.

She and Melita were about to climb into the carriage when Botano approached her. He kept his eyes down. "Forgive me, Misses, but would it be all right if I came into the meeting tonight?"

Daphne covered her surprise with a smile. "Why yes, Botano, you would be most welcome to join us." The servant nodded and hopped up front, beside Demas. She looked at Melita who looked like she harbored hidden treasure. "What is it, Melita? What has happened with Batano that I do not know?"

She grinned. "Cannot really say, Misses, but lately when he is not busy with Cyrene's servants, he has asked a lot of questions about our meetings."

"Have you told him about your coming to Jesus?"

"Oh my, yes. And I know he has watched you and me very closely. I can tell by his questions."

Daphne squelched a shiver of joy.

That night, the meeting started with an air of excitement. Daphne began by having Melita teach a song of praise to the Lord that ended with a declaration of God's deep love for all people. Her servant's lovely voice carried a special anointing of His desire to bless and set people free.

Those who had attended several times listened patiently as Daphne repeated her story for the new arrivals. She finished, surprised when Kerpos and his wife stood up. "Daphne, we are convinced that Jesus is the only true God and want to make Him our Lord, too."

Before she could react, several others stood. Each said they, too, wanted to make Jesus their Lord. She could hardly contain the joy that bubbled in her chest. Here was the breakthrough she had prayed for. "Please, all of you who have made this decision, come up here and we will pray." Four women and two men came forward. One was Baltos. Out of the corner of her eye, she saw Batano. He stood near the door, looking unsettled. She smiled and nodded, delighted when he joined the others.

"I am going to lead you in the prayer Lydia used when I made Jesus my Lord. And I want each of you to repeat what I say. God will hear each voice. All right?" Heads nodded and they repeated it, word for word. She hugged many women who wiped tears from their eyes.

Baltos lingered after the prayer. "I have known from the first night what you shared was truth, but I did not know what others might think. Now, I do not care."

She clasped his hand. "Welcome to God's family." Batano backed slightly as she stepped in front of him, so she simply nodded her joy.

Daphne could hardly sit still on the ride home. She whispered into the night sky, "Thank You, Lord. Thank You for that special anointing that broke the yoke of fears, doubts, and unbelief. I am so blessed to witness how you draw people into your kingdom."

The meetings continued with as much joy and enthusiasm as she had seen back home. Abiron set a night for her to speak to his slaves. Their interest piqued as they learned she had been a slave. Near the end, a man who appeared to be a leader stood. Everyone listened with expectancy written on their faces. "You say you have the Spirit of God in you now. How can you tell the difference between Him and the demon that once spoke to you?"

She chuckled. "Oh, My Friends, there is no comparison. The agenda of that demonic spirit was totally evil. It used me for its own purposes. It did not care that I hurt or was afraid or confused. All it wanted was to tell the lies of its father, the devil, through me. The Holy Spirit, on the other hand, brings me all the blessings of the Lord. He guides me, helps me, teaches me, and stands up for me against the lies of the evil one."

A woman asked, "You mean you still hear lies from the evil one?"

"Oh my, yes. Satan never quits with his efforts to discourage, lead you astray, or tell you God's mad at you when you mess up. But now I am free to refuse the lying, deceiving spirits that are more than eager to trip us up. All a believer has to do is rebuke them, in Jesus' name, and they flee."

"What do you mean by 'in Jesus' name'?"

"Well, while Jesus was still on earth, He told the believers that they could use His name when they asked anything of the Father. It is sort of like if you ask for something in your master's name. It makes all the difference, right? And the Father will surely give whatever His Son asks for."

Melita testified to the joy of having Jesus as her Lord and after a little coaxing Batano briefly told of his journey to belief. To hear it from those still in slavery brought a heartwarming acceptance, and more than half responded to Daphne's invitation to pray to receive Jesus as their Lord.

As the meeting closed, Abiron said, "They are wiser than I have been."

Daphne stopped and waved the others on. "We can pray right now if you are ready."

He dropped his head. "I do want the peace I have seen come into Orestes' life and yours and the others."

They went back into his study where he poured out his heart. "My father was a diligent follower of Apollo. He piled heaps of guilt on me if I even dared ask for clarification on why Apollo did the unseemly things attributed to him. Once, he had a servant beat me because I expressed doubt. That is why when I heard of your story, through Demas, I wanted to hear more. I hardly dared to believe there was a God who was truly good. I avoided even thinking about gods since my father died, but my nemesis, guilt, still hovers. It accuses me of what I struggle to believe. I cannot even explain it."

"Oh, My Friend, once you understand the two spiritual worlds that surround us, it will become clear. God is here, pulling for you to come to Him, but Satan is also at work. He sends whatever demonic spirits he senses will afflict you with their messages of deceit or condemnation. He knows exactly what will pull you down. Guilt is one of his favorites. I wrestled with that, too. But God is so much bigger than Satan, so willing to help you overcome anything the devil throws at you."

For several moments, Abiron stood with an arm across his waist and leaned his forehead against his fist. Daphne waited, silently acting upon the authority God gave believers to bind the spirit of guilt that tortured him. She prayed for God to expose the perpetrator of Abiron's indecision. Finally, his hand slid to his lips. He looked at her, longing in his eyes. "You are sure your God will accept me? I have not always—"

"Abiron, no one can ever be acceptable on his own. None of us has led a sinless life or deserves His love. It is a gift." She emphasized the word, *gift*. "It cannot be earned. It can only be received."

Like ice that dripped from the cliffs of Mt. Parnassus, his expression melted under the heat of God's manifested assurance. It changed his countenance from tortured to hopeful. "Then I want that gift. I need it...now."

She smiled, "And He wants you to have it." He followed as she led him in prayer.

He helped her into the carriage. "Thank you, Daphne. Thank you for obeying God's call and coming back to Delphi with this wonderful news. "As they drove out of earshot, the others plied her with questions about the delay."

Thank you for obeying God's call and coming, rang in her mind. The reminder of God's instructions through Paul drowned out the jubilant rejoicing over Abiron's salvation.

When they reached Cyrene's house, Demas asked her to wait a moment. The others went on ahead and he spoke in a whisper. "I am very concerned about some things I have heard in the city. Could I speak with you after dinner tomorrow night?"

Chapter Fifty-Three

Who is a liar but he who denies that Jesus is the Christ?
– 1 John 2:22

Cyrene gestured at the flower bed she contemplated rearranging. "I don't suppose it matters to anyone else what I have planted there."

Daphne chastised herself for continually pondering what worried Demas. "I am sorry, Cyrene. Tell me again what is it you want planted in this part of your garden. Mother oversaw all of the flowers and bushes around our home, and I hardly knew which were which."

Cyrene motioned to the stone benches that surrounded a small table. "It is all right. Let us sit there in the shade for a while." Within minutes, a servant approached with chilled citrus and pomegranate juice to refresh them.

"This is wonderful." Daphne licked her lips.

"My garden is just one of the few pleasures I find in life now that..." Her voice caught and she turned away.

"Now that you what, Cyrene? I can see you are unhappy. What is it?"

Her head drooped and she covered her face with her hands. "Mother continually reminds me I should be grateful and I have no reason to dwell in self-pity."

Daphne scooted close and put her arm around her friend. "It is hard to be grateful when your heart aches. What is it, Friend?"

"I am so ashamed. I should have..." Sobs choked her efforts to continue. "I see you strong and peaceful after all you went though. Why is it I cannot move on from the past? What is the matter with me?"

"Everyone faces a battle or two of some sort in this life. Without the Lord Jesus as my strength, I would have never made it through nor have been of any use to Him today. He makes all the difference in a person's life."

"But you were innocent. I... I should have—"

"Should have what? What is it that tortures you?"

Cyrene pulled herself upright. "I should have been more... more willing, a more submissive wife. He was desperate to have a son and I found reason after reason to put him off." She pressed her temples that pulsated with the painful confession. "I did not even feel sorrow when he died, and now here I am a widow after a brief marriage. I have no child to fill my life and little prospects of being married again. Few men want a woman who is not a virgin."

"But you nursed him through his injury. You were there when he needed your care. You did what you could, and you are not to blame for his death. Frankly, I do not think many arranged marriages become loving relationships, and if you failed in some areas it is because you are human. We all fail and miss the mark."

"But look at you. You—"

"You see me as I am now, after the fact. While I went through my trial, there were many times when I failed miserably to hang on to my integrity and to do what I knew to be right. I even lied to my master several times, or at least deceived him about the truth. But Jesus is the God of mercy and grace, He not only forgave me, He made me new on the inside and gave me the desire to please Him."

"But you are special, Daphne. Anyone can see that your life will count for great things."

"No, I am not special, but we all are unique in God's eyes. He has a specific plan for your life too, My Friend. It is not over, and I do not believe He wants you to spend it alone and lonely. Of course, you should be grateful for your lovely home and for being graciously provided for, but that does not mean you have to accept that this is all there will ever be."

"Really? You think your God knows and cares about people like me?"

"Of course, He does. He created you and has loved you since before you were born."

"Oh, I do want to hear and understand more about the goodness of your God." A gaze at the sun sent her to her feet. "It is time to get ready for dinner and I am going to hurry so I can join you and Demas tonight."

Daphne waved her off with a hug. "Lord, you never cease to amaze me. Thank you for touching Cyrene. Please let this be the night she walks away from all that guilt and into Your forgiving arms."

That night, Demas did not show up to take them to the meeting. Melita looked worried. "What do you think happened to Demas?"

Cyrene shrugged. "I suspect Father discovered that he has left some of the chores undone each night and is furious. But my driver can take us if someone can direct him."

To please Melita, they waited a while but when he did not come, they piled into Cyrene's carriage and asked Botano to guide the driver. An uneasiness swelled in Daphne's spirit. Lord, are we not to go, or is the Holy Spirit preparing me for what is to come?"

Remember I have promised to go with you and will never leave you.

The meeting commenced as usual with an enthusiastic response to the worship Melita led. Except for a few, most had attended before, so Daphne quickly covered her journey and opened the floor for questions.

A newcomer spoke up. "I want to know what happened after you were delivered of that demon right in front of all those people. Did everyone there accept what the man taught as truth?"

Daphne bit her lip. Did the man really want truth or was he hardened to it. "Well, there was great rejoicing among the believers and the nonbelievers moved closer, anxious to hear more. But one of my former owners, who was furious at the loss of my ability to earn him money, began to stir up trouble. Lydia, quickly, got me out of there. Later, I learned that Paul and Silas were arrested, beaten, and thrown in jail."

"So, that was the end of it?"

"No, actually it was the catalyst of many more who came to believe in our God. You see, a strong earthquake hit Philippi that night. The shackles fell from the prisoners and the jailer was about to kill himself when Paul yelled, 'Stop, we are all here.'"

"The man was so convicted he asked how to be saved. Paul ministered the truth to him and his whole household was saved. The next day, the officials learned the prisoners they had beaten and thrown in jail without a trial were Roman citizens.

They were terrified. Paul insisted they, personally, come free them and apologize. The whole town witnessed their humiliation, and before Paul left many came to believe."

The response to the magistrate's exposure was the same as when she told it to the original six. When the snickering faded, she answered a few more questions and asked if there were any there who wanted prayer for anything or to make Jesus their Lord. She was delighted but not surprised when Cyrene joined those who made their way to the front.

Daphne hugged her as they prepared to leave. "Your whole countenance has changed. I cannot wait for Demas to see you."

A newcomer who had sat in the back approached. He looked the age of Cyrene's father, scruffily dressed in a hood that shadowed a face nearly hidden behind a bushy, dark beard. "Just a moment, young woman. "

Abiron hurried to Daphne's side. "What is it Blanter?" At the concern in his voice Botano sprinted across the room. He wedged himself between Daphne and the man, folded his arms across his chest, and glared into his face. Most of the guests had left, but those who had not, turned their attention to Blanter.

The man huffed at the insinuations. "Cronos told me what has been going on here, but I found it hard to believe. Now I see it is true. Let me tell you, I have dealt with my son, and he will not be back to swallow this disrespect of Apollo. Everyone knows he is the only god to be worshipped here in Delphi. He is the son of Zeus, the most powerful god of all. This talk will bring disaster on our town and our crops, not to mention the reaction of the Romans."

His gaze swept those who remained. "And you should know, they disposed of this girl's troublesome family beforehand."

Daphne shot up a prayer for wisdom. "Good Sir, you are right that we were all taught that Apollo is a god, but now the truth has been exposed to show those we thought were gods are nothing but demons who pose as gods. The ancient text of our God says that all the gods made by people are just that, man-made idols. There is but one true God, the creator of all the world and He has sent His Son, Christ Jesus to—"

The man's glare shot throughout the room. "Enough! Zeus is god overall and Apollo is his son. And you, young woman are—"

Abiron grabbed his arm. "Blanter, what you believe or do in your house is your business, but what happens here is mine." He nudged him toward the door. "I suggest you leave...now."

He jerked away his arm. "I will leave all right. I will not listen to any more of this blasphemy." He pointed at Daphne. "But you can be sure, the temple priests will hear about this disparaging message you have spread. And they will not take it lightly."

Chapter Fifty-Four

He who has ears to hear, let him hear.
– Matthew 11:15

Daphne tried to put Blanter's threat from her thoughts. The sight of Talsta's sword as it plunged into the high priest had returned several times. Its terror haunted her. His lust for power had not been forestalled by the position of Apollo's first in command. Would he see her as one more threat to eliminate?

The crowds at Abiron's house grew to where it became impossible to accommodate everyone who wanted to attend. On an afternoon when he slipped away from his father, Demas encouraged her to speak from the *Bema*. "To stand on the platform right in the city is the only way to get the message out to those who have no connection to any of us."

Daphne smiled. His concern was real, but many visits included an opportunity to trek through Cyrene's courtyard where Melita encouraged slaves or helped them with chores. "I have never seen a woman speak from the Bema in any of the cities where I have been, Demas, not in Athens or Corinth. I do not want to offend anyone, especially the town magistrates."

"But how can people believe if no one tells them the truth? God has given you a voice and a message that resonates with people. You must tell them."

"I will pray about it. God has a plan. You pray, too. Promise?"

"All right. I need to get back before my father misses me. I do not want him to find more reasons to keep me from the meetings."

Melita jumped to her feet. "I will walk you to the gate. I need to see if more preparations are needed for dinner."

Daphne hid a grin and nodded her approval. The way they looked at each other and lingered at the gate made her heart long for Nicanor. "Lord, I can see they have developed deep feelings for each other. Please, do not let Melita get hurt.

After another night in which Abiron was forced to turn people away, he approached her. "It was a great night, but we have to find a larger place to meet. To refuse entrance to people, who need to hear of God's gift of salvation, is not right."

Demas had joined them. "I suggested she speak from the *Bema,* but Daphne is concerned whether people would accept a woman in that position."

She shrugged. "Could there be a large venue we could use or rent?"

Abiron chuckled. "Maybe the temple." Demas snorted at the thought. "What about the ruins of Athena's temple? Nobody goes there or uses it."

"No, I passed it on the way up the mountain recently. It is little more than broken down walls and has no roof.

"True, and I cannot see people traveling in the dark halfway up Mt. Parnassus." He looked at Abiron. "What about the palaestra? Nobody trains there in the evenings. Do you think they would let us use it? Could you check into it? I know your father was a major contributor when it was built."

Abiron stroked his chin. "That might be our answer. I will check first thing tomorrow." He singled Daphne out before she left. "My slaves have begged for another visit from Melita and Batano. Could you allow them to come and encourage them? They are hungry to hear more, and it has given them such hope."

She was thrilled they had asked for her slaves over her. "I know they would love to. Set a day and I will see that they get here."

At the next meeting, people were encouraged to get out the word they would meet in the gymnasium the following night. Excitement buzzed like flies in the fall, refusing to die or be silenced. Daphne asked the original three to stay with her and the others after most had left.

"All of you have been such a support to me and the message God has sent to Delphi. I would not be surprised if we are met with opposition tomorrow night, but remember God is greater than anything the devil uses to stop the Word from getting out. I ask each of you to find some time tomorrow to pray fervently, and fast for this outreach. Cover it with the powerful blood of Jesus for protection, and pray for those who hear the truth for the first time to have hearts open to God. We all need each other and I need your prayers for strength and clarity."

The early arrivals filled the palaestra's benches. The gymnasium had not been built for spectators. Some sat on the floor, but most appeared content to stand. Demas and the others encouraged people to find a spot, while they directed a few they knew to be wives of Romans or those who wore worn garments to the front. Daphne's heart leapt at the sight of those dressed like the Jewish believers in Philippi. Oh, Lord, could they be some of those I saw years ago on the way to the festival?

The team rejoiced as people continued to enter. Her heart raced. "Lord, please fill me afresh with Your Holy Spirit and show me exactly how to present what you have given me. I do not want anyone to miss Your hope-filled message.'" She nodded at the Lord's direction she tell the whole story, as many had not attended the meetings at Abiron's.

The time spent in praise seemed to touch God's throne. Melita had gathered Kerpos' wife and two men to help her lead the music. One played a seven stringed lyre while another played a double flute. Abiron briefly explained who Daphne's family was and what had happened to them, then introduced her. The room grew quiet as she climbed the platform they had constructed.

"Thank you, Friends and Neighbors. I have come with a message about the Almighty God who has sent His only Son, Jesus Christ into the world to teach us of His love and save us from our sins. As a resident of Delphi, along with all of you, I grew up with the understanding that Apollo was a god. But I have learned, along with people from as far away as Philippi to Thessalonica and from Athens to Corinth, that there are no other gods than the Great I Am. He is the one true God. All other gods are myths devised by the enemy of our souls and portrayed through his demonic activity."

An audible gasp wafted through the crowd.

"I know this may be hard to hear, but please be patient and I will explain why I know this to be true." She started at the beginning, explained her doubts and her venture into the adytum that exposed the temple's hypocrisy. She told of the murder and of being invaded by the demon of divination who had controlled the deceased pythia.

Heads shook or bent close to one another, shocked at what they heard.

She reminded them of the injustice to her father's estate and of being sold into slavery. "I was torn from my family." She choked as she described the pain of her little brother's sobs as he begged her not to leave them. Her voice dropped along with a few tears from the listeners. "I never saw them again. I ended up being used by the demon to tell fortunes for my owners' profits." She explained the horror of being manipulated and later controlled by the demon, forced to be a part of the downfall and even the death of many men. "I hated my existence and tried to end it but failed. I was totally without hope until a man named Paul arrived with the good news I have come to share with you. God had called him from the life of a successful scholar and molded him into a relentless apostle of the Lord, Jesus Christ. But the demon that possessed me was tenacious. He hated having this truth presented and did everything he could to stop it."

When Daphne began to describe her horror as she followed and harassed the man, as one, the audience leaned in to catch every detail.

"When I drew near to Paul's followers the demon began to transform me into a... into a horrible creature." An involuntary shudder diminished her voice. "Sorry." She cleared her throat. "You would not have recognized me. I could feel my shoulders hood like an aroused cobra and my eyes narrow into those tiny black beads that peer from the heads of reptiles. Onlookers stared as my arms wove up and down like a nest of snakes trying to escape a pit. They smelled the putrid stench that rose as I swayed past them. It sent them running to escape my evil eye. A foaming substance, I was helpless to stop, ran down my chin as I hissed curses and screamed threats that mocked the leader's message.

"I saw no end to this torture, but I thank God He had a plan to rescue me. After several days of this anguish, Paul came into the city to speak his message and the demon began his last tirade. He forced me right up to Paul, still screaming curses. That is when this godly man took the authority given him by our powerful Lord and commanded, in the name of Jesus Christ, that the demon leave me. I was violently thrown to the ground and with one last blood-curdling scream the demon was forced to leave my body."

Again, gasps and sounds of "Oh no!" resounded through the crowd.

Tears ran down her cheeks as she explained her immense relief and the joy that followed. "I was taught that God loved me just as I was. He knew everything about me, all my failures, my attempts to be good, my struggles. But now none of that mattered because He had sent His Son, Jesus Christ, to wash away all of my past. He carried my sins to a Roman cross where, in death, He paid the debt my evil had created with His own sinless blood.

"But the Almighty God, His Father, resurrected Him back to life. He lived again and hundreds saw Him walk about as He met with His followers and taught them about His kingdom. He opened the door to heaven for all of us, and those who choose to believe in Him will also be resurrected after our deaths. We do not have to go through some terrible dark struggle to get to the light. He is the light and we will, one day, spend all eternity with him.

"Friends, this great good news is spreading across Greece and into all the world as I speak. I know this is all new to you, but this truth will not fade away or be silenced by God's enemies who work through mere men. We are going to meet here every night. I invite you to come back and learn more of the Lord, Jesus. Now, if there are any here tonight who desire to receive Him as your God, please come forward. I will lead you in a prayer to ask Him to come into your heart and you will be born again into a new creation just as I was."

For a moment, no one moved. She held her breath. Lord, help them to be brave.

Near the back, an elderly woman began to make her way to the front. Daphne could see people watch her as their eyes shifted from her to each other. She had almost reached the front when two others stood and joined her. Then, as if a dam had broken, people came from every direction. A group of twenty stood in front of her looking expectant. She wiped the tears from her cheeks. "Lord, You are amazing. Look what You have done!"

Chapter Fifty-Five

...For the battle is the Lord's...
– 1 Samuel 17:47

Scores of people waited to thank Daphne and encourage her to continue. A woman who had been prayed for squeezed to the front. "I am going to bring my sister, tomorrow. She needs to hear this for herself." A tall, dark haired man in drab-colored clothing that draped from his head to his knees made eye contact. She studied his face and wondered why he looked familiar.

Demas and Abiron saw to putting the building back the way they found it while she talked with an elderly man dressed like the Jewish people she had seen in Philippi.

"Young woman, what you are saying is that our promised Messiah has come. Where has this news come from? Why should I believe this Paul, you spoke of, has really seen our Lord? Why should I believe, that after four hundred years of silence, God has kept His promise?"

"Sir, this great apostle was a former Jewish scholar who studied under Gamaliel. He was highly esteemed as a man zealous for the strictness of the law. When the Lord Jesus brought the truth to this world and claimed to be God's Son, Paul believed with the majority of the Pharisees that it was blasphemy. But while on his way to viciously persecute people who believed in The Way, Jesus spoke to him in a flash of light. It knocked him from his horse and made him blind. The Lord told him He was the Christ, changed his name from Saul to Paul and gave him instructions to follow Him.

Paul's heart spiraled a complete turn, and he became a champion for Christ's message."

"Gamaliel, huh? It has been a long time since we left Israel, but I remember that name. His father was head of the counsel about the time we left to escape Roman persecution."

"Were you familiar with a man named Epaphroditus who also left Israel about then?"

The man stroked his beard. "Epaphroditus?" His eyes lit up. "Yes, a faithful Jew. I remember him but his family settled farther north. I have not seen him since."

"Well, he is the leader of the church Paul founded when he visited Philippi. He accepted Paul's message as truth and became a believer right away. He loves the Lord Jesus. Most everything I know about Jesus and His Jewish heritage came from Epaphroditus' sermons."

"Really? Epaphroditus would not have come to this without proof. What convinced him?"

"Paul preached about the love of our Creator who spoke through the Pentateuch, the prophets and the psalms, of His plans to send the Messiah to redeem all mankind. He reminded Epaphroditus of the passages in each book that confirmed Jesus fulfilled every prophecy."

Tears welled in the old man's eyes and slid down his cheeks. "Then it must be true. I will tell all those I know and bring them to hear more of the entrance of our Redeemer."

"How I wish you could have met with Epaphroditus. He was in Corinth until a short time ago to study further under Paul, but he needed to get back to his flock in Philippi."

He murmured as he left, "Perhaps, I will go to Corinth and hear this Paul for myself,"

That night, Daphne's mind defied sleep. She wandered in Cyrene's garden where the bright, mid-summer moon cast a glow on her friend's flowers. Her heart sang at the wonder of how God had begun to spread His message, but her thoughts were on Nicanor. *When will I ever see him again, Lord? I miss him so.* She was about to leave when she heard footsteps.

A man's voice called in a loud whisper, "Demas, is that you?"

She held her breath, not sure what to do. *If it is someone who knows Demas, I probably need not be afraid.*

"Demas? It is I, Cronos. Are you there? "

Her hands flew to her chest. *Cronos? What was he doing here?*

Demas waved to him, "Over here, Cronos, by the fountain."

She stepped back into the shadows. *What could this be about? Demas never had explained what concerned him. Was Cronos a part of it?* The two men stopped not far from where she hid. She gasped at the sight of Cronos. His arm was in a sling, his face puffed with dark bruises.

"How's the arm? Looks like your face is healing." Demas touched his friend's shoulder.

"It is. The Lord is good, but things at my house are worse. If my father finds out I have even spoken to you, I—"

"He will not know. But tell me what you have found."

"I cannot probe much or he might get suspicious. I do know he made another trip to the temple and this time had an audience with the high priest. Did you notice any priests at your meeting tonight? I suspect he will send spies."

"None, unless they came in disguise."

"Well, I do not know what they plan to do but I could tell my father was pleased. You have got to protect Daphne. Those people do not want to lose their power over us and the truth she spread has caught on with many. Father sends me on errands since I cannot do much else right now, and people are talking about it in the square and at the market.

"All right. I do not want to alarm Daphne, but I will make sure all our friends are aware and alert to trouble. Do you think they really might harm her?"

"Friend, if they have my father's mindset, they will not care what it takes to stop her. They would blame it on the muses, and no one would question it. I am so grateful you helped me find Jesus for myself. You cannot imagine how badly I want to be there with all of you, to learn more about Him."

"You are doing Him a great service from where you are, Cronos. Believe me, I know how hard it is to go bravely against one's father. Get word to me if anything comes up and we will meet again."

Each left and Daphne wished she had not heard what they had discussed. But to hear Cronos had become a believer lifted her spirit. He was so fearful, Lord, and look at the courage he has now in You.

She went back to the benches she and Cyrene had used and fell to her knees. "What would You have me do, Lord? I cannot fight the whole temple guard or the high priest on my own."

The battle is not yours, it is mine. Release it to Me.

She prayed until assurance came that God would fight the battle in her place.

Things seemed a little tense as they prepared to leave for the palestra the next night. She was sure Demas had warned Batano of the possibility of trouble because he hovered even more than usual. On the ride over, the face of the man draped to his feet with clothing, returned, though she had not thought about him since. She gripped Melita's arm. "Now I know why that man looked familiar to me. You remember my mentioning it to you?"

Melita looked puzzled. "The one with a cape draped over his head that you thought you recognized?"

"Yes. He was at the temple the time I had to take an offering for my mother. He helped me get an audience with the high priest." She frowned. "Something I came to regret."

"So, why do you think he was there? To spy on you?"

"I do not know. I hope not. He seemed to be such a gentle soul."

"Maybe you should tell Demas and Batano about it. You cannot be sure what his intentions are."

"You are right." She made a mental note to do so, especially in light of what she had heard the previous night. To quench murmurs about a woman speaking of such a life-altering disclosure, she started each night with the testimony of one of her team or a new convert. Each told his story of how he came to believe in Jesus. The meeting went on longer than usual with an even larger crowd. Many asked her to repeat what she shared the night before.

To her delight, the Jewish man had brought many others with him." Lord, are You about to raise up another Epaphroditus right here in Delphi?"

The hour was late, and all the regulars helped clean up so they could leave. She tried not to notice

334

that the men whispered among themselves. I am trusting You, Lord. The battle is not mine.

On the fourth night, they arrived at the palestra to find the doors locked and Roman soldiers on guard. Abiron approached them, "What is this about?"

"Orders from the magistrates. It has come to their attention that people have been meeting here to spread beliefs contrary to Roman doctrine. That is against the law."

"But the palestra is privately owned by the city of Delphi. Nothing has been spoken out on the streets."

The soldier huffed. "Delphi owns nothing. Rome owns everything, so all of you had better leave before we decide to take you before the magistrates."

Abiron gathered Daphne and those who had arrived to set things up and explained the problem.

Baltos groaned. "What can we do? People will arrive soon. I hate to have to tell them there will be no more meetings."

"I know who is behind this." Demas' voice was loud enough for the soldiers to hear. "Satan has found an ally in this town, but our God is greater and He will fight for us."

It lifted Daphne's spirit to hear him confirm the message the Lord had given her. She smiled at him. "Paul taught that Jesus decreed that we must obey the laws of the civil authorities. So, for now, I think you men should intercept the people and inform them of what has happened. Tell them that we will get the word out when we find a place to meet. The rest of us will leave and devote the situation to prayer."

Everyone agreed, muttering disappointment but hopeful.

Chapter Fifty-Six

The fool has said in his heart, "There is no God."
– Psalms 14:1

Nicanor approached Epaphroditus after the meeting, anxious to tell him he was finally free to go and join Daphne. "Tell me again about that last morning you saw her. Did she look well? Has Batano kept a close watch on her? I could not bear it if she—"

Epaphroditus smiled. "Nicanor, Nicanor. You are going to wear yourself out before you get there if you do not relax. She was fine and both Melita and Batano were always right there with her. Now, when do you sail?"

"About a week. I have waited to make sure Patharus is ready to be on his own. He and Makendon, our overseer, can handle the estate, but my father truly loved Medea and I am concerned that when the reality that she is gone settles, the loss may hit him hard."

"Shall I drop in on him? Would he welcome a visit?"

Nicanor's lips twisted to one side. "I do not really know. I do know that on our ride to the port, Daphne told me he asked her about her faith. She thought he was quite receptive to what she shared. That kind of an opening has not happened between my father and me. I do not know why."

"God knows. His timing is always perfect. Anyway, I will try to see him. It could not hurt."

Nicanor rode slowly toward the estate. His thoughts whirled between concern for his father and his anticipation of the reunion with Daphne. She will be devastated to hear of Medea's death, but I cannot wait to see her face when she hears Kupios received Jesus just two days before she passed.

He pulled his horse to a stop at the ridge where he and Daphne had first embraced after Patharus freed her. "The view is grand, Lord, but without her beside me something is missing." The animal shook its head and pulled at the reins. He patted its neck. "All right, Boy, I am impatient too. Take me home."

Each day, he tied up more final details on projects Patharus had given him. To ignore the whisper that nagged in his spirit proved harder.

You need to tell your father about your last conversation with Medea.

"Lord, he always seems impatient or uninterested. I do not know how to approach him."

Just tell him how it came about. It is not up to you to open his heart. That is the work of My Holy Spirit. You are simply called to witness to My power to change lives.

Twice, Nicanor had stopped by with plans to tell Patharus about Medea's change of heart. The first time, he found him upset as he struggled to attach the wooden leg Halaten had made him. The second time, curses over his dissatisfaction with the size of the early wheat harvest turned the air purple. The scowl on the face of the overseer decided for him. He would come back later.

The day before he was to sail, he knew he had to make time. Why was I so bold with Medea and am so reticent with him?

Patharus looked up from his ledger. The smile he intended looked more like a grimace. "So, tomorrow is the day, right? Are you all set?"

"Yes. I decided not to take a personal servant. I can manage and when I catch up with Daphne, Batano will be with us."

"Did you take enough money from the treasury? I would not want you to run short, so far away. It would take time for a ship to reach—"

"I am all set, Father. There is something I have wanted to tell you ever since we lost Medea."

"Well, yes, I know. I cannot believe it has been almost a month."

Nicanor drew a deep breath and jumped in. "Father, I want you to know about my last conversation with her. Do you remember that you said you sensed a peace in her the day before she died?" Patharus nodded.

"Two days before she passed, she sent for me. Her servant had found your son's toy boat, and when I arrived she held it to her chest and clung to it like a lifeline." When he explained that Medea said Elias had asked her to take care of it until he saw her again, Patharus' eyes welled with seldom seen tears.

"Father, Medea believed it was the sign she had asked from the Lord, Jesus, to affirm He was real. There was no doubt in her mind that, well, 'this is it,' is the way she put it. She asked me to help her pray and receive our Savior as her Lord and I did. That is what brought the peace you saw in her." Patharus' head drooped and he covered his eyes with his good hand.

"I have shared this with you in hopes it will bring you peace about Medea. And, also, because as you said recently, we do not know what tomorrow will bring. I intend to return soon. But nothing in this life is certain. Daphne told me she talked with you about her faith, and I hope that you too will come to embrace what she and I, and Medea have accepted as truth. The eternity that follows our brief time on this earth is what matters and we all want you there with us."

Time lingered into an uncomfortable silence. Nicanor sighed. Did I miss it, Lord?

Patharus broke the stillness, his voice uneven. "Nicanor, Son, I am glad...appreciate that you told me Medea found her peace. You do know she was a Greek before we married, do you not?"

Nicanor nodded. Where was this going?

"Well, those of you who were born here and grew up with the importance of gods in your heritage have a different perspective than those of us raised Roman. Oh, we have our gods. But they are not the influence they are to you Greeks, and frankly not to me. My own mother put a lot of stock in Roman gods. When my father was called back to Rome to defend our emperor, she diligently called on Hercules for strength, on Felicitas the god of success, and Victoria the goddess of victory. Despite her trust in what she clung to, my father, the anchor of our family, died in battle. It destroyed her."

"But Father, I—"

"No, hear me out. Daphne tried to tell me this God of yours is different, a God above all gods, but to me they are all the same. There was a time I did all I could to honor a god who supposedly could heal Elias, but it did not help. Your God did not keep Medea from dying and I see no difference. You mean the world to me, and you know how fond I am of Daphne. If you are concerned about my future, go, and see that both of you return as soon as you can. That will give me all the peace I need."

Nicanor swallowed his disappointment and placed his hand on Patharus' shoulder. "We will return, Father, as quickly as possible. God be with you."

The ride to the port of Neapolis was bittersweet. His spirit leapt at the thought of being reunited with Daphne, but Patharus' refusal to accept the love of God weighed heavy on his mind. "Lord, I prayed, and I know Epaphroditus did too. Hearing of Medea's change of heart seemed to touch him. Did I do it wrong?"

Nicanor, do you trust Me?

"Yes Lord, I—"

Then continue to believe and know that I am in control.

Later that day, he boarded a ship bound for Corinth. He had traveled to Athens with Patharus while still a slave, bunked in the ship's bowels with servants and cabin boys. As a landowner, he mingled with the captain, enjoyed well-prepared food, and slept comfortably. The difference served to accent the changes in his life. He marveled with gratitude and his heart raced with expectancy as he leaned over the rail and the Corinthian Port came into view. "One step closer to Daphne, Lord. Thank you for a safe voyage."

Epaphroditus had filled him in on what to expect, the ride over the Isthmus and into Corinth. Daphne's last letter said she was setting out for Delphi by way of the Gulf of Corinth. How would he know where she was now... in Delphi or back in Corinth? Epaphroditus suggested he check in with those who attend Paul's meetings.

"I will need your help, Lord. Sounds like a big city to navigate by myself, but Daphne managed to get to Athens and back on her own and then to Delphi. I can surely do the same."

As soon as he stepped on the shore, he inquired about the place that handled messages. Maybe she left me a letter telling me where she is.

The same sleepy woman who lisped her reply to Daphne checked her stash of messages. "I am sorry. There is nothing here with your name on it."

Chapter Fifty-Seven

...My son, God will provide...
– Genesis 22:8

The next day, Demas decided to fill Daphne in on what Cronos told him. "We knew they were up to something and were concerned for your safety. It did not occur to us they would appeal to the Roman magistrates to stop us."

She shook her head. "It could have been worse. I am so grateful there was not any force or violence."

"But what are we going to do? We cannot meet in a public place and no one's home is large enough to contain all who want to be there."

"We must remember, Demas, God was not surprised by this. He knew it would happen before I arrived in Delphi with His message. If He wants us to go on, He will show us the way."

The original group met that night at Cyrene's to seek God's will and direction. After hours of prayer, Orestes spoke out. "The Holy Spirit has shown me a large outdoor space, maybe down on the gulf. Does anyone know where that might be?"

Impatience erupted from Demas. "No, no. That would still be public domain and we cannot use it."

Baltos held up his hands, "Wait a minute. Why could we not meet outdoors? I have a large field at the back of my estate that I did not plant this year. We could set up torches, bring the platform, and —"

Daphne's face lit up. "Do you think people would mind it being outside?"

Kerpos stood up. "Why not? The heat drops and the evenings are pleasant. We could tell them to bring blankets or something to sit on. I know my wife would not mind." Everyone was enthusiastic and added further solutions to possible problems. Baltos promised to cut down any brush or weeds that would make it difficult to enter or sit on the ground. "We can start tomorrow night. I will get my slaves to make torches and have them ready to light." He cocked his head. "I think I will even invite them to stand at the back and listen, if they want."

Abiron nodded. "Well, mine will be jealous. They have heard Batano and Melita several times and they love them. Orestes, Kerpos, will you help me get the word out? Start with the west and south parts of the city and I will cover the rest." He grinned. "It will not take much effort. News spreads like honey on fresh scones, around here."

Demas' brows framed a frown, so Daphne approached him after the others left. "What is it?"

"I was thinking about Cronos. It will not take long for our enemies to hear what we are doing. The high priest is not going to be satisfied with only keeping us from public places. I am concerned with whether my friend can uncover their next step without placing himself in jeopardy."

"We are to pray for our enemies but not that their schemes work. God has promised that no evil will befall those who put their faith in Him, so let us believe that for Cronos and ask for His protection."

Word had gotten out and, by dusk, Baltos' field filled with people. Daphne milled among them. She turned when someone touched her shoulder. The man whose long hood draped over his clothing stood face to face with her. "Do you remember me?"

She tried to disguise a quick search for Batano. "Yes."

"Do not be concerned. I want you to know my heart has been touched by what you have told us."

She nodded, her cheeks red.

"Menial tasks leave underling priests like me lots of time to think. I have suspected the temple's phony pretenses for quite some time. There is great evil in the heart of the high priest, and I wanted to warn you." He frowned and his eyes pierced hers. "He will not hesitate to find a way to silence you. I have a room at the inn until I can leave and rejoin my family in Athens. If I can be of any help, please ask."

He backed up and blended into the crowd. Her gaze followed. His need to discard his priestly garb and wear a strange disguise made sense now. She wanted to tell Demas and the others, but it was time to start. She introduced Baltos and thanked him for the use of his field and asked him to tell the crowd why he volunteered his property.

When he finished, she nodded to Melita. She and her helpers led the people in songs of praise to the Lord before Daphne shared her quest, then opened the meeting to questions.

A man stood. "So, this Jesus has gone back to heaven, but we are still here. How is He going to be a help for us? How is He going to do all the things we believed Apollo would do... bless our crops, protect us, ward off our enemies and such?"

Daphne could hardly make out the man's face in the wavering torch light. Was he there to cause dissention? "There is so much I did not know and am still learning, but I have learned that the Almighty God in heaven, who created this earth, sent His Son, Jesus to bring us a better kingdom. It is one of light and peace and He wants you to be part of it. Jesus did return to heaven, but while He was on earth, He could only teach, heal people, cast out demons and do miracles in one place at a time. He is the same today as He was then and will be forever."

"So, how is that going to assure my crops will not fail or my cistern not run dry?"

"He wants to meet your needs. Before He ascended into heaven, He promised to send us another Helper, one just like Him. And He did. He sent His Holy Spirit, the third part of the Godhead to help us with whatever we face. Jesus came to give us abundant life and His Spirit has the answers to all we need. You must simply ask. When you make Jesus your Lord, the Holy Spirit comes to be with you. He will be in you and will never leave you."

A woman to her right asked, "You said He did miracles, signs and wonders. What does that mean?"

Daphne took a deep breath. Could she explain it the way she had heard Paul or Epaphroditus do? ""You have heard me tell of being delivered from a demon that possessed me. That miracle or any wonder God does is referred to as a 'sign'. It is simply another word for the supernatural workings of the Lord. While Jesus walked the earth teaching the love of His Father, many miracles like mine and even more of healings of sicknesses and diseases followed."

"Then if He is the same, will He heal us here and now?"

"Yes. He loves each of you and wants you to be healed as well as set free. His sacrificial death fulfilled an ancient prophecy that said the wounds he suffered were payment for our rebellion. The brutal bruising he took paid for the moral depravity that lives in the hearts of unsaved men. He bore the lack of peace we experience without Him in our lives and by the severe flogging he endured, we are healed."

The woman's husband stood beside her. "But He is not here, so how can that happen?"

"It's available now and forever because while Jesus was still on earth, He gave that same authority over demonic powers and over sicknesses and diseases to His followers. Anyone who is a believer can take that authority and ask the Father, in Jesus' name, and because we have asked in God's will, He will answer."

A woman from the back limped her way to the platform. "My back is twisted from an injury that happened last year. Will God heal it and make it like it was before?"

"Yes. He wants you whole. She had seen Paul and Epaphroditus pray for hurting people. Did she believe the Lord would work through her? Holy Spirit, You are my help. Apart from You, I can do nothing. Please lead me in how to pray for this woman.

She stepped down beside her. "I am going to lay my hands on you and pray. Is that all right with you?"

The woman nodded. "Lord," Daphne said, "You went about doing good and cast out all demons and healed all who were sick while you were here. Now Father, we come to You to ask, in Jesus' name, for You to heal this woman's back and restore her to health. Thank You, Lord. To You be the glory. Amen."

The woman opened her eyes and tried to stand erect. Light flickered from her eyes and lit up her face. She looked at Daphne. "It happened! My back feels normal!' She twisted her chest from side to side. "It is straight, again! Oh, thank you, thank you, I—"

"No. No, do not thank me. Thank the Lord Jesus. He is the healer. He is the one who healed you."

Instantly, people flocked to the woman's side. They questioned her and demanded she touch her toes and rise again. She complied, beaming with joy. "Misses, I want your Jesus for my Lord, too. Will you pray for me?" Several others joined and Daphne led them all in prayer to receive Jesus as Lord. As soon as she finished, people rushed up and asked her to pray for a multitude of sicknesses. She took a few moments to explain that all healings are not instant, that some manifested over time, but they were to wait patiently and continue to believe healing would come. It was quite late when the last straggler left the field.

Daphne covered her eyes. "I am so spent, so ready to go home."

Melita put her arm around her waist. "You have had quite a night. Come, let us get into the carriage." They rode home with her head on Melita's shoulder.

At breakfast the next day, Cyrene suggested a change. "Daphne, would you like to go to the market with me today? It might be good to take a break. We can go see what's new and get back in time for you to rest before tonight's meeting?"

Each carried a small basket as they started out by mid-morning,. Batano insisted he come along, but followed at a subtle distance. Daphne examined everything, "Oh, look at those plums. Is it really time for them to ripen?" She put some in her basket, reminded of how long she had been away

347

from Nicanor. "Maybe your cook will make that wonderful plum dish again."

Cyrene laughed. "I am afraid you are going to get fat on his cooking and Nicanor will not recognize you when he comes."

They decided to cross the street and investigate the linens in a booth with a pretty swag across its front. Cyrene was but a few steps ahead of her when a carriage careened in their direction. The horses were nearly upon them when Batano leaped from behind and pushed Daphne from its path.

He had barely cleared the danger himself, but quickly worked his way up off the ground. He rushed over to her. "Are you all right? I am sorry there was no time to—"

"Oh, Batano, thank God you were with us." She looked over at Cyrene. She had not moved. Daphne crawled over and pulled her onto her back. "Cyrene, Cyrene, are you all right?"

She moaned. Her face was covered with blood from a gash on her head. Daphne spun toward Batano. "Please, help me get her over to that bench." He took one arm and she the other. Cyrene staggered and her legs buckled. Batano caught her, picked her up, and carried her to the bench.

Shoppers joined them, offering sympathy and disgust with the negligent driver. The woman in the linen booth brought a cloth dipped in cool water. "Here, put this on her head."

A man asked if they saw whose carriage had nearly hit them. Cyrene had lost consciousness and Daphne and Batano were not familiar with enough people to know. Disgust flashed across the man's face. "It looked to me like the driver aimed right for you."

Chapter Fifty-Eight

*...confirming the word through accompanying
signs...*
– Mark 16:20

Daphne could not stop shaking. Cyrene's mother paced. "What is taking the doctor so long?" Word had gotten around that it probably was not an accident. Her eyes pierced Daphne's. "Her father is going to be so upset. He has been very suspicious of this thing you have gotten her and Demas involved in." She frowned. "I do not mean to be inhospitable, Daphne, but..."

The doctor wiped his hands on a towel as he emerged from Cyrene's room. "I do not think there will be any ongoing problems. She has come around some, and has already asked what happened."

Cyrene's mother rushed over to him. "Can I see her? Are you sure she will be all right?"

"Her head will ache for days. I have stitched the cut over her eye. Change the bandage tonight or if it begins to seep. The potions, I left, will help her sleep but wake her every few hours until this time tomorrow, just to be sure. I will come by, in the morning, to check on her."

He left and Cyrene's mother made it clear that she, alone, intended to stay and monitor her daughter. Her tone quelled all hope that Daphne could look in on her friend, so she quietly left. Melita followed her back to Cyrene's house where Daphne fell in a heap just inside the door. She knelt beside her. "It is not your fault, Misses. "

"How could I have been so careless? I should have been more vigilant. I had been warned twice. Cyrene might have been killed."

Melita's gentle voice comforted her. "But she was not. Our God was right there with you. He even made sure Batano was along and alert. We all knew the enemy would try to stop the message from getting out, but God is our protector, and He displayed His faithfulness.

Daphne wiped her tears and slowly pulled herself to her feet. "You are right, but it is hard to dismiss the picture of Cyrene lying in the street, bloody and silent. I do not want any of you to be in danger because of me."

"We all know that. And do not forget, God chose each of us to help you. It is the reason He brought us alongside you. Here, let me get you into a fresh tunic. Your skirt is stained and torn. It probably ripped when you fell, but I am sure I can mend it."

She relaxed and let Melita mother her, grateful for her counsel and the Lord's assurance Cyrene was in His hands. She sent Batano to the others to inform them of what happened and gave in to Melita's coaxing she take a short rest. Later, she went to check on Cyrene. But again, her mother insisted she, alone, would keep watch and Daphne should not disturb her daughter.

It was time to leave for the meeting, but Demas had not shown up. He had made a brief visit to Cyrene right after the accident, but Daphne did not hear him say he might be held up. She stood at her window and watched. Lord, what should I do? All she heard was, *Wait and trust Me, I am in control.*

"I know, Lord, but what will they do if—"

Demas charged through the door. "I am here. Come on. Hurry. Sorry I am so late. Mother tried to get me to stay home, but Cyrene is doing all right. I told mother I knew she would take good care of her and assured her I would look in on my sister when we returned. She needs to understand Cyrene believed in what we are doing and would want me to go help."

They drove off, but Daphne did not miss the anguish on his face. She touched his arm after he helped her down at Baltos' field. "Are you all right?"

"I will be fine. We had best hurry. Baltos is probably worried."

During the worship, Daphne released her concerns for Cyrene and Demas and turned her thoughts to the task ahead. "Lord, so many people have come to hear about You. Help me make Your message clear and say only what You give me to speak."

Baltos' field was packed beyond reach of the torch lights. She concentrated on sharing the freedom from sin, the gift God's Son, Jesus brought to the world. The newcomers were full of questions. They wanted to hear what had happened to her. She tried to condense it for the sake of those who attended nightly, but no one seemed to mind listening to her testify of God's goodness to her again. When she opened the sessions to questions, a man asked why the demon within her had been so bent on deceiving people.

"Friends, the ruler of the kingdom of darkness knows what is to come. He knows that on the day when the Father sends Jesus back to earth, He will no longer come as the gentle Lamb of God, as we know Him today. He will come back as a Lion, a warrior who will send Satan and all his demons into the fires of hell for eternity. They know their time is limited and they want to take as many as they can with them."

A few more questions came before she invited those who wanted to receive Jesus as their Savior to come forward. Many of the new people responded. "Oh, Lord, how great You are!" She led them in a prayer for salvation, surprised at how many others joined after that to ask for prayer for healing. She looked over the lot with an awareness in her spirit. That is what brought so many here tonight, Lord. Word about last night's healings traveled fast.

Daphne looked at the expectant faces of those who stood before her and reminded herself that God promised miracles would follow the sharing of the Gospel. Oh Lord, thank You that this does not depend on me. You are the One who heals.

"Friends, God has given the authority to all believers to pray for the sick, so I ask Demas and Kerpos, whom you heard testify tonight, to come and help me pray for all of you."

The people lined up in front of the three of them and murmurs of prayer filled the air. She placed her hands on the ears of a man who asked if the Lord would restore his hearing. "Jesus, You who rose with healing in Your wings and healed the deaf while You walked the earth, please open this man's ears to hear again. We know healing is part of Your covenant with us, so we ask this Father, in Jesus' name."

The man's eyes grew wide. His mouth fell open and spread into a smile. He pointed at the man softly playing his flute. "I can hear him!" He hollered it again, loud enough for the whole crowd to take notice. They jumped to their feet and celebrated with him.

A lady with a protruding growth asked Kerpos for prayer. Disappointed when it remained, she came to Daphne. She hugged her. "Do not be discouraged. Be patient and keep believing and remember to praise God for your healing. It is His will for you to be healed so it will happen. Do not give up." After everyone had been prayed for and had left, the group gathered to thank God for His faithfulness.

Abiron spoke for the rest. "Daphne, we all know what happened today and are concerned. Word of these amazing healings will not stay within these people. The news will spread even faster than yesterday. We have all prayed and concluded it is best if you do not go back into the city or any place where you will be vulnerable to the enemy's attack."

"But Abiron, we have to get the word out. Even here in Baltos' field, who knows what the enemy might do? I will be careful and pray about where I go, but we cannot live in fear. This is God's mission and I cannot let Him down."

He nodded. "I know. Truth has to be told. We just do not want to lose you. You are the heart of this mission."

She clasped his hand. ""And all of you are a greater part than you can imagine." She gestured at the whole field where people had gathered. "Without your help, none of this would have happened. In fact, I would like you to give the message tomorrow night."

His jaw fell. "Really? I am not sure I—"

"But I am. The Lord spoke to me that people needed to hear from others, not just me. You have a great story of your own journey to belief, and there are those who will identify with where you have been. I promise to pray for you right up until the meeting begins."

He rubbed the back of his neck. "All right, I will hold you to that promise. He turned to leave but twisted back. "Tell me, how is Cyrene? I have not stopped praying for her."

"Her mother has kept me from her, but she says Cyrene is talking and has begun to eat and drink a little. Please pray for her parents. They resent the changes in her and Demas."

"Do you think her mother would let me visit?"

Daphne looked into his eyes and he blushed. "I think that would be wonderful, Abiron. But I would wait a day or two."

They left, but Demas followed her to Cyrene's door. He asked her how his sister looked to her, and she informed him that his mother had not, yet, let her see Cyrene.

"What? What is that about? Why has she not let you see her?"

Daphne tried not to sound critical. "I am not sure. She said your father was upset with you and your sister's involvement in why I am here. Perhaps it is time for me to leave."

"No, that is not what is going on. My father and I got into an angry discussion about it this morning, even before we knew about Cyrene's injury. He is very hard headed, stuck in the tradition of Apollo like his parents and grandparents before him. I finally had to tell him this is what I believe and I will not change. If he wants me to leave home that is his choice, but I have to do what is right for me."

I have come to set father against son, daughter-in-law against her mother-in-law, ran through her mind

"Demas, I am so sorry. It is distressing to be at odds with one's parents."

They talked for a while before he said he needed to check on Cyrene and intended to question his mother.

Chapter Fifty-Nine

...your young men shall see visions.
– Joel 2:28

Daphne turned to blow out her lamp when loud pounding, on the front door, alarmed her. She ran down the stairs with Melita close behind.

Demas looked frantic. "You must come! I had hardly slept when I heard my mother cry out. She said it was too soon to wake Cyrene when I first arrived, but then I found her bent over my sister, shaking her shoulders and screaming for her to wake up." I tried to help but Mother was inconsolable. She kept begging, "Please wake up Cyrene. Please, please wake up."

Both Daphne and Melita threw on robes and followed him back to his house. At the door to Cyrene's room, she paused and asked Melita to go find Batano and send him for the doctor.

Cyrene's mother had collapsed beside the bed. Daphne put her arm around her shoulders. "I have sent my servant for the doctor. Do not be afraid. Our God is with Cyrene."

The woman pulled herself up to her knees, agony and rancor contorted her face. "Your God? If it were not for the one you call your God, my daughter would not lie here near death." Deflated by the effort, her head sunk back to the floor.

Daphne did not recoil or make any attempt to defend herself. She bowed her head and placed her hand on Cyrene's forehead. "Father, I come to You in the name of Jesus. I know Your desire is for my friend to be healed. She is Your child Her sins and her healing were paid for on the cross. Lord, You said that by the blood that flowed from the beating You took, we would be healed. I believe it, Lord, and ask that her healing manifest, in Jesus' name."

She raised her head and spoke to the realm of principalities and the powers of darkness. "And I tell you, Satan, by the authority given me by the Lord, Jesus Christ, leave Cyrene and be gone in the name of Jesus. Every demonic spirit of infirmity be gone in Jesus' name"

Demas had roused his father and they rushed into the room as she finished. He glared at Daphne and pulled his wife up from the floor. "How is Cyrene? Has she moved or spoken?"

Daphne backed out of the way.

Demas put his fingers on Cyrene's neck. "Her pulse is strong." He put his ear to her lips. "And her breathing is even. Maybe she is in a deep sleep. There is healing in rest."

Cyrene's mother raged at her son. "That is not what the doctor said! He said we should wake her every few hours and I cannot get her to... to..." She cried out and collapsed again. "Maybe, she will never wake up."

Daphne joined Melita outside the room. She shivered at the ire in Cyrene's father's eyes. Help him, Lord. He is afraid for his daughter.

Demas bent to lift his mother. "This will not help. Father, please, let us leave Cyrene to rest and wait and see what the doctor says." As they prepared to go, a servant ushered the doctor in with Batano close behind. Cyrene's father growled in his direction. "What are you doing here?" To Batano's relief, the doctor gestured for the parents to accompany him to Cyrene's bedside.

Demas guided Daphne, Melita, and Batano into Cyrene's old room which overlooked the gulf. Daphne wiped her cheeks. "I am so sorry I brought this on, Cyrene. I wish I had —"

"Nonsense. There is no way you could have known of our enemy's evil plans. God is not going to let my sister die. He is a good God and He is with us."

The four of them held hands, Daphne on one side and Melita on Demas' other while he prayed. "Lord, You said if two or three gather in Your name and agree upon anything, it would be done for them. We agree that You are with Cyrene, healing her right now and will restore her back to us. Thank You, Father, for hearing the prayer we have asked in Jesus' name."

Melita's eyes welled. "Your sister is blessed to have you pray for her." He squeezed her hand, unaware both their eyes expressed the intimate connection they longed for.

Cyrene's father pushed into the room. "Demas, I am taking your mother to bed. The doctor said he will stay with Cyrene until morning, and that there is nothing we can do but wait."

"Good. Mother needs to rest. I will stay for a while and make sure the doctor has anything he might need." His father huffed and left without a word to the others.

The four of them sat in silence with Demas and Daphne occasionally peeking in to check on Cyrene. Each time, the doctor indicated no change. After a few hours, Demas encouraged the others to get some sleep. "There's nothing more we can do except continue to believe God heard our prayers. I will stay until morning and let you know if there is a change."

Daphne woke early and dressed while Melita still slept. She tiptoed down the stairs and let herself into Demas' parents' home where she found him curled on a settee softly snoring. Quietly, she opened the door to Cyrene's room and peeked in. The doctor hovered over her. She stepped close and whispered, "Any change?"

He startled, then motioned for her to follow him back through the door. Demas woke and brushed the cowlick from his eyes. "What has happened? Is she awake?"

The doctor shook his head. "I am sorry. There has been no change. She is at rest and that is a good thing. I suspect the blow to her head was harder than we thought. Sometimes the body knows better than we do and puts us on hold while it restores or completes the healing. I am going to leave her in your hands. Make sure someone is always with her and try to get her to drink if she rouses." He picked up his bag. "Tell her mother I will be back, this afternoon, to check on her."

She showed the doctor out. "Demas, you need to update your parents on what the doctor said. I will stay with Cyrene until your mother comes or for as long as she wants me to."

Melita soon joined her and they had breakfast in Cyrene's room.

That afternoon, Daphne struggled to release the heaviness in her heart. Cyrene's mother had taken over by mid-morning. She would not look at her and communicated no more than necessary. *Forgive her, Lord. It is her only daughter. I believe You have healed Cyrene. Help me to stand fast and not give in to the lies of the enemy.* She spent most of the day thanking God and praising Him for His faithfulness, as well as praying for her friend and the nightly meeting.

Demas arrived, earlier than usual, to pick up her and the others. He said he had ducked into Cyrene's room and tried to encourage his mother. "She said the doctor came by, but there was nothing he could do and told us to continue to keep watch. I told her there was something she could do, believe with us for her healing and put her in God's hands. She scowled but I ignored it, hugged her, and left."

The ride to Baltos' field was quiet. They were surprised when Batano asked them to wait by the carriage for a moment. "I want you all to know Cyrene is going to come out of this. While I prayed, the Lord gave me a vision. I saw her on her bench in her garden having breakfast like she does sometimes, still in her robe with her hair undone. That is how I knew it was after she came back to us."

Daphne clasped her hands to her chest. "Oh, Batano, that is wonderful. You have confirmed what we all prayed would come to pass." Joy and relief lifted everyone's spirits as they headed for the field.

Abiron called out as he ran up to them, "Demas, Daphne, I am so glad you are early. Something is going on. Look at the crowd." They followed the sweep of his arm. By this time each night, people packed in and placed their blankets to hold their spots while they mingled. But tonight, only a couple dozen people had shown up.

Demas frowned. "Where is Baltos? Have the magistrates shut us down again?"

"We do not think so, and those who are here have no idea what has kept people away."

Orestes rushed up to them. "Baltos took his horse and went to see what he could find. I would like to get my hands on the high priest and his cohorts, I know they are behind this."

Pounding hooves drew their attention. Baltos left his horse at the outer gate and ran over, his face pale. "Friends, I have bad news. Cronos' body was discovered just hours ago in the foothills of our mountain. Word has spread that Apollo is angry and has sent the muses to take revenge on any who listen to tales of a greater god. People are so frightened, I could hardly get them to tell me what happened."

Chapter Sixty

To do evil is like sport to a fool...
– Proverbs 10:23

Daphne gasped. "Oh, no! Poor Cronos. Who would do such a thing?"

"We may never know, but we know who is behind it." Abiron's face reflected his anger.

Orestes agreed. "And I have no doubt the high priest's cronies are the ones who planted Satan's thoughts in order to scare people off. We need to track down who started those rumors." He looked at Baltos. "Was anything said about how he died? Did anybody see anything?"

"It was no accident. One man said there was a rumor Cronos had been beaten to death, but he would not say where he heard it. Most were so afraid they would not open their doors. They even insinuated it was my fault, or ours, for teaching about a god other than Apollo."

Demas scowled. ""I cannot believe it. I warned Cronos to be careful, but he wanted to help." He pressed his lips and loosed a deep sigh. "I wonder if his father found he had passed information to us?" He searched the faces of his friends. "Could a man, actually, allow his own son to be a scapegoat in order to uphold his loyalty to a god bent on evil?"

Abiron put his hand on Demas' shoulder. "Think about what the Father allowed His Son to suffer. Thank God His sacrifice was meant for good. It is not your fault, Friend. You warned him of the danger. Cronos' father has always been a strong supporter of the temple. Remember how viciously he reacted at the meeting at my house?" He looked at Daphne and shook his head. "I think our city has its first martyr. Who knew persecution would be so ugly?"

Baltos glanced at those waiting for the meeting to begin. Some had wandered over or stared in their direction. He pointed it out to Daphne "What do you want me to do?"

"I have prayed for wisdom, and I believe God is saying we cannot let the enemy defeat us. We are to gather those who are here and tell them exactly what has happened. They need to know we have a wicked enemy, but more importantly, that we have a God who is greater than Satan and God will prevail."

Everyone agreed, so they went into the field and encouraged the people to gather close. Daphne bypassed the platform and stood among them. "Friends, we have received some very bad news." She told them about Cronos' death and what they knew about it. Many knew the young man, but few knew of his strong faith or his bravery.

"I want you all to realize Satan is not pleased that you have chosen to believe in his arch enemy, our Almighty God. Jesus told us to expect persecution, but He also said He would always be with us. He who is in each of you is greater than he who wants to destroy us. Cronos chose to do what God asked of him. He stood up for the Lord under difficult circumstances. He knew he might suffer, even lose his earthly life, but he has gained eternal life. That is something the devil can never take from him."

The face of a woman near Daphne turned white. "But we, too, are in danger then. If the high priest arranged for him to be killed, we could be next."

"Yes, it's possible but not likely. We believe this happened to frighten people into the belief that Apollo is real and can command mythical creatures. They do not exist and cannot kill people. You have learned Satan is behind that lie and each of you must decide who you will believe. The Lord will be with you, but if you choose to deny He is the true God, you will be subject to the wiles of the enemy."

Much murmuring and a few more questions were posed and answered. The meeting ended and most of the people affirmed their decision to trust God. Daphne waved them off. "Remember, God is for you, a very present help in time of trouble. Help your neighbors understand what we have shared with you and tell them we will meet tomorrow night, no matter what."

Daphne stopped to check on Cyrene when she returned. A cot had been set up with bedding stacked upon it. Distrust flared from Cyrene's mother's eyes as she rejected the offer to stay with her friend through the night. She longed to assure the troubled woman with Batano's vision, but her icy refusal drove Daphne away in silence.

The next morning, she sought the Lord about the sad turn of events. *Go check with the former priest*, resounded in her spirit.

She summoned Batano and he reminded her of her promise to not put herself in danger. "I know I said I would be cautious, but I kept getting these instructions and have asked the Lord to protect us."

The innkeeper's wife was out sweeping around the front when they arrived. Daphne approached with caution. "Excuse me, Madam, could you summon..." She had no idea what his name was and to refer to him as a former priest might jeopardize his well-being.

The woman looked at her strangely. "Are you looking for guest who might be staying at our inn?"

"Yes. I don't know his name, but he is quite tall with dark hair and a close-cropped beard."

She shook her head. "There is no one here like that."

Daphne wheeled around and faced Batano. "Oh, of course, now I remember. He said he planned to leave soon to join his family in Athens."

The woman cocked her head. "Are you sure he was going to stay here? We have not had anyone that looked like that in recent months. Maybe he stayed with friends."

Daphne thanked her and they walked, slowly, toward Cyrene's house. She mulled over a dozen possibilities. That must be it. He has already left, or he found friends to stay with. But why would God tell me to go see him? By the time they reached Cyrene's room, she decided God had a reason and she would know why in time.

Demas' father was with his wife when they made a quick stop. Hostility rose when they peeked in on Cyrene, so they went back to her house. A rap on the door brought dread. Had her father come to ask them not to come around again or to leave Cyrene's home? Daphne parted the curtains, relieved to see only Demas.

"Welcome. Come in. How is Cyrene? Your father was there, so we left."

"She is the same. I do not blame you for avoiding Father. He really is a decent man. He just finds change hard, maybe impossible."

She smiled at him. "With God nothing is impossible. Have you heard anything more about Cronos? Will the magistrates be looking for his killer or did they drop it?"

"Orestes has been out snooping around. You know he gets pretty upset when things are not what they should be. He shows a bit of a temper, sometimes."

"Did he find out anything?"

"Only that a sheep herder found Cronos right out in the open. He was bleeding but still alive, not hidden as you might expect. By the time he got help, Cronos was dead."

"Sounds like they wanted his body to be found. Is the herder the one who spread the rumors about the muses?"

Demas shrugged. "I doubt it. Most herders are loners. They do not mix much with city people."

"I wonder if Cronos said anything. Maybe we should find that herder, and see if he saw or heard something that would prove Cronos was murdered by a human. We need evidence to prove it was not some imaginary creature Satan trumped up."

"That's a great idea. I will see if Orestes can get the person who told him this to describe the herder or tell him who he is. Since Cronos was alive when he was found, it is possible the killer was still in the area."

That night, only about half of the usual crowd showed up. Melita surveyed the field as they entered. "At least some of the people have dared to believe God is with us."

Daphne nodded. "The men went to as many as would listen to pray with them and encourage them to stand strong and trust God. I wonder if Orestes was able to find the sheep herder?"

"You will know soon. Here he comes."

He wasted no time. "I know who the herder is, but it was too late to try to find him. I will set out first thing tomorrow. Most take their sheep out early on the same few routes. I will send word if I find anything that will help us."

She thanked him and they joined the others. Melita signaled to those who helped with the music and the meeting began. Before Daphne introduced Abiron, she repeated what she had shared with those who were there the night before. "Remember the void in your lives before you came to Christ. Be encouraged and stand strong."

Abiron affirmed his confidence in what she stated and began to share his story. People hung on his every word. They laughed at his honest failures and wept at his pain. Each response confirmed the Lord had instructed her to ask him to speak. The meeting ended without any new converts but with several undeniable healings.

Their carriage had traveled but a short distance when they came upon a man in the center of the road. He waved them down and asked them to stop. Daphne recognized the former priest. She reached for Melita's hand, her eyes wide with uncertainty.

Chapter Sixty-One

Evil will bow before the good...
– Proverbs 14:19

The man drew close to the carriage. Instantly, Batano placed himself between the man and Daphne. The former priest raised his palms. "I mean no harm. I must speak to Daphne."

She nodded and Batano moved to one side, poised and ready to pounce. She noticed the man had returned to wearing priestly garments. She asked, "What is it?"

"I must speak to you, alone. It's about the high priest."

Her brows rose. "But you said you had turned from the fallacy of Apollo's temple. How is it you know his plans?"

"Please, we both could be in great danger. Could you come down and speak with me for just a few moments?"

Demas stood up and answered for her. "No, we will not take that chance. We do not know you nor where you stand. There have been threats against Daphne and we are all in this with her. Whatever you know, you will have to say in front of us."

The priest looked disgruntled. He shifted his focus back to her and nodded. I talked with you that night and decided I could be of more help if I went back to the temple and listened for whatever the high priest planned."

She tempered a brewing accusation. "Yes, I went to find you at the inn. They said you had never stayed there."

His pause failed to hide his surprise. "That is true. I did not stay there. Back at the temple, I volunteered to clean or do other menial chores that would bring me into proximity with the high priest and his counsel. Today, I overheard him venting his frustration that some plan of his had been leaked. It seems he took advantage of a gruesome murder to spread fear that the muses had been offended by talk of god other than Apollo, and were behind the killing. He groused that his ploy had not been as effective as he hoped."

Demas grimaced. "So, he was behind Cronos' murder. We were sure of it."

"Yes, and when he realized I could hear what he planned, he told me to leave and come back later. But I heard him say, 'Enough is enough. It is time for her to go.'" Concern swept his face. "I knew he meant you."

Her hand flew to her throat. "Do you know what he has in mind or where he plans to attack?"

"They had been discussing Baltos' field and which roads led into or away from it. That is all I heard before he sent me out. He is very nervous about who surrounds him, aware his lofty position could be lost in the same way he gained it. He scrutinized me as I rose to leave so I am sure I will not be allowed near him again. I may even be on his list to eliminate. He has done it many times before."

"Then you must not go back there. It is too dangerous. Baltos has a big estate. I am sure he would let you stay there until we can prove the high priest is behind Cronos' death."

"Thank you. I am with a family friend tonight, but I will ask Baltos in the morning."

He backed away and Demas flicked the reins. "Daphne, I am not sure I believe him."

She shrugged. "God will show us. Will you get word about what he said to Baltos and tell him I suggested he stay at his estate? Or I could send Batano."

"I'll see to it. Batano needs to be close enough to protect you at all times."

By mid-morning the next day, Demas and Orestes showed up at Cyrene's. "I wanted you to hear this from Orestes, Daphne. He found the shepherd."

"Really? So soon? Was he of any help? Did he see anyone or anything unusual?"

Orestes grimaced. "He said he saw nothing out of the ordinary when he took his sheep out that morning. That evening, he was halfway down the hills when he saw a man come toward him from below. He passed on the opposite side of his flock, so he did not get a close look, but noticed the man was tall. He found Cronos shortly after."

She frowned. "A lot of people are tall.."

Demas glanced at Orestes. "Tell her the rest."

"The herder said he found it unusual that a man who hiked in the mountains would wear a long, hooded covering."

Daphne gasped. "Oh, Demas...no."

"This is more than a coincidence, considering last night. The priest was not at the inn like he said and has not been back to the meetings. So, where has he been the last couple of days...at the temple? And why did he come find you last night? Did he plan to kill you and Batano's size scared him off, or was he setting something up? I wish we knew if he really stayed with an old friend last night or if he dashed back to the temple for new orders."

"Do you think the magistrates would look into it and arrest him?"

"I doubt it. They do not involve themselves much with temple affairs. They have a live and let live agreement. And we do not even know the man's name."

Orestes promised to let the others know what he found, especially Baltos, "If that guy is the killer, I do not like the idea of him hanging around our friend's house or any of our people. We need to be on the lookout for whatever plan the high priest might have hatched for tonight."

More souls had faced their fears and attended the nightly meeting. Melita was well into leading the worship when Daphne whispered to Baltos. "I am afraid I need to use your facilities."

"We are just getting started. There is plenty of time. You can go up to the house, or behind that grain storage there is a smaller building where we set up a place for the crowds. It has all you will need."

The outer building seemed closer, so she slipped away and followed the torch-lit path to the small, windowless dwelling. She entered and twisted the small block of wood that locked the door. She was nearly ready to depart when she heard someone try the door. She called, "I will be right out." There was no response, only the sound of footsteps that circled the building.

The priest's warning returned. *I know he meant you.* Her heart began to hammer. She cocked her ear and held her breath. Nothing stirred. She checked the lock. Why had she neglected to ask Batano to accompany her? She rubbed at the icy chill that chased down her upper arms.

Brush or leaves rustled as the door suddenly rattled. Her knees buckled. She grabbed the wall and prayed the lock would hold. What can I do? I cannot scream. No one would hear me. An involuntary cry escaped her lips when the door suddenly rattled, and the hinges began to shake. She stared at the handle and held her breath. "Lord, please help me."

A voice called from a distance. "Hey, what are you doing?" The rattling stopped, replaced by pounding footsteps that grew faint. "Daphne are you in there? It is I, Batano."

"Oh, Batano! Yes, thank God."" She unlocked the door and flew to his side.

He put his hands on her shoulders "Are you all right? Do you know who that was? Did you see his face?"

She collapsed onto a nearby pile of coarse packing bags and held her temples. "No, I only heard footsteps after I entered the building and then the door rattled." She shuddered. "Thank you so much for checking on me. I should have asked you to come with me. Could you see who it was? Do you think it was that priest? Has anyone seen him or know if he showed up at Baltos'?"

"I asked Baltos and he knew nothing, but told me where you had gone. Whoever it was ran off into the shadows before I could get close enough to see anything." His tone changed, almost scolding. "Misses, I promised Nicanor I would protect you. Please do not go off without me like this again. Nicanor would never get over it if I let something happen to you."

Tears rose at his loyalty. ""I am sorry, Batano, so sorry. I promise I will not. I did not mean to cause —"

"I know. Let us return before they all start to worry. There are a lot of new people tonight who want to know what's going on, and are waiting to hear about the power of our Lord to protect us."

Daphne nodded and stood to her feet. What a joy to hear him talk about You, Jesus.

They arrived just moments before Melita asked the people to welcome her. She took a deep breath. Lord, my insides are still jumping. Please, Holy Spirit, help me. I yield to Your peace within me.

Batano took her elbow and helped her climb the steps up the platform, then left to inform the others of what had happened. The stand was not more than two feet above ground, but the height gave her an unobstructed view of the people. She scanned their faces and smiled. Her sweep ended in a quick gasp. Behind the crowd, Demas and all the others had the man in priestly garments surrounded.

Chapter Sixty-Two

Peace I leave with you, My peace I give to you...
– John 14:27

The people were waiting. "Lord," Daphne whispered. "I don't want to alarm anyone. Please help me to leave whatever is happening with You and concentrate on why I am here."

She began by acknowledging the crowd's bravery in coming and encouraged them to believe God promised to send His angels to protect them. Once again, she gave a brief testimony of the power of God that delivered her from the demon of divination and brought her into a relationship with Christ. She expounded on the love and faithfulness of the Lord Jesus to fulfill His every promise. Out of the corner of her eye, she saw Demas motion to Batano. He and Kerpos remained while the others hustled the priest off of the field.

Another quick prayer rerouted her mind back to the people. After she finished her message, a man stood with a question. "We are taking a huge risk to put our trust in a God that is so new to us. How did you know you had completely put your trust in Jesus after all you went through?"

She searched her memory. What had triggered such an important milestone? "It was after I left Lydia's. I intended to run away but came upon my owner who was in great danger. I found it impossible to leave him like that, despite consequences I would face if I remained. Later, the Lord helped me see it was at that moment that I chose to put my trust in Him. You all may be at a similar point. I doubt any of you are in imminent danger, but I believe each of us will come to a time when we have to examine our hearts and decide what we truly believe."

More questions followed. "What gave you the courage to discard the idol and come to Christ?"

"Oh, My Friend, you have it backwards. I turned *to* God and *from* the idol that represented the demon that possessed me. Once you make Christ Lord of your life, He gives you the courage to turn from the lies of the evil one, and anything that would take preference over Him in your heart. That truth was also impressed upon me as I ran from Lydia's. So, I took the *teraphim* I had used to deceive men and threw the idol as hard as I could. It landed in a herd of swine." She grinned. "You should have seen them scatter. They squealed like piglets torn from their mother."

The people laughed with her. Each new question brought another opportunity to witness how the Lord had drawn her to Himself and would do the same for them. She ended the meeting with an invitation for any who had not made a commitment to come receive Christ. She laid hands on the last one and opened it to prayers for healing and more responded. The men had not returned so she asked Melita and Batano to help her pray.

Surprised, they looked at each other. Joy beamed from their faces. Neither had expected to be considered an equal part of the ministry while yet slaves. Several people stopped to encourage her to keep on spreading her message. The men who had hustled the priest from the meeting had not returned, so Batano and Melita accompanied her and Daphne asked Kerpos to join them.

Demas met them part way. "Well, I guess we are back to the start. The priest insists he was asleep in a bunkhouse near the overseer's quarters when Batano scared off whoever it was. He said he only arrived just as the music ended."

Batano winced. "Did they check that out?"

"A few slaves said they saw him go in there, but none could say he never left."

"What about the overseer?"

Demas shrugged. "He said he was not there the whole time, but the priest was asleep when he left."

Daphne fidgeted. "What do you think, Demas? Do you think he is spying for the high priest?"

"I wish I knew. He seems sincere, but how can we know? Was he supposed to kill you tonight and will he try again tomorrow?"

She shook her head. "We cannot know, but God knows. Let us leave. I feel an urgency to get back and see how Cyrene's doing."

Demas walked along beside her. "Yes, it has been three days, and I am afraid the doctor and my parents have given up hope of a recovery."

She pondered their words most of the way home. *Lord, it seems like a lot of things have come against us. Have we missed something, or failed You? Please do not let fear or unbelief lead us into doubt or to grow weary in believing.*

When their carriage arrived at Cyrene's, Daphne knew something was amiss at Demas's house. She nudged him, "Look at all those lights at your house. Every room is ablaze."

He sighed. "On no. Looks like Mother has called everyone to join her in a vigil to awaken Cyrene. Do you remember the myth based on Apollo's power to heal? Candles are part of the process.

Supposedly, flames are sanctioned by the god of light, so Cyrene can see to come back."

"That is sorcery. What can we do to stop it?"

He rubbed the back of his neck. "I am afraid my mother would create a terrible scene if we tried to convince them of the evil behind it. Let us commit to our own vigil. We can pray to the only One who has power to heal and can protect Cyrene from Mother's misguided intentions. Remember, the Lord confirmed His word through Batano's vision. We need to stand fast and believe it."

Daphne grimaced but agreed. They would spend the night negating the demon's power, pray, thank God for the victory, and praise the Lord for Cyrene's miracle. Even from her friend's house, for hours she could hear the people wail and cry out to Apollo. She shuddered. *They sound like the paid mourners hired for my father's funeral.*

Late into the night, things grew eerily quiet. She startled at a knock on their door. Cyrene's mother stumbled in, nearly incoherent. "I have nowhere else to turn. Apollo does not appear to have heard us or just does not care, so I sent everyone home." She staggered and Daphne eased her onto a settee. She grabbed Daphne's hand, too distraught to hold up her head. "Please, will you ask your God to bring Cyrene out of this sleep? I cannot bear to lose her."

Daphne held her while she sobbed. "I know how hard this has been on you and I am so sorry it happened. But we have every reason to believe Cyrene is being healed even as we speak. God loves her and He has promised."

Swollen eyes lifted to hers. "I know you really believe that. But how can you be so sure? It has been three days with no water and —"

Daphne pulled her to her feet. "Come, let us go to her. I want to show you something." The woman trembled as she helped her down the stairs and over to her home. At the room where her daughter lay, Daphne drew her to Cyrene's side. "Come closer. Look at her face."

Her mother's lips quivered as she stared. "It looks like...she is almost smiling."

"What you see is peace. Even in this state, Cyrene knows she is in God's hands and she is at peace."

Her mother fell to her knees. "Please help me. I need that peace, I have been so afraid."

Daphne knelt beside her and told her about the love of Jesus and how He wanted to give her that peace. It was not long before the woman surrendered her life and her fears to the Lord. Peace swept over her and her face relaxed. "Thank you, Daphne. I am so sorry I was rude to you, I—"

"No, do not even think about that. You are a brand-new creation in Christ now, and every wrong thing you have ever done is forgiven and forgotten." She helped her up. "You go get some sleep. I will stay with Cyrene till morning."

Her mother pressed a wet cheek to her daughter's. "Rest, Dear One. I have come to know your God and I am trusting you to His hands."

They had almost reached the door when a raspy, weak cry turned them around. "Water...Mother?"

They nearly fell over each other as they rushed to her side. Daphne seized the water vessel, and her mother held it to her daughter's lips, laughing and crying. "Cyrene, Cyrene, you are back. Oh, you are back. Oh, My Darling, I thought I had lost you."

Cyrene's eyes flickered. "Mother? Where have you been?"

Both she and Daphne laughed, unable to contain their joy. They pressed the liquid to her lips and coaxed her to drink as much as she could.

Melita woke and found Daphne gone. She panicked and ran over to where the vigil had been, relieved to find her there. "I was so afraid. I should have called Botano. She rubbed her eyes. I was praying and I guess I fell asleep. Are you all right? What has happened?"

Daphne took her hands and danced her in a circle. "It's Cyrene. She is awake! And she is back. Thanks be to our powerful, faithful God."

Melita hopped over to see for herself and joined the celebration. "Oh, I must go tell Demas." She blushed and covered her lips.

Daphne's eyes sparkled. "I think we need to let his *newly born-again mother* tell him. What do you think?"

Melita's face twisted. She looked at Daphne, then at Cyrene's mother. Her face brightened. "Really?"

"Yes, I believe. I truly believe… and just in time to welcome my daughter back. Oh, I need to tell Cyrene all about it." She bent over her daughter, but she had fallen back asleep. "Rest well, My Little One. We have so much to share next time you wake."

Daphne encouraged her to go tell the family, assuring her again that she would stay with Cyrene. Her mother stopped at the door and twisted around. "Somehow, I feel that Christ held back her return until I was so broken, I would listen and surrender my life to Him. Thank you for not giving up on her, Daphne...or me."

Chapter Sixty-Three

Beloved let us love one another for love is of God...
– 1 John 4:7

It was mid-summer and compared to the soft breezes Nicanor had welcomed on the Aegean, the Cenchrean Port steamed. He found the small structure where personal messages were held and reread Daphne's last lines. The letter confirmed she had sailed to Delphi but did not indicate when she left or planned to return. Hopes for a quick reunion buried, he left her notice of his arrival and found a carriage about to leave for Corinth. How would he find her?

To travel over the Isthmus was new but he had been to Athens, so the size of the city and endless crowds did not intimidate him. The driver dropped him at the inn where both Epaphroditus and Daphne had stayed.

He unpacked his bag, feeling alone. The unobtrusive ways Batano had always anticipated his every need, left a void. It would be good to see his former servant, again. "To know he has been there to protect my wife was worth it, Lord. But what do I do now? She could be here in Corinth, still in Delphi, or on her way back again."

The innkeeper announced dinner. "Yes, I remember your wife and her party...nice people, easy to please."

"Did she say she intended to stay here when she returned or give you any idea of how long she planned to be gone?"

"Let me ask my wife." Moments later, the innkeeper returned from the kitchen and shook his head. "Neither of us can recall anything specific. Maybe you should check with the people at the nightly meetings she and her friends attended."

He thanked the man and turned in for the night. His mind raced with the joy the joy of being with Daphne again. He could, hardly, wait to hold her each night and awaken to her bright smile. "Oh, Lord, thank you for bringing her to me. To be part of Patharus' family would be so empty without her."

He ate a hearty breakfast of a ham and cheese dish with fresh bread, and then walked into the heart of the city. The number of Greek and Roman temples amazed him. Sailors, he had sailed with, jested and assured him the 1000 priestesses of Aphrodite's temple did not come out until evening. There had been prostitutes in Athens and some back home, but he found the sheer number of those who paid homage to this goddess by joining their bodies to men, hard to believe.

No one, he asked, knew of Paul or his meetings. He remembered that Epaphroditus mentioned he attended afternoon gatherings of God's people at the home of a woman named Chloe. He wandered until he found a man who directed him to her house. "That is where you will find her, but be careful, there are strange things going on there and those people can be pretty persuasive."

He chuckled. Well, that is a good thing, is it not, Lord? It was only mid-morning and there was no one around so he knocked on the door. "Excuse me Madam. Are you Chloe?"

She said she was and listened while he explained he was from Philippi, looking for his wife, who had stayed in the city before going on to Delphi. "What did you say her name was?"

"Daphne." He gestured, "She is about this tall with brown eyes and dark brown hair. You might have seen her at Paul's meetings. She was anxious to hear him and—"

Chloe's face lit up. "Oh, Daphne! My, yes, I know who you mean. Do come in."

They talked for over an hour. He told her how the Lord brought them together and of Daphne's call to come back to Delphi and tell people about Jesus. In turn, she told him how Paul turned her city upside down with the salvation message. "You would have been so proud of Daphne. She, courageously, shared her testimony at a meeting right here in my courtyard. My, what she had gone through."

"Really? That is wonderful...I wish I could have been here."

"I am sure you will hear her speak soon. Are you on your way to Delphi from here?"

He shrugged. "That is why I have come to Corinth. I need to find some clue as to where she is...still in Delphi, back here, or on her way. I hoped some of the believers might have seen her or that she told someone of her plans. The last message at the Port said she had gone to Delphi."

Chloe stood up. "Let me fix you some lunch. There is no meeting here today, as Paul is busy with some of the city's magistrates. But he will speak tonight. I suspect Daphne is still in Delphi because I have not seen her, and I am sure she would want us to hear what happened there."

He accepted her offer, and after a pleasant lunch left with instructions on how to get to the nightly meetings. A long walk through the city led to an afternoon nap until dinner was announced. He left the inn with plenty of time to find the meeting and hear Paul.

There is a God in heaven who reveals secrets.
– Daniel 2:28

Demas and his father charged into Cyrene's room shortly after her mother left. Daphne stepped, graciously, into the adjoining room as both rushed to her bedside. Cyrene's father called his daughter's name as Demas tried to calm him. "Just take her hand, Father. She will probably go in and out of sleep, but at least we know she is back and has had water."

Cyrene's eyes fluttered. When she uttered, "Water," her lips were so cracked they bled.

Demas put the cup to her lips. "Here you are, *Kalon*. Drink all you can."

Daphne smiled at the name, and blinked at tears the special term of endearment evoked. Demas' tenderness with his sister turned her thoughts to Alexander. "Oh, Lord," she whispered, "wherever my brother is, please bring him to Yourself and grant us a reunion."

Cyrene's mother returned with servants, loaded with breakfast trays. Cyrene fell back asleep while everyone except her father enjoyed the feast. Over and over, each one shared his excitement over what God had done. The servants leaked the news and soon Batano joined the celebration. Demas nudged him. "Tell mother about the vision you had while Cyrene slept."

He covered the side of his mouth with his hand. "Are you sure she will want to hear it?"

"Oh, I forgot. You do not know. Mother became a believer last night...or was it this morning?"

Everyone laughed at their mutual loss of time. Batano's smile lit up his face. "That is wonderful."

To hear how he had seen Cyrene healed and having breakfast in her garden sent tears down her mother's face, but her father just stared. Someone shouted, "She is awake again," and everyone jumped to see for themselves. Each patted her hands or hugged her with expressions of great joy at her return.

Her father grabbed Demas' arm. "It is time we get going. The animals need their food." He made his way out of the room, avoiding Batano as he passed.

Cyrene's mother insisted Daphne go get some sleep. "I know you have a meeting tonight and you need some rest. I am going to send word to the doctor and have some broth made up in case she is ready to take something besides water. Have you noticed how thin she is?"

Daphne agreed and she and Melita left for their rooms. Her thoughts crowded the pull of sleep and she lay wide awake. She prayed for Cyrene and for her mother and her father and revisited the possibility of the former priest being a spy. She thought about how happy Abiron would be when he heard about Cyrene. Finally, her thoughts settled on the Lord and His goodness, and she fell asleep.

Hours later she awoke in a panic, her heart pounding, and her tunic damp. She had run as fast as she could, but the high priest was nearly upon her. He rode in a black carriage and waved the knife that still dripped with his superior's blood. She tripped on a cobble stone and hit the ground. Mercifully, the fall jarred her awake.

She tried to orient herself. The room was full of sunlight. Why was she in bed in the middle of the day? The nightmare faded and her heart quieted. "Lord, it has been a long time since that dream tortured me. Please help me. I know fear is not from You."

The sweat-soaked tunic grew cold and made her shiver. She pulled it off and reached for a blanket. For a while, she rocked herself and whispered the name of Jesus. Fear left and peace seeped like warm syrup over corn cakes.

"Why did the dream return, Lord? I know the man means me harm, but the carriage did not touch me and if someone tried to kill me last night, he failed. What does it mean?" She spent the next hour in prayer. She asked for wisdom and understanding to know His heart and His will, then submitted to the cry of her spirit to pray. Out of her mouth flowed the rivers of living waters, beseeching God in words she had never learned. In time, she quieted and listened, comforted that the Spirit knew the Father's will and had prayed, accordingly.

I will tell you things to come when you need them. I did not send that dream, but your inner spirit has discerned that you not let your guard down. Listen to my Spirit and He will direct your path and counsel you. Be prepared to do the warfare I authorized you to do, and do not fear the evil one. Nothing shall harm you.

She rose from her knees, revived. "I trust You, Lord."

Chapter Sixty-Four

...He was moved with compassion...
- Matthew 9:36

Nicanor's feet, hardly, touched the rocky street on his return from Paul's meeting. "Lord, such wisdom given to one man...I could have listened to him all night." He laughed, "I guess it is well into the night." With quick steps, he dodged the dozens of bold prostitutes in revealing costumes who approached him. Their heavy perfumes nauseated him. He was not far from the outskirts of the city when the sound of someone sobbing diverted him.

He stopped and listened. It came from an area between a darkened temple and the palestra. Epaphroditus' warning flashed in his mind. Don't walk the streets of Corinth alone at night. Lots of evil waits there.

Compassion overrode the warning. "I do not think it is trouble. It sounds like a child." He moved, slowly, toward the sound until he could see a small figure hunched against the building. He stepped close as she jumped to her feet and backed, hands in front of her face.

He followed a few steps. "I did not mean to frighten you. I heard you crying. Can I help?"

She backed up farther. "No, no one can. Please do not come in here. Run. For your own sake, run."

"Why not let me accompany you home? This is no place for a young woman at night." He reached out his hand. "Come, I will..."

Footsteps rustled on the path behind him before blackness shut out everything.

He satisfies the longing soul.
– Psalms 107:9

Daphne rode in silence, contemplating the Lord's word to her. Don't let my guard down...follow the Spirit's counsel...be ready for warfare...I will not be harmed....

Everyone at the meeting who knew Cyrene and had been praying for her wanted to hear about her recovery, especially Abiron. "Did she remember the accident? Is she eating? What did her parents say? Do you think I could see her tomorrow?"

Daphne laughed. "Abiron, she just came out of it. I am sure she will be delighted with a visit, but I think tomorrow might be too soon."

He shrugged. "I know. It is just that I want to see for myself."

Orestes saw them and hurried over. "Daphne, Kerpos will not be with us tonight. You remember his father has been ill for a long time?" She nodded. "He has taken a turn for the worse, and Kerpos has asked that you and Demas stop by after the meeting and pray for him."

"Of course, and I will let Melita know Kerpos' wife will not be here tonight to help with the music. Baltos is speaking and perhaps we can leave a little early." The group, which included the priest, gathered briefly. They asked the Lord to bless the message and anoint Baltos with grace to speak what was on his heart. The worship ended and Daphne opened the meeting with prayer. She then turned it over to Baltos.

People responded to the humility of this wealthy landowner. Daphne sat in the back and rejoiced to hear this relatively new babe in Christ boldly declare his faith and hope in Jesus. Lord, You are amazing. There are almost as many here as before Cronos' death. You are greater than the evil in this city, and nothing can thwart Your plan to get the truth out through these strong believers. Perhaps it is time for me to return to Corinth and home. She smiled, surprised she no longer considered Delphi home.

She joined Baltos at the end to pray for those who wanted to make Jesus their Lord or for healing, then left the others to finish up. Joy and expectation accompanied them to Kerpos' father's estate Daphne hardly noticed when they passed the road to her former home. His wife brought them to the older man's door. "Kerpos, our friends are here.'"

Daphne hugged her. "We missed you tonight. How is he doing?"

Her eyes pooled. "It does not look good. He can be tough on everyone but hides a heart full of kindness from most."

Kerpos came out, shutting the door behind him. "His favorite servant is with him. He never adjusted to Mother's death, but this woman seems to help him cope."

Demas put a hand on Kerpos' shoulder. "Has he been open to the good news?"

"Somewhat. My father can be stubborn. I am not sure he would let me know what he thinks."

"Is he awake? Can we pray for him?"

"Yes, I would like him to have one last chance to receive Jesus. Maybe just you, Demas...I am not sure how he feels about listening to a woman."

Daphne touched his arm. "That is fine. The rest of us will wait here and pray in the Spirit."

In less than ten minutes, Demas came out chuckling. Kerpos rushed over. "What? Did he ask you to leave?"

"No. He said people have told him about Daphne and it is she he wants to talk to."

They all looked at each other, heads shaking. She rose to her feet. "Please cover me with prayer. God said he poured His Spirit on His sons and His daughters. Sounds like I will need a big dose."

Kerpos began to pace. Daphne had been with his father, a long time. Everyone stood when the door creaked. "Your father wants to see you, Kerpos. I believe he has something he wants to tell you."

He was through the door before she finished. She smiled "It is time to leave. This family needs to spend some time alone with their father."

On the ride home, she explained, "He knew my father very well and of our loss. It gave us common ground and Jesus used it to give me favor in his eyes."

"So, he was well aware of Kerpos' decision to trust in the Lord?" Demas sounded hopeful.

"Yes, he had taken in much more than he let Kerpos know. But he did warn me about Cronos' father. He said he would not put anything past him."

They were near home, about to exit the carriage, when Batano jumped up and pushed Daphne behind him. He pointed at a shrouded figure close to Cyrene's main entry. They all stared as apprehension rose. Demas whispered, "I am going to sneak around the back of the house and surprise him from behind."

Everyone held their breath as he approached the intruder from behind, crouched, and sprang. The force of his body knocked the man off his feet and Demas landed on top of him. Batano ran to help and the two of them turned the man on his back.

"Please," a weak voice pleaded. "I mean no harm. I just wanted to talk to the woman who speaks at Baltos' field."

A very present help in trouble.
– Psalms 46:1

A soft voice coaxed, "Young Master, Young Master, can you hear me?"

Nicanor tried to push himself up onto his knees but the pain in his head sent his face back into the dirt. He lay still, his breathing shallow.

A hand gently shook his shoulder. "Young...oh good, you are awake." The shadowed face of a young woman appeared then faded. Who was she and why was he here? He tried to remember but his thoughts jumbled like driftwood caught in opposing currents.

He felt her gently wipe the back of his head. Her words choked on tears. "I am so sorry. How does your head feel? Can you get up?" Without waiting for an answer, she helped him sit up.

The ground swirled. He squeezed his eyes and held his head in his hands. Where was he? He searched his memory. Nothing.

"I have a small place not far from here. Please let me take you there. You will be safe and can rest until you are ready to go home."

He nodded and allowed her to help him up. She pulled his arm over her shoulder and put hers around his waist. Together they stumbled the few blocks to her home. She led him into a small, one room abode and eased him onto a lone mat. His mind sputtered like the tiny candle he watched her light. Pain rejected all further attempts to remember anything. In minutes he slept.

Chapter Sixty-Five

...And we will take our revenge on him.
– Jeremiah 20:10

Daphne dashed over with Melita close behind. "Who is it? Is it the priest?"

Everyone gasped. The intruder was a woman. Demas stood over her, hands on hips. "Who are you and what led you to sneak around Cyrene's home?"

The woman staggered as they pulled her to her feet. She looked at Daphne. "I am Cronos' mother. Please, I must talk to you."

Daphne's jaw dropped as disbelief passed from face to face. "We must help her. She may have been injured." They led her into Cyrene's garden and onto a bench. She hunched over and rubbed her stomach. Daphne sat beside her. "Are you all right?" She wheeled toward Melita. "Hurry please, and get her some water."

Breathing hard, the woman held up her hand, "I...I will be fine. I needed to come...you need to know..." She gripped the seat and straightened. Sobs tore through her words. "He killed my son. He is evil and he killed my only son."

Daphne put her arm around the woman's shoulder. ""Shhh, you are safe here with us. Let me find you a place to rest for the night and we will — "

She jerked upright. "No! I need to get home before he discovers I am gone. He will kill me like he killed our son."

Demas knelt before her. "Are you saying...your husband is the one who killed Cronos?"

She nodded and, in gasps, told them that Cronos' father discovered that her son had leaked information about the high priest from her husband's visits. He had flown into a rage and beat him to death. "I do not know if he meant to kill him or not. I tried to stop him, but he knocked me across the room."

Demas groaned. "I am so sorry. Cronos was my friend...I am so sorry."

Tears coursed down her face. "Cronos knew he was taking a risk, but he wanted to help. Hours later when his father realized Cronos would not survive, he called on one of his friends at the temple and a priest agreed to carry him up into the hills. They hoped the muses would be blamed. An unspoken relief swept Daphne and the others. It was not the priest who claimed to want to know more of God.

Demas smacked his fist into his palm. "At first the muses were blamed, but God opened peoples' eyes to the lie."

She turned to Daphne, "Yes, but you must be aware of the evil plot against you. I have not heard of any specific plan, but they are furious and will not hesitate to kill you too."

"You are so brave to come and warn us. How can we help you?"

"I must get back before I am missed. I have not dared come to your meetings but when I saw such peace in Cronos I asked, and he helped me to see Jesus was the only true God. I want to help, too. I do not care what happens to me. My son is gone." She spat on the ground. "I just hope his father burns in that awful place Cronos said evil people go, after they die."

Sorrow for her unbearable loss engulfed each of them. Finally, she agreed to let Demas drive her most of the way home, assured that they would keep her in prayer.

Hope is lost and we ourselves are cut off.
– Ezekiel 37:11

The sun shone through a small window and sent trickles of light in a prism of dance across Nicanor's eyes. He blinked and looked around. Where was he? In one corner, a small wooden bench sat by a settee that leaned against the wall. Beside the door, a shelf held a few dishes and a cooking pot. Nothing of value stood out but the room was orderly and clean.

He pushed himself up on his elbows and sat up. His head pounded. He brushed the hair from his face and touched the sore spot on the back of his head. It felt sticky. He grimaced, looked for a water pitcher but found none. His eyelids drooped. "I need to...to what?" His confusion angered him. "Something is not right. I must get back to...to where? And how did I end up here?"

The door opened and a young woman backed in carrying a woven parcel. She turned and smiled at him. His jaw fell. What was wrong with her face?

She did not miss the stare she had seen dozens of times. She lay her package down and adjusted the veil that usually covered the left side of her face. "I see you are awake. How do you feel? Does your head hurt?"

He lowered his eyes, ashamed he had not covered his reaction. Except for the disfigurement, she was lovely. Shining dark eyes peered from under auburn hair that curled around her neck and down her back. "I will be all right, but please, who are you and how did I get here? Do you know what happened to my head?"

Guilt reared and squeezed her brows. She pushed it down, then told him she saw two men attack him from behind and leave him injured. "My name is Eunice. I saw them rip your money belt from your waist and shove you aside. As soon as they left, I came to see if I could help and brought you here."

He did a frantic check under his tunic. She was right. It was gone. But why was he wearing a money belt? What was it for? "That was very kind of you." His words faded into an empty tunnel that held no memory of the incident nor of how he made it to her home. He stood to his feet, surprised at the dizzy wave that made him spread his feet to keep from falling.

She reached over and helped him back onto the mat. "Please, do not rush it. You took a severe blow to your head, and it needs time to heal. You are welcome to wait here. I brought some fruit and bread. Do you think you could eat a little something?"

Where Satan dwells.
– Revelation 2:13

At the meeting that night, they all agreed that Daphne should tell the people they had an eyewitness to Cronos' murder but not who it was. Relieved, applause erupted and people hugged each other, their hearts eager to begin the worship. After most had dispersed for the night, the priest approached Daphne. "I am so glad you have found proof of the truth. The high priest has a tight group of supporters, but there are so many who are confused and full of doubt...as I was."

She sighed. "I wish we could reach them. The truth would set them free. Is there any safe way for you to go and encourage them to believe?"

"They do not know who to trust. I think it will have to come from someone else."

"Let us pray about it. We know God wants them to hear the good news."

Three days later, Daphne sat and brought Cyrene up on all that had happened. "Oh, My Friend, I cannot tell you how glad I am to see you able to eat and gain back your strength."

"Me too. My clothes hung like sacks of wheat, but I will fill out."

Daphne grinned. "Abiron did not seem concerned about it."

Cyrene flushed. "Can you believe he has been here, every day? He is so kind. I wonder why he never married."

"I think he has an ulterior motive, and his status may soon change."

A servant stuck her head through the door. "That gentleman is back. Shall I tell him you have company?"

Cyrene nodded, but Daphne sprang from her seat. "No, I have things to do. You go ahead." Abiron stepped in as she left. "Nice to see you, Friend. Have a good visit."

He waved her off. "Do not let me rush you out."

She had hardly reached her room when the servant knocked. "There is a man who wants to see you. Would you like to meet in the tower room?"

The priest entered and said he hoped he had not intruded. Briefly, he admired the view of the gulf before he sat opposite her and spoke as if their last conversation had been moments before. "I have given it a lot of thought, and last night I decided to go up to the temple. I wanted to see if there was any way I could get the priests who are questioning Apollo's deity somewhere safe, where they could secretly hear the good news. My heart aches for them."

"And did you find a way?"

"Maybe. Because I still have my robes, I was able to slip among them and see if they might have an idea. I have two men who I know are of like minds. Both really want to hear you and one of them suggested a storage shed where pots and grains for the sacrifice of bulls are kept. It would have to be in the night after everyone is dismissed from his duties."

Daphne studied his face. She no longer doubted his sincerity. "Do you think it would work? How could you arrange it or get there without being seen?"

"There is a path that leads around the spring and away from the temple, before you reach the sacred way. It circles back to behind the storage shed. I know it well and could lead the way if any would join me."

"Even in the dark?"

"It would not be easy but there is no danger of falling. We could go part way up the mountain and wait for dark to proceed."

"Do you think the priests would come?"

"My friends assured me they would get the word out to those they know they can trust and have the same doubts I had. In fact, they begged me to set it up for tomorrow night and I agreed. So, I hope you will come with me. If you do not want to risk it, I will go by myself but it will not have the same effect."

She signaled for a servant. "If Cyrene's guest is still here, would you ask him to join me?"

Abiron arrived in minutes and Daphne thanked him for coming. "I am sorry to interrupt your visit, but there is something I want you to hear." She turned to the priest, "Please, tell him what you told me."

Abiron's face twisted with skepticism. "We have been warned many times that the high priest intends to kill Daphne. To invade his territory sounds way too risky."

The priest looked disheartened. "I understand. I know I made it hard for you to trust me, but these men are so ready to hear the truth." He rose to leave. "Please, pray the Lord will give me the right words and maybe some will believe."

Daphne rose quickly. "Wait, Abiron is right. But if this is of the Lord, we do not have to fear. There were many times Satan tried to destroy me, but God rescued me from his vicious attacks. Our God is greater than the evil one. He is our shield and protector. Let us share this with the others tonight and we will seek God's will in it."

The priest's eyes filled. "Thank you. That is more than I could ask."

Chapter Sixty-Six

...bring to light the hidden things of darkness...
– 1 Corinthians 4:5

It took another day for Nicanor's dizziness to fade. Eunice offered to walk around the city with him to see if something would trigger his memory. They returned to her place and he lay down to rest. He wondered where she slept. "I'm so sorry to put you through this. I have no way to repay you for your help and for feeding me."

"No, do not be concerned. I can tell by your clothes you are a man of substance. You will make it right when your memory returns." Her voice dropped. "Besides I owe you."

"Owe me? Why would you owe me?"

She looked uneasy and scooted over to the cooking utensils. "Oh, I only meant that when I saw what happened to you, I knew any decent person would need to help." She busied herself with the food she had bought. "Have you any memory of family? A wife?"

His lids drifted to his cheeks and he sighed. ""I cannot tell you how many times I have tried to remember."

She reached for her only pot and began to cut up the lamb and vegetables. "I am going outside to cook this. Rest. Maybe you are trying too hard." Her veil caught on the door and ripped from her face. Once again, the mishap exposed the bristly, dark hairs that covered a ruddy section of her cheek. She did not stop to replace it.

He looked away but wondered at her disfigurement. Had she been born with it? Sleep captured his thoughts for over an hour. The smell of lamb stew roused him. "Daphne, what have you ordered for dinner? Is that my favorite?"

He opened his eyes. Eunice stood over him, her veil back in place. She smiled. "Who is Daphne?"

He sat with a start. "She is...she is...I do not know who she is. A cloud came and covered a picture that had been clear seconds before." He huffed. "That is worse than not remembering at all."

"No, no, it is not. Something came back to you and the next time maybe it will stay. Come let us sit on the bench and eat."

He shall call upon me and I will answer him.
– Psalms 91:15

Daphne expected opposition to the priest's request, so after the meeting she asked him to explain it to the others himself. In response, feet shuffled and heads hung. "Look, we have all been in this together from the start, and I want your input. God cares about these men and we need clear direction for His plan to reach them. I ask each of you to fast and pray with me through tomorrow morning. Let us meet at Cyrene's in the early afternoon to hear what the Lord has to say about it. If He opens this door, no man will be able to shut it."

Demas spoke up. "Daphne, we all care deeply for you and your brave effort to bring the good news about Jesus to us, but we cannot—"

She held up her hand. "No, I appreciate your concern, but we must see this from God's perspective. We may be the answer to His desire these men hear about Jesus. Please, put aside what makes sense to you right now and seek the Lord. He has promised to answer those who call upon Him."

The next morning, Daphne did not leave her room. She drifted from worship in song, to praise for all God had already done, to thanks for His goodness. All manner of prayer followed, and afterward, she prostrated herself and listened intently for His voice. No specific instructions came, but she was flooded with peace and assurance the Lord was in control and would reveal His plan.

At Melita's knock, she rose and dressed for the day. "Tell the others we'll meet in the tower room. Cyrene will join us, so let her servants know when to call her." Everyone gathered into the small space. "Thank you for coming. Demas, will you lead us into the Lord's presence?"

Following his prayer, she looked at each one. "Please share what you feel the Lord has said about going up to the temple." No one spoke.

Abiron cleared his throat. "I had a hard time praying through my fears, concerned about what would become of us if...well, if you did not return from the encounter. But the Lord heard my plea that I give that over to Him and fear lifted. I knew He would never forsake us."

Several others told of a similar experience. Each had received peace that God was in control, but none had received specific instructions. Daphne marveled at the consistency. "All right, let us pray in one accord. I believe, with all my heart, God will hear and lead us."

Some fell to their knees and others stood or paced the perimeter as each beseeched the Lord in the Spirit, using their prayer language. In time a hush fell, and the Holy Spirit prophesied through Cyrene. "Demas and Baltos are to accompany Batano and Daphne to the temple to share my love with the priests. Do not be afraid. I am with you always."

Every heart rested in confidence they had heard from God. Daphne beamed at Cyrene. "Thank You, Jesus. Thank You. Please, the rest of you, gather around and lay hands on the four of us and pray. We will need the Holy Spirit's anointing for the task He has called us to do."

Overwhelmed with confidence in God's directions, much rejoicing spilled before the group began to disperse. Daphne stopped Kerpos at the door. "How is your father?"

His lips clenched and he shook his head. "You would not believe him. We all know he is fading fast, but he cannot seem to rest. He wants to talk to everyone about Jesus."

Daphne grinned. "God is good! I think this might be a good night for the people to hear your testimony, Kerpos. Abiron and Orestes will be there to assist you and Melita, but the four of us will need to leave in a few hours to get part way up the mountain."

He agreed if she promised to pray for him. She smiled and shooed him out before she reminded Baltos to inform the priest that the four of them were going and would leave in two hours. She caught hold of Abiron before he left. "I am so glad the Lord assured you His work would go on regardless of who leads it. Kerpos will speak tonight, and I know I can trust you to keep things in order."

He gave a reassuring nod and walked Cyrene back to her room.

Will He speak softly to you?
– Job 41:3

On the third day, Nicanor let Eunice guide him around different parts of the city. He placed his hopes in that something would jog his memory. The cut on his head had closed and no longer ached or made him dizzy.

Eunice pointed to the left. "This street has many inns on it. Let us see if any are familiar to you. You do not talk like a Corinthian, so maybe you stayed in one."

They walked slowly. Nicanor gazed intently at each one. The street ended and he stopped, put his hands on his knees, and loosed a bitter sigh.

Trust Me, Nicanor, flooded his mind.

Eunice grabbed his arm. "What is it? You have a strange look on your face. Did you remember something?"

He straightened, "I... I do not know. Something came into my mind...a familiar voice but I do not know who it is or what it meant."

"What did it say?"

"It said, *'Trust me.'*"

Her brows almost met. "*'Trust me'*? Was that all?"

He nodded. "Let us go. I do not see anything here that looks familiar."

"All right, but there is one section of the city we have not explored. Shall we try it?" They stopped in the market and bought two small loaves of bread and cheese to eat as they went. The bustling part of the city gave way to neighborhoods.

Nicanor grimaced. "I do not think anything here is going to help me." They cut to the next group of homes and heard singing. It came from a courtyard. He scowled. "Wait." They stepped close and listened. "Do you know what this is, Eunice? Have you ever been here?"

"No, I have never been here, but I know there is a group who brought news of a new god and a great number of people have become followers. They meet in this area during the day and somewhere in the city at night. Do you think you might have been part of that?"

He cocked his ear in the direction of the sound and stared. Finally, he dropped his arms and shrugged. "I do not think so. The music seemed...like something I may have heard before. But I do not know where or how. Come on. Let us head back.

Chapter Sixty-Seven

...taking the shield of faith by which you will be able to quench all the fiery darts of the evil one.
– Ephesians 6:16

Daphne was familiar with the climb that awaited at the end of the roadway, but this time everything seemed different. Twilight dwindled shortly after their carriage stopped. They took time to eat the meal Cyrene's mother prepared, not wanting to proceed until dark. After a half hour, the priest announced, "It is time. Let us leave."

She stood and asked the others to join her in prayer. Everyone clasped hands and bowed their heads. "Lord, after I awakened from that disturbing dream, You told me that we were to listen to the Spirit's counsel. We believe we have. You said not to let our guard down but to do the spiritual warfare needed, so we have bound the evil spirits that would hinder our mission. We thank You for Your promise to go with us and that no harm will come to us. We put ourselves totally in Your hands, Lord, and trust that You are true to Your word. Amen."

The priest connected with each one's eyes. "Be as quiet as you can be. I will lead the way and lift my hand if I see any danger or see anyone along the way. Daphne, stay as close behind me as you can. The path is rocky once we leave the main trail."

The moon gave them just enough light to guard their footing and see their leader. Where the nearly hidden path deviated from the familiar route up the sacred way, he waited to make sure everyone followed.

Batano whispered, "How are you doing, Misses?"

"I am all right. I have climbed to the temple many times, but this route is different and the dark makes it seem long."

"I am right behind, so let me know if you need help."

She assured him she would. They pressed on up the obscure path. She could hear water splashing into the Kastalian Spring and felt the mist caress her face. Soon after, the priest stopped, "We are almost there. Be very diligent to stay low and keep an eye on me. If I see anything that does not look right, we will retreat.

He paused several times and listened before he beckoned them onward. They rounded a stand of trees and arrived at the storage shed. He gathered them close. "Wait here. I am going down and I will make sure everything is as planned. He bent low and moved quietly toward the building, then circled behind it.

Baltos nudged Demas when it seemed the priest should have returned. "We had better be ready to get Daphne out of here."

Demas nodded and motioned to Batano. "This could be a trap. We should — "

At that moment, the priest crept from behind the shed and motioned them forward. "Lots of men are inside, but thankfully, they only lit one small lantern. It looks good. Let us go."

No one moved. He looked from Demas to the others. "What is it?"

Baltos eyed him, his face wound into a squint "We have come up here because the Lord wants those men to hear about Jesus. "But if we are about to lose our lives for His sake, I hope you—"

The priest grimaced. "I cannot make you trust me, but Jesus is my Lord too. And if anything goes wrong, I will be as vulnerable as all of you. Please, this is not an ambush. These priests have risked a lot to hear about Jesus.

Daphne put her hand on Baltos' arm. "Jesus laid down His life and everything else so that we could be one with the Father. Let us do the same, if necessary. Remember, He promised to be with us."

Heads nodded and the group lined up behind the priest. Daphne's pulse raced as the magnitude of the dangerous encounter, she had endorsed, swelled with a vengeance. Doubt diverted her attention, and she tripped over a clump of weeds. Lord, If I have wrongly encouraged these men into danger, please protect them.

My sheep know my voice and will not follow another.

Confidence flooded her soul and peace returned. "Thank you, Lord. Satan, you are a liar. Flee along with your fear and unbelief. We have come in faith to do God's will, so you be gone, in Jesus' name." Turmoil evaporated like the mist near the spring. "Lord, please fill me afresh with Your Holy Spirit and help me make clear what these priests need to hear."

They arrived at the door and the priest motioned for them to follow. Everyone ducked through the narrow opening, aware the priest bolted and locked the door behind them.

A fellow priest greeted him. "Myron, you made it!" He nodded at the group of men seated on bags of grain. "I told you he would not fail us." He gestured at the visitors, "Welcome. Welcome."

Myron nodded at the men. "Make sure those few windows are covered and turn that lantern low. I am so glad each of you had the courage to come. You will not be disappointed. He beckoned for Daphne to join him. "This is Daphne. She and her friends have come, at great risk, to give you this chance to hear about the one true God. Please listen carefully. If there is time, she will answer questions. However, we must leave several hours before sunrise."

She began to tell them her story, her doubts about joining the temple, being assigned to marry a priest, and how she snuck into the adytum to find the truth. They nodded as she told them of what a farce the divination she had heard had been and gasped at how she saw the high priest murder the former leader. As one, they leaned in to hear how, after the pythia suddenly died, she was invaded by the woman's newly homeless demon of divination. When she said the new, high priest had chosen her to replace his dead wife, heads shook in sympathy.

"It was the beginning of my nightmare." She explained how her father's death had led to losing their home and the family being sold to pay off his debts. "I was bought by three men from Philippi. Their plan was to make money by my telling fortunes through the power of the demon in me, who posed as a messenger from Apollo. His relentless goal was to lead men away from the true God and into a commitment to worship what they thought was Apollo. Actually, he drew them into the realm of Satan, the enemy of the true God. "

"After a year of guilt and despair over my loss of integrity, I wanted to die. But around that time, I began to hear of a visitor to the city who spoke of a god named Jesus. His message revived my dwindling hope. I learned He was the God who created the world and desired me to be part of His family. I learned that He sent His only Son, Jesus, into the world to be a sacrifice... the debt of sin that separates each of us from Him. He taught us the sinless blood shed by the crucified Jesus would wash away the sin of any who chose to believe and receive His salvation. I found even I could be forgiven!

"The demon used me many times to thwart God's plan. He controlled my body, forcing me to harass the man who brought the good news. But when the threats proved a great distraction from the man's message, he took the authority God gives believers and commanded the demon to leave me. It threw me to the ground, screaming curses, but left me for good."

The men resisted the urge to cheer. Instead, bright smiles accompanied their nods.

She had begun to tell them how she had received Jesus as her Lord and of her decision to obey Him and return to her owner, when Myron approached. "I am so reluctant to have to stop you, but it is time, we should leave."

"Yes, could I take a few questions?"

He nodded. Several men raised their hands. Most wanted to know how they would qualify to be accepted by God. "Oh, My Friends, there is nothing you can do to deserve or earn His love and acceptance. He only asks that you believe He is the Son of God, died for our sins and rose again to open heaven for all who believe. I would love to pray right now with any of you who would like to make Jesus your Lord.

Tears washed her cheeks as everyone stood. As she prayed, they repeated each word. At their quiet *amens*, Myron spoke up. "There is so much more to learn. None of you need to stay here any longer. I have found there are people down in Delphi who will help you and those of you who have families. Just pack your things and—"

The door behind them crashed open. The high priest entered and sneered. "Well, Myron. How nice of you to bring your guests to visit." He turned to the temple guard and screamed, "Surround them!"

Chapter Sixty-Eight

Rest in the Lord, and wait patiently for Him...
– Psalms 37:7

Eunice bid Nicanor goodnight and left. He wondered how she supported herself but was not sure he wanted to know. He lay on the mat and let his thoughts drift.

"Daphne. She said I called someone Daphne. Is she my wife...my sister?" Strains of the music he had heard returned. "What was that, Lord? Was it..." He sat up with a start. "Lord? Who is Lord? Who am I talking to?"

I am Jesus, rest and put your trust in me.

He listened, intently, but heard nothing more. Rest...trust? How can I when I do not even know who I am? He lay back on the mat and finally slept.

Eunice arrived early the next morning with bread and boiled eggs. "Did you sleep well?"

He grunted. How do I explain what I heard when I do not understand it myself?

"I have to be gone most of the day. Sometimes the manager of the *palestra* pays me to clean the floors."

"Can I help? I used to..." He stopped. Used to what?"

"No, you rest. Expect me around dinner time. Will you be all right on your own?"

He nodded. "I will be fine. You have done so much already. I do not want to interfere with your life."

She left the bread for his lunch and shut the door. He wandered about the neighborhood for a while, hesitant to go too far from what had become familiar. The rundown buildings and squalor in the streets revealed a poorer part of the city. For a while, he watched two small boys playing a game with sticks and rocks, then decided to go back and wait for her return.

He stared at the ceiling, his mind a blank. Lord, what am I going to... He sat up. "There it is again. What does it mean? Who is *Lord*? Am I owned by someone? Why is it I cannot remember?" Confusion taunted like the pesky flies around his head until he gave up and escaped in sleep.

It was late afternoon when Eunice brushed through the door, rousing him. "I am back."

He stirred, "Where have you been, Daphne? Patharus expects us..."

Eunice dropped her parcel and knelt beside him. "You have remembered! Who are those people...and who are you?"

But thanks to God who gives us the victory.
– 1 Corinthians 15:57

For a few seconds, no one moved. The high priest grabbed Daphne's arm. "You will come with me, Girl." She tried to pull away, but he yanked her back and gestured to his guards. "Take the others to that nice high cliff on the east side and teach them to fly." He snickered at his own antics. "And include Myron in the party." His lips curled like an awakened guard dog. "Seems he forgot about the midnight bed check for new priests."

The temple guards lifted their spears and motioned for Batano, Demas, Baltos, and their ally to move. One of the younger priests yelled, "No!"

and hurled himself at the surprised guards. Before any of them could react, all the fledgling priests joined him. Sacks of grain deflected spears, and implements used to prepare the bulls flew and sent the guards sprawling. Pitchers of lustral water followed, smashing against any who were not quick to dodge the barrage.

Priestly hats flew and were trampled with writhing bodies. The high priest crawled through the fray, his eyes on Daphne. He pulled his dagger from his belt and headed straight for her. She had braced herself against a wall, where she shouted warnings to her friends in danger of being struck from behind. His pompous headgear caught her eye. "Lord, help me."

Use your authority in My name.

She screamed, "In the name of Jesus, you will not harm me."

He smirked and pulled himself to his feet. "Jesus huh?" He raised his weapon. "Now, we will see what your new god can..."

Myron heard her scream and spun around. He jumped to his feet and tackled the high priest from behind. His dagger flew from his hand and the two of them wrestled as each tried to get to the weapon. Daphne wound her way around the thrashing bodies and forced herself to grab the dagger. She shuddered at the memory of it plunging into the former high priest.

Batano leaped over a pair who struggled to best each other and relieved her of the weapon. The temple guards had been mostly decorative props that had never defended the high priest or themselves, so they were quickly overrun by the younger men. Beneath the fury of the new converts, the guards cowered or lost the desire to continue the fight. One lay unconscious.

Baltos joined Myron, pulled the high priest to his feet, and held him around his neck. Myron grinned. "Thanks, Brother," Their eyes met in an unspoken bond of newly acquired respect. With ropes used to control the bulls, the men tied the high priest and the guards with their hands behind their backs. They were then fastened to the legs of storage shelves to prevent them from untying each other.

Cheers, backslaps, and congratulations spread through the victors. The young priest, who started the fray, wiped the blood from under his nose and grinned, "I could not let him destroy you. You have given us a reason to go on."

Myron shook his head. "We would have been dinner for the crows without you. Thank you, each of you. Now, get your families and come down to the city."

Baltos echoed his message. "Come to my estate when you arrive. We will find places for all of you. Most of the people have heard what you heard tonight and have accepted it as truth. They all will want to help."

Someone pointed at the high priest "What do we do with him and the rest?"

No one spoke. Shrugs and questions passed from face to face. Finally, Demas spoke. "Leave them tied and let them stew over their losses till you are ready to leave tomorrow. Then tell anyone left where to find them. When the people hear about this, the temple's power over them will be completely destroyed. Jesus has replaced this false god for all eternity."

Exhausted, the group headed back to the carriage. Each delighted in the recount of one another's tale on how he called on the Lord for strength and triumphed. They speculated about the influence these newly born-again priests might have. Each possibility added to their joy and kept them moving.

Where then is my hope?
– Job 17:15

Nicanor struggled to hide his waning hope as they finished dinner. She put her hand on his arm, her face close to his. "Try not to be discouraged. It will come. You are welcome to stay here as long as it takes."

Her hair smelled of flowers and her lips were but inches from his. He thought of how satisfying it would be to take comfort in her arms, but a check within caused him to pull back.

She shrugged, drew to her feet, and gathered their dishes. "Sleep well." Without another word, she left.

He lay awake. What might have happened remained to taunt him, but something had not let him ignore the strong conviction it would have been wrong. It was dark when he awoke from a dream. He sat up and tried to recreate the scene. The house was large with many rooms. A young woman moved in his direction. He had called out, "Daphne, it is I, Nicanor."

The woman waved, and he could see she was about to leave on a long trip. In the dream, he called out again. "Daphne, wait. I will drive you to Neapolis."

He was on his feet now. His past began to pour through his mind like an unexpected spring shower. "That was Daphne! I must find her. We have to get back to Patharus."

Her passion to return to Delphi, his journey to come meet her, their plans to return together... everything rushed, with relief, to the forefront. Overcome with joy, and suddenly aware it had been The Lord who had told him to rest and trust Him, Nacanor cried out, "Oh, thank You, Lord!"

He wanted to leave and get back to the inn, but the darkness convinced him dawn was a good way off. He lay back down, and reveled in the joy of his renewed knowledge of who he was and what his life had been. At last, he slept, but stirred at the sound of the door opening.

Eunice entered and quietly shut it behind her. She was dressed in a light tunic that shimmered in the sparse moonlight. It hugged her figure and plunged nearly to her navel. He did not move, uneasy when she lowered herself to his mat. "Eunice, what...?"

She ran her hand down his chest. "You seem so lonely. I know the needs of men and I..."

Chapter Sixty-Nine

...and He has become my salvation.
– Psalms 118:14

Nicanor swept Eunice's hand from his chest. "No, this is not right. I owe you much and I will repay, but this cannot be."

She huffed. "Am I not enough? Is it my face that offends you?"

She backed and he followed. "Eunice, you would be more than enough for any man, a blessing to whomever you choose."

She jutted her chin, but her lips trembled. "But not you! Of course not. What man wants a girl with a beard like mine. She yanked off her veil, covered her face, and screamed, "I thought you were different, but you are like all the rest. You are—"

He grabbed her hands "Eunice, stop it. A few hours ago, I had a dream and all my past life rushed back in detail. I am married to a woman I love very much. She is sweet and gentle, kind, like you. I cannot be untrue to her."

"Sweet? You think I am sweet? You never knew that I was paid to lure you off the street so those men could rob you...did you?"

His face fell. "You did that? Why?"

She snarled. "Look at me. Would any decent man marry me? I must sell myself to live. Even the men I service do not know what is behind my veil." She lowered her eyes.

"Eunice, true beauty is not found on the outside. It is found inside, where it counts. You are beautiful. God loves you just the way you are and has a better plan for your life than this."

"God? Which god? I put my trust in several gods, but even Aphrodite's temple would not have me. No one has ever loved me, including my parents. They put me out as soon as I became a woman." Sobs sent her to her knees.

Nicanor pulled her to her feet. "Please, sit with me on the bench. I want to tell you about the true God who created you and loves you."

Dawn seeped through the tiny window before Nicanor told her all he knew about the Father. "He loved us so much he sent His Son to die so we could become His children." At first, she listened with arms folded and scowled. In time, snuffs filled the air as truth penetrated her aching heart.

She shook her head. "But I have lived in wickedness. Surely He could not love and forgive me. And how can a god, I cannot see, forgive my past and make me new? I once knew a woman who believed like you, but her situation did not change."

"When He comes into your life, He uses His powerful Holy Spirit to change your situations and your outlook for the better. He has given us hundreds of promises we can believe and make our own. Eunice, He knows all about you, and He loves you anyway." She started to object but he put up his hand. "All He wants is for you to believe He is God's Son and ask Him to be your Lord. He will forgive your past and transform you into a new creature in Christ... brand new, top to bottom."

She hung her head, her voice muffled. "Are you not angry with me for what I caused to happen to you?"

He strained to hear her. "No, there are times when we all make bad choices, but my God requires that we forgive others as He has forgiven us. Eunice, know that I truly forgive you."

She burst into tears, her head on her knees. "Please, I hate my life. I want what you have. I need it so much. How do I make Jesus my God, too?"

He swallowed the awe that rose in his throat and led her in prayer. She looked up, eyes shining. "Thank you. I cannot explain it, but I feel different, like I have a hope I have never known before."

He gave her a brotherly hug. "Eunice, there is so much more for you. Now listen, I plan to leave at dawn, but I want you to go back to that house where we heard the singing. A woman named Chloe lives there. Tell her about meeting me and that you have become a believer. She will welcome you with open arms and help you find a new life." He turned her face to his. "Promise me you will go at first light."

On the way to his former inn, Nicanor stopped by a large fountain for a drink. Statues of unclothed gods and goddesses spouted water from the center and the perimeter. He looked up at the sky. "Lord, if only everyone in this city could understand the demonic impostors behind those symbols. But I trust that Paul reached some."

And so have you, Nicanor. Everyone, like Daphne, is not called to preach to many, but you were obedient to share the good news with the one I brought under your influence. Eunice is now free of Satan's lies and is forever Mine.

No one saw the tears Nicanor wiped on his sleeve. "Thank you, Lord. She is not the only one you touched last night."

I will greatly rejoice in the Lord.
– Isaiah 61:10

Daphne's weary band arrived back in Delphi just as the morning sky lightened. To their surprise, Abiron, Melita, and Kerpos had gathered with Cyrene in front of her house. A cheer rose as they spotted the carriage. Melita was first to reach them. "You are back. You are here! Thank God. We prayed all night for your safe return."

Batano helped Daphne down. She fell into Melita's outstretched arms. "Oh, thank you, My Friends. I did not know you planned to pray all night, but we surely felt the effects."

Everyone gathered and hugged each of them, anxious to hear everything. Baltos called for a hush. "I think you need to hear it from Myron, our brother in Christ." He took the former priest's arm and pulled him to the forefront. "We only knew him as 'the priest,' before, but his name is Myron, and he is truly one of us.'"

Myron grinned. "I am so glad to be here with all of you, and I harbor no ill feelings toward any who doubted me. I probably would have done the same."

Abiron jabbed his upper arm. "Come on. Tell us. We are eager to know what happened up there."

Myron shared about the journey, how they found the priest waiting, how Daphne's message touched them, and that they came to believe in the Lord. "But we knew someone was praying when the high priest discovered us. He tried to abduct Daphne and kill the rest of us."

Everyone gasped, demanding to hear more. "The young priests took our side, blasted the high priest and his guard with whatever they could find, and defeated all of them. Questions, a hunger for details, flew from everyone until Demas spoke up. "Could we continue this tomorrow... I mean later, sometime today? We are exhausted."

Everyone laughed and agreed. It had been a long night.

But with God, all things are possible.
– Matthew 19:26

To Nicanor's relief, the innkeeper had tucked away his trunk, and everything was intact. The money he had not carried the night he was robbed remained where he had stashed it.

The innkeeper shook his head. "You are fortunate. After a week, I do not keep unclaimed things."

The next day, Nicanor hired a carriage and returned to the port with hopes he would find news from Daphne. Disappointment rose as he found nothing. He turned to leave, but the woman who handled messages called out. "Wait a minute. I remember you once had a message from Neapolis. Is that right? Let me check. I believe one arrived yesterday. I will look and see if it has your name on it."

Nicanor battled dread. If there was one, it had to be from Patharus. Something would have gone wrong. To his surprise, it was from Epaphroditus. Nicanor tore open the note and scanned the usual greetings and hopes for a successful trip. He hurried through a report on the church's joy in the newfound revelations their leader had brought back.

"Most of all, I wanted you to know I visited your father, in fact, several times. He asked me a lot of questions about the faith, and related how both you and Daphne had tried to convince him he needed a Savior. I knew you would be blessed to know on our last visit he let me pray for his weakened left side and his healing resulted in his giving his heart to Jesus."

Nicanor nearly dropped the letter. He stood there, mouth ajar and read it again." Lord! You are amazing! Who would have imagined Patharus would listen to Epaphroditus. And to think he cracked the shell that neither Daphne nor I could penetrate. Thank you, Lord! Thank You. Praise Your holy name."

Nicanor walked around, delighting in the Lord's goodness until he came upon an inn that served lunch. While he waited for his food, he reread the letter and tried to imagine sharing the things of God with his stoic father.

His thoughts drifted to Daphne. His mind swirled from one possibility to another on how to connect with her. Should he go to Delphi or wait in Corinth? What if he traveled and she had already left? He decided not to wait. The innkeeper directed him to the place where he could arrange passage. A ship was scheduled to leave in three days, so he paid the fare. He left a message to let her know his plans and hoped their ships would not cross.

Chapter Seventy

...I have finished the work You gave me to do.
– John 17:4

Daphne awakened to the smell of bacon. She sat up, disoriented by the bright sun.

"Good afternoon, My Friend. I thought maybe you would want to be up and about by now."

She rubbed her eyes. "Oh, Cyrene, where's Melita? I should have been up hours ago, I—"

"Nonsense. You had quite a day yesterday." She stretched out her arms. "A long, long day with an amazing and wonderful outcome. Here, let me put this tray over your lap so you can enjoy the special breakfast Mother made you."

"Oh, it smells wonderful and I am hungry. Thank your mother for me. She's an amazing cook."

"Well, it is not exactly my mother, but she oversees every bit of it."

Daphne made quick work of the bacon omelet and bread, spread with apricot preserves. Cyrene filled her in on how Melita had insisted they do the all-night prayer vigil. "She loves you so much, Daphne. How did you ever find such a devoted slave?"

"She was already a treasure when she was first assigned to me but since she came to the Lord, she seems happiest when she finds a way to put another before herself. She never complains and anticipates my every need. I would be lost without her." She started to tell Cyrene about how she had almost lost her to Medea, when she noticed her friend staring at her with a grin that stretched almost to her ears.

"All right...what is going on? You do not normally serve me breakfast in bed with a silly grin on your face."

Cyrene jumped to her feet and knelt close to Daphne's bed. "Well, I just thought you might want to know that while we waited for your return last night, Abiron asked me to become his wife."

Daphne's eyes filled. She threw off her tray and blankets and reached for her friend. "Oh, wonderful! I am so glad and so happy for you." She cocked her head and smirked. "But I am not surprised. He has been mooning over you for weeks."

They hugged and laughed, hardly aware Melita had come in, yawning. "Oh, Misses, forgive me please. I am so sorry, I overslept and forgot to—"

"No, no regrets today. This is a day to rejoice. Tell her, Cyrene."

Melita's face lit up at the news. "Really? I am so happy for you. How can I help you prepare for the wedding? Will it be soon?"

Cyrene started to answer, but Daphne chuckled. "Well, I know it will not be today. You go get some breakfast and then we will get ready for the day. The meeting tonight will be awesome. I've asked Myron to tell his story and share what happened at the temple. Besides that, he will introduce all of the priests who make it back to Delphi."

Melita helped her dress, arranged her hair, and left to help the other servants. Daphne spent some time in Cyrene's garden praising the Lord for His faithfulness. Thoughts of her friend's marriage brought Nicanor to mind. "Lord, I miss him so much. Please keep him safe until we are together again."

Why not go to him?

She jumped from the bench. "Now, Lord? Does that mean I have finished what You sent me here to do?"

You have been faithful in what I asked of you, and it is My joy to grant the desire of your heart.

She walked slowly among the flowers, while her thoughts leapt from the joy of being with Nicanor to how she could tell her friends. "I will miss them terribly, Lord. They have become my family in You."

Not wanting to distract from the Lord's victory at the temple, she decided not to say a word until after the meeting that night. On her way to her room, she passed Melita's open door. Her servant sat in a rocking chair and stroked one of the household cats. Her eyes were red and swollen

"Melita, are you all right? What is wrong? Have you been crying?"

The cat flew from her lap as Melita jumped to her feet. "Oh, Misses. I... I am fine. I should not have petted the cat. I know it makes my eyes run.

Baltos' field was packed that night. Word had gotten around about the trip to the temple, and everyone wanted a firsthand account. Daphne introduced Myron and credited his obedience to the Lord's desire they trust Him and gain the victory they now celebrated.

He fascinated his audience with tales of his life as a frustrated, unfulfilled priest. They delighted in how he came as a skeptic to hear Daphne share the good news about Jesus and left a new creature in Christ. He detailed their trip to the temple but played down his role. The crowd cheered when they heard how the young priests overcame the guards, and how the high priest ended up hobbled like one of the bulls prepared for sacrifice.

"It was the Lord who orchestrated the whole thing, from a disputable idea to fruition. He won the victory."

Daphne listened to him extol the Lord's intervention, with hardly a pause, before he sailed right into preaching of God's goodness and faithfulness. She smiled to herself. It looks like You have raised up another preacher, Lord.

Baltos and Demas sat in rapt attention not far from Kerpos and Abiron. Their commitment to the Lord and the faith they had put in her brought tears to her eyes. Lord, between the four of them and now Myron, I am confident Your work here will go on and spread well beyond Delphi.

Myron wound things up and called all the young priests who had left the temple to come forward. The people stood and applauded for several minutes. "Gentlemen, I encourage you to avail yourselves to what you can learn here at these meetings and get grounded in your new faith. I know some of you may want to return to your home cities. It is my hope that each of you will take the knowledge of Your Savior with you and share it with our needy country men and women."

Daphne came alongside him. "I want to thank Myron for his heart and courage to make sure all his fellow priests heard about Jesus." A roar went up from the young priests. "He, personally, risked his own safety back at the temple to rescue me from the high priest's intention that I did not leave there alive." With tears, he hugged her and left the stage.

425

She wiped her own tears, then continued. "Some of these young priests have families. They need a place to stay and a way to support themselves. If any of you from here or close by could help, please see Kerpos. He is right over there." She pointed him out and he was soon surrounded. The young priests cheered, encouraged by the number of those who volunteered.

Melita and her helpers led the group in a joyful song of victory that closed the meeting. Still, hordes of people lingered long into the night. Most wanted to meet Myron or hear Daphne's version of how she escaped the high priest's knife.

Daphne stewed on her bed much of the night, torn between her desire to leave and be with Nicanor and her joy in being a part of the Lord's movement in her home city. She released her struggle to Him several times but took it back before she fully surrendered it to His will. Sleep came but she was not yet awake when Melita arrived to help her dress for the day. "You are awfully quiet, Melita. Is something on your mind?"

Melita's eyes did not participate in the quick smile she flashed. "Oh, no. I guess I am still caught up in the awesome work God did at the service last night."

They finished and went down to breakfast. Cyrene joined them, full of dreams and speculation about how her life would soon change. "Mother is thrilled but Father is silent. I think he still resents the changes in all our lives, though Demas made it clear where he stands. Then Mother became a believer, which made things even more difficult." She gazed at some of the treasures she had accumulated. "I am sure we will live in Abiron's home. I am not sure what to do with mine."

Melita sprang to her feet. "Excuse me, please, I forgot to attend to some of Misses' things." She hurried from the room before Daphne could assure her it could wait.

Cyrene turned to Daphne. "That seemed strange. Is she all right?"

"I am not sure. She has not been herself. Perhaps I should try, again, to see what bothers her."

"I think it is Demas you should talk to."

"Demas?"

"Surely you've seen how they look at each other. I suspect all my talk of marriage has brought home her lack of freedom to choose a life with someone she loves. She may be a wonderful slave, but she is still a woman."

Daphne's hand shot to her lips. "How could I be so insensitive? Do you know where I can find Demas?"

Chapter Seventy-One

...you will be sorrowful, but your sorrow will
be turned to joy.
– John 16:20

That night, Daphne took extra time to share all
her journey for the sake of the young priests and
their wives. She told how she had gone from an
innocent girl who grew up in Delphi, to being
possessed by a demon at Apollo's temple. She
repeated how she became a slave. bought to tell
fortunes for the profit of her three owners.

The newcomers listened in awe as she described
being delivered of the demon and then freed by her
owner. At the end of her testimony, she said she had
an announcement. She took a deep breath and
looked over the crowd. "Friends, tonight will be the
last time I will be with you. God has told me my
time here is over and I am released to return to my
husband and family in Philippi."

A hush followed a collective groan from the
crowd. Melita and Cyrene were in tears, along with
many who had faithfully come for months to hear
about Jesus.

Daphne swiped at tears she could not stop. "I
will forever be grateful for your love and support.
God has poured His blessings on our efforts to get
the good news of the entrance of His Son, Jesus,
into our world. And I do mean our efforts. This
could never have happened without the help of my
good friends.

"Please, Demas and Cyrene, Kerpos, Baltos,
Abiron...and you too, Melita and Batano, please join

428

me." The seven of them made their way to the platform amidst cheers and applause. Daphne gestured at the former priest. "You too, Myron. Come join us."

She swept her arm toward them. "Each has played a big part in our success to overcome the lies Satan wrapped up in the guise of Apollo worship. I commit them to you now, your leaders of the church God formed here in Delphi." Cheers and applause rode on waves of joy and gratitude.

She raised her hand and the crowd quieted. "Most of these dedicated believers will remain here with you in Delphi. But God has a way of sending people out to share this unparalleled truth with others who need this as much as each of us did. So be ready for changes in His plans, and know God cares about all of us and will forever be with you, as each of you will be forever in my heart.

"Now, because of the strong influence of Apollo's temple in our city, as well as all of Greece, I want you to always remember this one thing. Anything sacrificed to an idol is actually being offered up to one of Satan's demons. This includes whatever you allow to come before your dedication to our Lord. That means family, money, position, people, and the Pythian games... everything. Whatever is prone to take first place in your heart can become an idol.

"Sacrifices are given to please, honor, or enrich someone or something. Bulls, treasuries, and libations please only the demons that hide behind them. There is only one God. The rest are counterfeits from the pit of hell. Let us each make sure our sacrifices are nothing but praise, worship, and thanksgiving to our Lord, Jesus Christ."

Agreement rumbled through the crowd. She swallowed the lump that rose in her throat and eked out a last request. "Please, let me pray for you one last time. Heavenly Father, in the name of Jesus, Your beloved Son, I ask You to watch over your children. Keep them safe and strong in You. Give them an extra measure of grace to recognize the wiles of the evil one who is sure to try to deceive or discourage them. Give each a heart to know You more deeply, every day." She paused and tried to minimize the quaking in her voice. "I ask...I ask that..."

Sobs filled her throat and she covered her face with her hands. Those on the platform gathered around her. They hugged and assured her the people knew her heart. Demas signaled to Melita. "Let us sing one of her favorite songs, you know, the one about God's faithfulness."

Melita shook her head, her hands pressed against her cheeks. "I cannot. I just cannot."

He beckoned to Kerpos' wife, and she stood and started the song. The whole crowd joined in. Spontaneously, they began to sway, arms circled around each neighbor's waist.

Baltos stepped to the front. "Friends, I know you are as grieved to see Daphne leave as we are, but it is God who has directed her back to Philippi for purposes only He knows. We need to send her off with joy and thanksgiving for His plan that brought her here to open the door of our hearts to receive Jesus as Lord. The greatest appreciation you can give her is your commitment to continue your walk with Christ. The rest of us will be here every night just as we have been. Perhaps we will even build a building, one with places to sit rather than on this hard ground."

Everyone laughed and applauded again. It was late into the night before everyone had bid Daphne Godspeed. She took time with each who wanted to tell her how she had blessed their lives, and laughed or cried at their memories of how Christ used her to reach their hearts.

All the people left. and her friends gathered around. Cyrene's chin quivered. "That was a bit of a shock. I did not expect—"

Abiron hugged her close. "No, but we should have known this day would come. Did you not tell me how much she misses her husband?"

Daphne nodded. "I have, so much, but I would not have traded this time with you for anything. I probably should have told all of you ahead of time, but I did not think I could go through it twice. I love each of you so much." Her tears returned and she sniffed. "But I know I heard from the Master and He has released me to join Nicanor. The only thing that makes it easier for me is the strong faith I have seen grow in each of you, along with my own. There is nothing that keeps you as dependent on the Lord as being called to stand before others and share your testimony or explain the many facets of our great God, as most of you have already experienced."

Everyone agreed. "I am confident He is going to use each of you to keep His truth going strong here in Delphi. So, I will arrange for the two of us to leave in the morning."

In unison, Melita and Batano's brows flinched. Daphne tried to hide a grin. "Demas, is there something you wanted to say to Melita?"

His face reddened. He went to Melita and took her hand. "Melita, this is not where I expected to say this, but I love you very much and ask you to be my wife."

Melita burst into tears. "You cannot. You know I am not free to be married."

Daphne could not contain her joy. She rushed over and pulled Melita face to face. "Oh, My Precious Friend, I meant to tell you it has long been my desire to grant you your freedom."

Agony colored Melita's face. "But you cannot. I am a part of Patharus' household. You cannot —"

Daphne shook her head. "No, no, Dear One. I should have told you long before that Patharus gave you to me. You have been my property since before we left Philippi. Melita, I set you free, just as Patharus, who once owned both of us, set me free."

Melita sank to her knees. "I am to be free. Really free?"

"You are completely free, My Friend...that is unless you are joined to a husband."

Everyone laughed as Demas grabbed Melita's hands and pulled her to her feet. "So, what do you say, My Newly Freed Woman? Will you marry me?" Melita fell into his arms and each of their friends hugged and congratulated them.

Cyrene squeezed Melita's waist. "Maybe we can have a double wedding, perhaps even before Daphne leaves.""

Daphne booked passage on a ship that was scheduled to leave for Corinth in four days. Cyrene, along with her mother and Melita, scrambled to make quick wedding arrangements. The night before she and Batano were to leave, the rituals took place in Cyrene's garden.

She took the hand of each bride. "You both look beautiful." The family and friends had gathered, and Daphne walked before them, matron of honor for both. The evening was warm and the sky perfect as the vows were spoken and each groom kissed his bride.

Cyrene's mother exclaimed. "Maybe now I will finally have grandchildren, since my family increased by two overnight." Her daughter blushed but hugged her before she made her way over to where a sea of awe had captured Daphne's heart.

Cyrene nudged her, "You know, none of this would have happened without you. I shall always be grateful.

Daphne chuckled and elbowed her back. "Well, see to it you name your first daughter after me. They laughed and hugged again. "Go on now. Enjoy your trip." She waved her and Abiron off and looked for Melita. She found her assisting the servants with the cleanup. "My Dear, Dear Friend, you will never change. That is what we all love about you. Demas is a very blessed man."

Melita's eyes filled. "How will I manage without you? I do not know how to be the wife of a free man, and Cyrene has given us her home. It is so beautiful. How can I—"

"You just be your lovely self, Melita. Cyrene's mother loves you and she will help you. Besides, you have been a blessing to me for a long time, and now you will reverse that role and be an example of love to your servants."

"But I—"

"No, no 'buts,' and I would not be surprised if every one of them becomes a believer as you hover

over them. They already know your heart from the way you jumped in to help right after we arrived."

Melita hugged her close. "Oh, Misses," she stopped and covered her lips. "I mean, Daphne." Her voice caught. "I will not be here to help you pack or get dressed and ready in the morning." She canvassed the room for her husband. "Wait right here. I need to tell Demas that I—"

Daphne pulled her back. "You will do no such thing. There are others who can help me. I will be fine." Her eyes filled and she drew her close. "I am going to miss you terribly, Melita. I could not have asked for a more loyal servant or endearing friend. Now, go find that man of yours and enjoy the time away he has planned for his bride."

Melita blushed and they embraced again before she hurried off to find Demas. Daphne sighed. Lord, how will I manage without her until I find Nicanor? There will never be another Melita.

Chapter Seventy-Two

A man's heart plans his ways, But the Lord directs his steps.
– Proverbs 16:9

Joyful sorrow seized Daphne's soul when Baltos, Kerpos, and Myron, along with dozens of the faithful showed up at the Gulf of Corinth to wave her off. Her heart still glowed from the hugs and well wishes they had poured upon her. When her friends looked no bigger than childish sandcastles engulfed by the surf, she released the tears she had disallowed and stopped waving.

Fixed to the rail, she wiped her cheeks. "I thank You, Lord, that Your hand is upon me. Even though I have no idea how to find Nicanor, what might await me in Corinth, or how I can bear to return to Philippi without my family, I know You will be with me." The pale surf turned to deep blue swells. Froth on the heightened waves drove her thoughts to the time she and her family had sailed from Delphi, bound as slaves.

The wind that teased her wrap, stole the prayer from her lips. "But, Lord, I thank You for upending the sorrow and grief of that day, into a joy filled life in You. Please help me find peace in my commitment to trust that You watch over my mother and brothers each day."

Batano came up behind her. "Your things are settled in the room reserved for women. They do not cater to passengers, so I hope the journey is brief."

"Thank you, Batano. Will they let you bunk with the crew?"

"They said I could, but I plan to sleep outside your door. Some rough looking sailors man this ship and I am not sure the captain has a handle on things."

She started to protest but he eyed her the way her mother did when Daphne should not have even asked. "I promised Master Nicanor. Remember? Anyway, they said lunch is ready."

That afternoon, they passed a ship headed in the opposite direction. She sighed. Could Nicanor be aboard? Her friends promised to send him right back to Corinth if he showed up there. Three nights in the oppressive quarters, with no facilities for bathing, passed. She was as relieved as Batano to find the journey shortened by good weather.

The Lechaem Port bustled. Ugly memories of being resold and forced to walk for days to Athens, with little food and water, resurfaced. The most difficult part had been her little brother's inability to comprehend why they did not return home. "Be with him, Lord. He probably still asks."

They departed and Daphne hurried to the message building where she found a letter from Nicanor. Her heart soared. He made it to Corinth! She tore it open and groaned at his plan to leave for Delphi. She read it to Batano and tucked it away. "Maybe he has not left yet."

Batano arranged passage into the city. She tried to remember the name of the inn where they had stayed with Epaphroditus, but it escaped her. The driver frowned at her assurance she would recognize it when she saw it."

They found the inn, grateful rooms were available. The innkeeper was out but as soon as he returned, she inquired whether Nicanor had stayed there. He nodded, "Yes, in fact he left just two, maybe three days ago. He was a nice young man."

Disappointment pierced like an arrow that embedded in a soft target. Indeed, they had missed each other.

"I was glad he returned for his things before a week passed."

He was away for a week? Her brows nearly touched. If he had come to Delphi, she surely would have known. "Where did he go?"

The innkeeper shrugged. "He did not say. But he did tell me he hoped to return with his wife. Is that you?"

She nodded. Three days? He probably arrived in Delphi as we pulled into port here. But how long will it be before he will be able to book another passage, and who knows if this weather will hold? It could be ten days before he returns. She climbed to her room with a heavy heart. Forgive my complaints, Lord, and give me strength to believe all things will work for our good.

O Lord, how great are Your works.
– Psalms 92:5

Nicanor found Delphi's only inn and inquired about a room. When he mentioned Daphne, he was met with the same unwelcome news. She had left three days ago. The innkeeper had been to the meetings and passed the news of his arrival to Cyrene's mother. Immediately, she came and insisted he stay at her home. Daphne's friends heard of his arrival and came to join them. A tall man, a few years older than himself, was first. He reached out his hand. "I am Baltos. I am so sorry your ship crossed with Daphne's, but we are delighted you are here."

Kerpos and his wife arrived shortly after. They could not wait to tell him how Daphne's message of Jesus had changed their lives. To hear that the number of believers had grown from five young men to hundreds of people amazed him.

Kerpos gripped his shoulder. "You must come to the meeting tonight and see for yourself. Baltos is scheduled to speak. By tomorrow, Cyrene's brother, Demas, and Melita should be back from their trip."

Nicanor cocked his head. "Melita? Do you mean Daphne's servant, Melita?"

"Yes. Of course, you could not have known but Daphne gave Melita her freedom and less than a week ago, she married Demas."

Nicanor was stunned. Daphne had freed Melita? Why? He did not like to think of his wife, alone in Corinth, without her servant's help. And what about Batano? Surely, he would not have let her go alone. As soon as there was a lull in the chatter he asked, "What about Batano?"

Baltos jumped on the question. "What a fine man. Let me tell you how he helped defend Daphne and all of us at the temple." Myron arrived before he explained the whole incident. "And this man is the one who saved Daphne from being killed by the high priest."

Nicanor's eyes widened. Someone tried to kill Daphne? Myron finished the story and added his gratitude for the truth Daphne had brought to their city. Nicanor's thoughts remained on the trauma his wife had experienced. He could hardly get his mind around all they shared, but was relieved that Batano was with Daphne and delighted that both Melita and Batano had become believers.

Cyrene's mother introduced him to her husband and settled him in a guest room. She accompanied him to the meeting that night. Nicanor rejoiced at the joy and enthusiasm of the crowd. Lord, I wish Epaphroditus could see this. Before the friends parted, Baltos insisted he share his testimony the next night. Nicanor's heart began to rush. That was Daphne's calling not his, but Baltos would not take no for an answer.

His heart took delight in the ways of the Lord.
– 2 Chronicles 17:6

Daphne spent each evening at Paul's meetings She gleaned all the insights he gave into the love and power of how God works in and through His own and tucked them in her memory. On the fourth, and every day after, she and Batano went to the port to see if Nicanor had arrived. Paul's meetings had grown so large, she did not connect with Aquila and Pricilla or Chloe until the second night. Each wanted a full account of her time in Delphi, so she arranged to meet at Chloe's house the next day.

Batano was invited, so the five of them sat in Chloe's courtyard and drank cooled wine. They told of their brief meetings with Nicanor and commiserated with her disappointment in their crossings. Daphne told them everything, from how God used five curious young men to start a movement, to their victory at the temple. Questions flew but stopped when Chloe stood and beckoned to a young woman who hesitated just outside the entrance. "Welcome, Eunice. Come join us."

The girl was introduced to Daphne and Batano as a dearly loved, new believer in Christ. Her hand shot to her lips, her eyes as big as the new moon. "You...are you the Daphne whom Nicanor spoke of?"

Daphne tried not to stare at the girl's veil and glanced briefly at Chloe. "Yes, you knew Nicanor?" Except for Chloe, the others had spoken of only brief encounters with her husband. How would this girl have come to know him?

Chloe seized the opportunity. "Oh, Eunice, you must share your story with Daphne."

Eunice blushed. "I am so sorry, I never meant to —"

Chloe jumped up and put her arm around her. "No, you must not dwell on the past. Remember, God has forgiven you and so did Nicanor." She led her to a seat across from Daphne, whose brain ran in frantic circles as she tried to imagine what Nicanor would need to forgive. "Just begin at the beginning."

Daphne's mind reeled. So sorry? For what? Unsummoned, a need to defend him rose.

Eunice twisted her hands in her lap, her eyes downcast. Finally, she looked up, began slowly, then blurted out the whole story. Daphne listened, horrified at Nicanor's injury and days of not remembering who he was.

"So, you see, I am alive in Christ today because of Nicanor's kindness. I will always regret that I led him into danger but will never cease to thank God He allowed him into my life."

Daphne rose, her eyes moist. She took Eunice's hands. "Thank you for sharing this with me. I understand. There was a time I, too, was desperate and did things I regretted, until I found hope in our Savior. I am so glad you asked Jesus into your heart, and I am sure Nicanor was too."

Eunice stood and hugged her. "Thank you for not hating me. I have never met a man like Nicanor. The only men I knew were..." she hung her head. In seconds, she raised it again and looked into Daphne's eyes. "If he were not such an honorable, considerate man, who treated me like an equal, I would not have listened when he told me about our Savior. You are blessed to have such a man."

She smiled and hugged her back. "I know, and I will tell him you said so."

Chapter Seventy-Three

...that I may open my mouth, boldly...
– Ephesians 6:19

Along with Chloe, Daphne and Batano enjoyed the worship that was a prelude to the Apostle Paul's message that night. He lay aside his outer garment and made an announcement. "We have a special ambassador, for Christ, with us tonight. I would like you to meet her and hear her story. Daphne, will you please come up and share what the Lord has done in Delphi?"

She gasped and shot a glance at Chloe, who simply grinned. She took a deep breath and slowly made her way to the front. How can I do this, Lord? This huge crowd came to hear Paul, not me.

The apostle put his arm around her shoulders. "I met this young woman in Philippi and challenged her to use her gratitude, for her newly found freedom in Christ, to serve Him. You need to hear how He worked, through her, to spread the Gospel."

She looked over the crowd, awed that he remembered her. "I will always be grateful to Paul, our leader, for his loving compassion and obedience to our God given authority." She swallowed her nerves and gave witness to God's intervention in her life. She shared His faithfulness from her misadventure in Apollo's temple, to being sold into slavery, to the day the apostle delivered from the demon." From that day forth, my heart's desire was to go back and tell those in Delphi about Jesus, and to expose Satan's plan to deceive through demons that pose as gods, like Apollo."

People applauded and praised the Lord. She thanked them and started for her seat, but Paul rushed up beside her. "No wait. We want to hear how things went in Delphi. How did you get people to listen?" He nodded at her and sat back down.

"It was all the work of the Lord. It started with five curious young men who listened, believed, and helped me get the word out."

Shouts of, "Praise You, Jesus," lifted from the people as they learned how her followers overcame obstacles created by the enemy and Roman officials.

"We started out in one man's home. But as word got around, dozens and then hundreds came to hear about the only true God." Loud praises arose as she detailed how God used them to destroy the temple's hold on people, along with its phony priesthood.

Paul commended her for her brave battle against the strongholds and encouraged the listeners to follow her example and dare to risk telling others about the Lord. Applause followed her to her seat where she gave Chloe a dubious glance.

Chloe shrugged, "I knew if I told you I had shared your story with Paul, you would shy from the attention. He did not say he was going to ask you to recount how it came about, but I am not surprised."

Daphne chuckled. "Some friend you are."

God resists the proud but gives grace to the humble.
– James 4:6

Nicanor arranged his trip back to Corinth the next morning. The Lord answered his plea, and he was able to book passage for the very next day. He wandered around the city trying to imagine Daphne growing up there. Upon his return, he came upon Cyrene's father as he struggled to corral a large ram into a fenced area.

He ran over and hopped the fence. "Here, let me help." The two of them soon managed to pull the animal into the enclosure.

Her father wiped his brow. "Thank you. He is a stubborn one."

Nicanor pointed at the pile of hay outside the fence. "Do you need that shoveled in with him? I can do it for you."

Her father eyed him. "No. You are Cyrene's guest. You need not —"

Nicanor picked up the pitchfork. "Oh, I do not mind. It gives me something to take my mind off tonight."

"What is tonight?"

He threw another load to the animal. "Well, they asked me to give my testimony at tonight's meeting and I guess I am a bit nervous."

"I do not go for that stuff, but you can practice here if it would help."

Nicanor finished with the hay, leaned the shovel against the fence, and sat beside the man. He told him how he had grown up a slave and was used to work. "But then, my owner adopted me and after I became a believer, a strain developed between us."

The man huffed. "I know about that. My son, Demas, was always obedient to my wishes until he heard that Jesus stuff. Then, he decided that had to come first."

"You mean he did not do his work?"

"No, he is still a hard worker, but I cannot get him to understand work has to come first."

Nicanor shot up a quick prayer. He related how he had found that to make time to follow Jesus was more important than anything. "It does not negate what has to be done. It just changes one's priorities. God cares about your responsibilities, and He knows your needs. But He wants you to surrender your life into His hands, simply so He can bless you."

They talked for hours. Cyrene's father asked pointed questions about things that concerned faith. Nicanor listened and shared the plan of salvation in simple terms, then excused himself to freshen before dinner. "Thank you for guiding me, Holy Spirit. And Jesus, please reveal The Father to this man and help him make a decision to follow You."

Kerpos came for Nicanor and Cyrene's mother right after dinner. "I thought you would like to get there early and get your bearings. Baltos will introduce you right after the worship ends."

He nodded. How did I get talked into this, Lord? To speak about You, one on one, is not such a threat. But to talk in front of a large group of people...

Baltos motioned to him after the music ended. Nicanor smiled at the warm welcome from the crowd, not sure where to start. Near the entrance to the field he spotted Melita. She was accompanied by a young man and, to Nicanor's amazement, Cyrene's father stood beside them.

His heart leapt and all nerves and fears of failure left. He gave them a slight nod. "Thank you all for coming. I know you have heard from my lovely wife, Daphne, whom I have not seen in months, and cannot wait to join in Corinth." Everyone laughed and he relaxed.

"Baltos asked me to give my testimony." Murmurs hummed and eyes darted as he explained he had been a slave in his father's estate before his owner adopted and made him his heir. "Slaves are not free to choose or openly pay homage to a god, but I had long stifled a hunger to worship something I did not yet understand. I heard of a very different God in Rome where I was sent to learn Roman ways, and then again in our city. They talked about this same God and being curious, and no longer a slave, I decided to go see for myself.

"I attended a few meetings and finally grasped that the God who created the world loved me and wanted me to be His child. It did not matter that I had been raised a slave and had fallen short of God's goodness many times. I gave my heart to our Lord Jesus. He forgave my sins, and I became a member of God's family, an heir, sealed by the Holy Spirit. His seal is a guarantee as irrevocable as the adoption by my Roman father. But I had to keep it to myself because he did not want any part of it.

"The strain in our relationship escalated until he was hurt in an accident, the same night Daphne became a believer. Because of her decision to help him rather than run away, he pledged to set her free. We had loved each other from a distance for over a year. That choice set her free to hear and respond to my love."

He saw Melita wipe her eyes. "Well, I was awfully new in my walk with Jesus, as was Daphne. It almost broke my heart when she said she could not marry me because the Lord wanted her to come back here and tell how she found freedom in Christ. I was devastated until the Lord said, *'Why not go with her?'* We married and booked passage, but my father had an apoplectic fit and I could not leave him. Daphne felt she should go on without me and we were at odds, me not wanting her to travel alone and she certain that the Lord had said, 'Now.'"

"Things got pretty strained until the Lord helped me see I needed to let go and trust Him. She left and I planned to join her as soon as my father was well enough. Meanwhile, his wife, Medea, who had been under the spell of false teaching, became very frail, near death. She had continually rejected the love of Jesus, but God answered our prayers, and she became a believer a few days before she died."

Melita's hand flew to her chest, and "Oh, praise Jesus," swept through the crowd.

"A few days before I left Corinth, I received a letter from Epaphroditus, our leader back in Philippi. He informed me that my father, too, had become a believer." Amidst the cheers, once again, he saw Melita's hand clasp her lips. He nodded and she patted her chest.

"Daphne does not yet know of these changes, but she will be thrilled when she hears of them. We plan to return to Philippi as soon as we can. God is good and I pray He will continue to bless what He began here in Delphi. Thank you for listening."

Baltos joined him on the platform. "Nicanor will leave tomorrow to join Daphne. Let us send him off with prayer." He laid his hands on him and prayed before Nicanor stepped down into the crowd. Baltos asked those to come forward who wanted prayer to receive Jesus or for any other need.

Nicanor smiled at Cyrene's father and walked over to him. "Is this going to be your first night as a believer?"

The man looked him in the eye. "You are the only one who made sense of this. Could you help me?"

"It would be an honor." He laid his hand on the man's shoulder. "Please repeat these words after me." Cyrene's father stumbled through the prayer, his voice unsteady. They had hardly finished when his wife and Demas surrounded him, with tears of joy.

Melita finished the music and found her way to Nicanor. She wiped her eyes. "Master Nicanor, I—"

"No, no more 'master.' I hear that you are a free woman now."

She blushed. "The misses, I mean Daphne, she was so generous to set me free. Here, I want you to meet Demas, my husband."

He put his arm around her and shook Nicanor's hand. "Thank you for the way you reached out to my father. Like yours, I could not imagine he would ever come to Christ. I am so glad for an opportunity to meet you and hear your story. It makes me wonder what God has in mind for you and Daphne. Whatever it is, I am sure you will spread the good news wherever He leads."

After everyone left and Nicanor was down for the night, he thought about Demas' words. *I expected to find Daphne and go home to Patharus, Lord. Do you have a different plan?*

Chapter Seventy-Four

Rest in the Lord and wait patiently for Him...
– Psalms 37:7

On her fourth morning in Corinth, Daphne hurriedly prepared for the day. She pulled on her peplos. "I had no idea how much Melita did for me. I should have found ways to show my appreciation and told her so." She sighed. "I do so miss her company."

She corralled Batano right after breakfast, and they left for the port in the first carriage he could summon. They watched with disappointment as people disembarked from the three ships expected that day. Nicanor was not among them. Batano cocked his head. "Maybe tomorrow?"

She grimaced. "I hope so." On their return she brightened. "Maybe if we hurry, we can get to the meeting at Chloe's this afternoon."

Out of the depths I have cried to You, O Lord.
– Psalms 130:1

All of Cyrene's family had gathered to greet Nicanor as he came down for breakfast. Melita was the first to reach him. "Master Ni," She blushed. "I mean, Nicanor, this is Cyrene. She and Daphne grew up together and were very special friends."

Cyrene beamed at him. "And this is my husband, Abiron. I am so sorry we were not here to hear your testimony last night. We arrived home very late, but I am so glad we could meet before you leave."

449

Nicanor took her hand. "Daphne mentioned you many times. You were the true friend that was there for her when her family was taken away. She never forgot that...or you."

Conversations started and halted as everyone strove to become acquainted with Nicanor at the same time. Cyrene's mother waved them all into the dining room. "I hate to interrupt but the food is ready. Nicanor's trunk is in the carriage, and we would not want him to miss his voyage."

Everyone laughed and found a place, surprised when Cyrene's father stood and announced he wanted to thank the Lord for the food. Tears splashed with joy as they listened to his simple prayer.

Cyrene hugged her father for the first time since childhood. She whispered into his ear, "And thank You, Lord, for bringing Father into the kingdom."

The meal ended and all the guests wished Nicanor well and headed for home. Cyrene stopped Abiron, "If it is all right with you, I would like to accompany Demas and Nicanor to his ship. We have had so little time to get to know each other." Her husband nodded and the three of them piled into the carriage.

Demas guided the horses while Cyrene peppered Nicanor about their life in Philippi. "Tell me about the first time you saw Daphne. How did you come to accept Jesus as your Lord? What is your father like? Did he mind that Daphne was not a Roman?"

Nicanor answered as best he could. He asked about Daphne as a child, what his wife's family was like, and what she thought when Daphne had, unexpectedly, shown up. The time flew and, too soon, they were at the gulf.

Cyrene hugged him goodbye. "I am so glad we had these few minutes. Take good care of my dearest friend and pass my hug on to her."

He boarded the dingy and climbed into the ship. As they waved him off, Demas sighed, "I wonder if we will ever see either of them again?"

Cyrene sniffed. "I hope so...but if not here, one day in heaven."

The second night out, Nicanor woke to the ship's violent rolls. He sat up and listened. The roar of the waves nearly drowned the sound of thunder. Until lightning flashed outside his small window, the dark sky could not be distinguished from the surf. The tempest did not fade but grew stronger, so he arose and dressed. "Maybe, I could be of some help to the crew."

He stepped out onto the deck, barely able to shut the door. Sailors hustled to lower the sails and strained to hear or see the captain's orders. Nicanor made his way down the deck. The wind plastered his hair across his eyes and made it hard to see. He found the captain. "Can I be of any help?"

"No. Everything is under control. It is not an *euroclydon*. This will pass soon enough. Those bigger storms are not due for a month or so. You probably should stay in your cabin. It will be safer there."

Nicanor nodded and headed for his room. A huge wave hit, and the ship rolled in the opposite direction. Everyone slid sideways. Nicanor slipped on the wet deck, reached for the rail, and missed. The next thing he knew, he was in the water.

The captain saw him go overboard and disappear. He ran for a rope with sealed, hollow gourds and blocks of cedar attached to one end.

When Nicanor bobbed up between waves, he flung it, but a wave caught the vessel and tore it from Nicanor's grasp.

He gulped water and began to sink. He coughed and cried out, "Lord, save me. I cannot let Daphne down or Patharus. I promised."

God has sent forth the Spirit of His Son into
your hearts.
– Galatians 4:6

Daphne awoke with a start. It was still very dark and the inn was quiet. In her spirit she heard, Pray for Nicanor. Or had she dreamed it? "Lord, I do not know what has happened, but I lift Nicanor to You. Please be with him and protect him from the evil one. Send your angels to surround him and keep him safe." She yielded to the Spirit to pray through her, comforted that He knew the Father's perfect will and would petition for God's best for Nicanor.

He is their strength in the time of trouble.
– Psalms 37:39

The captain instructed his strongest mate to watch, stay alert, and be ready to toss Nicanor the floatation device. The tall sailor spread his feet and stared into the water. He was about to give up when Nicanor bobbed up between two huge waves, with one arm raised. The sailor swung the rope twice over his head and whipped it in his direction.

Nicanor prayed, "Lord, give me strength." He kicked his feet and lunged for the float, but the smooth gourds slid from his grasp. On the second throw, he managed to grab one of the blocks of cedar. He hugged it to his chest until he was able to get a firm grip on the rope.

Once on deck, Nicanor lay on his stomach, panted, and coughed up water. The captain helped him into his cabin. "You are one lucky young man. Those waves made it hard to spot you."

Exhausted and breathing hard, Nicanor groaned. "It was not luck. It was the hand of God that saved me. But thank you for not giving up and thank whoever threw me that rope."

"It was my first mate, and I will pass on your thanks." He started to leave but spun around. "What do you mean by 'the hand of God'?"

Nicanor covered one last cough. "Come see me when the storm passes, and I will explain."

Do not fret, it only causes harm.
– Psalms 37:8

Sleep did not return, so at the first light, Daphne rose and dressed. It was the sixth day, and she was eager to get to the port. "Lord, You told us to be anxious for nothing but to pray about everything, so once again I commit Nicanor into Your hands and trust You are with him."

Batano met her outside but before they could board the carriage, a Roman soldier approached. He carried two large bags, his expression surly. Sweat ran from beneath his hair to the front of his ears, down his jaw, and disappeared into his tunic.

He called out to Batano. "You there. I charge you to carry this into the city for me."

Confusion sprang from Batano's face. He looked at Daphne. She spoke up. "This is my servant. He is not familiar with your laws. I need him with me. Please excuse him."

The soldier thrusts the sacks at Batano. "Well, I need him more. Get going, Boy."

At Daphne's shrug, Batano picked up the sacks. She told him not to worry, as she would wait for his return. Several hours passed with no sight of him. She found the innkeeper and told him about the soldier.

"It happens all the time, but do not worry. They can only make a man carry their load for a mile. Do you think he will be able to find his way back?"

She assured him they had traveled that way many times and Batano would remember. "But please, will you tell him I have gone on to the port and he should wait here?"

The port seemed even larger when she stepped alone from the carriage. The last of the ships, expected that day, docked with no Nicanor. She overheard passengers express their gratitude for surviving a raging storm. Her pulse quickened. Could Nicanor be on a ship caught in that storm? She returned to the inn and asked about Batano.

No one had seen him.

Chapter Seventy-Five

...all things work together for good to those who love God, to those who are called according to His purpose.
– Romans 8:28

Daphne was concerned for Batano. Where was he? After dinner she decided to go to Paul's meeting and ask her friends to agree with her, in prayer, for him and Nicanor. Chloe and Pricilla, along with Eunice, listened while she explained what had happened to Batano and of the storm Nicanor's ship might have battled.

Chloe took their hands. "All right, the Lord Jesus said if two or more agree as touching anything it will be done for them. Let us pray and agree." They found a quiet corner and prayed, fervently, that each be found safe and for Daphne to find peace in Jesus. Pricilla squeezed their hands. "Amen. It is done. Let us go worship the Lord."

Paul gave a lengthy message on trust. He explained that by faith they were able to call things that were not as though they were, and he urged them to believe in God's sovereignty. Daphne left for the inn, encouraged. "In Jesus' name, I call Nicanor and Batano well and safe from all harm."

The innkeeper met her at the door, "I am sorry, but your servant has not yet returned."

She thanked him, went to her room, and took charge of the evil spirit that harassed her. "You persistent spirit of fear, I command you in the name of Jesus Christ, to be gone and flee my presence." She settled for the night and meditated on God's promise to grant the prayer of agreement they had prayed. Peace descended as she reminded herself of Paul's final words that night. "All of God's promises are yes and amen."

The next morning, she left for the port without Batano. She thought she spotted Nicanor when the second ship arrived, and people began to disembark. A large man who paused, for what seemed forever, to help his disabled wife blocked her view. When he moved, no one was there. She studied the last of those who continued to straggle from the ship, but Nicanor was not among them.

She sat on a nearby bench and her lids fell to her cheeks. Lord, he is not here but he is in Your hands, and I trust you. When she opened her eyes, there he was, deep in conversation as he carried his trunk alongside a man in captain's attire.

Her heart leapt with joy and relief. She tore her way through those already on shore. On tiptoe, she waved until Nicanor saw her. He grinned, dropped his trunk, and waved back. Within minutes Daphne was in his arms. Both laughed and cried as he swung her off her feet. She drew back to look into his face, but he pulled her back to whisper how much he loved and had missed her.

The man with him bid them goodbye. "Take good care of your young man, Miss. He has the message of life that people need to hear."

Daphne stared after him, "What is that all about?"

"Oh, I will tell you later. We have so much to catch up on." He propelled her to arm's length and clutched her back again. "Did I ever tell you how beautiful you are?"

She laughed and snuggled close. He found a carriage about to leave and they boarded, both talking at once. They approached the inn, relieved to see Batano waiting on the porch.

He ran to help them from the carriage. "Master, welcome back! I am so glad you are safe." They embraced and he lifted Nicanor's trunk from the back. "Your arrival is the answer to many prayers."

Nicanor smiled. "And mine. I could not wait to be back with my wife, and I hear you are now part of God's family. That is great! But Daphne said you were forced away by a soldier yesterday. What happened? How did you escape?"

He faced Daphne, his face aglow. "I am sorry I gave you cause for concern, Misses. I noticed the soldier limped, so I offered to take his load the rest of the way into the city. Once there, he insisted I tell him why I would volunteer to do that. I told him of the One I serve, our Lord Jesus, and he pummeled me with questions all the way to his barracks. He then begged me to stay and tell him more. I knew you would understand." He grinned. "And now he is our brother in Christ."

Daphne pulled her hands to her chest and praised the Lord. She hugged him for the first time, and he blushed. "Oh, Batano, that is wonderful."

He hesitated, then addressed Nicanor. "Master, could I have a word with you?"

He nodded and Daphne went on into the inn. "Master, I have thought a lot about the life I led as your servant back home, and I...well, it is hard to imagine going back to that after all that has happened."

"I understand, Batano and—"

"Please, let me explain. I hold you and the misses dear to my heart and I do not know for sure what the Lord has in mind, but I believe meeting that soldier was part of His plan. He gave me this money."

Batano held out two drachmas. "The man said it should be enough to buy my freedom and he wants me to come stay with him. He believes there are a lot of men, in his company, that need to hear about Jesus. I have given it much prayer and I, too, believe it is what the Lord wants me to do. Could you consider it?"

Nicanor stared at the ground. He rubbed his forehead, and his eyes were moist when he looked up. "Batano, I will most joyfully grant you your freedom to serve our mutual Master. Return the money to the soldier or keep it. You may need it in the future."

Batano nodded, his voice husky. "Thank you, Master. My real freedom came the day Jesus became my Savior and washed away all the resentment I had built up against being someone's property." He put his hand on Nicanor's shoulder. "I want you to know I shall cherish this freedom. You were a kind master and I hope to pass your humble spirit on wherever God leads me."

Nicanor put his hand on Batano's. "Go with God, My Friend."

They said their goodbyes and Nicanor promised to repeat Batano's good wishes to Daphne.

He joined her in her room where he declared his need for a good night's sleep. "Maybe we could skip tonight's meeting."

A knowing smile spread over her lips. "Yes, but let us be sure to arrange our passage to Athens and to be back early, so we can attend tomorrow night. Everyone will be anxious to see you arrived safely."

She awoke in the night unaccustomed to someone sleeping beside her. She reached over and brushed the hair from Nicanor's eyes. Thank You, God, for answered prayers. Her thoughts ran to their plans to leave for Philippi, her joy dampened by the reminder she had not found her mother and brothers. She pictured how she had pleaded with one landowner after another, in Athens, to see if they could possibly have purchased her family. No match had been found.

From out of nowhere, suddenly she remembered that one of the owners said he had a woman that fit her mother's description. However, this woman had a baby as well as a young boy. Daphne jerked upright. It could be! Had not her mother been raped by the ship's captain about a year before? She grabbed Nicanor's arm.

"Wh... what? What is wrong?"

"Oh, Nicanor, I am sorry to wake you. But I think God has shown me where to find my mother and now I cannot wait to get to Athens."

They booked passage on a ship scheduled to leave the very next day. At the meeting that night, everyone was delighted to see Nicanor safely back and excited about the door that opened for Batano.

Chloe had told Paul of their plans and he called them to the front to pray over them. Their eyes met, awed at what he prayed, "Lord Jesus, thank You for the ministry You have started in these two. Please direct them, by Your Spirit, to the people who wait to hear about our Savior. Grant them the assurance that the grace You have given them was not in vain but will accomplish what You purposed. Amen."

Tears accompanied the many goodbyes and well wishes, along with "Godspeed" and pleas they come back for a visit.

Nicanor took Daphne's hand on the ride to the inn. "First our promise to Patharus and then what?"

She looked up at the star filled sky. "Only God knows but I am so glad we will be together in whatever He has planned."

Characters in Free Indeed

Daphne — thirteen years old
Tribia — Daphne's father
Hebee — Daphne's mother
Alexander — Daphne's brother, eighteen months
    her junior
Theo — Daphne's three-year-old brother
Belte — long time servant, friend to Daphne
Yahyah — Daphne's paternal grandmother, family
    matriarch
Zeus — believed to be Greece's highest god
Apollo — son of Zeus, god of Delphi, Greece
The Voice — a demon of divination who posses as
    a messenger of Apollo
Principality — the territorial demon over Greece
Cyrene — Daphne's closest friend
Talsta — high priest of Apollo's temple in Delphi
Bentalla — fellow slave in Athens
Patharus — leading owner of Daphne
Sergius — one of Daphne's new owners
Amplias — one of Daphne's new owners
Nicanor — slave/heir to Pathrus' estate
Kawit — fellow slave, Daphne's good friend
Stello — overseer of Patharus' estate
Jatel — manager of Patarus' household
Rybic — gatekeeper
Femi — fellow slave
Halaten — estate physician
Beresta — friend Daphne sees in market
Lydia — woman who hosts Paul and team
Botano — Nicanor's personal servant
Paul - Apostle to the Gentiles
Silas - companion of Paul in Ministry
Luke - author of the Gospel
Timothy - Paul's spiritual son

Carol S. Lacey

I hope you enjoyed Daphne's journey in this the last book in my *Snare of the Fouler* series. Writing takes a lot of time, but fills my many silent hours since my husband went to be with the Lord over two years ago. I delight in spending time at church, Bible studies, prayer groups, walking and with family. They keep me going, along with networking with other writers and a critique group I enjoy. Best of all is an uninterrupted (most days) time of worship, study, prayer, and communicating with the Lord each morning.

Perhaps I created Daphne as a person I want to emulate, ready to step out in faith and spread the gospel to my world. To bravely heed God's call, but before God found me, I was more of a follower. The Lord has had to push me into every position He's called me to do. From becoming my daughter's Girl Scout troop leader for five years, when an accident took the leader out, and no one else would do it. To lead the children's section at my church's missionary conference and recruit teachers. Later, I was coerced to take on a project in the Welcome

Wagon outreach I joined when we moved to a different city. Back in Michigan after a year, guilt led me to a stint on the board for a 120-member golf league. The most unimaginable task He brought into, after He became my Lord, was to become the teacher of two women's Bible studies. Hours of pouring over the word of God brought unexpected great joy and blessings.

I would have volunteered for none of the above. But I praise God that He positions us, flaws, and all, where He wants to use us for His purposes. He continually grows us into who He wants us to be, all designed before He placed us in our mothers' womb.

I have a website where I publish a blog called Nuggets From God's word. It contains tidbits of things He shows me in His word, or lessons, sometimes painful, that I share to encourage others. I would be so grateful if you would go to my website, carollacey.com, and post your thoughts about my latest book, or any other comments. For those interested, I have a new book, written but not yet ready to publish. I plan to put the first chapter on my website and hope you like it.

Blessings on your journey in Him.
Love, Carol

Made in the USA
Las Vegas, NV
10 May 2024

89762384R00256